TANGLE OF DESIRES

TANGLE OF MAGIC
BOOK THREE

J.E. NEAL

To all of the mamas out there—
This one is for you

CONTENTS

CHAPTER 1
LAVENDER NESTING
~DAN VINDICO~

By Halloween, very little progress had been made on either the test vault or the drug tests. Governor Vindico had called for a surprise drug test. The urine samples were watched over constantly by the heads of the lab testing facilities at Georgetown. There'd been no tampering, and none of the tests had come back positive. However, the afternoon before, three glass pipes had been found in one of the men's restrooms in the Occamy building by one of the maintenance staff.

Venton students were well aware of the school's policy on drug use, and most of them steered clear. If a test came back positive, the student was pulled from Venton and sent to one of the many drug rehabs run by the Auxiliary Department. They stayed there four months minimum and were then required to repeat the school year. Gifted powers would readily combine with chemicals. Often, that could lead to dangerous and sometimes deadly results. The testing system had worked for decades.

Other than meeting Clarence's derisive scowls occasionally in the corridors, Dan had no interaction with Pendergrath's son. Governor Vindico frequently reminded Dan that none of his mentors had filed complaints about him.

"Yeah, he's been here a week, Dad," Dan huffed.

The students were distracted most of the day though Dan wasn't certain why until he heard about the epic Halloween party being thrown by a few of the students that evening at one of the nearby country clubs.

Becca had returned to school half days with Jeff and Dan watching over her like a hawk as she managed her way through her classes and then returned home with orders from Adeline and Jeff to sit down and relax. She was beginning to show, and though Jeff tried to shield her as much as he was able, the other students were not very kind.

Jeff and Becca often ate lunch with Dan in his office instead of in the lunchroom, which meant that Jeff wasn't overhearing much about either of the cases they were still working.

"Are you okay?" Dan panicked as he answered his cell on the first ring before he took a bite of the sandwich he'd packed for his lunch.

"I'm fine," Fionna sighed. She was growing weary of Dan's frantic watch over her. She'd grown to a size where she was hardly able to stand without help or for any length of time. She could no longer see her feet, and she was unable to go longer than a half hour between bathroom breaks.

As she put it, the once sweet round ball that contained her baby girl now looked more like skin stretched over a body. According to her, Halia had dropped so low she felt like she was walking with a cantaloupe between her legs.

She was uncomfortable most of the time and not in that great of a mood though she did try. Dan constantly assured her that he wasn't offended that she would snap at him for no real reason. He just wanted to make certain she was as comfortable as she could be.

Walking across the room seemed to exhaust her and though she was starving, she wasn't able to eat more than a few bites of food as there wasn't much room left. She'd lost four pounds at her checkup Monday, and Adeline had informed Dan that if she continued to lose weight, they would be inducing labor within the next week. This was also due to the fact that Fionna was having intense Braxton-Hicks contractions. Dan kept her casted in the evenings to try and drown the pain. She was already dilated nearly three centimeters and was spotting from the gunshot injury to her uterus.

Dan was in a constant state of frantic terror. He was so concerned that she was going to go into labor while he was at work that he broke out in a sweat every time his cell phone rang. He'd arranged for Aida to go trick-or-treating with Olivia and Oliver under Meredith's supervision. Fionna's chances of managing to stand and give out candy to the marauding band of goblins, witches, wizards, superheroes, and princesses seemed fairly slim. Dan wasn't leaving her to take Aida trick-or-treating.

"I was just wondering why we don't have any more of those pickles that I want. I'm cleaning out the refrigerator and they're gone," Fionna demanded.

"I don't know, baby, but I can get some on my way home," Dan soothed instead of pointing out that they were out because she'd eaten them all in two days' time.

"Okay, and those protein bar things that Adeline wants me to eat a little at a time, and we're out of the lavender bathroom cleaner stuff I like."

"You got it. I'm cutting out early, so I won't be much longer."

"Don't get the eucalyptus scent again."

"I promise I'll get lavender." Clearly, he was never going to live down buying the wrong bathroom cleaner a few weeks before. He wondered momentarily how she'd used an entire bottle in the last month.

"Thank you. I know I'm probably completely miserable to be around," she fussed, on the verge of tears all of a sudden.

Letting his eyes close in defeat, Dan rubbed his temples. "You are not miserable to be around. I love you. I hate that you feel so badly. I want to come home and take care of you."

His plea, however, brought on a deluge of tears that had Dan deciding to cancel his last class. As soon as he got out of the meeting with the other Ioses mentors, he flew to his Ferrari.

Racing into the kitchen, Dan's eyes goggled. "What are you doing?" he demanded. He was unable to believe what he was seeing with his own eyes.

"I'm cleaning behind the refrigerator," she scoffed as if the fact that the rather large refrigerator in their kitchen was moved away from the wall was completely normal. The doors were flung open, all of the food previously contained in the fridge was now covering the countertops, and his extremely pregnant wife was behind the refrigerator with the vacuum.

"How did you get back there?" Dan tried not to panic.

"I climbed. How else am I going to clean it?" She sounded like Dan was suddenly the most unintelligent person she'd been around in a while.

"Holy fuck," he whispered as he nodded his understanding.

Studying their home, he rubbed his forehead. "Uh, Fi, honey, what have you been doing today?" He did his best to sound nonchalant.

"Well,"—Fionna, however, was suddenly quite perky—"I vacuumed the whole house, cleaned all of the bathtubs, reorganized Aida and Halia's closets, cleaned the ovens, scrubbed the bathrooms, and reorganized the entertainment center. Oh, and I cleaned the grill."

"Wow." Dan willed his heart to beat in rhythm. Before he could make another comment, Fionna was climbing back up on the countertop to escape from behind the refrigerator.

"Whoa, okay." Dan guided her into his arms. She turned to try to force the refrigerator back into its proper location.

"Baby, stop. I'll move anything you want, okay? Just tell me what you want to clean."

"I just got to thinking we watch movies all the time, so obviously the media center needed to be cleaned," she explained as if she'd heard nothing Dan had said.

"Obviously." Dan began to watch over her frantically.

"Do you think we should get a dog?"

"Probably not today." Dan willed patience as he extracted the telephone list from the refrigerator door that Fionna had made weeks before of who was to be called when she went into labor. He was going to need it very soon.

He touched Garrett's name on his phone and slipped into the living room.

Garrett answered with a chuckle. "Figured I'd be hearing from you soon. She called me about ten this morning and told me that it was absolutely necessary that she have Clorox wipes immediately. I thought it was a little strange that she didn't go get them herself. So, I left work and went to get her those and then took them to her. She was definitely Shield seeking. Sorenson called me back in about a half hour ago, or I would've stayed until you got home. I hugged her a few times trying to get a read on her, but her rhythms never tensed from any contractions, so I figured she had a while."

"Thank you for doing that. Are you working all night?"

"I'm supposed to get off at ten, but call me when you need me. You know I'll be there."

"Wait, what is Shield seeking?"

"Mom used to do it right before she went into labor. I think it's probably a Receiver thing, even though that's not Mom's primary Predilect. It might be every pregnant woman though. I'm not sure. They just seek out someone they're comfortable with when their hormones start flowing rapidly. They aren't usually thinking all that straight, so it can be erratic."

Dan wished she'd called him, but he kept his mouth shut. "I'll give you a call when we head to the hospital."

After Fionna methodically loaded all of the food back into the refrigerator, she decided she wanted to clean out her vanity in their bathroom. This provided Dan the perfect opportunity to watch over her while he packed his bag for the hospital and phoned her parents. They were of course excited but needed to stay at the bakery for the dinner rush. Dan promised to call them when they left for the hospital.

Aida arrived home thrilled to go trick-or-treating. She'd never done anything like that before and was eager to try it. Dan hated that he couldn't go with her, but there was no way he was leaving Fionna in her current condition.

"Can I put on my hula costume now?" she begged as soon as she'd had her snack.

"I vacuumed it for you," Fionna informed her. Dan tried not to laugh as Aida stared at her mother like she'd lost her mind.

"Just go with it. Mommy's really wanting to clean today," Dan assured Aida in a quiet whisper. She nodded but was well aware that something was off.

In the split second it had taken Dan to reassure Aida, Fionna had disappeared into the laundry room and was trying to move the washer and dryer.

"Fionna." Dan raced to her. "Baby, please sit down, okay? I'll clean up in here. You just relax."

"I'm fine. I feel great. I need to clean. Get out of my way." With a dramatic roll of her eyes, Fionna laid the wet rags she'd been using to wipe down the appliances on top of the dryer. She turned and made yet another trip to the bathroom.

Dan's cell rang. As if he'd needed more confirmation that his baby girl was going to be in his arms instead of in his wife in days instead of weeks, he answered Tutu's call.

"And how is my Maylea, Daniel?" she quizzed with an excited lilt in her voice.

Unable to halt his grin or calm his nerves, Dan chuckled. "Why don't you tell me?" Tutu laughed. "Uh…" Dan checked to make certain Fionna hadn't come out of the restroom. "She's cleaning like a mad woman and not making a great deal of sense."

"The day Elisabeth gave birth to Maylea, she yelled at Papa because the spring planting rows weren't straight enough and, as I recall, because the dirt was dirty."

"Like mother, like daughter then." He followed Fionna back into the laundry room and pulled the washing machine forward for her while cradling the phone between his ear and shoulder.

"Thank you." Fionna kissed his cheek like he'd just given her a great gift.

"She'll be all right. She needs you to be calm and to be the rock she clings to. Her receptors are off. She's feeling everything from you, from herself, from the baby, from everyone around her, and it's going to overwhelm her. Try to keep her calm and give her the raspberry chamomile tea I sent her home with. It will help her balance everything and prepare her to deliver. She's going to be off for a while. Remember you are her stronghold. You are her Shield. That's what you've always been for her, and she needs you now more than ever."

"There's nowhere else I would ever be." After heating a mug of water with his hand, he searched through the boxes of tea stored in the pantry from Tutu that Fionna was to drink before labor. "I'm sure I'll be calling you soon," he managed as he leaned back to make certain Fionna hadn't decided to perform other feats of gymnastics.

"Yes, you will," was Tutu's parting line.

He could hardly believe they'd made it this far. It seemed so surreal. He'd wanted it so badly, and Halia was most certainly on her way. His heart ached as he watched his astounding wife try to prepare their home for their baby girl.

He took her hand. She smiled, but she continued to scrub with the other.

"I was just thinking maybe after you have some tea we should pack a bag for you for the hospital and maybe one for Halia." He studied her energy as he held her hand. It was just beginning to give slightly rhythmic pulses. Dan felt one and pulled Fionna into him. He hoped to hold on to her long enough to feel the next and get a time.

Her stomach was hard as a rock as he held her to him, but she pulled away before he could read the next pulse indicating the very beginning of her contractions. Still, he assumed it was going to be a while. He offered her an adoring smile.

"Why? She's not coming for three more weeks, and I don't need tea. I need the vacuum."

Dan had to force himself not to laugh. His Receiver, the strongest of their generation, with her body so flooded with birthing hormones, and her energy reading in erratic, unusual pulses, was unable to feel what was happening. Her own mind couldn't read its way through her hormones.

Dan drew a deep breath and tried to think of a way to convince her to pack. Debating, he decided to go with the way that was most certain to get his wife upstairs and packing.

"I'd feel better if we were all packed, so I'll do it. That way you can keep cleaning. Halia really just needs those T-shirt things, right?" *One, two…*he grinned.

"No, wait. It's going to be freezing when she comes. She needs more than a T-shirt." Fionna rolled her eyes. "And my girls do not leave the house in a T-shirt. I'll do it." She was now highly irritated as she marched toward the nursery with Dan hot on her heels. He carried the tea into the nursery and encouraged Fionna to sip as she packed.

But fifteen minutes later, Dan stared down into the large diaper bag she'd picked out for Halia. Thus far, she'd packed seven receiving blankets, two pairs of tiny black patent Mary Janes, a rattle, a cloth doll, and nine stretchy hair bands complete with large silk flowers in varying colors.

"Daddy, could you help me?" Aida whisked into the nursery carrying her grass skirt. She was already dressed in the turtleneck and tights that had been negotiated if she was going to wear her hula gear from the classes she attended when they were in Kauai for the summer.

"Yeah, baby." Dan watched Fionna stare into Halia's closet but not appear to see anything at all. He guided Aida into her skirt and had just tied it up around her waist when the doorbell rang.

Biting back a curse word in front of his daughter, Dan raced down the stairs to deal with the first trick-or-treaters. He grabbed a bag of mini Butterfingers from the pantry where the Halloween candy had been stored. With a chuckle, he noted that over half of the bag was already gone.

He opened the door and was given the customary response. As he began dropping candy into plastic pumpkin heads and pillowcases, Fionna appeared.

"What are you doing?" she demanded.

Dan wasn't certain how to respond.

"Those are mine." She jerked the bag of candy bars away from him, then reached in one of the pumpkins and removed the Butterfinger from a little girl dressed as a fairy. Fionna then held them protectively to her chest and glared at Dan.

The trick-or-treaters were thoroughly confused.

"Just one second." Dan tried to remain calm as Fionna fell onto the sofa and began unwrapping candy bars. He raced back into the kitchen and prayed that his wife had no emotional attachment at that moment to Tootsie Rolls as he quickly distributed the candy. He flew up the stairs and retrieved the tea from the changing table.

"Here, baby. Just relax for a few minutes and drink this."

"Fine," Fionna agreed with a sigh as she began studying the living room furniture.

While she was distracted, Dan called Zach.

"Hey, man. Everything okay?" His brother-in-law's calm, cool demeanor did nothing to soothe him.

"I don't know. Did my sister go insane right before she went into labor?" Dan rushed into the kitchen to pour the bags of candy into a bowl to set by the front door.

Unabashed laughter poured from Zach. "Uh yeah. She most definitely did. Why don't we come over to see if we can't help you out?"

"Thank you." Dan decided to accept as Aida followed him into the kitchen carrying her haku crown for her head and her wrist and ankle leis. The doorbell rang again. Dan rushed back to the front door. He began dressing Aida while simultaneously handing out candy to a gaggle of toddlers arranged on his front porch.

His cell rang, and he answered without seeing who was calling.

"Daniel, it's Stephen. Is this a good time?" the Crown Governor requested.

"Uh," Dan wasn't certain what the correct response might be. He checked the living room again and nearly dropped his cell phone in the candy bowl.

"Fionna, do not move the sofa!"

"I think we should rearrange the living room furniture," she informed him loud enough for the governor to hear her.

He laughed hysterically.

"Baby, please just sit down for me, okay?"

"Lillian, do you think the twins would mind trick-or-treating over in Crescent Hills?" Governor Haydenshire called through his laughter. "Why don't we see if we can help out a little? I was calling to see how you were doing with Clarence, but I'd say you're not too worried about him at the moment."

"You don't have to do that, sir." Dan tried to sound reassuring, but the doorbell rang again, and Fionna slid the coffee table across the room.

"Daddy, I have to go to the bathroom," Aida lamented. That meant she would now have to remove her grass skirt. Dan fought not to whimper.

"I've done this several times. Let us help," the governor tried to soothe. "Why don't I phone your dad? They're supposed to keep Aida when you leave for the hospital, correct?"

"We're not ready for that, I don't think."

"We'll see you in a few."

Zach and Kara arrived with little Aiden dressed as a pumpkin. Meredith was next to take Aida trick-or-treating. Aida and Olivia were thrilled to be hula girls together while Oliver had chosen a Spiderman costume.

Fionna's cell phone rang. "Hey Em," she squealed.

Dan shook his head and had to laugh. Receivers from around the globe who all adored his wife could all feel her oncoming labor while Fionna herself could not. "No, I feel great. I'm thinking about rearranging the living room. You know, just for something different," she informed one of her best friends. "Why does everyone keep telling me to sit down?"

Zach and Dan tried not to laugh.

"Wait, she hasn't eaten," Dan remembered just as Meredith was about to take Aida out.

She gave her brother a soothing smile. "I think this is going to be a big night. Why don't you let me take care of Aida? I'll take her by the house. The kids ate hot dogs. We have plenty. She can spend the night."

Dan knew his girls better than anyone. He shook his head. "She won't want to stay overnight. She'll feel what's happening as soon as Fi's rhythms pick up just a little more." He gestured his head to Fionna as he spoke quietly. "She's going to want to come back home."

Meredith nodded. "Okay, I'll bring her back whenever she wants to come, but you might want to go ahead and call Dad."

"Yeah, maybe so." He kissed the top of Aida's head, working around her floral crown, making her giggle. "Have fun, sweetheart." He was still heartbroken that he couldn't take her trick-or-treating for her first time.

Aida clung to Dan's hand. "Okay, but promise to take care of Mommy, please. I don't think she feels quite right," she confessed in a concerned whisper.

Dan knelt down to stare into his precious little girl's soulful, brown eyes. "I know, baby. I don't think it's going to be too much longer until you're a big sister, okay?"

A broad, delighted grin spread across Aida's face. "I'll help." She set down her own pumpkin bucket.

"It's okay. It won't be for a while. You can trick-or-treat and then we'll take care of Mommy together."

"Are you sure?"

"I'm sure."

Aida studied her mother.

"We'll be back before Mommy and Daddy go to the hospital. I promise," Meredith vowed.

"Okay."

Dan knew she didn't want to go. "I promise I'll take care of Mommy."

Willing bravery, she let Meredith guide her down the steps.

"Fionna!" Zach leapt as Fionna attempted to climb up onto the coffee table to dust the fan.

The Haydenshires and fifteen trick-or-treaters arrived at that very moment.

Zach guided Fionna down from the table and back onto the sofa. Dan distributed mass quantities of candy. The Crown Governor guffawed as he shook his head.

"Lillian, I want you to take this all in," he commanded. "Ten times," he reminded her.

Mrs. Haydenshire cocked her eyebrow upward. "Until you have

experienced the kind of hormone and energy bursts that cause this, you will have no vocalized opinion," she informed him.

Shaking his head, Governor Haydenshire turned to Dan. "Logan and Connor took the boys trick-or-treating near the farm. Adeline decided she would try and get some sleep. She's expecting your call in the near future. We dropped Abigail off with Rainer and Emily. She adores her big sister. Emily understands her better than any of us," he explained with a delighted smile. "And your parents are on the way," he concluded.

"Thank you." Dan tried to sort through his erratic thoughts and more emotions than he was capable of understanding at the moment. "Fi, baby, please drink your tea. Here, I'll reheat it for you."

Fionna finally accepted the tea. "There's so much to do, and now all of these people are at our house. Why are all these people at our house?"

"I know," he soothed, "but just for me, take a break and rest. Drink the tea. I think it'll make you feel better."

Fionna eased down onto the couch. "My back's bothering me. I probably tweaked it when I moved the fridge."

Dan and Zach shared a knowing glance with Governor Haydenshire.

Mrs. Haydenshire stepped in. "Sweetheart, why don't I see what I can whip us up for dinner, and you sit and let Dan rub your back."

"You don't have to do that. I'm sure I'll be fine in just a minute," Fionna assured her.

"I would really like to." Mrs. Haydenshire directed Dan to the couch.

He sank down beside Fionna. Emotion clogged his throat. All of the love he felt for her and all that she was about to go through had him in a sudden chokehold. His body couldn't contain the overwhelming adoration he had for the woman seated beside him who couldn't make sense of what was happening all around her.

"Come here, baby." He guided her to him as he heated his hand and began absorbing the pain of her body beginning to prepare for labor.

"Where's the car seat?" Zach asked in a barely audible whisper.

"In the nursery," Dan mouthed. With a nod, Zach disappeared upstairs and returned with the car seat and the base.

Trying to keep Fionna from concentrating too much on what he was doing, Zach rushed out into the garage. Dan rubbed Fionna's back and inhaled the delicious smells suddenly coming from their kitchen. Mrs. Haydenshire was truly an astounding Occamist.

"I have to pee again," Fionna whimpered. Dan guided her up and watched over her obsessively as she waddled to the bathroom.

"What can I do?" Kara asked as she glanced at Aiden sound asleep in his own car seat.

Dan ran his hands through his hair and tried to formulate a plan. "I'm assuming that my little girl will need to wear more than flower headbands and tiny booties home from the hospital."

Giggling, Kara made a quick return to the nursery.

"Dan, sweetheart, do you have a few towels you don't mind being ruined that you want to put in the passenger seat of your car?" Mrs. Haydenshire's question held a great deal of knowing wisdom.

"Yes, ma'am." Dan rushed to the laundry room and handed the towels to the governor who assured Dan he would get them into the car.

"Here Kara, let me help you," Mrs. Haydenshire said. "She's a few weeks early. She's going to be small."

"I think she put some preemie stuff in one of the dresser drawers," Dan remembered. "Fi, are you okay?" He knocked on the bathroom door and tried not to panic. She'd been in there too long.

Mrs. Haydenshire paused on the step as the governor halted in the kitchen.

"No," Fionna choked.

"Let me in." Dan shook the doorknob. She opened the door. Terror was etched on her features as she trembled. "What happened?" Dan tried to soothe her, but he was frantic himself.

"Something came out, and it was gross," she managed in a terrified whisper.

Dan pulled her into his chest.

Mrs. Haydenshire gazed at them sweetly. "That was your mucus plug. It's fine. It's supposed to happen. Nothing's wrong," she reassured.

"Remember they said that in the class," Dan reminded her.

"It can't be." She shook her head. "I don't know how to have a baby." Fionna melted down in his arms. She sobbed as she clung to him. She buried her face in his neck and grasped fistfuls of his shirt in her terror.

"It's okay, baby," he soothed. "You're going to be amazing. You always are, and I will be right there with you every step of the way."

Mrs. Haydenshire nodded. "He's right. You're going to be just fine. Your body knows precisely what needs to happen, and you still have a while. Maybe even a few days, okay?" Mrs. Haydenshire lied well. "Why don't you go sit down and let Dan cast you for a little while? We'll take care of everything. You're already an amazing mom, and this will be no different."

"What if I don't know how to love her as much as I love Aida? And what about our other baby?" she pled to Mrs. Haydenshire.

"Sweetheart, I know it's scary, but it's going to be okay. I promise." Mrs. Haydenshire guided her into her capable arms. "I have eleven children, and several others that I didn't give birth to but I'll definitely claim, and I've had multiple miscarriages. I love each and every single one of them so much I cannot possibly begin to quantify it. Your capacity to love grows with each one. Please don't worry about that. You're going to amaze yourself."

"Come here, sweetheart." Dan guided Fionna to the couch, settled her beside him, and let her resume her fierce grip on his shirt. He set his shield firmly in place over her.

"Fi." Kara eased back into the living room and set the now fully packed diaper bag near the door to the garage. "I know it's really scary, but I swear it's a completely amazing experience." She was on the verge of tears herself as she watched Fionna cry and cling to Dan.

He cradled her head in one hand and held her to him with the other while trying to whisper how much he loved her and that he would never let anything happen to her.

"Why don't I pack your bag for the hospital as well?" Kara offered.

Fionna sat up and scrubbed her hands over her face though her terror was evident to everyone in the room.

She managed a trembled nod. "I laid out some skinny jeans and a cute sweater on the bed when Dan was trying to get me to pack earlier. I want to wear it home from the hospital, since I'll be able to wear them again now."

Kara and Mrs. Haydenshire tried to hide their chuckles.

"Uh, okay," Kara placated. "I'll get those and maybe a few other options as well."

"Oh, and those brown high-heeled boots that go with my skinny jeans," Fionna ordered as Dan shook his head.

"Uh-huh." Kara covered her mouth to hide her laughter.

Mrs. Haydenshire joined them in the living room after she checked the huge pot of homemade chicken noodle soup she'd somehow managed to fix in all of the chaos. She was careful to avoid Dan's shield cast.

"When you feel a little better, maybe let Dan help you upstairs and you and Kara pack the biggest bra you own and some underwear you'll plan on throwing away after you get back home."

"Okay," Fionna agreed in a fretful whimper. She tried to stand, and Dan immediately dropped the cast. He guided her up the stairs to their bedroom.

Kara was packing sweats, Dan's oldest T-shirts, thick socks, and the few pairs of cotton underwear that Fionna owned.

"No, I don't like those. Just grab some of those thongs in there." Fionna began digging in her bra drawers.

Kara shot Dan a horrified look. "She cannot wear thongs for a long, long time. Oh my God, I don't even want to tell you how much blood is going to be coming out of her hoo-hah and how badly thongs would hurt."

Dan nodded his understanding. "She's freaking out, and she can feel every emotion from every person in about a ten-mile radius at this point. To say she's not thinking clearly would be a serious understatement."

Kara drew a deep breath. "Okay, I am willing some inner Zen. She doesn't need to feel anything from me but calm." She headed to the master bathroom and began setting Fionna's hairbrushes and ponytail holders on the counter.

"No, don't pack those yet," Fionna demanded. "I don't know why my back hurts so bad, but I am not having this baby tonight." She turned on Dan. "Why are you not rubbing my back?"

"I'm sorry, baby. Come here." Dan pulled her close and began massaging her back with his heated hand. A sudden thought had him smiling. If his students thought PMS was bad, they should wait until labor.

"Come on. Let's go get some soup and maybe just chill out. Like you said, everything's fine for a while."

But Fionna caught him lying the second the words fell from his lips. "You don't believe that. Why don't you believe that?" she demanded.

"Fi, please." Clearly begging was going to be the best option. "Just come downstairs with me so I can keep rubbing your back until you feel better."

"Keep packing," Dan mouthed to Kara as he guided his wife downstairs.

Zach grimaced. "Your parents just pulled up, and Meredith called. Aida wants to come home. She's pretty upset."

"Fi's rhythms are shifting, and Aida picked up on it. They're closer than any two Receivers I've ever seen. They're practically symbiotic," Dan tried to explain the relationship between his daughter and his wife.

Governor Vindico waltzed through the front door sporting a proud grin. "I take it you won't be at work tomorrow," he teased Dan.

"I don't think so." Dan lifted a crying Aida up into his arms from the front porch.

"I want Mommy!" She wiggled out of his arms and rushed into the house.

He watched her soothe Fionna while Fionna soothed her. They cuddled closely, and Fionna seemed to calm.

"Here, Lillian, let me help." Mrs. Vindico headed into the kitchen as Mrs. Haydenshire was preparing soup bowls and pulling homemade biscuits from the oven. As long as Mrs. Haydenshire prepared it and his own mother only served it, Dan could foresee nothing wrong with that scenario.

He settled on the couch to try and offer his girls his undying love, devotion, and support. He began rubbing Fionna's back again. He could feel her rhythms pulsing in quick bursts that were coming closer together.

"Do you want to try and eat something?"

"I guess so."

Governor Haydenshire handed her a tray prepared with soup and biscuits along with a seltzer water.

Aida stuck close to Fionna while she managed to eat the soup.

Kara placed Fionna's packed bag beside the diaper bag. "Don't forget her pillow when you leave." She seated herself on the floor in front of the coffee table to eat soup while Zach fed Aiden a bottle.

But suddenly, Fionna was shoving the tray toward Dan. All of the blood in her face drained in an instant.

Dan panicked as she sprinted to the bathroom. He raced after her. "Baby," he soothed as he helped her stand erect and wipe her face with a cool cloth as she shivered convulsively from vomiting.

"She needs to stay in here," Fionna begged. "I don't know how to have her. What if I do it wrong, and she isn't okay? What if something goes wrong or she doesn't like me? Or Aida doesn't like her? Or she gets mad at me because I made her be born? And,"—she began to sob against Dan's chest again—"it's gonna hurt so bad." She tucked herself as tightly as she was able into his strong embrace.

Dan kissed her head. "She's going to love you and Aida so much. And you're going to be amazing, sweetheart. You are already the most amazing mom. I will be right there the entire time. I'm not going anywhere. I will cast you through every single contraction. We will get through this together just like everything else, and soon we're going to be able to hold her in our hands, okay?" He kissed the top of her head. "I can't wait to meet her, and I know she can't wait to meet you."

Nodding against him, Fionna seemed to have no desire to leave the guest bathroom. She just wanted a moment of solace in his arms.

"And you'll help me get back to normal and lose all of this weight?" she demanded.

"I'll help you do anything in the world you want, but you have to let your body recover."

"I want to take a bath."

Dan hated to tell her no to anything, but he shook his head.

"You can't take a bath, sweetheart. The plug is out."

"I want everyone to go away. It's horrible. I can't think. It's so confusing," she convulsed out her plea.

"Okay, that I can do." Dan couldn't imagine what she must be feeling with her powers on the highest of alerts. "I think we should let my parents stay in case we have to leave Aida here overnight. Why don't you lie down for a little while? I'll get you some relief."

"My back hurts so bad." She trembled against him as her tears soaked through his shirt.

Feeling like he was being physically rent in two, Dan began rubbing her lower back again. He tried desperately to ease her pain. Thinking quickly, he led her to their bed. He heat casted the sheets, blankets, and comforter. He helped her pull off her maternity jeans and guided her into the heated comfort.

"I'll be right back," he promised.

Dan raced back down the stairs, dispensing with his soaked shirt as he went.

"Is she okay, son?" Governor Vindico eased.

"Not really." Dan shook his head. "Thank you all for your help."

"But we need to go because she can feel every emotion coming from all of us," Kara supplied for him.

Dan turned to his parents. "I need you to stay. I think we'll be leaving in the next few hours, but could you try to stay calm and happy? She's overwhelmed."

Mrs. Haydenshire patted his cheek. "Just call us if you still want us up there, and she's going to be perfect. I promise." She pulled the Crown Governor out the front door.

"Thanks," Dan offered again.

"Our pleasure, son." Governor Haydenshire slapped him on the back.

"I'm going to try to get her to sleep as much as she's able," he explained to everyone left in his living room.

"How about if Aida and I get her ready for bed, and then we'll all go to the hospital after your baby sister is here, okay?" Kara encouraged Aida.

"I want Mommy," Aida fussed.

"Let's let Mommy sleep a little and then you can see her."

"Is there anything else we can do?" Mrs. Vindico offered very sweetly.

"I don't think so, Mom, but I'll let you know."

Kara led Aida up the stairs and began giving her a bath while the governor and Mrs. Vindico cleaned the kitchen.

Zach offered Dan a kind smile as Aiden slept on his shoulder.

"It gets intense, but it's really awesome too. Just try to cast her through the contractions. Keep eating so you can keep it up. It's unbelievable how much pain they feel. I don't know how Kara survived, but just try to pull as much as you can on you."

"Do you want to take these with you?" Governor Vindico brought in a large box of protein bars and added them to Dan's bag by the door.

"Yeah, thank you." Dan nodded.

His father grinned. "We'll get Aida to bed. Go on and take care of her. She needs you."

"I will," Dan vowed to his father and his brother-in-law before he raced back up the stairs.

CHAPTER 2
INTRUSIONS

He fell asleep several hours later after keeping Fionna tucked in his shield that he filled with heat to ease her pain and soothing energy to keep her calm. He regulated his emotions as best he was able so that she felt nothing from him but his undying love.

After he'd soothed her to sleep, Dan let the thoughts he'd kept at bay form in his mind. Everything his life had been right up until the moment he'd followed her home from that bar. Every loss and every gain tabulated in his mind. The baby they'd lost and his little Halia who was mere hours from being born. His precious Aida asleep across the hall. Kauai and DC and so many places in between. What it would be like to have his baby girl in his arms and out in the cold, cruel world. *I have to keep her safe.* The thought filled him from the tips of his fingers to the deepest, darkest places of his soul. His shield readied itself for the responsibility. It was who he was. It was why he'd been put on the earth—to protect his girls.

Suddenly, he questioned everything. He questioned his desire to go back into law enforcement, his father's pleading request that he not take his family to Kauai, how this night would change the course of their lives forever.

He fell asleep amid his ponderings. Dan awoke with a spasm as he felt Fionna move away from him. "Are you okay?"

"I have to go to the bathroom," she managed through an exhausted yawn. "Oh my God, why am I wetting my panties?" She sounded horrified.

Leaping from the bed, Dan made it to her in two long strides. She was soaking wet.

"Make me stop!"

"You're not wetting your pants, baby. Your water is breaking." He tried to remain calm but failed.

A knock sounded on their door as he helped her into the bathroom. It was three in the morning.

The governor was wearing the robe and slippers he'd worn every day of Dan's entire life. "I heard you explode from the bed. I take it we're having a baby." He chuckled with a pride-filled grin.

"Her water just broke." Dan ordered himself not to panic.

"All right, son. She'll be fine. Get her to the hospital," Governor Vindico soothed.

Fionna appeared wearing her favorite robe, a purple terry cloth number with large green polka dots. She'd had it for years. It was a gift from Tutu. Dan had always considered it Fionna's security blanket.

"I'm taking a shower and shaving my legs," she informed Dan and his father defiantly.

"Your water is breaking. We have to go. We are having a baby. You are not taking a shower," Dan commanded.

"The baby will have to wait until I've shaved my legs."

"Dan." Governor Vindico shook his head as Dan's eyes goggled in stunned disbelief. He set to argue with his wife again, but his father grabbed his arm. "It's something she can control," the governor whispered, "and there is a lot right now that she can't. Take a deep breath and go take care of her. I'll put your bags in the car. She'll be all right."

"Fine," Dan sighed. "I will take a quick shower with you, and then we are leaving."

Carrying his cell phone into the bathroom, Dan phoned Adeline and Garrett and then helped Fionna step into the shower. Leaving the phone on the counter, he stepped in behind her and watched over her obsessively. He helped her wash and then held her steady while she shaved her legs as well as she was able. He casted her through the beginning contractions, but the sheer amount of pain had her more willing to go to the hospital than anything else.

After what seemed like a lifetime while Fionna dressed, then changed clothes again, blew dry her hair, and put lotion on her recently shaven legs, they were in the car flying to Georgetown. Garrett gave them a police escort and made it to Georgetown in record time.

Adeline was waiting with a wheelchair and a kind reassuring smile.

"Are you ready?" she soothed as they were whisked toward the elevator.

"No," Fionna whimpered and clung to Dan's hand.

Garrett knelt down in front of the wheelchair. "Hey," he soothed. She released Dan's hand and threw her arms around Garrett. He embraced her readily.

"I'm so scared."

"I know. Listen to me. Nothing's going to change. Okay? Not you and Dan, not me and you, not you and Aida. It's just going to get even better. I promise."

"And you'll love the new baby as much as you love Aida?" she pled.

He squeezed her tighter. "You and I will both love the baby as much as we love Aida."

He always knew what it was that she so desperately needed to hear. "You go climb in the hospital bed and take some deep breaths. Dan and I will be right here the entire time."

A contraction overwhelmed her suddenly. Dan reached for her, but Garrett pulled the pain into his own shield. "I've got you."

Adeline nodded her understanding. "We need to get her up there, Garrett."

They climbed on the elevator, exited on the obstetrics floor, and were quickly escorted to a room.

"Go ahead and take everything off for me," Adeline instructed. Garrett made a quick exit to the waiting room.

It was a true testament to the state of his wife's psyche that she asked, "Do you want me to take my panties off too?"

Dan fought the urge to double over laughing. Fionna Vindico was most certainly not prudish or even that modest, but the sterility of the hospital room coupled with the extreme stress she was under had her confused and panicking.

"Here, baby, let me help." Dan eased her out of her clothing, helped her into the gown, and covered her in the hospital bedding.

Adeline had covered her chuckle well as she moved to Fionna. "I'm just going to hook up your monitors and then we'll see how far you've dilated."

Fionna clung to Dan's hand with both of her own as Adeline hooked up the monitors to measure Fionna's contractions, her vital signs, her energy rhythms, and the one to measure Halia's vitals and energy.

"Everything looks good," she assured Fionna. Adeline seated herself in a rolling chair and moved to the end of the bed.

"Okay, Dan's going to uncover you, and we'll just see where we are, then he can cover you back up." She was clearly concerned over Fionna's reaction to her underwear being removed.

Fionna tensed as another contraction took hold of her.

"Dan, just cast her. That's a pretty mild one. You can probably pull most of the pain from her if you'd like," Adeline guided.

More than happy to take his wife's pain, Dan concentrated and replaced Fionna's fear with his calm and pulled the pain from her body into his shield. As the contraction passed, Dan eased the sheets and blanket upwards to uncover her legs. He seated himself on the bed beside her and tried to give her a little comfort over being exposed.

Just as Adeline's glove snapped on and her fingers were inserted into his wife, the door to the hospital room flung open.

Adeline jerked her hand away, making Fionna yelp as she cringed into a kind of ball, and Dan attempted to cover his wife up and shout at whomever had come in unannounced. "What the hell do you think you're doing?" he thundered viciously.

He was stunned as Bob and Linda Barge, the horrible couple from their birthing class debacle, stood in the doorway of Fionna's labor and delivery room. "Why does she get this room and I only get a little one?" Linda was on the verge of stomping her feet.

"Mrs. Barge,"—a nurse tried to drag her away—"Mrs. Vindico's labor is much farther along than yours. We told you not to come to the hospital for another few hours. You wouldn't listen, and she's the governor's daughter-in-law."

Dan yanked the covers back over Fionna as he marched toward the Barges all in one sinewy move. "Get the hell out of my wife's room, and do not come back." He shoved Bob Barge out of the room and slammed the door behind them.

Drawing a deep breath, he tried to refocus on his wife and the pain she was experiencing. He reset his single-minded focus on Fionna.

"I'm so sorry," Adeline continued to apologize. Fionna was so bewildered she was shivering in her shock.

"I'm right here." Dan laced his fingers through hers, letting her draw from him in heavy doses.

"Okay, good. Just keep doing that." Adeline nodded. "You work up there. I'll work down here. We'll have a lovely night." She lifted Fionna's sheet from the end of the bed, keeping her covered, as she checked Fionna's cervix this time.

Suddenly, Fionna contorted in pain. Dan casted her. He felt his shield shimmer slightly from the sheer amount of pain she was experiencing as he tried to siphon it onto himself.

"That's a big one." Adeline grimaced. "You're at a six. If you'd like, I'll have an anesthesiologist come in and cast your spine. That will block the pain receptors and let you relax somewhat until you're fully dilated. Your energy will soothe for a while anyway. Then we'll let Dan pull as much as he can while you push, okay?"

Dan sincerely hoped Fionna would agree. She was still gasping for breath from the last contraction.

"You're sure it won't hurt Halia?" Fionna asked.

"Not at all, and I'm a little worried about your previous wound. I think keeping you as calm as we can for as long as we can will actually be best for Halia."

"Okay."

A minute later, a guy who appeared to have just come out of the academy made an entrance. He was a little too cocky for Dan's liking, and he was sporting quite a smirk.

"This is Cade McNamara. He'll be your anesthesiologist," Adeline introduced. She didn't particularly care for Cade either, Dan noted.

"Fionna Styler," Cade drawled. He was entirely too excited to be working with Fionna.

"NO," Fionna shouted. "Fionna Vindico, and this is my husband." She jerked her hand up, still laced in Dan's. "And I'm a ridiculously strong Receiver and I'm in labor, obviously, so I can feel all of the gross things you're thinking about." She turned to Dan. "Make him stop."

Dan stood with his eyes ablaze in fury as he marched toward Cade. "You know, I think we'll be needing another anesthesiologist," he growled. "Because you're going to be admitting our friend Cade here very soon." Adeline's eyes goggled as Cade slunk backwards trying to make an escape.

"I'll...just see who else is on call tonight," she assured Fionna while casting her and trying to help her calm down.

A few minutes later, another medio appeared. She was shaking her head. Adeline beamed as she issued into the room. "This is Carla Parakin. *She'll* be your anesthesiologist," she tried again this time with a delighted smile.

Carla was British and very maternal. She fussed over Fionna and promised that she would ease the pain in just a matter of moments.

True to her word, Dan casted Fionna through another contraction, and after that, Carla set to work. She ran a solid blue energy orb up and down Fionna's spine which allowed her to relax from the pain for a while.

"I like it when she calls me dearie." Fionna settled back against the pillows as everyone left the room for a few minutes.

Chuckling, Dan kissed her forehead. He was relieved she seemed settled for the moment. "I'll take anyone over Cade." Dan was still infuriated over the medio's lack of ethics and the Barges' intrusion. "Are you ready for me to start calling people?" He had no idea if she wanted him to let everyone know she was in labor or not.

"Dan." Fionna's chin trembled. She tried to blink back tears as she clung to his arm.

"What, baby? Are you hurting again?" Dan started toward the door to locate Carla.

"No." She shook her head. He eased himself back beside her. "It's just…" she tried to explain but more tears escaped her eyes.

"It's just that we're going to have a baby." He knew perfectly well what had settled in her mind in the absence of the pain.

She began shivering, both from the magnitude of what was happening and the cast on her spine. Dan cradled her to him.

"I know and I'm overwhelmed. I could never love anything more than I love you, and I can't believe that you're gonna make me a dad again. I don't deserve this."

"Don't say that. I love you and you're an amazing man and an amazing husband and the most amazing dad."

Dan wiped away her tears as he blinked back his own. "I love you more than life itself, and I will be there for every single thing, baby. I swear to you."

"I love you too and I know." She rubbed her head against his chest, needing him to be her soothing shelter from the world if only for a little while. His shield spilled out over his wife.

"Will you lie beside me?"

"Of course." Dan had at least done this much before. When she'd been hospitalized from the gunshot wound and the miscarriage, he'd lain beside her upon her request and held her while she slept.

Pushing those thoughts away, Dan cradled Fionna on his chest and wondered if he could get her to sleep.

"You can call people," she whispered as she clung to him. Dan extracted his phone. He began with the Stylers and worked his way steadily through the list.

Carla checked on Fionna often to make certain she was feeling no pain though the contraction monitor continued to spike off the scale.

She sat beside Fionna, held her hand, and reset the cast slightly.

"Is this your first?" she asked kindly.

"Oh, uh…well, kind of," Fionna offered.

Dan beamed at his wife and kissed her head again as he extracted himself from beside her. It felt oddly uncomfortable to be lying in bed with Fionna while someone that reminded him of his grandmother was beside her.

"We adopted our oldest daughter last spring," he explained to Carla.

"Right, so I've never done this part. I was pregnant before, but we lost the baby," she confessed in a heartbroken whisper. She seemed to want Carla to know everything.

"Everything in its own time and its own place. We're going to get you set to rights in no time."

Fionna smiled. She seemed to let Carla's reassurances wash over her like a healing balm.

She offered Carla a hesitant smile. "This is probably a really weird thing to say."

"What's that?"

"Your energy, well, really it's your spirit…it feels nice. It makes me feel better." Fionna tucked herself physically back in her pillows. She seemed to brace for rejection. "You remind me of my little girl."

But Carla didn't look off put in any way.

"That's pretty huge coming from her." Dan held Fionna's hand. He gazed at her as he brushed her hair away from her face.

Carla looked deeply touched as she blinked back tears of her own. "Thank you for saying that. I love this job. I get to meet beautiful people just like yourselves at a time when I can help them. I think that's what makes me tick. I enjoy making new mommies and daddies feel better however I can, and taking away others' pain the best that I'm able."

CHAPTER 3
SISTERS

Adeline returned to the room as Carla checked Fionna's monitors to make certain everything was stable.

"The Vindicos just arrived with Aida. She'd really like to see you. Let me check you again, and if it's okay, I'll bring her in. Rainer and Emily are here as well, along with most of the Angels. Garrett's anxious to get in here, and Mrs. Haydenshire, oh, and your parents," Adeline enumerated the sheer number of people all wanting to wish Fionna well. "Would you like some ice chips?"

"Is that all I can have?" Fionna asked. She didn't seem hungry, just curious.

"Yes, while you're under anesthesia." Adeline checked Fionna's cervix again. "Okay, you're at a seven and a half now. If you're going to let people visit for a few minutes, it probably needs to be within the next hour. You're seventy percent effaced, so everything is getting ready."

"Can I just see Aida for a few minutes first?" Fionna begged.

"Of course. Dan, why don't you go get her. You making an appearance might help," Adeline suggested.

"Is that okay?" Dan studied his wife.

"I'll stay right here with her, Dad," Carla assured him.

"It's okay." She wanted Aida badly enough to let Dan go for a few minutes.

"I'll be right back." He kissed her cheek.

Dan smiled as he greeted all of the people that loved them enough to show up in the early morning hours to wish them well.

"Daddy!" Aida wiggled out of Garrett's lap and raced to Dan. He lifted her up into his arms.

"Do you want to go see Mommy for a minute?"

"Yes, please."

"Is everything the way it's supposed to be, Daniel?" his father asked.

"Yeah, she's doing great. I'll come back and let everyone visit for a few minutes after we're done." He gestured his head to Aida. "She was a special request."

Understanding chuckles spread throughout the crowd. As he carried Aida back to Fionna's room, he encountered the Barges yet again.

Linda was dressed in a hospital gown pushing an IV pole and yelling at Bob as he followed her. "Tell them I do not want to walk anymore. Tell them to make Aakerman Robert come out now," she demanded of her bewildered husband.

"You're supposed to breathe. They said walking might help you do that thing they said."

Shaking his head, Dan was unable to believe that Linda Barge had gone into labor the same day as Fionna.

"Hi, Mommy." Aida leaned out toward Fionna as soon as Dan entered the room.

"Hi, baby." Fionna looked as if Dan had just laid the world at her feet as he handed Aida off to her mother. She cuddled her in the bed.

"When will baby Halia come out?" Aida studied all of the monitors hidden under the blankets on top of Fionna.

"I don't know exactly, but I don't think it'll be too much longer."

"And you'll be all right?" Aida's voice shook, and Dan's heart fractured.

"Mommy's going to be fine, baby girl. I'll be in here right beside her the whole time," Dan promised. This seemed to bring Aida some peace as she nodded and then nuzzled her head against Fionna's neck.

Suddenly, huge tears began leaking from Aida's eyes.

"What's wrong?" Fionna cradled her as tightly as she could.

Dan leaned down in an effort to lift Aida into his arms, but she clung fiercely to Fionna.

"What if you like Halia too much more than me and you want me to go back to the orphanage?" she finally managed through her terror-ridden tears.

"Aida, no," Fionna tried but her chin trembled, and suddenly the two women that meant more to Dan than anything or anyone in the world were both sobbing. Not certain he'd be able to withstand much more, Dan tried not to wonder what it would be like if Halia was in the mix with salty tears pouring down her sweet face.

"Aida, baby, listen to Daddy," Dan guided her. Fionna attempted to wipe away the downpour from Aida's eyes as she tried to quell her own. "You are our little girl, just like Halia is our little girl, and nothing will ever change that. You are never ever going back to the orphanage or going anywhere except with me and with mommy. Because you are ours and we love you and Halia the very same, okay?"

"And I'll still be Uncle Garrett's girl?" Her breaths shuddered from her.

Fionna grinned through her tears. "You will always, always be Uncle Garrett's girl."

"And Tutu will love me and Halia, and Aunt Malani will still be my Aunt Malani too?"

"They both love you so much and nothing will ever change that. Everyone on the farm and all of your friends that you met when you helped Tutu and Mommy run the store, they all love you." Fionna assured her.

"And Halia will love me?" Deep concern reverberated in her whisper.

"Halia will love you so much," Dan pledged. "You'll be her big sister, so she'll need you to show her how to do things and to take care of her and keep her out of trouble."

"Like you did with Aunt Kara, and Aunt Meredith, and Aunt Lindley?"

"I...tried." Dan was certain he hadn't always done a great job of taking care of his little sisters.

Aida was still clinging to Fionna. "I want to stay in here with you and Daddy. I can help Halia be born because I'm her big sister." She turned Dan's words back on him in an instant.

Fionna looked crestfallen as she cradled Aida closer. "I think Daddy is going to stay in here with me while Halia is born, and then once they take her out and get her all cleaned up, then Daddy will come and get you and you can come in and hold her, okay?"

"How did she make a mess inside your tummy?" Aida looked both concerned and intrigued.

Chuckling, Fionna kissed the top of her head. "She didn't really make a mess, but she's been inside of me, and they'll have to clean her up before we can play with her."

Aida nodded. It was clear she wanted to ask more but wasn't certain she should. Dan decided that was probably enough information for a seven-year-old, so he tried to change the subject.

"Do you want to come back to the waiting room with me and let Garrett come back in and see Mommy?" Dan asked her.

"Okay." Aida sat up off Fionna.

"Will you be okay while Daddy and me are gone?" She kissed Fionna's shoulder as it was closest to her mouth.

Clara came back to check Fionna again. "I think Clara will probably check on me and on Halia while you're gone."

"Well, hello there. My name is Clara." She beamed.

"My name is Aida, and I'm their little girl too and Halia," Aida vowed.

"Of course you are, Miss Aida," she assured her. "You know there is something very, very special about big sisters." She leaned down to make Aida feel that she was being let in on a very big secret. Delight lit Aida's features. "But you must never tell the secret to baby Halia, because it's only a secret for big sisters."

"Okay." Aida was enthralled. Dan and Fionna shared a grin as Dan laced his fingers back through hers. "I won't tell."

"Did you know that even though your mummy and your daddy will love you and your baby sister the very same, there is something that you have that baby Halia won't."

"What?"

"No matter what, my sweet little angel, your mummy and daddy will always have loved you the longest because you will always be their very first little girl."

Aida seemed astonished as she thought that through.

"And do you know how I know this?" Clara asked her. Aida shook her head. "Because I am a big sister, and I think we are very special indeed."

"I think so too," Aida whispered. With that, she extended her hands up to give Clara an exuberant hug.

"Thank you," Fionna whispered. It soothed her soul that Aida knew what she would always mean to them. The relief colored her eyes and eased the tense lines on her face.

"Want to go see if a few people might want to come see Mommy for a few minutes?" Dan urged again.

With a broad grin, Aida wiggled off the bed. Clara studied the monitors closely.

"It won't be long, Dad. I'd hurry."

Dan tried to mentally prepare himself though he had no real idea how. He reached for Aida's hand and felt the slight spark when their hands connected. She was trying, with all of her limited might, to soothe him. Though she couldn't access her energy yet, she wanted desperately to reassure her father. Unable to help himself, Dan lifted her up into his arms as they made their way down the corridor.

"Do the things on Mommy's tummy tell Clara when baby Halia is all finished and ready to come out?"

Dan tried not to chuckle at the thought that the fetal monitors were a kind of oven timer.

"Kind of. When Mommy's body is ready for Halia to come out, Clara and Adeline will know."

Dan informed everyone that they could stop in and see Fionna for a few minutes, but that they didn't think it would be much longer.

Suddenly, Aida was reaching her hands out to Garrett. With a delighted smile, Garrett hoisted her up into his arms.

"I need you to stay with me while Daddy stays with Mommy," she explained in a fervent whisper.

"You got it, baby girl. I'll stay with you the whole time. We might even have time to build a fort in the waiting room out of the chairs."

"Can we help?" Rainer teased Aida as he gestured to himself and Logan.

She giggled her delight as she nodded. Dan could never have asked for better friends. Aida was a Receiver, and she was frightened and unsure about what was going to happen. She wanted a Shield and though Dan knew he would have been her first choice, she sought out Garrett, an extremely powerful Shield himself. He was always her second choice, and he always would be. Rainer's offer was to her a guarantee that she would not only have Garrett's shield but his and Logan's as well. The offer visibly reassured and relaxed his little girl.

"Take me to see Mommy," Garrett said.

"It's this way," Aida directed.

Garrett and Emily stayed longer than anyone else, which seemed to thrill and distract Fionna from her fears, so Dan was happy for them to keep her laughing. Adeline appeared and explained that she needed to check Fionna's progress, which had everyone blowing her kisses and waving their goodbyes as they made quick exits. Garrett carried Aida in his arms. She wrapped her entire little body around his. Dan saw Garrett's powerful green orb surround his baby girl in the arms of his best friend.

CHAPTER 4
HALIA

"They're at two minutes," a nurse informed Adeline. She nodded and pulled on another pair of gloves. Fionna was trembling and holding on to Dan's hand with all of her might.

"I'm right here." Dan kissed her forehead and let her draw from him in steadying streams.

"Okay, you're at a ten and you're almost fully effaced," Adeline soothed, but Fionna began to panic. "We're going to wait another few minutes and let you work through the transition while I get everything ready. Then we're going to push, okay?"

"No." Fionna shook her head. She gasped for breath as her eyes locked on Dan's in terror.

"Sweetheart, you are going to be perfect. You're so amazing, and I could never love anything more. I'll be right here. I'll pull as much of it off you as I possibly can."

Adeline pushed what looked like a rolling dresser with three drawers and a clear, plastic structure on top that contained a small mattress. There were several baby blankets, tiny diapers, extra cloths, and a nasal syringe. Behind her a nurse rolled in a metal cart that contained numerous instruments for either Fionna or Halia. A baby scale was pushed in as well, along with a cart big enough to lay Halia on and work on her if need be.

Dan's heart thundered as he watched the methodical precision of the delivery nurses and Adeline. He tried to remain calm. He knew Fionna could read every emotion his body contained, but he wasn't able to relax.

Adeline checked Fionna once more. "All right, I'm going to have Clara slowly lower her cast on your spine. Then when you feel the contractions, Dan will try to pull some of the pain away as you push with everything you've got, okay?"

Tears leaked steadily down Fionna's beautiful face as she managed a slight nod. She was shaking in her terror, and Dan tried desperately to calm her down.

"Dan," Adeline warned, "you can take as much away as you're able. I know how powerful you are, but she has to be able to feel the contractions coming so she can push through the pain. That's how we do this."

It was akin to her instructing him to abandon his wife and children. He had to let her hurt. He wasn't certain he would be able. It wasn't in him. Keeping her from pain of any kind was who he was. He was her Shield.

Clara began lowering her cast, and Fionna convulsed in pain. Focusing solely on her, Dan casted and pulled the pain into his shield. He spread the pain throughout his ample muscle structure. He spread it as far as he was able so he could take on more. He cringed in agony. It was horrifying to think that his precious Maylea was experiencing this as well.

"Push, Fionna, hard, right where you feel my hand," Adeline commanded. Fionna's body curved in as she squeezed Dan's hand and pushed with all of her might.

"Good. Now breathe," Adeline ordered as Fionna fell back against the pillows and sobbed.

A nurse handed Dan a cool cloth and directed him to Fionna's face that was covered in sweat. His hand shook as he tried to wipe her off and comfort her. His muscles twitched from the force of the strain he'd pushed into them.

Fionna convulsed again, shaking her head back and forth as another contraction consumed her. "No, please stop, it hurts" she begged, and Dan's own tears fell in her hair.

"They're coming fast, Fionna. It won't be much longer. Push now," Adeline ordered. Dan pulled the harrowing energy from her again as she bore down and forced her body's will over her mind's.

This went on for the next ten minutes with Dan biting back shouting demands that Adeline do something to make this stop hurting his wife and to get his little girl out. Fionna fell back once more, gasping for breath and begging Dan to make it stop. It nearly killed him as he tried to console her.

Suddenly, Adeline nodded. "She's crowning. Give me a big push in five, four, three, two,…one," she urged as the contractions continued hard and fast.

Fionna leaned forward and pushed again.

Suddenly, Adeline's eyes goggled in horror as she glanced at the nurse beside her. A horrifying guttural groan tore from Fionna. She paled dramatically.

Panic seared through Dan's veins as Fionna's eyes began to spin.

Adeline summoned and projected her voice throughout the hospital. "Medio Harrison Sawyer to birthing room four stat."

"What's wrong?" Dan demanded.

"She's bleeding. The scar tissue tore. It's the gunshot wound, and the baby just crowned. We've got to get her out so I can heal Fionna's uterus. She can do this but not alone. You have to stop pulling the pain away and start supplying her with your strength. Now," Adeline demanded. "Dan, right now!"

"Come on, baby, push." Dan sobbed as he forced his sheer power through Fionna as she writhed in abject horrifying pain.

"Again," Adeline demanded.

"No, please no," Fionna begged.

"Dan, she could bleed out. We have to do this now," Adeline commanded them.

Medio Sawyer rushed into the room. He looked bereaved.

"Maylea,"—Dan stared into her eyes—"look at me. You can do this. Now push, baby, just push."

"Listen to him, Fionna," Medio Sawyer soothed. "One more big push for us, okay?"

Drawing all of her resolve from Dan, Fionna's face contorted, and she screamed through the pain. He forced his strength through her, and suddenly he heard a tiny wail.

Adeline quickly handed Halia to the nurse and began working on Fionna. Dan couldn't make sense of all he was seeing. Several blue orbs moved over Fionna's abdomen. Nurses were healing her birth canal and delivering the placenta while Adeline and Dr. Sawyer re-healed the wound in her uterus.

Fionna seemed unable to remain conscious.

"Fi!" Dan shouted as his heart stuttered in his chest. A nurse strapped an oxygen mask over her face.

"She's going to be all right. Give us a minute," Adeline assured him as she and Medio Sawyer continued their intensive casts. The minutes seemed like hours, and suddenly Adeline moved away and gave Dan a soothing smile.

Another minute crawled by before Fionna blinked her eyes open, confused and frightened.

"You scared us," Medio Sawyer admitted. Chloe's father had known Fionna since she was a teenager. She'd been friends with Chloe all through the academy and the Angels. He appeared deeply shaken by what had happened.

"Are you okay?" Dan tried to console her though he was inconsolable.

Suddenly, a nurse moved beside them. She was holding their tiny, precious, baby girl. Halia had dark brown hair just like her mother's, and Fionna's adorable nose. The nurse laid her in Dan's arms.

He held her in front of Fionna. Halia's little eyes blinked several times. Her forehead furrowed in confusion.

"Hey there, baby," Dan soothed through his sobs as he tried to hold her safely and wipe away his tears.

"I want to hold her," Fionna choked. Dan gently laid her in her mother's arms.

She soothed as soon as she felt Fionna's energy. Her tiny hand shot out, and Dan placed his index finger in her grip. She began to yawn as she lay against her mother's chest.

"She's four pounds, eleven ounces, eighteen and a half inches long, and she's perfect," Adeline assured them. "You need to relax, Fionna. You gave us quite a scare. And I think this time, I'm going to say let's not have another one for a while. You need to let your uterus fully heal." Dan and Fionna nodded their agreement as they swallowed back tears, unable to look away from Halia.

"I can't let her go home until she's over five pounds," Adeline continued. Dan listened, but Fionna didn't seem able to concentrate. "We need to get her eating. She'll need to be on enhanced formula or breast milk. If you don't want to nurse, would it be all right if her daddy gave her the first bottle? That way you could rest. After that, if you're feeling up to it, you can let people in to see her."

"Okay," Fionna agreed somewhat begrudgingly.

Adeline moved away from them to prepare the bottle.

"You are just absolutely amazing." Dan was still unable to speak without crying.

"She's really here." Fionna seemed unable to believe that to be true. "She's perfect." Halia's mouth formed in a wide yawn as she snuggled in her mother's embrace. Dan ran his fingers tenderly over her tiny, beautiful face. Her back arched toward her father's hand. She felt his energy, and it soothed her.

"I told you she was gonna be a Daddy's girl." Fionna choked back tears as she gazed down at their precious baby. Dan was unable to believe that he'd somehow managed to gain himself all of the astounding women that were in his care, but he knew he would never ever let them down.

CHAPTER 5
AFTERBIRTH

Adeline showed Dan how much to heat the tiny bottle. He lifted Halia up into his arms and seated himself in a rocker right beside Fionna's head. Adeline lowered the lights in the room.

"Put her on your chest, skin-to-skin, Dan," she instructed. Dan managed to maneuver Halia from one arm to the other while he pulled off his shirt.

"In a little while, if you want her in the nursery so you can sleep, that's perfectly fine. Don't be afraid to tell us that you need a little time. You have to heal. You lost a lot of blood, and the energy and hormone level drop for the next twenty-four hours will be dramatic," she warned both Dan and Fionna. "Relax and take it a little at a time. Medios will be in to cast you every couple of hours. They'll try to keep your energy stable and to help your uterus back to its original shape. That's a little painful," she admitted. "We gave Halia a couple of shots while we were working on you, but in a few minutes they'll be in to give you a potassium shot. It's necessary to your energy levels as they make their recovery."

Dan tried to listen to everything Adeline was saying, but Halia's sweet suckling grunts as she inhaled the bottle held most of his attention. He hadn't been aware that his baby girl was given shots. It was all a blur.

"Feed her every two and a half hours, and we'll need to check the first few diapers." She turned to Fionna. "Being sore for the first several days is common. Like I said, take it easy. Let Dan take care of you and Halia."

"Okay." Fionna smiled through her exhaustion.

"I'm going to leave you for a little while. Spend some time together, then we'll bring Aida in, or you can take Halia out to meet her friends and family."

Dan and Fionna nodded their understanding. Adeline eased to Dan and turned her back to Fionna. "She's exhausted. The normal energy pulses that come after birth aren't as strong as they normally would be because she lost so much blood. Try to get her to sleep if she can." Adeline offered them a quick wave as she left.

"I don't want her to go to the nursery. I want her here with us," Fionna fussed.

"Okay, I'll take care of her as long as you sleep."

"Don't forget to burp her." Fionna was frantic suddenly.

"I will, sweetheart. You sleep." He lifted Halia up onto his shoulder and patted her back gently. To Dan's knowledge, she didn't burp, but it seemed to soothe Fionna. Exhausted from helping his wife birth their child, Dan laced his hand in Fionna's and pushed as much calm into her as he was able. A minute later, she couldn't fight it any longer. Her eyes closed as her neck went slack. She was out.

Working with a great deal of finesse, Dan kept Halia cradled to him and extracted the box of protein bars from his bag with one hand. He managed to unwrap one with his teeth. He needed to eat if he was going to cast Fionna through the pain of medios forcing her body to heal rapidly.

Halia began to wiggle as he reseated himself in the rocker and laid her in the crook of his massive arm. She was so tiny and vulnerable it terrified him. Her eyes opened and blinked several times showing off her long eyelashes. Then she went slightly cross-eyed.

"Hey, baby girl," Dan whispered. She stuck her tongue out several times to taste the air around her. Dan heated his hand slightly. He concentrated and could pick up on the tiny burgeoning energy of his newborn daughter.

She grunted. She could feel his as well. Her rhythms picked up, and she arched her back toward his hand. "I'll always keep you safe, sweetheart. I promise you. I'll never let you down. I love you so much."

With a few heavy blinks, Halia fell asleep safely in his arms. She looked so much like Fionna when she slept it took his breath away. Her skin was suddenly only a slight shade or two lighter than Fi's, and her tiny nose was the precise shape of her mother's.

Her eyes, though they were the color of her mother's, were shaped like Dan's along with the delicate angles of her face. She was his, and he could never possibly deserve something so precious. All he wanted was to hold her, to know she was safe in his arms and protected from the world. He dozed off as he rocked Halia.

"Dan." He heard Fionna's voice though it sounded distant. He shook himself awake then panicked. He made certain Halia was still safely asleep in his arms. "I have to go to the bathroom," Fionna confessed with more tonality to her voice this time.

Before Dan could stand, she shuddered and her face contorted in pain.

Dan panicked as he laid Halia as tenderly as he was able in the cradle and raced to his wife. She was drenched with sweat, and there were pools of blood on the sheets between her legs.

"Hold on, baby, I'm getting Adeline," he assured her as he sprinted out into the corridor.

The hopeful faces of their friends and family wouldn't come into focus as he grabbed a nurse.

"Something's wrong. She needs Adeline," he demanded.

"Let's see what's going on," the nurse offered patiently.

Fionna was pale and drawn. Her eyes were still slightly bloodshot from pushing. The nurse pulled the bloody sheet away from her.

"We just need to set another healing cast. Get your body a little closer to the way it was before you conceived. Lack of bladder control is completely normal along with night sweats for the first few days.

We'll work on those muscles for a while, all right? There's nothing wrong, Mrs. Vindico."

Adeline sprinted back into the room. "What's wrong?" She rushed to Fionna's side.

Fionna was horrified and appeared to try and melt into the bed. Her face colored rapidly as she squeezed her eyes shut.

As Dan had been watching liquids come out of his wife for the last twelve hours or so, she certainly had nothing to be embarrassed about. He was in absolute awe of what she'd done, the pain she'd endured, and how her body had somehow birthed his child.

"Just make me stop doing that, please," she begged, still unable to open her eyes.

"Fi, baby," Dan tried, but she shook her head and covered her face with her hands.

"Dan, why don't you take Halia down to the waiting room and let her meet Aida? I'm going to cast her for a while. I'll try to restore her bladder control, but she probably won't get a lot of warning. We can assign a nurse to stay with her if you'd like."

"I can take her to the bathroom," Dan assured the women staring up at him. He was trying not to see the bruises covering his wife's vulva as they made him rather queasy.

"I'll restore as much as I'm able until you want me to stop, okay?" Adeline negotiated, and Fionna nodded. Dan knew she would let Adeline work long past the point of pain.

"Fionna, listen to me. You don't have to be back to normal today. We can't even leave until she weighs more, so just take it easy for me, please."

"Take Halia down and let everyone see her while they get started. Then bring her back and you can cast me." Fionna hadn't heard a word he'd said. Dan sighed. She had just enough energy to let her embarrassment call the shots.

Adeline nodded her approval of the idea.

"Are you sure?" Dan quizzed.

"Yes, I want Aida to see her, but then I want to hold her. I haven't gotten to hold her much."

"Okay," he soothed but then turned on Adeline. "Do not hurt her, and she's not going to tell you when it's too much," he commanded.

Adeline laughed at him outright. "This isn't my first delivery."

"Dan," Fionna scolded.

"What? I know you."

Adeline patted Fionna's shin. "The entire process is really tough on Shields. I'm not offended, but I think you upset Aida when you ran out of here. She could use some reassurance."

Feeling guilt wash through him in heavy doses, Dan still didn't know how to divide his time between his wife and his daughters.

"Once they're done, she can come back in with you," Fionna continued her instructions.

Dan leaned and kissed her head, then scooped Halia up from her cradle. She remained sound asleep.

"She'll sleep like that for the first week or so. She's a preemie, so you might be waking her up to eat instead of the other way around," Adeline explained as she helped change the linens on Fionna's bed and then made her comfortable before she began the casting.

"I'll be right back." Dan carried his tiny baby girl out to meet all of the people who loved and adored her.

"I want Mommy! She needs me!" Aida was on Garrett's shoulder with Emily trying to comfort her.

"Mommy's okay, sweetheart," Dan vowed.

"Aida, look," Emily urged as Garrett turned Aida in his lap so she could see her little sister. Shuddering breaths escaped Aida as she stared down at Halia. Dan held Halia in front of her big sister.

"Mommy's just fine. Adeline's getting her all fixed up, and then you can go see her." Dan continued to calm her.

Aida timidly touched Halia's tiny hand. "Hi, baby Halia," she whispered in awe.

"I'm Aida, your big sister." Everyone moved closer to see the girls together.

Governor Haydenshire slapped Dan on the back as he handed Garrett a handkerchief to wipe away Aida's tears.

"Is Mommy really okay?" Aida asked again.

"She's perfect. She wants to see you."

Halia's eyes opened hesitantly which delighted her big sister.

"Hi," she offered again with a broad grin.

"You have a beautiful family, Daniel," Governor Haydenshire vowed.

"Thank you." Dan blinked back another round of tears as he watched his girls get to know one another.

"Nice work, man." Garrett nodded his agreement.

"Believe me, Fi did all the hard stuff." Dan elicited chuckles from the crowd.

"I want to hold her," Aida begged.

Garrett raised his eyebrows in question. Dan nodded. Garrett showed Aida how to form her arms into a kind of cradle. Dan grinned as Garrett set to make sure the baby was perfectly safe with his own arms while letting Aida hold her.

Dan laid Halia in their combined arms.

"I'm holding her," Aida gasped to Emily who beamed at her.

"You're doing such a good job."

"She looks like you." Governor Vindico grinned as he watched the girls.

Dan chuckled. "Poor kid."

"Could we get some pictures out of that? I'm so freaking tired of people asking if she's mine." Garrett rolled his eyes.

"No pictures for a while, but I'll see what we can do to assure the Realm that Fionna's baby is mine."

"You think that's bad?" Governor Haydenshire edged away from Aida. "They keep asking me if I'll love and accept Fionna Styler's baby? Now, tell me, how am I supposed to answer that? Of course I love and accept her. She's yours." He gestured from Halia to Dan. "But she isn't my granddaughter if that's what they're getting at."

"I'm sorry, sir." Dan wasn't certain what to do with all of the press.

Rainer pointed out the windows of the hospital waiting room. "They're already out there. I'd keep them both in the room if I were you." He draped his arm over Emily's shoulders.

"I need to get back in there. They're doing an intense cast on Fi to try to heal everything."

"I want to keep her," Aida begged.

"Let me take her back to Mommy for a little while. Then you can come and stay with us. We'll let everyone else see Mommy too."

Aida nodded her begrudged agreement as Dan lifted Halia back up into his arms.

"How much did she weigh? She's so tiny." Kara moved in to see her newest niece.

"Uh, four pounds, eleven ounces," Dan recalled as he began bouncing Halia gently. She was starting to awaken.

Governor Vindico chuckled. "Well, you've got that down." He gestured to Dan's swaying form. "We're so proud for you, son, and we do want to see Fionna."

"Let me go get them settled."

MAJOR AWARD

Over the next two hours, Dan casted Fionna through a dramatic healing process, learned to change a diaper, how to apply diaper rash cream, and how to rub alcohol on Halia's umbilical cord stump, watched Fionna give their little girl a second bottle, and then changed another diaper.

By the time that was over, Fionna looked dramatically better, and Dan laid Halia in her mother's arms after helping Fionna pull on a large sweatshirt and sweatpants along with socks. She declared that Kara was not only brilliant but also a lifesaver as Fionna was having a difficult time regulating her own temperature due to her rapid energy fluctuations and the blood loss.

Dan raced out to the waiting room to find Aida. She was in a fort constructed of chairs and couch cushions along with Garrett, Rainer, Logan, and Governor Vindico. Dan laughed as he took this all in.

"You were gone a long time." She looked thoroughly put out as she climbed out of her fort.

"I'm sorry." Time seemed oddly variable. He couldn't keep up.

Aida sat on the bed with Fionna and Halia while a steady stream of people moved through their room. All of the grandparents held Halia. Dan's mother fed her a bottle and Fionna's stepmother burped her and rocked her back to sleep. Rainer and Logan brought Dan copious amounts of food but didn't seem too comfortable being in the room with Fionna so soon after giving birth.

"Why is Rainer afraid of me?" Fionna asked Emily after Rainer made another escape.

Emily giggled. "Because he knows what part of you Halia just came out of, and it freaks him out. Occasionally, he and Logan have the combined maturity of a five-year-old," she explained as the ladies cracked up.

Tuttle and Lindley made an appearance near dinner time. They brought a present for Halia much to Dan's surprise. His impressed hopefulness quickly abated as Fionna lifted two pink onesies from the gift bag.

"My God, Lindley, are you serious?" Dan spat. The first onesie had, "Daddy told Mommy he loved her," on the front. Shaking her head, Fionna moved on to the second that declared, "If you're cute, I'll let you change my diaper." Infuriated wrath poured from Dan as he jerked the outfits out of Fionna's hand.

"This is sick," Dan roared. Halia startled and started to cry.

Dan scooped her out of Garrett's arms where she'd been sleeping soundly. Fionna looked exhausted, and Dan was at the end of his rope.

Kara stepped in. "Aida, would you like to come spend the night with Uncle Zach and me?" His sister seemed to know that Dan was on the brink of throwing everyone out of the room.

"We're gonna go," Mrs. Haydenshire decreed as she and the governor kissed Fionna goodbye.

"Halia gets to stay here with Mommy. I want to stay too," Aida huffed.

Governor Vindico stepped in. "Why don't you and me and Grandma go back to your house? We'll stay with you there. Then tomorrow morning, we could go out and get some breakfast, and I think we should go to the bookstore and get you some new books and a few that you could read to Halia. Then maybe we should go to the toy store. It's hard work being a big sister, so I think that deserves a prize. Then we'll come back up here, and you can show her what you picked out."

"Okay." Aida looked pleased with the plan.

"Thanks, Dad," Dan whispered.

"And then I can bring Sophie to meet Halia."

"Maybe we can pick Halia out a baby doll to be Sophie's friend," Governor Vindico offered.

Dan walked Aida out to his parents' Land Rover and promised to take care of Fionna for her. He had to sprint back into Georgetown as the press moved in.

By the time he made it back to Fionna's room, Halia was sobbing, and Fionna was easing herself from the bed while holding Halia and trying to reach the bottles to heat them.

"Baby." Dan leapt as he fixed the bottle and took Halia in one quick move.

"Adeline said I need to walk around, but everything inside of me feels like Jell-O."

Dan brought the nipple to Halia's mouth, effectively ending her crying. "Let me get her fed and then we can walk around a little."

"I want to feel normal. I want to take her home and be there with Aida and just not be here." Fionna sighed.

Dan willed patience as he kissed his wife's forehead. "A few hours ago, you gave birth to our beautiful little girl. So, for me, because it exhausted me just watching what you went through doing that, please just rest for a couple of days. Let's let Halia get used to the world outside of you and maybe try to get a little sleep, okay?"

"I had a lot of help there, Mr. Vindico," she reminded him.

"You were absolutely amazing." He'd done nothing by his estimations.

Adeline knocked quietly on the door. "How about if Halia and I go to the nursery for a few minutes when she finishes that bottle? We'll let the pediatrician give her a checkup. I won't let her out of my sight. And maybe you and Dan could take a very slow walking tour of the maternity ward. Then if you still want me to cast you again before you go to sleep, I will."

"I do. I want to feel normal again."

"That's going to take at least a week or two. Don't push it or it will be longer," Adeline warned.

"Keep telling her that," Dan demanded.

He finished feeding Halia and then helped Fionna to the bathroom. This time, he helped his wife change her diaper. Adeline changed the pad on the bed again. Every time Dan saw the sheer amount of blood and fluid coming out of his wife, he longed to hold her just like he held Halia, to protect and comfort her after all she'd been through.

"Adeline, these diaper things are horrible," Fionna lamented as she let Dan help her up and out of the restroom.

"I know. I'm sorry. They're the only kind we have, and they are the most effective."

"Maybe Kara will get me some big pads or something."

"I'll call her after our walk," Dan assured her.

"When you get back, we can either put ice packs on your vulva, or if Dan doesn't mind having his hand there for a little while, he can cool it down, heal the bruising, and reduce most of the swelling," Adeline commented with a wry grin..

"I'm certain I can handle that," Dan assured them.

Fionna held Dan's arm as he guided her very slowly around the Georgetown Labor and Delivery Ward.

"Thank you for taking such good care of me," she gushed as he watched over her obsessively.

"Sweetheart, I love you. You and Aida and Halia are the only things that matter to me. I want to take care of you and do and be everything you need. But Fi, baby, you've got to relax. Let me take care of you while you rest and heal."

"Okay," she sighed her begrudged agreement as they continued their painfully slow pace.

Suddenly, she began giggling. There, in the Georgetown newborn nursery, were numerous little rolling dressers with plastic cradles on top just like Halia's. They contained the babies born there in the past few days. But in the front window was a little boy that looked like he was four or five months old instead of four or five hours.

Fionna's hand covered her mouth as she tried to stop laughing.

"Oh my gosh, I feel terrible for Linda Barge," she gasped under her breath.

There was a large sign taped to the cradle. "Aakerman Robert Barge born Nov. 1 at 5:36 pm weighed in at 14lbs. and 12 oz. Biggest baby born this week at Georgetown. Biggest baby contest sponsored by Bob Barge Used Cars."

"That's almost fifteen pounds." Fionna shook her head. "That makes me hurt. I need to sit back down."

As they stood at the windows, they saw their little Halia being reweighed and checked out by Adeline and a pediatrician. Suddenly, they were bustled out of the way by Bob and Linda Barge.

"Excuse me, my wife just gave birth. Do you think you could watch where you're walking?" Dan demanded hotly.

"Our little Aackerman Robert was the biggest baby born here in over a year," Linda informed Dan snidely although she did look rather worn.

"How nice for you."

Adeline smiled at Dan and Fionna as she laid Halia back in her cradle and rolled her out of the nursery. "Let's take her back and get you casted and then let you sleep before she needs another bottle."

"Look at her, Bob. You can hardly see her she's so little," Linda sneered.

"Oh, you mean in the way that she doesn't look like the youngest member of the International Sumo Federation to hold title weight," Dan spat. He was infuriated that the Barges felt at liberty to comment on his baby girl's weight.

Adeline bit her lips closed to keep from laughing as Fionna's eyes goggled.

"Dan," she soothed. "Let's go back to the room. I'm starting to hurt again."

"Come on, baby." Dan guided Fionna away. They followed behind Adeline who was pushing Halia in her rolling bassinet.

"That's because she ate fish while she was pregnant," Linda huffed indignantly.

Dan spun, but Fionna grasped his forearm. "No. Just come on."

They made it back to the room, and Dan helped Fionna back into the bed.

"How is she already up walking around?" Fionna asked Adeline.

"She didn't lose a tremendous amount of blood after she gave birth, and her medio told her not to get up yet, but she won't listen. She's going to regret that tomorrow."

CHAPTER 7

SALT WATER TEARS

A deep yawn contorted Dan's face. He eased out from under Fionna. He wasn't sleeping all that well with his wife in a hospital bed, and he doubted she was either.

Halia was working herself from grunts to louder wails.

"Shh, baby girl." Dan lifted her into his arms. She was soaking wet. "Let me change you and then I'll feed you, but let's let mommy sleep." Before Dan could clean her up and dry her off, she was sobbing. Fionna slid from the bed and eased toward them gingerly.

"Here, I'll feed her," Fionna offered as she heated a bottle.

"I got her. You go back to sleep."

"Are you sure?"

She was exhausted. Her body had not only given birth but had also lost a tremendous amount of blood and had been pushed through a series of intensive casts.

"Go back to sleep."

Fionna brushed a sweet kiss on Halia's head and then one on Dan's jawline as he seated himself back in the rocker. She eased back into the bed and was out a moment later. Dan glanced at his watch as he gently rocked Halia and watched her inhale the bottle.

It was just after three. He let the past twenty-four hours reel through his mind. Halia stared up at him for a moment before her eyes closed again. Her little hand reached for his. Bracing the bottle with his chin, he placed his index finger in her grasp.

"I'm right here, baby." He listened to her rhythmic pulls of the bottle.

When she'd finished, he patted her back. She was asleep long before she'd burped. Dan eased her back into the cradle and rejoined Fionna in the bed. She sought him immediately and curled up on his chest. She was moving with more ease which gave him a great deal of solace.

The next time he awoke, he rubbed his eyes and sat up in the bed, shocked at how well he'd slept. It was almost seven in the morning, and Fionna was seated in the rocking chair with Halia.

She was singing a Hawaiian lullaby with her soft illuminating Receiver's cast covering Halia who was sound asleep. The image touched the deepest wells of Dan's soul. He saw tears leak down Fionna's cheeks as he padded to them softly.

"I just wish she could meet her," fell from her trembling lips in a sobbed plea.

"I know, sweetheart." Dan knelt down before them and rubbed Halia's head.

"She's a Scholera Predilect just like my mom."

Smiling up at her tenderly, Dan brushed her hair away from her face, not certain what to say or what Halia's Predilect would mean for her life.

"I need her. I don't know how to do this," Fionna pled.

He caressed Fionna's beautiful face. "Every time you hold her, and rock her, when you sing to her the same lullabies your mom sang to you, when she feels how much you love her, she is meeting your mom. Because I know that so much of what makes you the incredible woman and the incredible mother that you are came from her," he vowed. "I promise we'll figure it all out together."

This brought on heaving sobs that awoke Halia. Dan tried to comfort his wife and his baby girl by placing one on each shoulder.

Adeline chuckled as she slipped into the room after a slight knock. "You have no idea how many times I've walked in on this same scenario."

Dan handed Fionna tissues and kissed the top of her head.

Halia was no longer attached to her mother's energy though. Dan recalled that Halia would kick her disapproval whenever Fionna was upset when she was pregnant. But as Fionna had just explained, Halia was not a Receiver, and she couldn't pick up on the emotions of Fionna's energy the way Aida was able to.

"Why don't you lie down and we'll see Dan's work?" Adeline tried teasing Fionna and did elicit a giggle from her.

Dan had kept his cooled hand over Fionna's mound and lips for nearly an hour the night before. He'd worked her body through the tender swelling and healed the bruises. When Fionna was able to move her legs and abdomen without pain, he'd brought it back to the correct temperature and then soothed her to sleep.

"He's always done amazing things with my vaj," Fionna informed Adeline. They both giggled hysterically as Dan shook his head.

"My little girl doesn't need to hear this." He pretended to cover Halia's ears, only bringing on more laughter.

"From my medical perspective, you did do a very good job. Everything looks much better," Adeline informed him.

"Naturally," Dan scoffed just to hear Fionna's laughter again.

"Remember, we'll be casting you a few additional times today, and feeling emotional is completely normal. It will take a while for your hormones and energy levels to steady." Adeline gestured back to the rocking chair where Fionna had been sobbing a few moments before. "We need to keep Miss Halia gaining weight, which she is doing nicely. As long as the gunshot wound looks good and she's over five pounds, tomorrow evening you can take her home. But if I'm going to let you go home, you must promise me a few things."

"Okay," Dan took the bait.

"You must solemnly swear that you will not engage in intercourse for at least three weeks, and it must be after your postpartum checkup. When you do decide to initiate that portion of your relationship again, you must work slowly and take it easy for the first few times. The way that I'm able to heal you sort of tightens everything back up. Lots of foreplay and lubricants are good. It might be a little painful, similar to your first sexual encounter," she explained but moved on without awaiting a reply. "You must also swear that you will use the cast for at least a year so we can make certain that your uterus has completely healed this time before we put it to task yet again."

"Yes, ma'am." Fionna smiled.

"I solemnly swear," Dan agreed as he bounced Halia who'd worked her left hand to Dan's mouth and had taken hold of his bottom lip.

CHAPTER 8

HEALING

By the next evening, Fionna had been casted repeatedly until her body had dispensed with the excess blood and birthing fluids. She was elated to switch from diapers to the pads Kara had provided her.

With her uterus back to its original shape and healing along with her internal organs resettling back in place, Dan was astonished by how much weight she'd lost. Not nearly enough to have gotten back into her skinny jeans, which she laughed hysterically over with Dan and Kara as they'd quoted a few of her instructions to them before she'd gone into active labor.

Dan carried their bags along with the Hawaiian floral bouquet sent to Fionna from Tutu and Papa to the car. He added it to the box of preemie diapers the hospital had provided them along with a box of enhanced formula.

He was bombarded as soon as he made his appearance.

"Mentor Vindico, will your wife and little girl be headed home today?"

"Can you confirm that the baby is in fact yours?"

Dan rolled his eyes.

"What's her name, Dan?"

"Are you getting ready to take her home?"

"Has the Crown Governor seen her? Is he demanding an energy scan?" came at him from all sides.

As Dan had been asked about Halia's paternity each time he'd left the hospital in the last forty-eight hours, most of the time to acquire Fionna non-hospital grade food and coffee, he was no longer surprised by the audacity.

After loading up the Mercedes, he wondered how badly they were going to be swarmed when Fionna made her exit. He backed out quickly, making reporters and cameramen leap out of his way, as he drove to the exit where he was to pick up Fionna.

Racing inside, he smiled as Fionna was fitting blankets around Halia inside of her car seat.

"I don't want her to get cold," she fussed.

"The wind's picked up. We need to get her home."

Adeline appeared with a wheelchair for Fionna. Dan draped an additional blanket over the car seat to block Halia from the chilling November winds and from the cameras. He carried her out as Adeline wheeled Fionna to the car.

The press swarmed. Dan ordered them away as he helped Fionna up into the car. One reporter was ballsy enough to reach for the blanket on the car seat. Dan summoned. His shield cast pulsed in an angry orb in his hand. He narrowed his eyes. "Move or be thrown."

The reporter backed away.

Dan studied the clouds as he drove them home. If his predictions were correct, they were going to get an early snowstorm. "I'm going to get you inside and then go out and get a few more boxes of diapers and some more formula."

"Okay." The two syllables shook from her.

"What's wrong?"

"What if I do something wrong? She's so tiny and helpless, and there were lots of people to tell me how to do everything at the hospital and now…" she drowned out in her own worry.

"We'll figure it out. If we can't, we can call a bunch of people who will gladly help us."

The Stylers were at the house. It smelled heavenly when they entered. Mr. Styler had been baking most of the day. Dan was so tired of eating fast food, his mouth watered as he took in the dinner spread on their kitchen table.

"Thank you." Fionna hugged her parents tightly. She was ordered to go and sit on the couch by her father.

"I'll bring you a plate, Maylea. You rest," he commanded.

Rolling her eyes, Fionna agreed. She grabbed Aida's hand and pulled her onto the couch beside her. Aida was delighted to have her mother's undivided attention for a little while.

Dan handed Halia off to the Stylers to make his quick run to the store to pick up anything they might need should they be snowed in for any length of time. When he returned, Fionna was sipping the tea Tutu prescribed to ward off depression and anxiety and to rebalance her hormones that Gretta was insisting she drink per Tutu's orders.

Dan summoned heat from around him, lit the fire, and watched Fionna help Aida give Halia her bottle. Tutu had explained that Halia needed to be close to Fionna often, so Fi held her after she ate.

Dan had everything he would ever need. Fionna was right beside him with his arm around her. Aida was lying in his lap watching TV and telling them all about her days while they were away. Halia slept soundly in her mother's arms as lightly falling snow began to etch the window panes outside.

"Look." Fionna pointed out the windows. "Have you ever seen snow before?" she asked Aida. Fionna seemed thrilled to be able to show their little girl something she'd never experienced before.

Aida shook her head and crawled into a chair near the window.

"What is it?" Her expression was a mix of wonder and fear.

Dan moved to her. "It's like rain, only it's so cold outside the water droplets are frozen when they fall and then they stick to the frozen ground."

"I didn't know what it was either until I moved here." Fionna wrapped her arms around Aida. "It doesn't snow in Hawaii except on the very, very highest volcanoes, and we don't really go up there. It scared me when I first saw it, but it won't hurt us. If it keeps snowing and it sticks, then tomorrow maybe Daddy can take you out to play in it."

"Of course, but it's really cold so you have to bundle up," he warned. She might be the only child on the block that had Iodex grade heat syncs in her winter coat and mittens, but Dan saw no issue with that.

"I'll wear my coat," Aida promised as she stared out into the darkened night and watched the snowflakes perform their rhythmic dance to the ground. Halia began grunting.

"Why don't you and I go get your bath and put your warmest jammies on and then we can read Mommy's books that Pops brought for you. Daddy can give Halia her bottle and put on her jammies," Fionna explained. She'd sensed Aida's desperation for a little time with her mommy.

Aida loved her grandparents and certainly she loved Dan, but she wanted Fionna all to herself for a little while. Fionna's father had discovered several Hawaiian children's story books in a box he'd been unpacking. He'd brought them over for Aida to read.

Aida was visibly thrilled with the idea. "Come on, Mommy." She grasped Fionna's hand and yanked her toward the steps.

"Whoa." Dan scrubbed Aida's hair with his hand. "Be careful with Mommy," he reminded her.

"I'm sorry." Aida's face fell.

"I'm okay." Fionna cupped her hand under Aida's chin and leaned down to press their foreheads together in a *Honi*, an exchanging of breath in Hawaiian.

Dan grinned as he took the baby from Fionna. She was working her way into quite a temper.

"She's hungry." Fionna kissed Halia's cheek on her way up the stairs.

Dan wasn't certain how other people dealt with newborns, but being married to a powerful Receiver was extremely helpful. According to his phenomenal wife, babies spoke in emotions. As that was most definitely Fionna's native language, there was very little guessing as to what Halia might need at any given moment.

Dan wrapped a blanket around Halia and carried her to the kitchen. She was sobbing and curling herself up into a tiny ball as he quickly heated her bottle.

"I'm hurrying. I promise," Dan tried to soothe her. A moment later he reclined her in his arm and placed the bottle to her tiny rosebud lips.

Fionna swore to Dan that Halia was happiest in his arms. The thought delighted him, but he'd pointed out that she adored Fionna as well.

Fionna read *Too Many Mangoes* and *The Hawaiian Rainbow* to Aida.

After that, Fionna eased back down the stairs, yawning and hunched forward.

"I think I better put all of my girls to bed," Dan urged.

"I'm just so exhausted. I want to have energy. I want to bond with my little girls and spend time with you and do stuff," she fussed.

"Fi," Dan sighed. "How old is Halia?"

"Three days." Fionna rolled her eyes. She knew perfectly well where this was headed.

"Actually she's not even quite that yet." It was only eight o'clock and Halia had been born around ten in the morning.

"And that means you need to take it easy and rest. You'll be back to normal, sweetheart, but it's going to take a few weeks."

"I know, but you don't understand. I haven't really felt like myself in months, and now I can see my feet and my stomach doesn't arrive in rooms five minutes before the rest of me. It seems like getting back to normal is just out of reach, and I want to be me again. Or maybe I want to figure out who I am now. I really, really want that."

"I know," Dan soothed.

"You do not know."

Chuckling, he nodded his agreement. "Okay, I don't know, but I can imagine," he corrected. "How about this—why don't we put our tiniest baby girl in her crib as I have successfully fed and burped her and been spit up on, which I have decided is a way that she professes love and generally means that she will probably sleep for a couple of hours." He reveled in her giggle. "Then we could take a bath and I will put you to bed just before miss Halia decides that she would like another bottle."

"You're the best husband ever," Fionna declared as she kissed his cheek. "But my boobs still feel like flaming bowling balls."

Dan winked at her. "I will selflessly volunteer to cool them with my hands just like I did last night while the rest of you relaxes in the bath water."

"So far, my birthing our child has gotten your hands on several of your favorite things," she sassed with a gleam in her eye.

Dan waggled his eyebrows. "It's my job to soothe any pain you may have, sweetheart. I take that job very seriously. When you're feeling all better, I'll see if I can soothe anything else that you might like."

Fionna shuddered. "That makes my brain happy but my va-jay-jay terrified."

"Not for a while." He'd wait as long as she needed. "Let's go take a bath. You're supposed to use those oils and that pad thing Tutu sent. You know that will help."

"As if she doesn't remind me enough that she's always right, now she has you doing it too."

Chuckling, Dan carried Halia up to her nursery. He successfully wrapped her in the swaddle sleep sack they'd been instructed to use.

He moved to the ornate white iron crib that Fionna had picked out for their littlest princess. Fionna removed the decorative pillows that had been placed in there before Halia's birth. She summoned a heat cast and ran her hand over the mattress, warming the spot where Halia would lie. Dan leaned and laid Halia tenderly in the crib. They both stared at her uncomfortably. She was so little, and the bed appeared gargantuan. His baby girl looked lost amongst the floral crib sheet.

Fionna shook her head and reached for Halia. "She's scared. We can't just leave her in here all alone. She needs us." Fionna's voice shook. Halia was beginning to stir. Her face contorted toward a terrified peal. Lifting their little girl out of her bed and cradling her tenderly, Fionna's cast soothed Halia back to sleep.

"I have an idea." Dan rushed from the room. He grabbed the brown wicker bassinet that had been in their living room. It was certainly light enough for Dan to carry up and down the stairs each day that he was home with his girls. Halia would be dramatically bigger by the time he returned to work. Maybe she could sleep in her crib in a few weeks.

Forgoing the nursery altogether, Dan set the bassinet up right beside their bed. He heat casted the mattress and the basket itself.

Relief eased Fionna's entire body as she laid Halia back in her bassinet and covered her tenderly. She kept her soothing cast pulsing from her hands as their little girl settled into the tiny bed and entered a restful sleep.

"Okay, but not in our bed and not in here for too long," Fionna reminded Dan of the Haydenshires' advice to them when they'd adopted Aida.

"I know, but we're going to be getting up with her for a while anyway. This way she won't wake Aida." He grabbed the monitor, guided Fionna into their bathroom, and closed the door before turning on the bath water. Next, he extracted a wooden crate from the closet that contained the oils, rubs, and other things Tutu had prescribed for Maylea after giving birth.

It also contained a tub of coconut oil to be used for Halia's backside to ward off yeast and diaper rash and lavender baby washes and massage oils for the little princess. Dan set those aside and lifted out the box labeled specifically for Maylea.

Fionna took over. She pulled something that looked like the large bed pads she'd sat on in the hospital bed while her body had been casted and all of the afterbirth forced from her uterus.

"Tutu fills these full of oatmeal, and Epsom salt, and yarrow, and shea butter and stuff, and then you sit on them in the bath and it makes everything feel better." Fionna looked rather forward to the relief.

"Are you still hurting that bad, baby?" Dan tried not to panic, but her being hurt wounded him.

"Kind of," she confessed.

After adding lavender oil and two other oils Fionna said would tighten her skin back up, Dan guided her into the tub as she seated herself on the bath pad.

"Are you sure you want me in there? I can just let you relax, sweetheart."

"No, I want to sit with you. It's important. I don't want to get all caught up in the girls and forget us." She sounded like that fear had been bothering her for a while.

"Fi." Dan shook his head as he climbed in the tub behind her and settled her back against him. "We will not let that happen, but you literally *just* gave birth. I'm gonna be home for the next three weeks. Then I'll go back just long enough to get the kids ready for their exams and then I'll be home for another four weeks for Christmas break. All in all, I'd say our precious little girl has impeccable timing in terms of getting me out of work."

Fionna smiled as she reveled in the relief her body was experiencing and being in Dan's arms.

"I never thought I'd hear you excited about missing so much work."

"If that's not a sign that I'm not meant to be at Venton, then nothing is," he lamented. He wanted to do a good job. He'd made a commitment.

As it turned out, their bath was cut short in light of Halia's fussing.

"You stay and soak. I'll get her," Dan commanded.

"She's not hungry, just lonely. Just let her snuggle with you."

He extracted himself from the tub and dried off while he rushed back to the bassinet.

CHAPTER 9

SLIPPERY SLOPE

Light was pouring in the bedroom windows when Dan awoke. He'd gotten up to feed Halia at eleven thirty and then again at three. Fi had gotten up with her just before six and had taken her downstairs to let Dan sleep. As it was nearing ten o'clock, it wasn't a horrible schedule. He pulled back the blinds on the windows to discover several inches of snow covering the ground. Pulling on a pair of sweatpants and a T-shirt, he went off in search of his girls.

Fionna had relit the fire, and Aida was seated on the couch holding Halia under Fionna's supervision.

"Look outside." Aida pointed out the window. "It's like magic!"

Chuckling, Dan nodded though he thought the sight before him on his sofa was far more magical than the snowfall.

After carrying Halia's bassinet back down to the living room so she could nap under her mother's watchful eye, Dan bundled Aida up for playing in the snow. He filled the heat syncs with his hand and arranged them in Aida's winter coat and boots before he donned his old Iodex snow jacket and set the heat syncs to keep him warm as well. Fionna helped Aida with her knit cap and gloves and waved to them as Dan helped Aida onto the porch.

"Go nap with our littlest one, Mama," Dan ordered as Aida patted the snow on the porch railings.

"Yes, dear," Fionna sighed as she closed out the wintery cold and returned to the warmth of their home.

Dan showed Aida how to pack a snowball, and she let the still-falling snowflakes land on her tongue. She joined some neighbor kids as they constructed a snowman with Dan's help.

"Hey, I'm Chris Leslie." The children's father extended his gloved hand to Dan.

"Dan Vindico." He smiled.

"I'm sorry we haven't met before now. I guess we kind of keep to ourselves," Chris tried to explain.

"No problem. We have the same thing going on."

"I have a new baby sister," Aida informed Chris's daughter who looked to be a year or two older than Aida.

Chris smiled. "Congratulations," he offered Dan.

"Thanks. She was born Thursday morning."

"Is your wife doing okay?" Chris seemed to understand that it was Fionna that had done all of the hard work.

"Yeah." Dan nodded. "Little sore and really tired after all that."

"Yeah, it takes Carrie a little while to get her equilibrium back, but we have five, so we're significantly outnumbered."

Dan chuckled.

After an awkward pause, "Hey, can I ask you something?" spilled from Chris's mouth.

"I suppose." Dan was wary. He kept his eyes trained on Aida. Once a cop, always a cop.

"Not to get into your business or anything, but have you met those people who bought the Adamses' old house?" He pointed to Fred Scheckles's new home across the street from Dan and Fionna.

"Yes." Dan sighed with an eye roll.

Chris laughed. "Okay, good. I thought you seemed completely normal, but he keeps telling everyone that you're some kind of spy or something and that you have weapons in your basement and that you're going to be starting some kind of neighborhood watch."

Shaking his head, Dan laughed. "I used to be the head of an Elite Force that worked out of the CIA," he gave the most recent Non-Gifted explanation of Iodex.

Sometimes they were FBI. Sometimes Navy SEAL teams. Dan was fairly certain if Logan Haydenshire ever got his way, they'd be the Avengers next. "Not that I advertise that too often, but Fred showed up at my house and tried to detain one of my former officers," he bent the truth further. "And I don't even have a basement. The back door leads to a single storage room that's not tall enough to hold anything but lawn equipment, which you are welcome to check out if you're worried. I understand you want your kids and wife safe. I got out of the CIA a while ago. It's not exactly the kind of job I wanted once I got married and started having kids. We adopted Aida back in April, and, like I said, Halia was born a couple of days ago." Whatever Fred Scheckles had told Chris, it had him visibly concerned.

"Thank God," Chris gasped his relief. "I didn't know what to think, you know. Carrie said she'd met your wife a few months ago at the grocery store, and that she seemed like a perfectly normal, nice, kind person. I'd seen Aida playing at the park and getting off the bus in the afternoons. But you know you hear about people everyone thought were normal going crazy or whatever. There are people with arsenals in their home." He shook his head.

"I'm really sorry." Dan wondered what could be done to shut Fred Scheckles up. "Unless you can build some kind of weapon of mass destruction out of dozens of preemie diapers, gallons of formula, and my wife's extensive shoe collection, I can't help you." He made Chris laugh heartily.

"That Fred guy is nuts then, right? A few days after he announced that he was going to join your neighborhood army, I caught him leering over the fence at my wife while she was raking leaves for the kids to jump in."

Dan could tell it had infuriated Chris, but he must've not wanted Dan to think he was overbearing or overly protective. Dan wondered what Chris would think if he and his wife got to know the Vindicos a little better. You could take a Shield out of Iodex, but you couldn't take the Predilect out of a Shield.

"If he doesn't stop getting our mail just to hand deliver it to Fionna while he tries not to drool all over her, I might come up with that arsenal," Dan huffed.

"Now, that's a cause I could get behind. He rang our doorbell at six Saturday morning to inform us that there was a Land Rover he hadn't seen before parked in your driveway and to deliver our paper to us in his bathrobe." Chris shuddered. "Like I said, we have five kids. If they're all asleep at one time, we throw a party, and here this guy is ringing my doorbell at six on a Saturday morning."

"Trust me, I do now understand how precious sleep is," Dan assured him.

"I thought my wife was going to strangle him. She told him your wife probably had the baby and asked why he cared what cars were in your driveway."

Joining in the laughter, Dan nodded. "That was my parents' car. They kept Aida while Fi and I were in the hospital." He felt he owed Chris an explanation. He was immensely thankful that Chris had decided to approach Dan instead of just going along with whatever Fred Scheckles was telling all of their neighbors.

"You said preemie diapers," Chris recalled. "Is she okay?"

"Yeah, she was three weeks early. She weighed less than five pounds so we're keeping a close watch on her, but she's doing really well. We probably won't have her out too much for a while." Dan hoped to ward off any rumors as to why the Vindicos stuck close to home and weren't especially social.

"Hey, I get it. Annabelle was six weeks early." He gestured his head to his youngest little girl. She appeared to be around two or three and was trying desperately to keep up with her older sisters and brothers. "She had to stay in the NICU for two weeks. Then Carrie and I wouldn't let her out of our sight for about the first six months. I had to convince Carrie to go out on the weekends and have a little fun. I was worried she would forget the world outside of our house."

Dan instantly liked Chris Leslie. He offered him a kind smile. "She looks like she's gotten it all figured out," he pointed out as he watched Aida pack a snowball for Annabelle and place it in her mittened hands.

"Are you kidding me? She wears us all out. I can't keep up with her." Chris chuckled as Annabelle toddled over to him, showing him the snowball Aida made for her.

"Did you tell Aida thank you?" Chris reminded her.

"Dan tu," Annabelle gushed.

Annabelle began exploring the front yard and picking up tiny sticks that had fallen from trees under the weight of the snow.

The older children followed after her, and Dan and Chris relocated to keep an eye on them.

Suddenly, Dan heard a car approaching rapidly over the slick streets. In a deafening moment, he heard the brakes screech. The car slid on the ice. The driver lost control in the cul-de-sac where the kids were playing.

Dan raced to Annabelle. He threw his shield. It forced Aida and the Leslies' youngest son away from the car as it careened where Annabelle had been standing not two seconds before and was forced away by Dan's cast. It dented the bumper. Dan prayed Chris didn't notice that.

He held Annabelle wrapped in his shield.

As he studied the passengers, he noted six or seven young men from Venton Academy. Seated in the middle of the backseat, he saw none other than Clarence Pendergrath as he tried to slink down in the car as it sped away, swerving all over the icy roads.

"Oh my God, thank you," Chris choked as he made his way to Dan and Annabelle.

The little girl was sobbing. Dan dropped his shield and handed her to her father.

"Wow, you're really strong," the Leslies' son admired. Dan prayed his cast hadn't hurt the little boy.

CHAPTER 10

COMFORTS

Fionna raced out onto the front porch carrying Halia who was crying and wrapped haphazardly in a quilt. Chris's wife, Carrie, sprinted out of her house at the same moment.

"What was that?" She raced through the freezing snow wearing nothing but jeans, a sweatshirt, and house slippers. It seemed no amount of snow was going to keep her from her children if she thought they were in distress.

"Dan!" Fionna gasped in terror over Halia's wailing.

"I'm coming, baby. Stay right there." Dan didn't want her carrying Halia down their snow-covered brick steps when she still wasn't all that steady on her feet. "I'll call the police," Dan offered Chris who was fighting back tears. He and Carrie held Annabelle between them along with their other children in an odd, congregated hug.

"Thank you so much." Carrie broke away and threw her arms around Dan. She must've felt the heat syncs in Dan's jacket. Her brow furrowed.

"No problem." He stepped back and lifted Aida into his arms as if that was the reason he'd fended Carrie off.

As Dan carried Aida back through the snow toward their own front door, he heard Chris explain, "Oh yeah, it's probably that thermo-tech stuff. He's former CIA. I told you that Fred guy was a moron."

Still reeling from what happened, Dan found it odd that he was chuckling.

Fionna was trembling from fear and cold as Dan bustled all of his girls back into the house.

"Why did the car do that?" Aida's chin shook as she clung to Dan.

"I don't know, baby." He helped her off with her coat and returned the heat syncs to the charging station hidden in their coat closet. He lifted Halia from Fionna's embrace and set a heat cast through his hands. He calmed her from the freezing cold she'd been exposed to. Fionna was still shaking as she helped Aida change into warm clothes and settled her on the couch with her blanket and Sophie.

"Who was that? I know you know," Fionna asked as she and Dan headed to the kitchen with Halia.

"Three guesses and the first two don't count. I'm calling Dad and then Portwood." He handed Halia back to Fionna once she was calmed.

"Are you freaking kidding me? I have to send guys out in this on Sunday because of that little prick?" Portwood spat.

"For the record, I told all of you letting him out was a huge mistake," Dan reminded him.

"You and me both, but when the Crown Governor says, 'Landon, this is what we're doing,' I say, 'Yes, sir,'" Portwood lamented. "Did he see you?"

"Oh, he definitely saw me."

"And is the house going on the market or are we okay with that?"

"I just brought my baby girl home, remember? I can't sell it right now." He sounded angrier than he'd intended.

"All right, I'm on it. I'll see if we can't find Junior and his little gang of idiots."

Dan wouldn't let Aida go back outside to play. He simply couldn't. He noted that the Leslie children never made another appearance either. He lay on the couch for the rest of the afternoon with Halia sleeping soundly in a little ball on his bare chest while Fionna and

Aida cuddled on the love seat watching *Calamity Jane* and a collection of *Gidget* movies.

"Mommy, you made my shirt wet." Aida leaned away from Fionna in the middle of *Gidget Goes Hawaiian.*

"Oh my gosh. I'm so sorry," Fionna panicked as Dan tried not to laugh. Aida had been lying against Fionna's chest, and she'd leaked all over both of them.

"Go change," Fionna sighed and then turned to Dan. "When will it go away?"

"Adeline said a few days. It's okay," Dan assured her as she stomped up the stairs to change. When she returned, she made herself yet another cup of the sage tea Tutu had sent that was supposed to dry up her milk.

Dan's heart seized as a knock sounded on their front door at dusk. Aida was seated at the coffee table playing with Dan's iPad. Halia was asleep in her bassinet.

Fionna stood. She and Dan shared a concerned expression.

"Take the girls upstairs," he ordered. Fionna guided Aida up the stairs and lifted Halia from the cradle.

Dan considered the pistol hidden in the coat closet, but he set his shield and eased the front door open. He immediately dropped his shield and relaxed. "Hey, Fi, it's the Leslies." He opened the door wide to allow Chris and Carrie Leslie into their living room.

Fionna reappeared carrying Halia.

Tears formed in Carrie's eyes as she eased inside. "I just wanted to bring you some dinner. I know it's so hard right after they're born, and we wanted to thank you again for saving Annabelle."

"You didn't have to do that." Fionna looked truly honored.

"We wanted to," Chris assured her.

Carrie was gazing at Halia longingly.

"Would you like to hold her?" Fionna offered.

"Do you mind?" Carrie looked as if Fionna had offered her oxygen after drowning.

"Okay, but five is enough," Chris reminded her as everyone chuckled.

Carrie settled on the edge of the love seat and accepted the little bundle of Halia and her blanket.

Dan carried a huge pot of chili along with all of the sides into the kitchen. While they'd been in the hospital, the Stylers and the Haydenshires had loaded up their freezer and fridge with dinners for the next week, but chili was perfect after the day they'd had.

Fionna began probing Carrie for information on when she would stop leaking and when her backside would stop hurting.

Chris and Dan stayed in the kitchen and tried not to overhear.

"Do you want to stay and eat?" Dan offered since they'd made the chili.

"Oh no, we can't. We left our oldest in charge, so we have to get back before he declares lordship over his siblings and tries to force them to become his slaves, which always shockingly ends in revolt," Chris explained. "My house is very much like the Roman Empire."

Dan chuckled. "I talked to the police. They sent out a few cars."

"I still can't believe it. It happened so fast." Chris shook his head.

"Yeah, well, they had no business joyriding over ice." Dan was still furious over the morning's events.

Every time he thought about Clarence Pendergrath knowing where his home was, it made his stomach churn. He shuddered slightly as he followed Chris back into the living room.

"Don't you just want one more?" Carrie asked Chris as she gestured to Halia.

"Not two days ago you were threatening to put three of ours out for the garbage pickup when they finger painted the antique rocking chair."

"I know, but she's so cute and she smells like a newborn and a little baby coconut," Carrie cooed.

Fionna laughed. "That's probably the scented coconut oil we rub all over her little tushy to keep her from getting diaper rash," she explained.

"Oh, does that work?" Carrie sounded intrigued. "I've heard of that."

"It works great."

"She's just so sweet." Carrie kissed Halia's forehead as she slept.

"Okay, but if you want to try for another one, we have to go home and let the Vindicos eat."

"Yeah, please don't work on that here." Dan brought on more laughter.

"That was so nice of them, and now we have friends that are here and nice." Fionna seemed thrilled with the Leslies as she devoured a bowl of chili.

By eight thirty, Dan and Fionna were both exhausted. Aida was worn out from the snow and the terror she'd experienced that morning. Dan helped her with her bath, and she fell asleep halfway through the first story he read her.

Dan fed Halia her bottle while Fionna soaked her aching body in another bath. He checked Aida in her room and tucked her quilt around her. He heat casted it as he kissed her cheek. He brushed another kiss on Halia's cheek. Her little tummy was full of the warmed formula. He grinned and fell into the bed exhausted. He was asleep when Fionna crawled in the bed. She curled up on his chest, and he managed to kiss the top of her head before they both fell sound asleep.

CHAPTER 11

CURIOUS

Dan shot upward as Aida raced into the bedroom, and Halia began sobbing loudly.

"What was that?" Fionna gasped as Dan handed her the baby, and Aida crawled into bed beside her. Dan slid the pistol from the nightstand.

"Stay in here. Do not come out until I come to the door and I tell you your birthdate," Dan commanded. "When I leave, slide the chest in front of the door. I'm going to cast it when I leave." He pushed the blanket chest that sat at the end of their bed as close as he could get it to the door so that Fionna wouldn't have to move it far after he left the room.

"There it is again," Fionna whispered as Halia continued to wail and Aida shuddered beside them.

The banging was coming from the back of the house. Dan edged into the hallway. He waited until the lock on the knob turned, and he heard the chest slide across the carpeted floor.

Pressing his back to the wall, he slid down the hallway with his arms extended downward, grasping the Browning semiautomatic in his hands. He summoned and threw a shield over the bedroom door. He drew again and surrounded himself in his shield by pushing it out of his pores. He listened intently. He cleared Aida's room and then the nursery. The sound was coming from the floor below.

He eased along the wall and down the stairwell, clearing the kitchen when he heard a crash that sounded like it was coming from below him. *The storage room.*

"He's here," Dan spat as Portwood answered the phone. Dan glanced at the clock on the ovens. It was just after midnight.

"Where?"

"He thinks he can get in the house from the storage room."

"I'm at the office. Mike's up here with me. We'll be there in five. I'll call you when we get there."

True to his word, Dan's cell rang three minutes later.

He raced out the front door as Ericcson and Portwood sprinted around the house from the driveway, pistols drawn and shields pulsing a vibrant green.

A split second later, Ericcson had someone by the scruff of his neck. He hurled him on the ground and planted his boot in his chest. "Are you fucking stupid enough to think you'd break in Vindico's house, kid?"

Dan summoned and lit his outdoor lights, illuminating the area. He saw the footprints through the snow that led to his storage room door that was badly dented.

But it wasn't Clarence Pendergrath lying on the ground. It was Fred Scheckles.

Chris Leslie raced over from next door. "Is everything okay? I got up with Hannah. Her stomach hurt. I heard something banging and saw your lights come on."

"I was just curious," Fred was pleading. His eyes goggled over Dan's gun aimed at his head and Portwood's aimed at his heart.

"You weren't kidding, were you?" Chris also seemed bewildered by the fierce demeanor of the Elite Iodex members and the high-powered guns they were all carrying.

"I was just curious. I didn't mean to wake them up. I slid on the ice," he lamented. "I was gonna check it out when they were gone, but there's always someone here." Fred couldn't get his confession out fast enough.

"Are you fucking kidding me?" Dan snarled. "You woke up my babies and scared my wife to death because you were curious." Incensed rage spiked in Dan's shield, not that Fred Scheckles could see that.

"Curious about what?" Portwood demanded.

"He used to be in the CIA," Fred tried to explain to Portwood though he sounded more like a tattling child.

Portwood nodded and visibly worked to keep from laughing. "Guess who we work for?" He gestured to himself and Ericcson.

Fred paled dramatically. "He has some kind of elaborate security system. I decided that's what threw me back that day when I came over with Betty's cookies. I was just trying to make sure he wasn't some kind of crazy."

Realizing what had obviously happened, Portwood shook his head and shared a quick glance with Dan.

"What's his name?"

"Fred Scheckles," Dan and Chris supplied simultaneously.

"If you're arresting him, can I add some kind of charge for him loitering around my house, staring at my wife and kids, and basically being a pervert?" Chris still seemed shocked by the situation.

"I'm sure I can come up with something." Portwood narrowed his eyes at Fred. "Do you know what this is called, Fred?" He gestured to the half door that Fred had been trying to pry open. "We call this breaking and entering, not to mention trespassing, and it sounds like Mr…." Portwood waited on Chris to supply his name.

"Chris Leslie," he stated.

"Mr. Leslie might have a trespassing charge in the works as well," Portwood informed him.

"Oh, and add intercepting mail belonging to another," Dan spat.

"Damn, man, that's ten years or up to $250,000. Do you have that kind of cash?" Ericcson questioned Fred.

"I was just picking up their mail. It's a neighborly thing to do," Fred argued.

Portwood rolled his eyes. "It's against the law. As is trying to enter another person's property in the middle of the night while he and his wife and his kids are asleep. So, listen up, unless Mr. Vindico or Mr.

Leslie want to press charges, I'm gonna let you go. But you already know Dan's former CIA, so if I were you, I'd stay the hell away from his house and I'd make damn certain that I stay away from Fi and his girls. If you can't do that, when he gets done with you, you can take on all of Dan's Elite team. I promise that will not end well for you."

"Back in Pilmore, we don't keep things from our neighbors. We're nice and open. If Betty's in the back yard, I wouldn't get upset if he took a gander." Fred threw his hand out to Chris who scowled his disapproval. "I'm just keeping an eye out. Keeping the crime away from the neighborhood."

"You are the crime in the neighborhood, moron," Ericcson defied as Dan stifled a chuckle. His acrimony returned quickly when he thought of Fionna up in their bedroom having been awoken from a deep sleep only four days after giving birth to comfort and protect their children.

"Guess what," Dan growled furiously. "This isn't South Dakota. Do not come back on my property. Stay the hell away from my wife and my kids, and keep your nose out of my life," he demanded as he leaned inches away from Fred's face.

"You don't have to be rude." Fred managed to stand when Ericcson released him.

"Go home, Mr. Scheckles. If I get called back out here, I'm not going to be so nice," Portwood assured him.

Fred made a quick escape. He slipped on the ice every few feet as he fled. Everyone standing in Dan's backyard shook their heads in stunned disbelief.

"So, you can just call the CIA out whenever?" Chris stammered.

"I try not to abuse that privilege," Dan assured him.

"No, no, I'm good with it. I'm just not certain if I feel really, really safe being your neighbor or just a little freaked out."

Portwood, Ericcson, and Dan all chuckled.

"Dan's a good guy," Portwood vowed. "As long as you don't mess with Fi or the baby girls, you're golden."

Chris's hands went up in mock surrender. "I have no issue with that," he promised. "I'm just gonna go." He gestured his thumb back toward his own home. "And, no joke, that Scheckles guy is crazy, but I didn't mean to intrude. I guess I'm still a little freaked by the car thing this morning." He sounded as if being horrified by the thought of your child being hit by a car was something he should apologize about.

"It's fine," Dan soothed. "It's nice to have neighbors that aren't insane."

With a wave, Chris rushed up the steps to his back deck and disappeared inside his own house.

"You know he's gonna keep trying shit like this," Ericcson sighed.

"Yeah, I know. Hey, what were you doing at work so late?"

Portwood grinned. "I hired Jeff on the contingency that he passes his exams, right?" Dan nodded. "Right, so I figure I've got a freaking tech genius. Why not really see what he can do? In the past week, we've rounded up three high-end retail hackers and several fraudulent credit card cyberstalkers. I don't remember what he called them. Then Friday, he figured out that there's been attempts on Iodex files from unknown IP addresses. He managed to find the guys, but they're in Myanmar, so we were negotiating with Iodex there. Anyway, he and Logan and Rainer were looking over the Venton stuff one day at lunch. The day Halia was born actually," he recalled. "Somebody's trying to hack the school's databases. Jeff's pretty certain it's Wilshire.

"But every time we set something up to catch whoever it is, some kind of good guy hacker or whatever Jeff calls him keeps getting in the way. Governor Haydenshire wants Wilshire caught if it is him. He just filed for separation to force his paychecks to be divided since your dad set it up so his wife's getting the money right now," Portwood explained the urgency. "I'm sure Jeff would've told you, but we figured you wouldn't want us to interrupt Fionna's pushing with 'hey Dan, we got something on Wilshire.'"

"Yeah, I was a little preoccupied," Dan admitted wryly.

"I figured."

"Speaking of Fi, I need to get back inside. She's holed up in our bedroom with the girls."

Ericcson shook his head. "I'm sorry, man. Neighbors are either great or horrible. They are never anything in between."

After thanking them for coming so quickly, Dan raced back inside. "Hey baby, it's me, and April 26th."

The door flew open as Fionna and Halia fell into his arms with Aida wrapping her arms around his waist.

"It's okay," he soothed all of the girls. "Our neighbor decided he'd like to check out the storage room." He took Halia from Fionna and began trying to soothe her back to sleep. He seated himself on the blanket chest Fionna had pulled away from the door. He pulled Aida onto his lap and balanced both of his little girls while giving Fionna adoring gazes as she began to pace.

"That Fred person?" she shrieked. Dan was well aware of the fact that if it hadn't been for Aida's presence *person* would not have been her chosen word. "Did you arrest him?"

"I can't arrest anyone anymore, and we don't exactly have much jurisdiction over Fred Scheckles other than turning him over to Non-Gifted," Dan reminded her. "So, we just scared the…"—Dan glanced at Aida—"we took care of it for tonight anyway."

Aida yawned and nuzzled her face into Dan's chest.

"Here, baby, I'll take you back to bed. It was just our neighbor in the backyard. Nothing scary, okay?"

"Why?" she managed through another deep yawn.

"People get nosy and want to know things that aren't any of their business," Fionna explained.

"What's nosy?"

"Let's talk about it more in the morning." Dan handed Halia back to her mother and lifted Aida into his arms.

"Will you lie down with me?"

Fionna nodded her encouragement. "I'll give Halia a bottle, and Daddy can lie down with you and then maybe everyone can sleep until morning."

As it was only a little after midnight, Dan doubted that Halia would make it until morning, but he appreciated her optimism.

He returned to their bedroom just as Fionna was laying Halia back in her bassinet. They stood together, staring at their little girl sound asleep in the moonlight reflecting off the remaining snow drifts.

"She's so beautiful," Fionna whispered.

"Just like her mama and her big sister," Dan vowed. "Come to bed with me." He was desperate for her to relax and sleep. She needed to heal.

Whimpering with a mock pout, Fionna climbed into bed and resumed her position cradled on Dan's chest.

"You used to say that to me and we got to do more than sleep. Now sleep is all I dream of, and we've only been home two nights." She sounded like this was something she'd been worrying about.

"Fi, baby, your grandmother, Adeline, Mrs. Haydenshire, Malani, everyone told you that it would take a couple of months to get back in your groove. I'm not pressuring you to do anything at all. I want you to take your time and heal. Let's just lie here together, okay?" Taking all of the pressure off Fionna Vindico was the only way he knew how to get her to really relax and begin to gain a little perspective.

"You are so hard on yourself. For me, please relax. I'm home for the next few weeks. Let me help. Let's do stuff together with the girls and then whenever you're ready for the two of us, we'll ease into that. Whatever you want is fine. You are a phenomenal wife and a phenomenal mom, so let's just take it a day at a time. Please. For me."

"Okay." Fionna nodded against him, but she sounded like she was accepting bitter defeat.

CHAPTER 12
OVERPROTECTIVE DISCRETION

A few weeks later, McCarron was having a teacher workday, and Fionna was going for her postpartum checkup with Adeline.

Dan wanted to go with her, but Fionna wasn't ready to leave Halia with anyone besides Dan. She decided she would rather have him stay home with the girls and she would go by herself.

"I will agree to this only if you promise me that if Adeline tells you that you need to relax more or rest or whatever that you'll tell me what she said. I am not afraid to call her," Dan informed his wife as she got ready.

Fionna wound her arms around his neck and gave him a sassy grin. Dan fought the need that had been gradually increasing with each passing day. Her color had returned. She had more energy. She took long skin-to-skin naps with Halia each afternoon. Halia was sleeping better at night.

Fionna was no longer in any pain, and after calling Tutu the Monday after their nighttime intrusion to inform her grandmother that she still felt rather unbalanced and that her hair was falling out at what she considered to be an alarming rate, a large box from Kauai had arrived Wednesday morning.

She'd readily taken the teas and adaptogen supplements along with soaking in the bath with the oils her grandmother had sent. She'd followed the diet prescribed by Tutu that had Dan wondering if they should take out stock in avocadoes, walnuts, salmon, and leafy greens.

The diet had resulted in a little weight loss that had restored at least some of her waning confidence. Tutu had phoned Dan to inform him that Maylea needed a little time to rebalance herself and to see that she took time for herself, which he'd insisted on.

Fionna had gone for a quick lunch with Emily and Mrs. Haydenshire, and she'd gone to the salon for haircuts and pedicures which seemed to have worked wonders.

She felt better and looked amazing. Dan could hardly keep his eyes off her.

"I promise I will tell you everything she says while I'm naked underneath you tomorrow night," she sassed. Groaning in ardent desire, Dan forced the imagery from his mind.

"Not unless she says everything is okay for that," he corrected her with a silent prayer that Adeline would give her the go-ahead. "And we're taking it incredibly slowly."

"Yes, sir." She waggled her eyebrows, and Dan shuddered in need acute to the point of pain.

After Fionna headed back to Georgetown, Aida begged to go to the park and take Halia in her stroller. The temperature had risen gradually since the snow storm, and Dan was eager to get out of the house himself.

He realized, with some relief, that he wanted to work. He hadn't lost his drive to accomplish, but every time he pulled his laptop out of its case or attempted to complete his lesson plans for the rest of the year, his mind seemed to resist. Playing with the girls or just cuddling and talking with Fionna was a vastly more appealing way to spend his paternity leave.

Jeff and Becca were coming over that evening to discuss what had been going on at Venton in Dan's absence and to see Halia.

As Dan began packing the diaper bag, he realized that taking his children to the park now required more logistical planning than a search and rescue mission.

Trying to think through all of the possible scenarios, Dan dressed

Halia in the warmest outfit he could locate in her closet. He was certain Fionna would have been able to tell him immediately which stretchy hat went with the outfit, but he wasn't too concerned. He heat casted several blankets and laid them in her car seat which he attached to the stroller.

He changed her diaper and packed a bottle while Aida put on her coat, hat, and gloves, then Dan helped her tie her boots. Dan threw in a pacifier that Fionna had been trying on Halia though she seemed to prefer her fingers. Dan laid his baby girl in her car seat and bundled her up against the cool weather while she slept and sucked her index and middle finger vigorously.

"Let's go, Daddy," Aida urged. Though she adored her baby sister, there had been moments of her slight disdain toward Halia. She'd pointed out with regularity over the past few weeks that Daddy and Halia got to stay home, but she had to go to school.

To try and not only reassure Aida but to also ward off any further jealousy, Dan would spend the morning either napping with Halia or playing with her for the little amount of time she was awake and then spent the afternoons with Aida. He hoped to ease her into big sisterhood gently but was aware that she was going to have to share Fionna once he went back to work.

They began down the path to the parks behind their house. Dan pulled the hood cover over the car seat and the one on the stroller, blocking Halia from the brisk air and from view of any prying eyes.

"Are we still deciding to move to Tutu and Papa's after school is done?" Aida asked. Dan chuckled. She'd overheard his and Fionna's discussion of what kind of home they might like to build on the farm if they should move, and they'd told her they were still deciding whether or not that would be a good option for their family.

"Would you like to move to Kauai, baby?"

She pursed her lips in her consideration. "I think mostly yes and some no."

"Okay, which parts no?"

Aida began skipping beside the stroller. "Tutu and Papa's farm is my most favorite place, and it makes the sunshine in my tummy just like you do," she informed him, making Dan's entire day. "But I would miss Haley, and Ms. Powell, and I would miss Garrett most of all, and all of my grandparents here, and Aunt Kara, and Olivia," she listed.

Dan nodded his understanding. "Mommy and Daddy would still need to be here sometimes because we have to come to the Angels meetings. We would come back to visit, and all of those people could come to the farm and visit us. And next year, you would have a new teacher, not Ms. Powell."

"Why?" Aida panicked.

"That's how it works, sweetheart. When you go to the next grade, you get a new teacher."

Aida nodded but looked disheartened. "And Garrett will come to the farm?"

"I definitely don't think it would take too much to get Garrett to agree to vacation in Hawaii, especially if you're there."

They arrived at the park, and Dan waved to Chris Leslie who was helping Annabelle up the stairs to the slide. Her big brothers and sisters were racing around the monkey bars, and Aida ran to join them.

Chris sauntered over after settling Annabelle in the sandbox.

"This is Carrie's favorite part about me working from home," he joked. He ran his rather lucrative web design job out of his home, so he could occasionally spend his afternoons outside with the kids and then work after they'd gone to bed at night.

"I'm not looking forward to going back to Venton, trust me," Dan lamented as he waved to Aida at the top of the jungle gym.

Chris chuckled but didn't comment.

A few minutes later, Carrie pulled up in the Leslie family Suburban. She parked on one of the side streets beside the park and joined her family.

Dan grimaced as he took in the back of the Leslies' Suburban. He tried to hide it from Chris, but he'd seen Dan's concerned expression.

"What?" he pled. "That's bad, right? I knew it. But why?" He gestured to the many varied stickers of the Leslies' children's activities that their proud mother displayed on the back of her car.

Dan shook his head.

"No, it's dangerous or something, right? Just tell me," Chris demanded.

Dan pushed Halia's stroller closer to the Leslies' car. "This is really just me being overprotective because of some of the cases I worked over the years." He tried to soften the blow of what he was about to show Chris.

"Got it. Now tell me."

"You have the family stick figure people." Dan pointed to the lower left corner of the Suburban's back windshield. Chris nodded.

"So, I already know that you have five young kids and you live in Arlington County." Dan pointed to the license plate. "If the car is parked in your driveway, I know you have five young kids and I know where they live." He sighed as Chris's neck tensed with a harsh swallow.

"Anyway," Dan moved on. "You have the McCarron sticker there." He pointed to the Caring Mama Bear from McCarron sticker on the back door. "Now I know you have five young kids and at least some of them attend McCarron Elementary. But then you have Matthew and Hannah's name on the fast pitch softball and the soccer stickers. So now,"—Dan drew a deep breath and pulled his cell phone from his pocket—"I don't even have to know your last name, but if the car is in your driveway then your last name would be very easy to come up with," he pointed out. "I Google Hannah and Arlington Dynamites and I now have Hannah Leslie, shortstop at 10 and,"—he touched another page on the Dynamites' website—"I see that the ten and under Dynamites practice Tuesday and Thursday afternoons from five to seven o'clock." He showed Chris the website.

"It's about to get worse, isn't it?" Chris choked as Dan nodded.

"You have the Hilton Head sticker there." He pointed out the HH sticker on the opposite side of the windshield. "I Google Leslie and Hilton Head review," Dan continued. He shuddered at how quickly the information was fed back to him.

"And a review here says that your family enjoys spending the last week of summer at the Sea Pines resort at Harbour Town." He cringed. "I know when your family is typically out of town and more information about your family.

"On top of that, the half marathon sticker probably means that either you or your wife are active runners. So, if I Google the Arlington Moms' Running Club looking for a Leslie,"—he typed in the search—"I find Carrie Leslie who is registered to run the upcoming 10K. That probably means either the whole family will be out of the house and that your children, one of them a toddler,"—he pointed to the stick figure sticker representing Annabelle—"will be in a large crowd of people attending the 10K.

"This also tells me that Carrie runs in the Monday, Wednesday, Friday running group just before school would be letting out. That tells me that if I were to show up at McCarron early, I could probably access your children before she picks them up or meets them at the bus stop, and I already know two of their names. I also know where you go to church." Dan pointed out the magnet for a popular nondenominational congregation in the area.

"I know that you both went to Chapel Hill. I have Carrie's name and that means I can at least access a picture of her or perhaps more on several social media sites. I Google the graduating classes of Chapel Hill with your names and then I send a follow request saying I'm so and so, just set up a new account, and I'm from Chapel Hill, after I've checked to make certain you aren't already friends with the person I've chosen to impersonate. I choose a different major than yours, once I've figured out what you majored in, so you wouldn't have had a lot of classes with this person. You may not remember them, but they must've gone to school with you, right? You accept the request no big deal," Dan explained. "Now, I have access to every single piece of information or picture you put on social media."

"Okay, stop." Chris looked sick.

Dan offered him a sorrowful gaze. "It's not just you. Everyone has them, and no one realizes that with just a little bit of knowledge and a computer, you can learn just about anything.

"I used to pull up the Facebook pages of people we were working cases for, and I wanted to scream. 'You posted when you went to the gym every day at the same time, and then that you and your husband were going out of town and that you were nervous about leaving your kids home alone.' Sharing everything about your life is dangerous," Dan vowed adamantly.

"And now it's gotten worse. You can advertise on all of the social sites what you just purchased from an online store or, hell, even that you just ordered a pizza. I see that you just purchased a dozen princess books, so now I have the lure." Dan shuddered slightly from thinking like the kind of person that would abduct a child.

Chris methodically checked all five of his children before calling Carrie over and explaining to her what Dan had just explained to him.

She paled visibly.

"People really do that?" she choked.

Dan gave her a sorrowful nod.

"How do we get them off?" she pled frantically to her husband which made Dan feel even worse.

His cell rang in his hands, and keeping a close eye on Aida, he answered Fionna's call.

"Hey, baby doll, how'd it go?"

"Good, but I had a clogged milk duct or something on my nipple," Fionna explained. "It was kind of fevered and felt weird, but I wasn't sure why. I just spent like five minutes with Adeline's hand on my left boob. We're really good friends, but that was odd. She healed it all up though."

Dan shook his head slightly to remove that image from his mind. He called himself a pervert for good measure before he chuckled.

"I'm sorry, honey. I'll be happy to check that out for you when you get home," he offered, listening to Fionna's adorable giggle.

"It was hurting a little, but like I said, I didn't know what it was," Fionna explained why she hadn't had Dan look at it earlier. "It was better because my milk is mostly dried up."

"Gotcha. Was everything else okay?" He watched Aida slide down a tube slide with Annabelle.

"Yes," Fionna drawled with a great deal of sass.

"Adeline said everything was good, ready, or whatever?" Dan restated.

"Uh-huh." She giggled. "Actually, she said everything looked great, but to remind you to be careful because apparently after all of her healing, I am now, and I quote, 'virgin tight.'"

Dan's entire body seized and his heart flew. He reminded himself that he was at a park with his children. He stifled the thundering groan gathering in his lungs.

"And I was wondering if you would mind if I ran by Guinevere's since I'm downtown. I'll be quick. I miss my girls, but I was kind of thinking I might pick up something for tomorrow night."

Dan's mouth began watering to add to the rest of his body's responses that her conversation had elicited. It had just been too damn long. He forced himself to refocus on the park in front of him.

"The girls are fine. We came to the park. Halia's still asleep, so take your time." Dan tried not to let the Leslies pick up on the desire evident in his tone.

Guinevere's was Fionna's favorite lingerie store. It carried everything imaginable to cater to the sensual pleasures. If she wanted to dress up for him for their reunion the next evening, nothing would make him happier.

"What are you in the mood for, Mr. Vindico?" she purred over the phone, making Dan ache with the all too familiar pain only she could soothe.

Dan drew a deep breath. "Yeah, I'm out here with the Leslies." He knew full well that the information, meant to make her change course, would only drive his Maylea further.

She laughed. "Really? You know I could do silk, lace, black, something saucier for our big debut? What are you hoping to see tomorrow night?"

"Fi," Dan pled as the images she created made his breaths shorten and his jeans tighten.

"Tell me," she commanded.

"Baby, it's been over two months, okay? Believe me, anything at all is perfect." He backed the stroller away from the Leslies who were watching the children on the playground closely.

"I'm kind of in a red mood," Fionna informed him.

Dan managed to turn his groan into an odd sounding cough.

"Okay, I'll be nice…for now. Take care of my babies, and I'll be home quick."

"I love you. We'll be home before you get there. Halia's already grunting."

"I love you too, and I miss her," she fretted.

"Go enjoy your afternoon. You haven't even been gone an hour. She'll be fine. I'm kind of getting the hang of this," he teased.

"You're amazing with her and with Aida. And I look forward to using all of your amazing abilities for my own pleasure tomorrow night. I love you. I'm here, and I'm walking in," she sang as she ended the call.

Allowing himself just a moment to contemplate all of the deliciously carnal things he wanted to do with his wife, he wondered if there was some way to bribe their newborn into sleeping for longer than her typical three-hour span.

Shaking himself from his erotic reverie, Dan rolled Halia toward Aida on the slide.

"Come on, baby girl, it's time for Halia's bottle," Dan called.

"We can bring her home, Dan, if she wants to stay a little while longer," Carrie offered.

"Do you want to stay and play with Annabelle and Elise, or do you want to come home with me and Halia?" Dan studied Aida closely.

"I would like to stay and play, please," she answered readily.

"You're sure you don't mind?" Dan asked the Leslies.

"No, we've got her," Chris assured him.

"Thank you."

Halia began fussing. Dan lifted her into his arms.

"That's the worst part about bringing them out when they're tiny. There's no way to heat a bottle," Carrie lamented as she waved to Dan.

"Yeah." He tried not to smirk as he paced home quickly.

CHAPTER 13
HUNGER

Unable to maneuver the stroller while holding Halia and giving her a bottle, Dan laid her back in the car seat portion. This only served to make her cry harder which effectively broke her father's heart. He quickly heated the bottle he'd packed and a moment later she was devouring her meal.

He managed to park the stroller in the garage and extract Halia while keeping the bottle in her mouth. Rather impressed with himself, Dan carried his baby girl inside and let heat flow from his pores. He warmed her as she wiggled farther into his embrace.

Dan's cell rang and he rebalanced everything to answer while feeding Halia.

"Dan, it's Glenn Sullivan. How are you?"

"I'm good. Is everything okay?" Dan tried to come up with a plausible reason why his substitute would be calling other than the fact that someone had gotten into serious trouble.

"I suppose that depends on who you ask," Mentor Sullivan quipped. "Listen, I don't want to be a pain in your ass, son, but I'm about to be incredibly rude."

"How's that?"

"Jeff Strenton mentioned that he and his bride are having dinner with you this evening to discuss the Venton soap opera."

Dan laughed. That was an excellent description of everything going on at the school currently.

"Yes, sir."

"I was wondering if you think Miss Styler would forgive me for tagging along?" Mentor Sullivan hesitated. Certain that Mentor Sullivan must've called Fionna Miss Styler when she was in his classes, Dan chuckled.

"I'm certain Mrs. Vindico wouldn't mind that at all."

"I stand corrected," he allowed wryly. "And how are your lovely wife and all of the girls you've gained yourself this past year?"

"They're all doing well. Fi's out running a few errands, and Aida is at the park with some friends. Halia is finishing her bottle in my lap."

"You know, you feeding a baby a bottle isn't something I ever thought I'd see."

Dan was sure that when he'd been attending the academy, the very thought of doing anything at all with a baby would have repelled him instantly.

"I'm certain if you join us for dinner tonight you'll see what my beautiful wife has helped me learn."

"If she managed to teach you anything, I'd say she does astounding work," Mentor Sullivan goaded. "You're certain Fionna won't mind my intrusion? I won't eat. I just wanted to discuss a few things and make a confession or two."

"It's fine. I really appreciate you covering my classes for me, and Fionna would never let you come over and not eat." Dan hoped that Fionna wouldn't mind an extra guest.

"If she'd rather it just be Jeff and Becca, I'll understand. Just let me know."

"It shouldn't be a problem. We'll eat around six."

"I'll be there."

"See you then." Dan ended the call and hoisted Halia on his shoulder to burp her.

She was sound asleep a moment later. Still thinking about his plans for the next evening, Dan decided to see if Halia might nap in her crib.

She'd gained a good bit of weight in the last two and a half weeks thanks to the enhanced formula she was drinking. Dan knew he would probably have an easier time making the transition from the bassinet to the crib than Fionna would.

He eased up the stairs, kept Halia tucked close with one hand, and heat casted the sheets and mattress in the crib. He wrapped her in her swaddle wrap, laid her down, and then tiptoed from the room. She seemed fine as she settled into the warmth of the mattress. Dan eased the door almost shut.

Returning to the living room, he began picking up burp cloths, Aida's books and toys, and other random things Fionna wouldn't want lying around the house since they were having guests.

He took out the trash and then carried a pair of Fionna's flats up to their bedroom. His eyes landed on his bedside table and a thought struck him. His groin tightened. He moved to the top drawer in the table and pulled the small brown leather photo album from its depths.

Sitting down on the bed, he decided to go ahead and torture himself. As he opened the album, his heart picked up pace as he studied one of his Christmas presents. It was a full photo album of pictures of Fionna either in barely there lingerie or in nothing at all. He flipped to the shot of her in nothing but a white lace thong. Taken from the back, she was looking over her left shoulder as she pulled one side of the thong downward seductively.

He fought the imminent groan the photo always elicited from deep within his chest as he stared at it unabashedly. Desperate for more, he pulled his phone from his pocket. He entered the password to get into the file where he kept the video they'd made early in the summer locked away since Aida played with his phone often.

His cock throbbed in desperate need. He pressed play. God, he could almost feel what he was seeing. His hip bones driving into her lush ass as he took her hard from behind. She turned back to stare him down.

"Harder," she challenged.

"Such a good girl," Dan growled.

"Hey good lookin', what have you done with our children?" Fionna entered the room.

Dan dropped the phone, not certain why he felt like he was doing something wrong.

A broad, delighted grin spread across her face. "Whatcha got there, Mr. Vindico?" She moved to him. Her eyes danced with a hunger all her own.

Dan shook his head and returned the album to the drawer. "I miss you, baby doll. I needed a fix."

Fionna stared at him for one endless moment and then angled her head in for a kiss. Dan grabbed her. He crushed her into him, kissed her with covetous need, and devoured her mouth.

"Where are the girls?" she breathed just before tracing his lips with her tongue.

"Uh…" Dan shuddered in his frantic need. "Halia's in her crib, and Aida's at the park with the Leslies," he panted.

Suddenly, her hand grasped his strain through the zipper line of his jeans, and a growl he couldn't quell erupted from his chest. He was hung so tight he ached just from watching the video.

"Lie back," she commanded as she continued to grope him. It took every fiber in his body to shake his head.

"No, not until you're ready," he ordered much more for himself than for her.

"Dan, lie back right now. I want to suck you and lick you. I want to drink you." Her voice was low and needy in her desire.

He couldn't do it. He couldn't fight it. He needed the release only she could give. His extended showers weren't cutting it anymore. He needed her.

Watching her hands work as she popped the snap on his jeans and then lowered the zipper in a second flat, his entire body begged for her with every thrumming pulse of his energy.

"God baby, I swear I'll make it up to you tomorrow night. Just suck me." He broke all of his own rules about never allowing her to give him pleasure unless it was returned.

His need seemed to drive her wild as she pushed him back on the bed and lowered his jeans and boxers until her face was mere inches from his throbbing cock pulsing in her face.

She kissed her way down his chiseled abs, letting her ample

cleavage brush over his strain. Dan writhed. His body thrusted of its own accord, desperate to permeate her.

"Fi, please," he begged as he laced his fingers in her hair.

"What?" Her hot breath caressed over him as he continued to throb.

"Suck me, baby doll. Right now. Let me see my cock in your hungry little mouth. Be a good girl and suck it dry for me. Take it all."

"Oh god," she groaned in desperation as she licked from his sack to his head.

Starving moans thundered from him as she pulled him deeply in her mouth.

"Fuck, baby, more, take more, pull more," he ordered, desperate for her to pull the erotic energy coursing copiously through his veins into her mouth straight from the source.

She moaned as she did as he asked, sucking him hard, swirling her tongue over his head, then delving back drowning him in her mouth. "That's it," he grunted. "So fucking good."

Then in an embarrassingly short amount of time, at least by Dan's estimations of himself, he exploded inside her mouth.

"Drink me, baby doll. Every drop," was his last verbal command echoed through his thundering moans as she sucked him dry.

He shuddered and quaked as she released him with a sexy smirk spreading across her beautiful face.

"You are incredible, and I swear I will make that up to you," Dan vowed yet again.

Before she could reply, they both panicked as "Daddy" rang through the hallway.

"Uh, hang on, baby," Fionna called.

She raced from their room to greet Aida and thank the Leslies for bringing her home while Dan tried to catch his breath and redress. He let everything he'd just been treated to replay slowly in his mind.

CHAPTER 14

ROLLER COASTER RIDE

Still feeling guilty over his requests, Dan headed downstairs to apologize again. Aida was regaling Fionna with everything she'd done at the park. She grinned as Dan made his sheepish entrance.

Dan's phone rang from the coffee table, and he answered before it could awaken Halia.

"I'll ask her and call you back," Dan agreed as he ended the call.

He winked at Fionna and elicited a grin, though concern tensed in her rhythms.

"Olivia wants Aida to come over and play for a little while this afternoon before everyone comes over tonight," Dan explained the phone call from Meredith.

"Yes, please," Aida begged.

Fionna nodded her agreement, but Dan saw the disappointment color her eyes and tense in her rhythms. She must've really missed Aida that morning, and she seemed to still feel guilty over shopping after her appointment. Dan joined them on the couch. He slid his hand up and down Fionna's back.

"It'll just be a couple of hours, sweetheart," he soothed.

"I know. I just...don't know how to balance everything." Fionna laid her head on Dan's shoulder.

Aida had been their primary focus for quite a while, and everyone was having to make a few adjustments. Dan texted his sister back, and a few minutes later, Meredith and Olivia appeared at the door.

Aida raced down from her room carrying Sophie, a bag of doll clothes and play bottles, along with a catalog from a rather expensive doll company that manufactured dolls that both Aida and Olivia were hoping to find under the tree at Christmas.

Aida hadn't had the courage to ask for the doll. She was often afraid to ask for anything at all, but she would gaze longingly at the catalog, and had dog-eared the pages that her favorite dolls and all of the accessories were on.

Each time she was taken to the library, she would come home with the stories about each of the dolls. She would read them with dogged tenacity and then start over once she'd finished.

The particular doll she most wanted was already hidden up in Fionna's closet along with several outfits and accessories awaiting Christmas morning. Dan and Fionna had also added the hardback collections of stories to put under the tree.

"Okay, you two have fun." Fionna forced a smile.

"Can I peek in on my newest niece?" Meredith asked.

"Of course," Fionna assured her as they eased up the stairs quietly. Dan followed them. He wondered how Halia was doing in her crib.

"I didn't know her daddy was going to up and decide that she's big enough for her crib now." Fionna's comment let Dan know she wasn't exactly pleased with his decision.

Meredith threw Dan a knowing glance as her brother was being reprimanded. As if to show allegiance to her mother, Halia began fussing before Fionna had the door opened.

Fionna rushed to the crib as Dan began lambasting himself for scaring their little girl.

"I'm sorry. I just thought maybe I'd try it," he offered hopefully. Fionna shot him a grin that said he was forgiven but not to let it happen again. Meredith chuckled as she gazed at Halia.

Fionna moved to lay Halia on her changing table. "Actually, she's not scared," Fionna admitted with a touch of melancholy. "She's just wet."

"So is the crib." Dan began removing the crib sheets and the blanket that were now soaked.

Meredith kissed Halia's head. "I'm going to go and let you two work this all out. But if I may be so bold, Fionna, she eventually needs to sleep in her crib. Trust me, you do not want her in your room for long. Been there done that, and as you both saw not so many weeks ago, it became a much bigger problem than I ever imagined it would. And it's a long, long road back," she lamented.

"And Dan, your child is not quite three weeks old. Be patient and try to think with that head"—she pointed to Dan's face—"and not that one." She dropped her pointed index finger to Dan's crotch. "Let her be a baby. Trust me, the days are long but the years are very short, and listen to your wife."

"Got it," Dan admitted sheepishly as Fionna cuddled Halia, which seemed to be all she needed for her normally laid-back sweet kindness to make a return.

They waved goodbye to Meredith and the girls and returned to the couch. Fionna cradled Halia, tenderly kissing her head and gazing at her.

Finding himself suddenly able to think much clearer than he'd been able in the past few days, Dan gazed at them, unable to believe they were somehow his. He was certain he'd never deserve something so miraculous and yet they were there right beside him. Fionna nestled herself and the baby against Dan. He quickly wrapped his arm over them.

"I'm sorry about the crib thing, honey. I never would have done that if I'd known it bothered you."

"I know. I don't know why that threw me so much. I guess…I'm just still a little… emotional," she hesitated.

"I swear I'm not trying to push her to grow up or anything. I just kind of thought you might not want her in our bedroom tomorrow night with everything we were planning. I uh…wasn't really thinking all that clearly," he admitted.

Fionna laughed and kissed his jawline. His heart beat disjointedly for a moment.

"Okay, how about this? Let's leave her in the bassinet for a little while longer, but we'll put the bassinet in the nursery at night. I know it's stupid. She doesn't care where she sleeps as long as it's warm and she feels safe, but it makes me feel better."

"Then that's what we'll do."

"She'll sleep through the night eventually, right?" Fionna choked slightly as Dan chuckled.

"That was my understanding."

Suddenly, Dan recalled Mentor Sullivan's phone call. "I almost forgot, but Glenn Sullivan kind of invited himself over with Jeff and Becca tonight. Is that okay?" He was concerned over the emotional roller coaster Fionna seemed to be experiencing that afternoon.

Worry spun in her rhythms as she kept Halia tucked in her safe embrace.

"Oh…uh, okay." She glanced around the house and then down at herself.

"Sweetheart, I'll help do anything at all. We can order out if you want, and you can just relax. He wants to talk about Venton. I'm sure he's not expecting some kind of elaborate dinner party. We just had a baby." He patted Halia's back tenderly as she lay on Fionna's chest.

"I know." Fionna forced a smile. "I just haven't seen him in a long time, and I don't think I've ever had dinner with one of my mentors. I didn't do all that well in his classes," she admitted.

"I promise he's not going to give you a test, and you're the strongest Receiver of our generation. No one would have expected you to ace your defense classes."

"I am not. Stop saying that."

"I think I managed to pull a low B in my Energies of Emotions classes and that was the grade I dropped before graduation so I could graduate with a 4.2," Dan explained.

"You should have asked me for help."

Dan chuckled though he couldn't fathom her suggestion. Everything had been so different then. He'd hardly known the woman he was destined to marry, and he'd been in love with someone else.

He leaned and kissed her cheek. Her eyes closed softly as she reveled in the sensation. "Want to talk about what's really bothering you? I've gotten a little better with emotional energies since I fell madly in love with and married a phenomenal Receiver."

"I know you think I've gone insane," she sighed as she kissed the top of Halia's head as she slept soundly on her mother's chest.

"I don't think you've gone insane. I think you just had my baby, and that there is a little bit of a difference between what happened in our bedroom and the way you're feeling now. I just wondered if you'd talk to me. I want to hear each and every thing, even if you don't think it's important." Dan kept her tucked beside him and tried to soothe her.

"I don't know," she confessed. Confusion swam in her rhythms.

"Do you not know or you don't know how to tell me?"

She stood suddenly and moved to the bassinet. Heating the small mattress with her hand, she laid Halia tenderly in her bed and covered her as she slept.

"I think maybe I'd like to be the one being held for a little while." Tears swam in her eyes.

CHAPTER 15

LOST AND CONFUSED

"Come here to me." Dan motioned her to him. He reclined on the sofa and pulled her onto his chest. Grabbing a nearby quilt, he covered them in its warmth and held her tightly. "How about this?" He pushed his shield out from his pores and encased her in all of him. The very air she breathed contained his rhythms. His safety and his love encircled her, and she drew deeply from the air around her. "Better?" She nodded against him, and her rhythms began to calm. "Okay, now you talk, and I'll listen."

"I don't know. I feel so many things. Mostly, I just feel confused."

"Let's start with the first thing you're confused about, and we'll work through them all, okay?" He wouldn't let her block him out ever again. He would be there for each and every thing, and he would wait patiently for her to explain to him what was going on in her mind and in her body.

Fionna seemed to decide that perhaps she did need to talk. "I went to Guinevere's," she began. "I was so excited because I've lost a little weight, but then I stood in the dressing room and looked in the mirrors and…" she drowned out in her own disappointment and in her defeat.

"Fi, baby…" Dan shook his head. It physically hurt him when she found fault with herself. He wished she would acknowledge what it did to him physically not just emotionally. He knew she could feel it. She squeezed her eyes shut and forced away her tears.

"I talked to Adeline, and I was like, 'I want to lose another twenty or twenty-five pounds and get back to a little less than what I weighed before I got pregnant.' She said that I was okay to exercise and diet, but that it wasn't going to come off instantly and that I shouldn't ever expect to weigh what I weighed before. That I would never see that number again.

"And I was like, no, she's wrong. I lost eight pounds when I had her and I lost another six the last few weeks, so I can lose the rest no problem. I left the office and went to the lingerie shop. I picked up stuff that I normally would have slipped right into and none of it fit. I had to get bigger sizes. The saleslady was really sweet. She was like, 'so what if you need a bigger size. You're a beautiful woman,' and she said, 'I bet your husband thinks you're gorgeous.' I got a few things, but I hate the size that they are. I also hate that I've let society tell me that my size matters at all, but I can't shake this feeling no matter what I do."

Dan felt the tears dampen his shirt.

"Then I came home, and I found you upstairs with those pictures, and you have no idea how badly I needed that. It made me feel so good that you went and looked at those and watched that video we made. I need to know that you think I'm sexy, but then after I finished..." She shook her head.

"I came downstairs and dealt with the girls and was a mom again. I may never look like I did in those pictures. I may never be that again. I'm so thankful for everything we have and for you and my girls, but I won't ever be that woman again. It scares me.

"I don't know who I am anymore. I don't know how to be so many different people and do them all right." She finally laid out the terror that Dan felt flowing from her heart and permeating her rhythms. Her foundation had been shaken, and he'd done nothing to reassure her. He'd only asked and taken. He hadn't given back, and he certainly hadn't made her feel beautiful in what they'd shared.

"Sit up and look at me," Dan commanded. Her brow furrowed as she sat up, and Dan moved with her. He dropped his shield and gazed into the depths of her eyes.

"Fionna, you are the most beautiful woman on this planet," he vowed, watching her eyes roll. "Stop it," he ordered. He wasn't playing. She was going to listen to him and hear what he was saying. "I don't give a damn what size you are or what the number on the scale reads. The only reason I let you do that up there"—he pointed harshly to their bedroom—"my God, I clearly shouldn't have done that, but I swear all I've been able to think about for days is being with you," he vowed adamantly.

"Not just having sex. I don't ever want to just have sex again. I want to be with you. I want to share that with you. I want to feel all of you around me. I want our energy to join so thoroughly that I can't tell where my shield stops. I want to be one with you.

"You're my wife, and you know what—sitting right here, right now, having just laid my little girl in her bed and taken care of our daughter before she ran off to go to her cousin's house, you are more beautiful to me than you were that night I followed you home from Anglington's wearing a tight leather skirt with everything on display.

"Sweetheart, right here, right now, lying with me on our sofa with tears falling down your beautiful face breaking my heart, you are more beautiful than you were on our wedding day. Don't you see, baby? You are everything to me. I love you—your beautiful body and your beautiful soul and your brilliant mind.

"So, you're right. You will never look just like you did on the day you posed for those pictures because you just keep getting more and more beautiful, every moment of every day. You are the fantasy, and you can be a great mom and a phenomenal wife and my wild seductress, but you have to take everything a little bit at a time. We'll strike a balance just like we had to do when we adopted Aida.

"I know it's crazy right now, and you're exhausted. You know that you should go out and do stuff for you but you feel guilty when you do it, and that's got to stop," Dan soothed. "You don't have to do this alone. They're my girls too. If you'd like a night out just the two of us or if you'd like to go away for a weekend, that's okay. Just say the word, and I'll make it happen. But you've got to stop beating yourself up for the things you want. If you stop doing everything that makes you my Maylea, you will end up right where we found Meredith a couple of months ago."

This finally seemed to get through the drowning confusion in Fionna's emotional state.

"I know," she admitted. Drawing a steadying breath, she leaned back into his embrace. "I just feel so exhausted. It's like I don't know my own body anymore. I was an athlete for my whole life. I was either doing hula, or surfing competitively all the time, or I was challenging. I knew what my body could do, and I don't recognize this version of myself. I want to learn to love her the way I used to love me, but I'm really struggling. And the tabloids..."

"Are cruel and full of shit. You know that."

"It's not just the weight. I miss the energy I used to have. I feel sluggish all the time, and it's not just the lack of sleep. It's like everything in me runs slower or something. Even my energy arcs are slower than they used to be. It scares me."

"Would you like to start running together? We could put the princess in the jogging stroller in the mornings after Aida gets on the bus and then again in the evenings, and Aida can ride her bike with us. If you want to gain some of your energy and strength back, then I'll help you do that. But I need you to know that I have everything I've ever wanted and have ever needed in my arms right now. This version of you is everything to me. Every version of you is everything to me."

"Thank you." He felt her energy begin to lighten and lilt toward solace and contentment once again. "You'll probably hate running with me. I haven't run since I challenged. I'll be slow."

"I'll love running with you, Maylea, because I'll be *with you*."

"I was thinking if I ever actually feel awake again, maybe I could take a few classes at the gym. They have a nice nursery for the kids. I feel guilty about leaving her for that though."

Dan lifted her chin tenderly with his hand. "If you don't do anything for you, you won't have anything to give her."

Seeming to consider for a minute, Fionna drew a deep breath. Nervous energy rolled off her in waves. "Can I ask you something?"

"Anything."

"Okay, first, please don't freak, and second, please, please know that I do not mean this disrespectfully at all for people that do this for a living."

Now thoroughly confused, Dan nodded his acceptance of the conditions.

"Kara wants me to take this new exercise class with her on Tuesday and Thursday mornings for an hour, and I kind of really want to, but I'm afraid it would be weird for you."

Dan's brow furrowed. "What is it?"

Fionna mumbled something that Dan had no hope of translating.

"Sweetheart, just tell me." He lowered his head, hoping to get her to raise her own.

"It's a pole dancing strip class, but it's not like for going into that line of work. It's because it's fun and to lose weight and sort of feel sexy again. You know, maybe learn some new moves that will rock your partner's world," she explained with her cheeks glowing hot from her embarrassment.

Dan tried to envision the class his wife was desperate to join. He wanted to tell her yes, but his shield tensed, and she'd not only seen it, but she'd also felt it.

"Would any men either be in this class or be viewing this class?"

"No, it's a women's only class, and it's in the same room where the nude yoga classes are held so no windows on the inside that would make it viewable from the gym. It's on the fourth floor with blinds," she assured him. "I really want to try it. I think it would be fun, and I think maybe it would help me feel sexy again."

She should have started with that. "Sure, baby." Dan was more comfortable with the class now that he knew no one would be seeing his baby's provocative dancing save maybe him. "Do I need to install a pole in our bedroom, or will you just dance around me after these classes," he teased, making her laugh sweetly. The sound delighted him.

"You're sure? I didn't want it to bother you about...you know... everything." She grimaced.

Dan racked his brain. He wondered why she thought he would

mind this. What husband in his right mind wouldn't want his wife to take erotic dance classes?

"What everything?" he asked.

She looked bereaved. "With…you know…other people you dated." She refused to meet Dan's eyes. He nodded his immediate understanding. *Bridgette.* He shuddered slightly.

"Sweetheart, look at me." She turned her timid gaze on his. "I never really thought about what she did for a living. I really only ever thought about her as an intel source, quite honestly."

Fionna laced her hand in his, and he felt her soothing energy flow through him, bringing him peace and absolution.

"I do take partial responsibility for her death, and that's something that I have to live with for the rest of my life. But her being a stripper had nothing to do with you or with us or even with the circumstances of her death. So, no, you learning to pole dance won't remind me of her or even make me think of her.

"I never went to see her strip. I never went to The Tantra at all other than to occasionally make sure she got home from work okay and the day we arrested a few guys there and then again at the takedown. I used to meet her in the basement so that Wretchkinsides's guys wouldn't see me picking her up. That's how I knew where she was. But honey, that's in the past, and I told you I'm tired of living inside of tombs. God somehow saw fit to give me a real life out here with you and with my girls, so let's just leave it where it belongs in the past, please," he begged.

"Okay." Fionna flooded Dan's energy with her own soothing rhythms, and somehow magically giving to him seemed to fill her as well.

"Okay." Dan kissed her cheek. "You learn to strip, and I'll keep right on stripping you because you are so damn sexy, and somehow we'll make all of this work. I promise."

"Thank you for being you and being amazing and for everything."

"Taking care of you is my job, baby doll. And you take excellent care of me," he reminded her.

"Will you help me get ready for tonight? I want to look like I'm not freaking out about my life and the baby and not sleeping. I don't want to scare Becca, and I kind of want to make Mentor Sullivan see that I'm not a complete boy crazy ditz that can't throw a shield because I won't put down my lipstick tube long enough to learn how."

"I take it that was something he said to you in class," Dan fumed.

Fionna nodded, and fury ignited in his shield. Glenn Sullivan had always been Dan's favorite mentor. He was gruff and no-nonsense and didn't put up with much from the students. But that was before he'd insulted Dan's baby.

"You threw a hell of a shield when it mattered most, and I don't really care what Sullivan thinks. You're mine, and I am constantly in awe of you, Fionna."

She drew from Dan deeply. It made his longing to be with her grow tenfold in a matter of moments, but she stood and dragged him off the couch and into the kitchen.

They spent the rest of the afternoon dusting, mopping, and polishing the already clean house and then hiding the loads and loads of backed-up laundry in their closet. Then Dan insisted that Fionna take a short nap while he gave Halia her bottle and laid her on a quilt for some tummy time per Fionna's instructions.

Fionna woke an hour later looking much more refreshed, and she and Dan were making her famous crab cakes when Aida returned from Olivia's.

"I want to help." Aida dragged the step stool Fionna kept in the kitchen, so that she could help cook, to the counter.

Dan set Halia in her bouncy seat and moved it to the kitchen table so the whole family could make dinner together.

CHAPTER 16

TENSIONS

Though they'd had a wonderful afternoon, Fionna still seemed extremely nervous about Mentor Sullivan's coming over for dinner.

Dan followed her up the stairs to change clothes. He was still trying to reassure her. "I'm sure he's just going to go over what he's been teaching and probably give me even more bad news about Wilshire or some shit going on at Venton and that will be it."

With a sigh, Fionna tugged on one of the only pairs of jeans that she could currently fit in.

"You look beautiful, baby," Dan immediately complimented. He planned on doing that far more often. She clearly needed to hear it as she was woefully unable to see it when she looked in the mirror, much to Dan's chagrin.

"I'm not in my best form right now, and he's kind of abrupt and a little impolite sort of." Fionna tried to soften the fact that she just didn't like Glenn Sullivan.

He *was* abrupt. Dan thought back over the dozen or so defense classes he'd taken from Mentor Sullivan. It occurred to him that perhaps he was rude to those that struggled, and because Dan had always excelled he'd never really noticed. If Sullivan dared to comment on Fionna's weight or on anything at all that didn't meet his liking, Dan would throw him out, no questions asked. No one messed with his girls. He didn't care who they were.

Jeff and Becca arrived a few minutes early.

"How are you feeling?" Becca leapt as soon as Fionna entered the room.

Fionna glanced at Dan. "Uh, well…everything feels good. I'm a little tired still, but I'm sure that will get better once she's sleeping through the night. Mrs. Haydenshire gave me tons of ideas on how to get her to sleep a little longer, but we have to wait until she weighs a little more."

"She's beautiful," Becca gushed. Jeff studied Halia with a great deal of curiosity as she slept in her bouncy seat.

"Have you ever held a baby?" Dan asked.

Jeff shook his head.

"Do you want to try it?" Dan thought Jeff should probably get a little practice in before April. Panic cascaded through Jeff's shield.

"Uh…maybe in a little while."

"May I hold her?" Becca begged Fionna.

"Of course. Go sit down, and Dan will bring her in there. I need to start browning the crab cakes."

"Let me do that, baby," Dan offered.

"I can help," Jeff volunteered.

"If you're sure you don't mind." Fionna lifted a very sleepy Halia from her seat and moved to the living room with Becca following closely behind her. Aida trailed after them regaling Becca with all of her big sisterly complications.

"Baby Halia is very sweet and lets me hold her like this." Aida formed her arms in a cradled position. "And I get to give her bottles sometimes, but she has to drink them a lot and that means Mommy and Daddy have to feed her because I tried to teach her to hold her bottle but she kept dropping it." Aida sighed.

Dan and Jeff chuckled as Dan extracted a large platter of formed crab cakes from the refrigerator and set them beside the oven.

"And then a couple of days ago, I woke up in my fairy princess bed because I don't get to sleep in Mommy and Daddy's room even though baby Halia does," Aida informed Becca with a heavy note of injustice. "I went into the kitchen, and Halia looked like she had oatmeal in her hair."

Jeff's brow furrowed as he glanced at Dan.

"Cradle cap," Dan explained quietly. This didn't ease Jeff's confusion. "It's kind of like baby dandruff, only it was pretty bad."

Fionna had impressed Dan yet again. She'd promptly rubbed Halia's scalp down with coconut oil, gotten in the shower with her, and washed her hair. The problem cleared up the next day. Jeff nodded his understanding though he looked momentarily overwhelmed.

"You know, only babies sleep in their mommy and daddy's rooms," Becca explained.

"Are you sure?" Aida didn't sound too certain.

"Yeah, because if you're a big girl, then you don't want to sleep with Mommy and Daddy unless you're sick or something. Your fairy princess bed might get lonely and miss you. You're such a big girl that you and Daddy and Mommy and Sophie and all of your stuffed animals won't fit."

"Okay, make me look good now. Which pot thing do I cook these in?" Dan whispered to Jeff.

"Uh." Jeff searched the pot rack over the oven. He seemed pleased to be helping. "Probably this. Does she use it a lot?"

Dan nodded. Fionna's large set of cast iron cookware, that she'd purchased long before she'd begun dating Dan, were her favorites. Dan had loaded the skillet in the dishwasher once, not long after they'd moved in together, and she'd nearly come unglued.

When she'd told Dan the cost of the cookware set and what putting cast iron in the dishwasher would do, he'd understood her reaction. But she loved them, and the things she created using them were phenomenal. Dan was looking forward to her cooking again, though he would certainly never mention it to her.

She couldn't create the elaborate meals he'd quickly become addicted to when she was feeding his little girl every few hours and trying to catch up on sleep in between.

Jeff laid the large skillet on the stove and summoned to light the gas.

"What oil does she use?" he asked Dan.

"Uh..." Dan shrugged and pointed to a bottle of oil beside the oven.

"That's olive oil. Are you sure that's what she uses?"

"Baby," Dan called. "What oil do I cook these with?"

Fionna giggled. "Tell Jeff I use canola oil."

She returned to the kitchen to sauté asparagus and create a dipping sauce for the crab cakes, while Becca gave Halia her bottle.

"Oh, Mrs. Vindico, I wanted to apologize." Jeff began methodically flipping the crab cakes in the skillet until they were a beautiful golden brown. "Mentor Sullivan asked if he could come over with us tonight, and I didn't know what to say. I mean, you just had a baby. I told him that actually, but he didn't seem to care."

Fionna shot Dan an 'I told you so' look.

"Do you know what he wants to tell me?" Dan asked.

"Not really. Portwood's had officers up there a bunch this week, still kind of watching the kids and their reactions. He makes sure someone is there while Becca's there, but she gets out at ten now. She just tested out of her humanities class."

"Great," Dan commented. He was enthralled watching Fionna cook. She seemed delighted suddenly to be back in the kitchen creating. It was definitely a passion of hers, and her eyes lit with zeal as she worked.

"Yeah, well, don't ask her about it. She barely passed," Jeff lamented. Dan noted the customary guilt etch his face.

Suddenly, Becca appeared in the kitchen carrying Halia with a great deal of skill.

"Are you talking about Mentor Sullivan?" She lifted Halia to her shoulder and patted her back. She swayed her slightly as if taking care of an infant was something she did on a regular basis.

"Yeah." Jeff nodded.

"Please tell me he at least called you, and he's not just going to show up." She sounded as if such a thing would be unforgivable.

As Dan considered her reaction, he knew that the Sapmans would certainly have bred their children to be overly polite growing up under the watchful eye of the Realm who were often disparaging about the children of the Realm Governors.

"He called just before lunch," Dan assured her. "Classes are going okay, right?"

"Yes, sir, just like all the years before. Most of us had him last year, so it's okay, I guess." Jeff shrugged. Dan's brow furrowed as did Fionna's. She'd picked up on the slight disdain.

"But…" Dan urged.

"I don't know."

"Just tell him. He probably already knows. He taught Mentor Vindico," Becca explained.

"I guess he's just kind of old…a little," Jeff faltered. "Like he threw out all of your lesson plans and went back to his old ones. So, everyone's like, we learned this last year. I know senior year is a lot of review, but it's the same lesson plans."

Dan drew a deep breath as Fionna offered him an irritated gaze.

"Great. Now, I get to go back to work and I have two weeks to get everyone ready for my exams which are based on my lesson plans."

"Right, and everyone figured that, and the syllabus told us what would be covered on the exams. So, everyone's looking at the lists and that's not what he's teaching, and it's not really completely covered in the textbooks. We're all freaking out because we have to keep our GPA up to get a recommendation to any of the Iodex branches. People have started begging the guys Portwood sends up there to help them while they're there. It's kind of crazy."

Dan nodded dejectedly. Suddenly, Halia threw her hand out and craned her neck around. She spotted Dan and began to cry. Shock washed over him as he rushed to her and lifted her from Becca. His baby girl calmed in his arms.

"Don't feel bad. She's definitely Daddy's girl," Fionna reassured.

"Me too," Aida fussed as she moved to Dan. He wrapped one arm over her, hugging Aida to his waist while he cradled Halia on his shoulder.

"You're both my girls," he vowed. Jeff offered him an understanding gaze as he continued to cook the crab cakes to perfection. Fionna casted them to stay warm.

"I rewrote every lesson from the plan book he gave me when I signed my contract," Dan explained. "I wanted you to be ready to sign on at any Iodex and be able to jump in with both feet. Most of the curriculum was badly dated. I tried to think of everything I had to teach Logan and Rainer when I hired them onto Elite that I thought they really should have been taught at the academy. Things have changed in the last thirty years. I need you to at least be presented with the information before I can test you on it."

CHAPTER 17

STUDENTS AND TEACHERS

Before anyone could answer, the doorbell rang. Dan carried Halia with him as he answered. Aida tagged along. Dan vowed to himself that he would make certain to reassure her more later.

"Glenn, come on in," Dan bristled. He wasn't a student anymore. He was a grown man with a wife and children. Clearly, he needed to demand a little respect from the man he'd replaced. He would no longer refer to him as Mentor Sullivan.

Fionna joined him at the door, drying her hands on a towel and smoothing her hair.

"Mentor Sullivan, how are you?" She smiled politely though Dan caught the disdain rolling in her rhythms.

He cleared his throat. "You already know my wife, and this is my sweet baby girl, Aida," Dan made certain to introduce her first which did at least elicit a broad grin.

"Hello sir, it's very nice to meet you," Aida offered as Dan closed out the chilly night air. He cradled Halia in his arms as he warmed his hands to sooth her shiver.

"Hi there, dear. It's nice to meet you as well." Mentor Sullivan seemed to study Aida quizzically.

"And this is Halia." Dan turned so that Mentor Sullivan could see Halia's sweet face which was currently bobbing up off Dan's shoulder and then falling back onto her father in an effort to be able to hold up her own head.

"Why is she doing that, Daniel?" Mentor Sullivan looked concerned.

Becca chuckled as she moved into the entry way as well.

"Newborns do that to strengthen their neck muscles until they're strong enough to hold up the weight of their own heads," she supplied knowledgeably. She may not have done that well in humanities, but clearly she'd excelled in her Scholera Predilect classes.

"Oh, I didn't tell you Halia's a Scholera predilect as well." Fionna beamed at Becca.

"Really?" Becca squealed as Fionna nodded.

Dan caught the slight eye roll from Mentor Sullivan as Fionna took his coat.

To Glenn Sullivan, there was only one Predilect that mattered. If you weren't Ioses, he had very little use for you. Of all the other Predilects, Receivers were the most annoying by Sullivan's standards. Dan had forgotten all of his derisive quips about Receivers until that moment.

Sullivan had never married or had children. To Dan's knowledge, he'd never even dated much. Mentor Sullivan was a few years older than Dan's father, and the governor had commented to Dan once, when he was in school and fired up because Sullivan had encouraged him to dump Amelia in effort to train more often, that Sullivan never had much to do with girls when they were in school.

"Can I get you something to drink, Mr. Sullivan?" Fionna asked.

"Whatever you have is fine." He glanced around Dan and Fionna's home.

"Daddy." Aida tugged on the leg of his pants.

"What, baby?" Dan settled on the couch. He kissed Halia's cheeks before he reclined her to let her fall asleep once again.

"May I please have some juice?"

"You can have some water. Ask Jeff or Becca to get you some," Dan directed.

As she moved quickly into the kitchen, Mentor Sullivan studied Dan cradling Halia tenderly in his arms.

He shook his head. "Does she know she's adopted?"

Dan's entire body tensed as he drew a deep breath. "Of course. She was seven when we adopted her."

Fionna returned carrying a bottle of beer and a mug she'd chill casted. She settled beside Dan to begin playing hostess. Dan heard Jeff teasing Aida in the kitchen and her giggling.

"Well, Ms. Styler, it seems you went and broke him good." Sullivan gestured his head to Dan as he drew a sip of the beer.

Dan sighed audibly as Fionna's jaw cocked to the side. She narrowed her eyes. Dan laced his hand through hers to sooth her.

"I really see it more as her pulling me up out of the pits of hell than her breaking me," he corrected his mentor with challenge pulsing in his shield.

"S'pose that depends on your definition of hell now, doesn't it?" Sullivan goaded.

"As it is my definition that we're working from, I'd say the sentiment stands," Dan fired back. He wasn't backing down. No one was going to attack Fionna and walk away unscathed.

～

Jeff Strenton

A smirk crossed Jeff's features as he overheard Mentor Vindico promptly inform Sullivan what he could do with his opinion about Fionna. Jeff was still angry about Sullivan's quip that he'd let Becca's carnal feminine wiles distract him, and now she had him for twenty-one years. As Jeff was about to take a test from Sullivan, he'd bit back the retort that Becca had him for the rest of his life. She always had.

Thanks to Dan, Logan, and Rainer, Jeff had gotten a 98 on the lab exam which had irritated Mentor Sullivan.

Emily was in Brazil working in an orphanage with the Angels for a few weeks, so Rainer had been helping Jeff study for the last few days. Jeff had learned a tremendous amount. He planned to take his end of the year exams as soon as he possibly could. Then he would be finished and could officially accept his appointment to the Elite Squadron and the paycheck that came with that.

Jeff removed the next batch of crab cakes, which smelled heavenly, as he laid the last of them in the pan to fry. He continued to listen.

❧

Dan Vindico

"You've still got your temper, I see." Mentor Sullivan gave a hearty laugh.

Dan narrowed his eyes as he kept Halia cradled in his arms. She kept him calm just like her mama.

"How are my classes going?" Dan demanded.

"They're not exactly what I expected to find, but they're fine."

"I just…think I'll go get dinner on the table." Fionna made her hasty retreat.

"Nice setup, Daniel. You've got your students cooking dinner. This wasn't exactly what I had in mind when I practically forced Wilshire to hire you on."

Dan patiently laid Halia in the bassinet. He debated his retort as everyone settled in to eat.

"Oh, no, Mentor Sullivan. Bec and I love to be over here. Mentor Vindico pretty much saved our lives. He's the reason I got the Iodex internship and that I'm being given the opportunity to be an actual officer soon. We're happy to help do anything we can. They just had a baby," Jeff pointed out.

"You earned the internship, Jeff, and your hard work and tremendous skill set got you hired on early," Dan corrected him. "And,"—he turned his glare on Sullivan, wondering how on earth the man he'd admired all through school could possibly seem so different —"Jeff and Becca are close friends of ours. I appreciate their help tremendously. I think of Jeff as an Iodex officer and a confidant of mine. I no longer consider him a student. If all goes well and we keep working,"—Dan gestured his head to Jeff—"soon he'll be out of Venton and on the Elite Squadron. At which time, I sincerely hope that they will still count us as close friends."

"Oh, that reminds me." Fionna smiled in an effort to keep conversation light and upbeat. "Becca, I boxed up all of my maternity clothes for you to take home."

"Oh my gosh! Thank you, thank you, thank you." Becca leapt from the table and threw her arms around Fionna's neck. Jeff and Dan were both thrilled that their wives were so happy despite the tense conversation thus far.

Mentor Sullivan shook his head as Aida politely passed the salad Fionna had fixed earlier in the day.

"These are very good, dear," he commented before going on. His tone and his rhythms were perforated with derision, and the look on his face said everything his compliment hadn't. "*At least she's good at something*" rang from his features. Fionna's face fell as she'd picked up on the ridicule in Sullivan's emotional bands, which confirmed Dan's suspicion.

"Thank you," Fionna offered kindly as she drew a deep breath.

"Fionna's a great cook. She's given me tons of recipes, and we love them all." Becca came to Fionna's immediate defense.

"Fi's an incredible person," Dan echoed, making his wife blush violently as she shook her head.

"Thank you both."

"One of the reasons I demanded that Wilshire hire you is that I knew he was screwing around on his wife, and I suspected the books were suffering for it," Sullivan drawled.

Aida's head shot up, and her brow knitted.

Fionna panicked. "I'm sorry, sir, but we'll have to discuss that after the girls are in bed."

"What does that mean?" Aida asked.

Jeff rolled his eyes as he shot an annoyed look at Sullivan.

Sullivan's jaw clenched. He sent a resentful look Aida's way. Drawing a deep breath, he seemed to refocus. "I certainly don't want to upset you, but I do have several things I need to discuss with you.

Would it be all right if I stayed a few minutes after the girls are in bed?"

"Certainly," Dan commanded. "If you think you can treat my wife and my child with the respect they deserve."

"I have done nothing otherwise." Mentor Sullivan made a concerted effort to calm his tone.

"She's an extremely powerful Receiver, Glenn," Dan quipped. "You don't get anything by her."

"We'd be happy to help get Aida and Halia ready for bed," Becca offered sweetly.

"Can I wear your hat again while we make up stories?" Aida begged.

Blood pooled rapidly in Jeff's cheeks. Jeff and Becca babysat Aida twice before, so Dan assumed she was referring to one of those times.

"She wanted to wear my Venton ball cap when we kept her last time, so I let her and then Becca came up with a game where whoever was wearing the hat got to add to the story. She seemed to have fun," Jeff managed to explain though he also seemed to brace for rejection.

"That's a great game!" Fionna looked thrilled. "You're both really good with her. Whenever I work up the courage to leave Halia, I'm calling you," she assured them. Becca was overjoyed, and Jeff looked relieved.

This brought on another head shake from Sullivan, but Dan didn't comment.

"I didn't wear my hat tonight. Maybe we could borrow one of your dad's," Jeff suggested.

"Can we, Daddy?"

"Of course," Dan assured her.

"Did Mr. Strenton tell you that he earned himself a 98 on your lab exam, Daniel?" Sullivan sounded loath to admit this.

"Nice work," Dan complimented.

Jeff couldn't quite hide his pride. "Rainer's been helping me for the past week. Emily's out of town." Dan glanced at Aida and shook his head minutely. Jeff nodded his understanding.

Dan and Fionna certainly knew that the Angels had made a return trip to the orphanage in Brazil where they'd worked the year before.

They'd packed up an endless number of clothes, books, and toys for the kids. It was the orphanage where Fionna had met Aida and their fates had been sealed. Dan and Fionna decided that with Halia's arrival, perhaps they wouldn't mention where the Angels were heading. They weren't certain how she would take the news.

CHAPTER 18

SWORD, SHIELD, AND SMOKE

They made their way through dinner with Dan complimenting Fionna's cooking repeatedly. Jeff and Becca echoed his praise. Jeff consumed seven crab cakes, which delighted Fionna more than all of the acclaim.

"These are so good," Jeff vowed. "We used to make them at that diner where I worked last summer, but they just tasted like soggy bread crumbs."

Fionna grinned. "I'm glad you like them. It was fun to cook again."

With that, Halia grunted from her cradle and quickly worked herself into quite a dejected sob.

Dan and Fionna both stood.

"I'll get her," Dan soothed.

"Would you mind just getting her bottle?" Fionna asked though it sounded like more of a dire plea than a request. Dan knew she wanted to escape the heavy emotions the room had to have been drowned in. "I think I'll take her upstairs and get her ready for bed, since Jeff and Becca are going to play with Aida for a little while."

With that, Fionna lifted Halia out of the bassinet, and Dan saw her soothing energy calm Halia as she nestled herself against Fionna's chest.

"Of course," Dan agreed. "I'll get the table cleared and the dishes cleaned up," he offered as soon as he handed Fionna the warmed bottle. "Glenn, do you mind hanging out for a little while?"

"I'm all right," Sullivan sighed as he cleared his own plate. He looked rather annoyed that he was going to have to wait for Dan's attention.

Becca helped Aida with her bath, and then Jeff joined them upstairs to play the game with one of Dan's Iodex baseball caps. Fionna returned downstairs with Halia. Dan beamed. Fionna had wiped Halia down with some of the lavender baby wash formulated by Tutu.

Halia was wide awake after her bath. She was babbling all kinds of adorable sounds wearing a long-sleeved onesie that proclaimed that she was daddy's little princess, along with pink knit pants. She looked adorable, and Dan couldn't quite hide his delight as her eyes locked on him again and her cooing grew in intensity.

Fionna laughed and handed her to Dan. He cradled her to him.

"Hey there, baby girl." She yawned as she settled into Dan.

"Can I get you another beer, Mentor Sullivan?" Fionna offered.

Dan wished Glenn would go home. He wanted to spend a little time with Halia. She changed so quickly, and she was finally really awake. Dan wondered if he played with her and kept her awake just a little longer if perhaps she might extend her sleep as well.

"I think that's probably a good idea," Sullivan huffed.

Fionna returned with the drink and handed one to Dan preemptively as she settled beside him on the couch.

"All I was trying to say earlier was that I expected you would have put forth a little more effort in sorting out this nonsense with Wilshire and Katherine Bryant for your father. Instead, you seem to be turning students into your new best friends, letting them cook for you and keep your kids, not teaching the curriculum, and lounging around here playing housewife and mommy," Sullivan quipped.

"Excuse me," Dan gasped.

"Dan." Fionna flooded Dan with her soothing energy as her eyes goggled.

"I am not teaching *your* curriculum," Dan roared, "because it was badly dated not to mention wrong. It will not prepare my students to accept appointments in any capacity of law enforcement."

"You may be showing them how to perform technical maneuvers in the field, but you are not teaching them much of anything. You're training officers not guiding students. They won't all end up in an Iodex office, and you've left out large chunks of the history of Iodex, why they need to do what they need to do, and why it will work."

"I teach history to my history of defense class," Dan fired back. "The majority of my classes are defense classes meaning that I teach the art of defense. Practical skills that these kids can actually use so they don't get themselves killed in the field. You know, I can't recall a single time when I stared down the barrel of a pistol that I thought, if only I could remember the Inner-Realm Treaty of 1946, that would surely save my ass!"

"See, there's the fire." Sullivan threw his hands out toward Dan in exasperation.

"What?!" Dan was unable to believe what he was hearing.

"The fire," Sullivan chanted. "I don't know what's happened, but this isn't you." He gestured his hands out to Fionna and Halia.

Dan prided himself on being a man who was rarely shocked, but his mouth hung open in stunned disbelief.

"What happened to the youngest head of Iodex, the guy who tore the Interfeci apart with his bare teeth, never wavered, never got distracted by a pretty face?" He indicated Fionna once again. "That's the guy Venton needs. Get in there, Daniel. Hunker down. Figure all of this shit out. I've done some of the work for you, but my God, I hardly recognize you at this point."

Halia's precious face contorted in terror from the shouting, and she trembled in Dan's arms, only adding to his fury. Drawing a deep breath, Dan waved Fionna off as she tried to take the baby.

He lifted her onto his shoulder, letting her curl into his neck as she located her fingers and began sucking vehemently.

"It's okay. Daddy's got you." Dan cradled her in the safety of his embrace. He noted that he could no longer hear the laughter or any noise at all from Aida's room. Everyone was listening.

"You're right," Dan lowered his voice to a menacing murmur.

Fionna turned her shocked expression on Dan. "I'm certain I don't look anything like what you saw for the last decade of my life," he agreed with the assessment. "Because *that* wasn't me.

"I worked twenty-three hour days, slept in my office, followed every lead, and took them apart piece by piece. It nearly cost me the love of my life and it did cost me a child, not to mention everything else they'd already taken." Dan wrapped his arm around Fionna, keeping Halia cradled closely, still soothing her.

"But that isn't what I signed on for when I agreed to step into your position at Venton. I agreed to teach, not to form my own version of Iodex with only myself to command," he snarled.

"Precisely." Sullivan didn't seem to even hear Dan. "You're the guy that can do it all. Teach, figure out who the hell is stealing those tests, what's going on with the drug testing, and whether or not Wilshire and his mistress cooked the books. That's why I got you the job," he shouted vehemently.

"Well, that's sure as hell not what you told me when I signed on." Dan handed Halia to Fionna. He wasn't going to be able to calm. "Because hear me say this, if you had, I wouldn't have taken the job. That isn't me anymore. This is." He mimicked Sullivan's move of gesturing to Fionna and the baby. "My wife, and my kids, and a real life, that's what I want. I somehow managed to get it after all of the hell I went through and that I put her through." His incredulity grew with his fervor.

"I don't want to work like that ever again, and you know what? I won't," he vowed. "Never again. I told my father I would help figure out what is going on at Venton, but I was quite clear that it wouldn't interfere with my family time. I'm sorry if I'm not getting it taken care of as quickly as you might like, but I'm doing my best."

Sullivan shook his head. He fell back in his chair with a huff. "So, you're just gonna throw it all away. All of the training, all of the hard work, top of Ioses, highest GPA in the order, youngest Chief of Elite ever, everything I taught you. She swaggers by and blows you a kiss, and you're just gonna walk away." He rolled his eyes.

"My God, listen to yourself," Dan demanded. "I'm not a twenty-year-old kid anymore. I'm not the head of Ioses order, and I don't give a damn what my GPA was. If you brought me back on because you thought I would work day in and day out to clean up someone else's mess, then I'm sorry, but that wasn't what I signed on to do. You seem to have forgotten that I grew up a little in the past fifteen years." Dan glared at the man that had given him his start.

"The life, if you could even call it a life, that I lived for the last decade took everything I had, and it gave me nothing back. All of the men I put away, hell, the men I killed didn't change what they'd done. It didn't bring Amelia back for her parents. It didn't bring Aida's family back to her," he hissed. "But what I'm doing now is a life.

"She gave me that. She is responsible for all of this. She changed me all for the better. She's helping me actually give back and make up for all that I'm responsible for taking away. No one should live the way I existed. And yet, she somehow saw through all of the pain and all of the volatility and pulled me out of hell. She showed me that life was worth living as long as I had her. She's all I want.

"And she's given me more than I'll ever be able to repay, but me leaving her here with my kids so I can work endless hours chasing down pointless leads and hitting roadblock after roadblock? That's not going to happen. I will not live to work anymore ever again. I want a life—a real life. I want her and I want my girls, and I want to be here with them. I suppose I'm sorry you're disappointed, but honestly, I feel sorry for *you*. I'm not the young, pompous asshole who shook your hand when Wilshire handed me my diploma then strutted off that stage thinking I had the world by a string. Things change. I changed, and you know what, so did you."

"You are more than this, Daniel. This is a waste of your skills and your training. You aren't living up to your potential or making use of the tremendous talents you were given," Sullivan vowed in a fervent choke.

"You're wrong," Dan vowed adamantly. "I have never been more than I am right now sitting here with her."

A huff and eye roll were the answers to his vow.

"You may have changed, Dan, but I haven't." With that, he pulled a large file from his briefcase and flung it on the coffee table. "I knew when I demanded that Wilshire hire you, teaching would never satisfy you, but there were cases that Venton needed solved. I thought that would drive you until you got your footing again, figured out what to do with the cards you'd been dealt. I thought you loved your alma mater, and that you were the man that would right the wrongs. I never imagined the only thing that would light your fire would be giving out sex advice to a bunch of horny academy upperclassmen and picking one student to actually connect with." He gestured his hand up the stairs, referring to Jeff.

Shaking his head in shock and fury, Dan jerked the folder off the table. "What the hell is this?"

"I thought we needed a little more data. I made a big show of how I was throwing out all of your stuff. I didn't really do that. I just worked it in with my own. I know they have to pass your exam. I told every class we were changing things and then I assigned another test for today. I told them the grade would count as a large percentage of their pre-exam grade, and that your dad had approved it, meaning that I'd submitted the test and the answer key and that it would have been in the safe." He explained his actions. Dan nodded. It was a brilliant idea though he loathed to admit that.

"I gave the test. I made it more difficult than it needed to be, but you've already figured out why that would need to be the case. The correct answers were the least obvious. I figured we might as well catch ourselves a bunch of cheating liars.

"So, Chief Vindico," he stated pointedly. Dan tried desperately to show no emotion, but Sullivan knew him too well. "Yeah, you like that, don't you. It's who you are, no matter how many times you tell yourself it isn't," he spat. "Here's the list of everyone that received a perfect score." He handed Dan a list of students' names. "And guess whose name is on that list?" He jerked his thumb toward the stairs.

Fionna shook her head. "No, I would know if he cheated, and he would never do that," she vowed adamantly as she patted Halia to sleep.

"And how would you know that, Miss Styler?" Sullivan scoffed.

"Because despite your obvious prejudice against the entire Auxiliary Predilection and Order, that's what she does. Let me also add that on more than one occasion my wife's incredible powers have saved my life. Literally saved my life and our children's lives. Now, I will admit that I haven't done everything that should have been done at Venton, and you were right that teaching isn't doing much for me. I plan on quitting at the end of the year, but I will not sit here and let you belittle my wife or her extraordinary abilities. If you want us to continue this conversation and our relationship, then you owe her an apology, and for God's sake, she married me. Her last name is Vindico! She is not your student anymore."

Fionna's mouth hung open as she stared bewildered at Dan.

Dan jerked the list of names from Sullivan's hand and gave it a cursory glance.

"Only three students in your senior Ioses classes made a perfect score." Mentor Sullivan was still trying to incriminate Jeff.

"Jeff, Ben Cobson, and Maya Patel," Dan came right back without having to read the list. "And none of them are stealing tests or purchasing answers online."

"More than half of the rest of each of your classes also received a perfect score so…most of that list is cheating, and you follow the smoke long enough…" he drawled.

"You'll find the fire," Dan concluded one of Sullivan's well-known phrases.

"There's a job to be done, and I don't care what you and your wife"—he gestured to Fionna, giving a concerted effort not to show his obvious disdain—"decide you're going to do when the school year is over. I know Dan Vindico doesn't walk away unless the fight's over and he's won. Then he gets up and dusts himself off before he lets a pretty girl lick his wounds for him."

"Excuse me," Fionna spat. Dan couldn't quite hide his smirk. "I have endured your derision and pompousness about not only me but also my husband for as long as I intend to. I am not here to lick his wounds, nor am I here to serve as his distraction. I am his wife. I'm the person who loves him and has chosen to go through life with him and that includes all of the highs and all of the lows. It doesn't matter if you care what he does at the end of this year. It has nothing to do with you at all.

"We did not ask for your opinion, and we don't want it. You don't get to dictate what we do or when we do it. I understand that you feel replaced and lost without the position that you allowed to define your life, but that isn't what Dan is going to do. His family will define his life. I also understand that you wanted desperately to come over here tonight to reassert your importance in Dan's life. Yes, I can feel exactly what you want despite the fact that you believe I'm not good for anything more than being a sheath for his sword," she shouted.

Dan stared his former mentor down. "Either apologize to her or leave. Your choice."

Sullivan considered for the length of one heartbeat. "Please forgive my lapse of memory, Mrs. *Vindico*. I do see and respect everything you've obviously done for Dan, and you have given him a lovely family. I wish you nothing but the best," Sullivan directed to Fionna in a somewhat gentler tone. "And I hope you'll forgive me as well, Dan, once you shut down that engine and let the afterburners cool."

Dan let the harrowing confusion wash through his veins. There were just enough truths in all of the hurtful absurdity that he wasn't certain how to fight.

Drawing a deep breath that was filled with bitter regret and abject rage, Dan nodded.

"I suppose somewhere among all of that pure, sexist bullshit you just spoke in my living room, there are a few truths," he admitted. "I will step up my game at the academy, but it will not take away from my girls and it will not take away from my wife."

"I've always tried to help you even if you haven't always agreed with the way I've gone about it. You've never been all that good at listening to any voice other than your own anyway." He reminded Dan of just one of his more fatal flaws.

"Yeah, well, that's changed as well." Dan held his hands out to Fionna in exultation. Sullivan chuckled and nodded his agreement.

"Then I stand corrected because anyone that makes you listen does have extraordinary abilities."

For a moment, Fionna kept up her infuriated glare, but she turned to Dan. She must've sensed the lost confusion swimming in his energy.

"We need to figure out when these kids are getting in the safe and how," Dan commanded though his voice sounded distant and hollow even to himself.

"Gotta be coming back up to the school after hours. Portwood's had guys monitoring the corridors and I've been watching the key codes, but dozens of mentors come and go. I suspect they have multiple codes that they're using to gain entry." Sullivan confirmed what Dan already suspected.

"Uh, sir," Jeff's voice shocked Dan momentarily. "Could I just say something?" He was standing on the stairs.

"Of course." Dan nodded.

Fionna offered him her kind, reassuring smile as she stood and carried Halia into the kitchen to prepare her next bottle.

"I've been thinking," he began and then he drew a steadying breath. "I asked Logan about it, and he said it was a solid theory." Dan suspected that Logan had praised Jeff heartily if he was willing to bring it up at all, but that Jeff was downplaying his abilities once again. "I'm pretty sure the entire test vault thing is a distraction. What if the electric pulse and the key codes are to make us think these idiots are actually breaking in and stealing tests from the vaults.

"Portwood, Rainer, Tuttle, and I have all taken fingerprints and energy scans repeatedly, and we've never found anything we shouldn't have. Logically, it tells me they're never going near the vault. There's no way they went into the test vault that night because the time between when the lock was blown and Iodex showing up was just a few minutes. Then I remembered what you and Portwood asked me when we went to the relay station. 'What does it do for them? What does it get them?' I think the vault is a distraction. Think about it— whoever this is, they're amazing hackers. What if they're hacking your laptops and stealing the tests and answers from there? The vault gets all of the attention, and they're getting away with murder. What it gets them is a way to completely throw us off. And it was set up the day your dad took over Venton. They knew they had to do something that would distract us because he was going to be up there investigating everything. That's why they did it the night of the dance. They wanted all of the attention on the vault." He turned to Mentor Sullivan. "So, this time, sir, the smoke didn't lead us to the fire at all."

Sullivan was visibly stunned with Jeff's brilliance and seemed to reassess his impressions of Jeff Strenton in a moment flat.

"Uh, Bec's reading one of Aida's books to her. She said it was her favorite," Jeff added as Fionna returned with a bottle and a fussing baby.

"Thank you. I'll go up and check on her in just a minute," Fionna assured.

"Give Halia to me," Dan directed. "Go check on Aida. I'm sure I scared her."

"I'm gonna go. You have your hands full. Like I said, I wish you both the best, Dan. But I've always been more of the opinion that women are a great distraction from the work we're here to do. Perhaps I'm a little jaded. I've seen the dismantling a few too many times. Take it from Wilshire." He grabbed his coat off the rack in the entryway.

"That was just as much Wilshire as it was Bryant," Dan assured him. "He ran headlong into that fire. It wasn't just her." Jeff nodded his adamant agreement. "And I think it's high time we all ask ourselves why Wilshire and Bryant decided to throw away their marriages instead of just standing in judgment of them. That might actually lead us somewhere."

"Maybe so, but something about Katherine Bryant has always bugged me. She's got something sour brewing and has for longer than she's been letting Wilshire do the stirring. Mark my words, she's all for playing the ends against the middle as long as she comes out on top."

Dan factored all of that into everything he'd heard that evening. He laid Halia on his shoulder and patted her back gently as he walked Sullivan to the door.

"You can be mad or you can do something about it. Being mad at the messenger isn't going to solve anything."

Dan shook his head. "No. I can be furious because of how you treated my wife. I'm her Shield. No matter how much you hate that, it doesn't change the fact that she is why I'm on this earth, that she is who I'll always protect above all others. It doesn't matter what you want me to do."

"Shields were put here to protect the world, not only the object of their desires. Stop believing Realm legend and start doing your job."

"I can do both."

"Then do it."

Dan closed the door behind him. Becca gave him a hesitant smile.

"Fionna's lying down with Aida. We'll just go." She pulled Jeff toward the front door.

"Thanks," Dan managed and then opened the door for them as well.

CHAPTER 19

UNITED

He couldn't think. It was too much. He was drowning in his own swirling mass of confusion and regret. Promises he'd made waged war against his own deep desires that had been so violently thrown in his face. He kissed Halia's sweet cheek as she slept soundly on his shoulder, safe in her daddy's arms.

Not certain where to begin or where they would end up, Dan knew the only thing that he needed desperately in that moment. Without thinking or planning, he gently laid Halia in her bassinet and carefully carried the bed and baby to the nursery. He positioned it near the door and heat casted the bedding. He smiled as his tiny baby girl sighed contentedly in her slumber. Performing a different cast on the baby monitor, Dan carried the listening portion with him as he closed the door.

Fionna met him in the hallway. She was pulling Aida's door closed. Her eyes were red-rimmed and exhausted. It cut Dan to the quick.

He took her hand and guided her into their bedroom. He closed their door and locked it. Pulling her into him, he didn't speak. He was more forceful than he'd meant to be, but the hungry, desperate groan that echoed from her lungs urged him on.

"I need you," he growled just before he tempted her lips with his tongue. She parted them, and he swept it through her mouth tasting her, feeling her energy fill and bind him. She responded heatedly as she began to pant.

"Don't you want to talk?" she gasped as her fingers laced through his hair and she angled her head for more.

"Tomorrow." He began kneading her backside and positioned her provocatively against his strain.

"Dan," she tried again, but he kissed her, effectively ending her wondering if she should try harder to get him to talk to her.

"Later, whenever, just not now." He jerked the sweater over her head.

"Oh god, yes." She gave in to the desire pulsing and thrumming between them. The air around them was so thick with need, Dan could hardly breathe.

Working like a woman on fire, she flung his belt off and had his jeans undone in seconds flat. Her hand was on him, and a thundering growl spilled from his lungs as she began working him over.

"I want it. I want you inside me. I need it. I've needed it for so long. Just make it go away. Take me. Fill me full. It hurts to be without you." Her confession was riddled with urgent desire. "Make me better," she commanded, and Dan nearly lost it all as her fingers worked the buttons on his shirt and then located his hardened chest aching for her touch.

It was just a few days. Adeline and her three-week rule faded rapidly into a distant murmur.

"I'll be so gentle, baby doll. I swear I will. Just let me make it feel better. Just be with me, Maylea. Everything else can fucking wait because the only thing I'll ever need is right here, and I want her."

She trembled in his arms. His promises and his desire nearly drove her over. Her energy arced in jagged pulses, desperate to be soothed.

Hoisting her jeans off, Dan lifted her into his arms and carried her to their bed. She was his, and she held the only cure to his confusion and his aching pain.

"My god, you are just so fucking beautiful," he vowed reverently as he gazed at her lying before him, awaiting his tempting shelter and his strong embrace.

Her trepidation about her weight and her faltering self-esteem still plagued restlessly in his mind. He'd use his words and his body to show her how incredibly stunning he thought she was.

He watched her chest rise in rapid pants, and her breasts swayed in heavy fevered mounds that needed to be sucked and tended. Dan couldn't wait any longer. He hooked her panties with his thumbs and dragged them down her legs.

"I want to see you—all of you. You're all mine, and you are so fucking gorgeous you make me ache." He pulled open the drawer on the bedside table, removing the jar of lubricant. If she was virgin tight, then he needed to work slowly. With a fervent prayer that Halia would just give him a little time, he dipped his fingers in the jar.

"I'm gonna cast you, and then I'm gonna open you up for me. I'll make certain nothing hurts you, okay?"

She spread her legs farther and bucked, desperate for him to begin.

Dan summoned from the copious amounts of erotic energy that seemed to bleed from every surface of her body. He sealed her closed. It had been so long since he'd performed that cast, he paused and remembered to flood her womb with his own tender, soothing energy so that she felt no discomfort.

"Does that feel okay?"

She nodded. Her eyes begged him. Her body writhed. Her deep olive skin glowed enticingly, and he watched her beautiful lips glisten in preparation and need to be filled full of him.

He began tracing her mound and slit with his fingers spreading the lubricant slowly over her. He built her tenderly and made her wetter.

He lay beside her and made slow, languid movements with his tongue over her nipples as his fingers opened her ever so slightly.

"Oh god, please. Please now." Her body trembled as he began to suck the pulsating tips of her breasts, pulling hard, preparing her, as he pulled the erotic energy from the storehouse and then moved to her right breast to perform the same task.

"Relax for me, baby doll." He kept his voice calm but in control. He summoned soothing energy as he dipped his fingers deeply inside of her. "Fuck," he gasped. He'd never felt her so tight. It was simultaneously astounding and terrifying. He didn't want to hurt her.

But she seemed to feel no pain as he edged her open slowly, reaching deeper with each stroke.

"Yes, yes," she urged him on. He knew she could feel his fear.

"You're so tight, baby doll," he warned her. "So fucking tight for me. I don't want you to hurt."

"Open me. Make me yours," she ordered fiercely. "I want you inside of me. You could never hurt me. You're my Shield."

"It's gonna be like the first time, sweetheart. It's going to hurt. I'm gonna go slow, take it easy until you're ready for more," he explained as her back arched in desperation. "But I'm going to make you mine."

He dipped the length of his fingers deep inside her, spreading the lube as far as he was able and coating her in its healing salve.

The motion brought her. She came hard and fast. The need had been building for so long she couldn't fight the tidal wave that ripped through her violently. Dan growled his adamant approval.

"My god, there is nothing more gorgeous than watching you come undone for me."

Listening to her shuddering cries of ecstasy, Dan forced himself to wait though every fiber of his very being wanted to crawl over her. He'd wanted her underneath him for so long. Wanted to cover her body with his own, to shield her from the world, to make her feel nothing but all-encompassing passion at the flick of his tongue, the touch of his hand, and the force of his cock.

He throbbed against her thigh, desperate for her attention. A hungry groan spilled from her lips as she reached and grasped him.

"I want you inside of me," she begged with aching need. The lush scent of her and of sex filled his lungs. The soft quilt on their bed was a distinct contrast to how hard he was hung.

He leaned and grabbed the lubricant from the table.

"Rub me down before I make you mine," he commanded.

A moan in the tenor of a hungry scream poured from deep within her as she dipped her fingers in the jar and groped him.

"That's it." He panted for breath as the exquisite feeling coursed through his veins. She spun her index finger over his head, and he pulsed hot and heavy in her hands. He needed to fill her like he needed to draw his next breath.

Trying desperately to make certain that he caused her no harm, he kept his fingers opening her and stretching her slowly before he formed her around his length.

"Are you ready, baby doll? I need to make you mine."

"Now," she demanded. Dan moved over her and allowed himself just a moment to watch her body squirm in anticipation for him.

"All mine, baby doll. All fucking mine." He rubbed his strain over her clit, still trying to prepare her for the force.

"Please," she whimpered, and he could deny her no more.

He dipped his body low and edged her open. He let the lube guide him. Keeping his body braced on one forearm, he moved his other hand over her mound, sending soothing pulses throughout her as he pushed her open and felt her liquid perfection devour him and form tightly around his strain.

She trembled as he opened her. It had been too long. *Take it slow, not too much,* became his constant mantra as he pumped her as gently as he was able. He felt her open and a shuddering growl echoed from his lungs.

"More." She bucked to meet his every thrust. He transitioned until he was pounding into her, burying his need deep inside her, feeling her energy fill him and restore him. It healed him as he provided her with his unfailing love and devotion with every rhythmic thrust.

"So damn tight. My god," he groaned his ardent appreciation. "And so damn beautiful. I'm gonna lose it all, honey. You're just too much," he assured her as he felt his release build fiercely in his groin.

"Yes," gasped from her as she felt his love and his lust fill her and make her whole once again.

He soothed the plaguing murmurs of her heart and of her mind that she wasn't enough. Dan knew he'd never seen anything more beautiful as he watched her body respond to his rhythms, fuse them together, and thrum out of her in an erotic cadence.

Suddenly, she lost it all. Her body shuddered and pulled him deeper. The consuming flames of her climax seared through him, and with a final ragged push, he spilled himself inside of her, burying himself deep within the perfection of her.

"Are you okay?" He withdrew gently and fell to the bed beside her, then he pulled her onto his chest. He casted his shield around them letting her recover in his energy that was always filled with love for her.

"Perfect." She clung to him.

"Little sore?" he asked though he already knew the answer.

"Just a little," she assured him much too quickly.

He kissed the top of her head. "Our little girl still has an hour or so until her next bottle. With any luck at all, I could give you a bath and see if I can't take away what I just caused."

"Okay, but we better hurry." She wiggled from the bed, and Dan grimaced as she winced when she walked. He followed after her and turned on the water. He casted the faucet to warm the water instantly and then guided her in.

He returned for the baby monitor and then climbed in behind her.

"I'll rub you down again with the 'Ōhi'a lehua after we get out. Hopefully you won't hurt tomorrow." He kept his hand circling her mound, trying to ease all that he'd done.

She smiled sweetly, settled into his safe embrace, and reveled in his tender care.

"You're pretty much the best thing ever," she vowed, making him chuckle as he shook his head in adamant disagreement.

CHAPTER 20

STRATEGIC DECISIONS

When she seemed to no longer feel any pain, Dan settled back. He could feel her working up courage. He wondered where to begin and how to answer the inevitable questions that were coming.

"You know," she began as she felt his panic set in. She could feel everything he felt now. His release was inside of her. "I've known for a while that you missed law enforcement and that you were afraid to admit that even to yourself. That's why I hadn't brought it up. You seemed like you didn't want to talk about it."

"All I know is that you didn't like my old job, and that I told Aida I didn't chase bad guys anymore. When I resigned, Governor Haydenshire told me anywhere but law enforcement because he said it's not good for me." He finally decided to simply talk, to allow the disorienting concerns of his heart take flight on his tongue. She was his other half, and he knew somehow that she would make sense of his chaos. She always did.

"Keep going." She let her soothing cast form over him this time.

"But my God, I hate my job. I really do," he finally confessed. The weight of the burden grew lighter with every word that exited his lips. "And I don't ever want to do anything that would make you scared or worried, but when Kai said that the sheriff's position was mine if I wanted it, I felt like he was throwing me a lifeline. The idea of it made me able to breathe again. I just don't know what to do or what you want me to do."

She turned in the tub so she was leaning against the opposite end. She gave him his smile as he reached and held her hand. He wanted to be joined to her constantly.

"But I do love the farm, and I think that I could learn from Papa and really keep it going when they can't anymore," he eased, not wanting to upset her. "I'm just a little worried…"

"That you'd still be doing something that isn't what you were meant to do."

He nodded. "But, if you don't want me to take the sheriff's position, then I still think we should move to Kauai and live on the farm. I really do if that's what you want," he tried to explain everything swirling rapidly in his mind.

"Okay, my turn," she soothed. He studied her intently. He wanted to hear her words and feel her energy as she said them. "I've been thinking about it a lot too. And as crazy as everything was that Mentor Sullivan said and did, he was right about one thing. It is who you are, and I know part of what you hate about Venton is that you feel like you're wasting all of your training and your knowledge," she offered hesitantly as she studied him as well.

"Maybe." He glanced away from her though he certainly couldn't lie to her.

"Here's what I think for right now at least. I know that you're always telling people that I saved you and took you out of hell," she explained in a strangled whisper.

"You did."

"But don't you see? You saved me too. Remember how I was when I was pregnant the first time and not telling you?" She convulsed slightly from the memory. Dan reached for her, but she shook her head. "That's kind of how I was getting before that night at Anglington's. I was a mess. I was doing things I knew I would regret, and you took me out of that bar and you made me feel like Maylea again. Not only that, but you loved me as Maylea not Fionna. You make me whole. You make me better. You love me like no one else ever has. You make me feel things I never thought I would ever feel. You gave me Aida and Halia, and you are the most amazing husband ever. And, sweetheart, you changed everything about your life for me.

"I don't really want you to go back to National Iodex where you're hunting down mass murderers every day," she vowed adamantly, "But I don't really think that's what you want either," she stated knowingly. He nodded his agreement.

"And what you said to Mentor Sullivan about not taking time away from me and the girls and the way you've been with all of the crap going on at Venton, you've proven to me that you can do it all. You can leave work at work and not let it consume you. What I'm saying is that I fell in love with *you*. I want you to be you. I should never have asked you to be anything other than who you are. You love me for me. I want to do the same. I just need you to promise me one thing, and then I really think you should take the job." Her brow furrowed. "Although, there's more coming with that, and I'm not sure what it is yet."

"I'll do anything, baby. You name it."

"If I feel something is off or have a bad feeling, because you know when I'm on Kauai I'm even stronger," she reminded him. Her cheeks glowed pink, but Dan was thrilled she was finally embracing the magnitude of her awe-inspiring power. "If I ask you not to go to work or not to do something, that you won't do it. I need you to trust me," she laid out her demands. "If you'll really listen to me always, then I want you to do what you love. You were fine with me quitting the Angels, having a baby, and getting married. You're moving me back home all because you love me. I think it's time I do a little changing for you. I owe you that. I don't want you doing something you hate for me."

"Yes, absolutely," Dan agreed instantly. "Thank you." He was unable to contain his overwhelming emotions. "Thank you so much. My God, how did I ever get so lucky?" He reached and pulled her back to him.

"Now, I have a few questions, Officer Vindico," she prosed just to feel his energy respond to his new title. "Or will it be Sheriff Vindico?"

"I don't give a damn as long as it's not mentor."

She grinned and seemed to revel in his elation. "You know you can't lie to me," she reminded him though he certainly had no intention of doing anything of the sort. "Do you want to figure out what's going on at Venton and then buy out your contract? Do you want to move before June?" She let her eyes close in concentration as she read him.

"I don't know." He gave her the most truthful response he could access. "I don't want to disrupt Aida's school year, not that I've been all that impressed thus far.

"I think it's going to take a few months at least to get our new house built, and truthfully baby, I don't think the girls can share a room until Halia's older. That cottage might get pretty cramped with an infant and an eight-year-old. I'd like to have an office at home. I know that I won't have to be at the precinct every day, but I'd like to be able to work from home a good bit." He continued to allow the streams of consciousness to flood from his mouth.

Suddenly, the monitor carried Halia's sweet grunts of hunger to them in the bath. "I'm going to go get her, but I want to feed her in the bed and keep talking, please," Fionna begged.

Dan nodded his instant agreement. They hadn't really discussed much in the last few weeks, constantly interrupted by bottle making and feeding and diaper changing and trying to catch up on sleep. He was thrilled that she'd missed him as much as he'd missed her.

Dan helped her out of the tub. He heated the towel he handed her before letting the water out of the tub and toweling himself off.

Fionna crawled into bed with a bottle and their littlest princess who was red-faced and wailing.

"I'm hurrying, baby girl, be patient," Fionna soothed as she seated herself and supplied Halia with the bottle

Her fury subsided instantly as she inhaled the warmed formula. Dan rubbed Halia's head as she suckled. Her eyes blinked slowly in her contented state.

"How does this work? Do we get Papa to start on the house or hire a crew or something? Do we sell this house first?" Fionna was full of intrigued questions. Dan smiled. He loved the way her eyes danced when she was learning something new.

"We don't have to sell this house if you don't want to. We could rent it out and contract it through Patrick Haydenshire. He runs his parents' rentals and does an excellent job. Or we can sell. It doesn't matter to me. It's a pretty prime piece of real estate and would bring top dollar, but the market is down and rentals are up. That would be a constant source of income, and of course it would give us the option of moving back if we ever wanted to.

"I don't really want to ship either of our cars over. I'd rather buy when we get there, but I'd kinda like to keep my bike." He watched his beautiful wife giggle as she brushed a tender kiss across his little girl's forehead.

"That's fine, sweetheart. I know not to come between you and the Agusta." She seemed delighted that they were talking and planning their future together. "Hey, do you think Jeff and Becca would like to rent from us? I totally trust them, and he'd be so close to the Senate. He'll be Elite before we move, right?"

"We can certainly ask. I can tell you that when Jeff Jr. makes his show, that house they're in is going to get cramped quickly."

"They're going to name him Aaron," Fionna informed him. "And I really hope Jeff Jr. isn't what he calls his member," she teased as Dan shook his head at her.

"You're terrible and should probably be spanked, and I've really missed your deliciously naughty sense of humor." He waggled his eyebrows at her. She beamed at him and seemed just as thrilled with his flirting as he was.

"Did you ask Papa about the job any after I left?" Dan asked.

"A little…I thought I told you."

"You were a little preoccupied." He gestured to Halia who was finishing up her bottle and already back asleep.

"He said that the Deputy Sheriff is Josh Riker. I went to school with him up until we moved. He was always really sweet, and he shoved this awful bully, Alex penis-head, into the lockers one day when he popped my bra in middle school and broke the back strap. That's how hard he pulled it. He made my back red." Fionna rolled her eyes.

Dan cracked up. "Please tell me the kid's last name was not actually penis-head."

Fionna began laughing with him. "No, that's just what Malani and I always called him. How did I not realize I said that? His last name is Penstead."

"Well, I like Josh. Where does Alex currently reside?"

Fionna giggled as she attempted to get Halia to burp. "He works for the state senate in Honolulu now." She shook her head. "I'm assuming he got over his obsession with popping bras and breast development."

Dan shook his head and kissed her cheek and then Halia's. "Nah, we never really get over it. We just try to be a little more discreet at least until we get a set that are all our own that we can play with anytime we want."

"Anytime you want. Is that what you think?"

"If we're good." He traced his index finger lightly down the curve of her breast over her nipple. She shivered slightly.

"Do you think you could not feel me up while I'm burping our child?" She shook her head at him.

"Not really. They're gorgeous, and I haven't had my hands on them nearly enough lately. She's asleep so…."

"I'll be back. Do not go to sleep," she commanded him as she stood and carried Halia back to her bassinet.

"Now, I want to hold you," Dan informed her as soon as she returned.

With a broad grin, she lay against his chest as they continued to talk.

"Josh was apparently excited that you were thinking about taking the job. You've probably met his mom. She shops at Tutu's store almost every Friday. His wife is one of the advanced hula teachers at Miss Leialanie's where Aida dances.

"But he's agreed to step in as interim sheriff if Papa can get you to agree to come on as sheriff. Papa said there are about seventy-five Iodex officers on the island and that they would all report to you and then you would report to the state Iodex precinct in Honolulu."

"I feel like I should discuss this with Governor Haydenshire. I could have gone to jail for what I did." He fought the involuntary shudder that always worked through his body when he thought about summoning the life force out of Dominic Wretchkinsides.

Fionna nodded. "I'm pretty sure Josh and everyone kind of knows that you did that, and they still really want you," she assured him.

Dan was overwhelmed by the mercy and grace other people were willing to extend him.

"What kind of house do you want to build?" Fionna changed the subject.

Dan considered that. "Papa sent over several plans he thought you might like. I haven't really looked at them. I didn't want to get my hopes up in case you didn't want me to take the job," he confessed.

"I knew you wanted the job."

"And I knew you'd push me to take it because you knew I wanted it. I had to make certain that was what *you* wanted. Not all of us are phenomenal Receivers, baby doll." He dragged his fingers gently through her hair.

As he said this, a thought occurred to him. He called himself stupid for not thinking of it before.

"Hey, when I go back to work next week…"

"Mm-hmm," she urged him on.

"Do you think you'd be comfortable with my mom or Kara keeping Halia for a few hours and you coming up to Venton with me? I should have asked this a while ago. It seems to me that I have my own personal lie detector lying in bed beside me. So, Officer Hot Lips, would you want to come play detective with me and see if we can't wrap this up?"

"Sure, but don't forget I'm taking those classes with Kara Tuesday and Thursday mornings. I don't want to miss. And what if the people doing all of this aren't in your classes?"

"How close do you need to be to get a really accurate reading?"

"It depends. I get the most accurate reading one on one, but I can feel deceptive energy from everywhere. I just might not be able to pinpoint it exactly. It depends if that's what's on all of their minds. When people are actively lying, the distortion in their rhythms is very specific. It always, always includes relief."

Dan nodded. "Because at least for a moment, the lie got them out of whatever they're in."

"Exactly. But if people feel guilty for doing something, that's a very strong emotion as well. It weights their bands with desperation to get away from what they're worried about."

"If we decided to eat in the cafeteria during lunch hour, could you point out a few candidates?"

She nodded. "This might even be fun except that I'll miss my little coconut," she lamented. Dan chuckled. He thought that was a perfect nickname. "But she'd be a great little distraction."

"No," Dan spat. "Not no, fuck no. The girls are not coming up there anymore. Not with Pendergrath's spawn there. I'm sorry, baby. I really don't want you anywhere near him, but I don't think he'd pull anything with you in a school full of people, and like I said, you throw a hell of a shield when you need to but not my babies. No."

"All right, all right," she sighed with a slight eye roll.

"Hey." Dan kissed the top of her head. "Overprotective is kind of my schtick," he tried for a joke though he meant every word he'd said. His girls would not be back up at Venton ever.

Her giggle was cut off in the wake of an all-encompassing yawn. Dan slid farther down in the bed and cradled her to his chest.

"Go to sleep, baby. We can talk all day tomorrow and look over the house plans. I'll get up with Halia. You sleep."

"Best husband ever." Contentment and happiness lolled in her rhythms as she slipped into a deep sleep.

CHAPTER 21

POSSIBILITIES

Renewed vigor surged through Dan's veins. He had a goal. He and Fionna spent the weekend discussing house plans and upgrades she'd like in their new home. She'd spent hours on the phone with Tutu and Papa and Malani and Kai.

Dan had phoned Josh Riker and introduced himself and thanked him for being willing to step in as interim until Dan could get his family moved out there. Josh seemed like a great guy. Dan had agreed with Fionna's assessment. He was thrilled Dan was taking over, and Dan was flattered by his exuberance.

Josh didn't seem to be a fan of tourists, which he explained was at least half of the crime on the island. He'd jokingly informed Dan that the officers would love him because they apparently all knew and held deep respect for Tutu and Papa. Their families shopped at the store on the farm regularly, and they all thought Maylea was not only a great friend but was also a knockout and had been saddened when she'd moved away.

Josh asked Dan to please give Maylea his condolences about her mother. He'd explained that he hadn't had the courage to approach her at the funeral.

Dan had taken Fionna jogging each morning for the past three mornings. She finally even admitted that she was having fun.

Aida rode her bike ahead of them, circling back every few minutes while Halia slept in her jogging stroller. She seemed to enjoy the rhythmic movement as Dan pushed her along.

Thursday morning, Dan kissed Fionna awake. He carried Halia in to help awaken Mommy. She cooed excitedly which delighted Fionna.

"Hey, baby girl." Fionna pulled herself upright and took Halia from Dan.

"She slept four and a half hours," Dan announced. The extra couple of hours of sleep was worth hundreds of dollars.

"You can tell Daddy I'm not running his marathon today," she teased.

Dan sighed. "Fi, baby, I can only go on what you tell me. You said you wanted your energy and stamina back. If you don't want to run with me, it's fine. I'm not a Receiver, remember?"

"I'm just teasing," she assured him. "I just mean that this morning I'm dancing." She sounded exuberant.

"I was kind of hoping you'd dance tonight," he informed her. A broad delighted grin lit her features.

"Not after the first class. I have to be good. I'm not giving you a mediocre lap dance."

"I've never known you to do anything mediocre especially when it comes to my lap."

She giggled delightedly as she checked the clock on her phone. "I need to get ready. Was Aida upset I didn't get up before she left?"

"She was fine. I promised you'd play with her when she got home. And Halia and I are going to nap on the couch while you go shake your sexy ass."

"I really don't want my little coconut's first word to be ass," Fionna informed him as she crawled out of bed. "Okay, you go play with Daddy, and I'll get ready." She handed Halia back to Dan. He grinned as she attempted to get her own fingers in her mouth with a great deal of struggle. Dan aided her, and she began sucking.

He watched Fionna strip out of one of his T-shirts. He wondered how much longer it would take for their little coconut to sleep through the night so that her mama could go back to sleeping naked in his arms.

Fionna pulled on a pair of booty shorts and a sports bra. A shuddering groan escaped Dan's lungs. It delighted his wife.

Giggling, she topped the shorts with a pair of jogging pants and an Arlington Angels T-shirt. Moving quickly to the closet, she began flinging shoes until she located the ones she was searching for.

"We are going to build bigger closets in Kauai, right?" she called from the depths of the closet.

"I'm even adding in Maylea's shoe closet," Dan informed her.

She emerged looking excited by his announcement.

"Okay," she nodded but then changed her tune, "but all I wear there are flip-flops. I'm going to save all of my boots for when we come back to visit here though." She hoisted a pair of black heels with ankle straps and her running shoes into the crook of her arm and headed down the stairs.

"I'm nervous," she admitted. She fixed herself a piece of wheat toast and a poached egg.

"You'll be great, baby doll. I can't wait to see."

She rolled her eyes and kissed his jaw as she moved to the door to let Kara in.

"Oh, there's my teeny, tiny niece." Kara pulled Halia from Dan's arms. "I'm Aunt Kara, and I'm your favorite."

Halia seemed fine with Kara being her favorite aunt as long as she got to continue sucking her fingers.

"I signed us up for the thirty minute pole class and then the thirty minute strip," Kara informed Fionna as she swayed Halia rhythmically.

"Hmm, wonder what you and Zachy will be doing tonight, Care Bear." Dan shook his head at his sister.

"Do not call him Zachy. He hates that."

"Do I need to separate you two?" Fionna sassed in her best impression of Dan's mother. He and Kara cracked up.

"You're sure she'll be okay?" Fionna asked again.

"I'm starting to get a complex," Dan chastised.

"Okay, sorry, sorry."

"Zach's working from home today, so we can check out the nursery really well. Make sure Halia and Aiden will be fine after Dan goes back to work," Kara soothed.

"We'll be back in a little while," Fionna assured as she kissed Halia's cheek and then Dan's mouth.

"Have fun, baby doll." Dan waved and carried Halia with him to the door.

Though he'd given great effort since he'd awoken with Halia at five thirty and stayed up to get Aida off to school, Dan couldn't quite get his mind off what Fionna was going to be learning to do.

It had been many, many years since Dan had been to a strip club for the purposes of seeing a show. He'd gone with Will and Garrett a few times in the months that followed Amelia's death. They'd been trying to yank him forcefully out of his self-imposed sentence to hell. But other than using it as yet another way to consume masses of alcohol, desperate to drown out the harrowing pain, Dan had never found strip clubs all that appealing.

Strippers were hit on constantly all day, every day, and they were completely immune to even the best pickup lines. The majority of them had no interest in their clientele and wanted to go home alone. Dan never liked to have to work too hard to get a woman into bed as that was all he had any real interest in. It didn't seem worth the effort. He just didn't care that much. Having a woman grind on you and dance in your lap all night but going home alone was frustrating.

Bars proved vastly better pickup grounds. Dan shuddered as he strengthened the safehold he tried to keep on the memories of himself in the past.

He seated himself on the couch and laid Halia in his lap. He gazed down at her.

"What's Mommy doing?" He watched her eyes light as he talked. "You probably don't need to know that actually," he stated out loud as his baby girl seemed to love the sound of his voice.

His mind went back to Fionna being the woman to give him a lap dance or to strip for him.

Halia yawned. He moved to the recliner and rocked her to sleep then laid her in her bassinet. His mind was too full of erotic images of his wife whipping off her lingerie in heels and dancing in his lap for Dan to nap, so he pulled out his laptop.

He opened the multiple house plans Papa had sent over for them to consider. Dan began listing the things he and Fionna liked about each.

Going back to Tutu's cryptic announcement that Dan's sons would be born on the island, he decided they'd need a fourth bedroom. They wouldn't need guest rooms since the farm held several guest cottages.

Papa would add a large screened-in porch off the master bedrooms of whichever plan they chose that would contain the vast outdoor tubs that all of the homes on the farm had.

This brought his mind back to being in the bath with Maylea. All summer long, Dan had given her nightly baths. She would add oils to the water and then use its lubrication for the purposes of running her hands up and down his potent erection. Dan shuddered from the fantasy that played in great detail in his mind.

Shaking himself, Dan refocused on the house plans. Fionna liked the idea of the girls sharing a bathroom, so Dan added that to the list of likes. He'd asked her about her grandmother's prediction about their having more than one son.

"She isn't always right," Fionna vowed though Dan hadn't really gotten the impression that she believed her own statement.

He dozed off a few minutes later until he heard the lock on the garage door pop. Sitting up, he rubbed his hands over his face and moved to check on Halia. She was still sound asleep in her bassinet.

"Fi, she offered you a job. Obviously, you were amazing," Kara was announcing.

Dan greeted them at the door. He pulled Fionna into his arms and immediately noticed that she was glowing, and her energy was rolling in ecstatic waves.

"Hey, baby doll, how was class?"

"Kind of painful but really fun. I bruised my inner thigh. I need you to heal it," she informed him.

"He can heal you later. Tell him," Kara demanded.

"How did you bruise your thigh?" Dan asked.

"It's not bad. I just got a little overzealous whipping my leg around the pole," Fionna explained.

Kara shook her head. "I look over and Fionna has her legs wrapped around the pole, spinning around like she owned the place and then spinning down in something called a descending angel. My mouth hung open, and I fell over because I can hardly do the hand stand thing on the floor, and she's all 'oh no, I bruised my thigh.'" Kara rolled her eyes. "She was amazing. It was like she'd been pole dancing for years. The teacher wants to train her to teach the classes. She offered her a job on the spot."

"What did you say?"

Fionna headed to the kitchen and fixed herself and Kara large glasses of lemon water.

"That I had to think about it and talk to you. I told her that I'd just had a baby, and that I didn't know if I wanted to be away from my little coconut any more than just taking the class," Fionna informed Dan readily.

"But Katarina told her that she could train her in thirty or forty-five-minute sessions after our class and that she thought Fionna would be a great teacher," Kara added.

"It was really fun," Fionna admitted.

"And Katarina said that Fionna could just sub for her sometimes if she didn't want to take a full-time job. It would just be a few times every couple of months," Kara continued to gush. She was clearly impressed with Fionna's abilities and the praise she'd received.

"I told you the hip thing I learned from taking hula for so long. I danced most of my life until I started challenging at the academy," Fionna reminded Kara.

"Are you gonna do it?"

"I don't know. I never ever even thought of dancing again and certainly not teaching other women to dance."

"Call me when you decide," Kara demanded.

"Bye, Care Bear." Dan held the door open for his sister. She rolled her eyes as Fionna shook her head at Dan. "Go play with Zach."

"Call me. I love you," Kara chanted to Fionna. "And you, I like occasionally," she informed Dan.

"Thanks." He tousled his little sister's hair as she headed out the door.

CHAPTER 22

ATHLETIC EXCUSES

"That's totally crazy, right?" Fionna asked. Her cheeks colored as Halia began her scheduled fussing.

Dan stood, but Fionna grabbed his bicep. "No, I'll feed her. You've been taking care of her all morning."

"Sweetheart, I took care of her for an hour and a half, in which time, we talked and she napped. Now, I want to hear about your class." Fionna retrieved Halia, and Dan warmed a bottle. "Sounds like you made quite an impression. I'm offended that I never knew you had such skill."

Fionna sank down on the couch and spoke in Hawaiian to Halia just before giving her the bottle.

Her face ran a steady shade of crimson as she began. "Well...I mean...I guess I've kind of always been a little bit athletic," she hemmed.

He rolled his eyes outright and shook his head in abject disbelief. "Somewhere in this house is a cup that you made me take off the mantel that says that you were the greatest Receiver in Summation in the entire American Realm. I think 'I've kind of always been a little bit athletic' would be a serious understatement."

"That was just tacky on the mantel."

"Fionna," Dan scolded.

"I took hula at Miss Leialanie's until I was fourteen, and we moved away. Then when Dad and Gretta got married, she kept telling me I should hula again because I'd always loved it. She found these traditional Hawaiian classes, which wasn't easy in Texas, let me tell you. Anyway, she would drive me an hour to and from three days a week so I could keep learning."

"Keep going."

"I don't know. It was this kind of huge moment for me."

Dan grinned. She looked like whatever had happened in her class had made her entire week.

"It was like I was in there with, like, twenty other women I've never met and Kara of course. And there were women much older than me and younger than me and that weighed way more or less than me. I'm looking around, and I'm, like, all of these women are really, truly beautiful because they want to try something new and have fun and spice up their love lives and just be the sexy, amazing women they are, you know?" She studied him for a moment. "Do you remember the first night we were in Paris?"

Dan fought the shudder that always rocked through him whenever he thought of their family trip to Paris. "Kind of."

"When we were staying in that apartment that Fitz got for us," she reminded him.

Dan recalled some of the conversation they'd had in bed that night. That's when he'd told her that he thought they should name the baby Halia Elisabeth after her mom, and she'd promptly requested that they name her Halia Elisabeth Amelia Vindico, effectively shattering Dan's heart and healing it all in the same moment.

"And I told you about how I didn't feel like I fit into the way motherhood was going on around me and how frustrated I was."

"I remember."

"The women in my class today want to take time for themselves and their bodies, and we started learning and it was like watching all of them sort of blossom into these whole entirely sexual creatures. Like it didn't matter if you were a mom or a grandma or a lawyer or a waitress. In there, we were all just people, and it was okay to have a healthy view of sexuality, and it was okay to admit that we like having sex. A lot of women won't do that." Fionna sighed. "Most women complain about it. It's like we're afraid to be sexual beings. I think because for so long we were told that we weren't good enough or that if we liked sex we were bad. Women buried their sexual identities. Society can't seem to figure out what they want from us, but they're always quick to tell us whatever we're doing is wrong.

"But in there, it was like we were beautiful no matter how much we weighed or how old we were or which life paths we'd chosen. There was kind of this really neat unity to it. I really, really liked it."

Dan joined her on the couch. Her eyes were sparkling as she talked. Her entire body glowed with confidence and purpose. Dan couldn't take his eyes off her.

"Sounds like it fit your spirit. Now you keep talking, and I'm going to take your jogging pants off."

"Are you now?" She giggled.

"I'm healing your leg, baby doll," he explained. "You keep going."

She lifted Halia up against her chest, and Dan grasped the elastic waistband of her pants, pulling them off along with her tennis shoes.

"When she offered to teach me, I was really excited but..." Fionna hesitated.

"But what?" Dan was still enamored with the spark in her rhythms that she always held when she was learning about something that interested her.

"That's another hour a week I'll be away from our little coconut, and we're getting ready to move, and I want to help you at Venton, and she said it would take me several months to learn the moves and much longer to perfect them," spilled from Fionna's mouth. It dampened her spirit and her energy.

"You'd be away from our little coconut for three of the one hundred and sixty-eight hours each week," he pointed out as he edged her thighs apart, but the rest of his argument was drowned in his gasp. There was a large purple and green mark on Fionna's inner thigh. "Is this even safe?"

"You should have seen what I looked like after some of our Angels challenges. It does hurt worse now than when I did it though."

"Relax for me." Dan summoned from himself. His eyes closed as he touched his hand to the bruise.

Her leg tensed as he worked.

"Sorry, baby, but you banged it up pretty good."

"What do you think I should do?"

"As long as you don't keep coming home bruised, I want you to do whatever you want to do. You had a good time, and somewhere under all of those excuses I think you want to try this out."

"Do you think your mom would flip?" Fionna seemed to brace herself for reprimand.

"On a pole or just in general?" He reveled in his wife's abashed laughter. "How would she ever find out, and she's managed to deal with the fact that Lindley is working at a sex shop," he reminded her.

"That's true, but I think she mostly just pretends that Lindley has some kind of church secretary job, or a nurse, or librarian, or something. Someone told me that she told them Lindley was working at that huge church on G street."

Dan rolled his eyes. "My mother is insane, but I'm certain Lindley could get costumes for all of those positions at her shop. But you just told me that women are afraid of their sexuality, so don't let my mother's fears stop you from helping other women embrace their own."

"Good point, but what if I learn all of this stuff and then what am I going to do with this knowledge in Kauai?"

Dan kissed her inner thigh as the remnants of the bruise disappeared. "I could add a pole room to our new house if you'd like."

"I'm going to be learning pole and stripping." Fionna waggled her eyebrows.

Dan finally released the thundering groan he'd been holding in ever since she'd walked back through the door.

"I always want to be supportive of anything you want to do," he vowed as she tried to quell her own laughter as not to awaken their daughter. "I am perfectly willing to help you practice anything you need an audience for."

"You are always so willing to give," Fionna mocked as they continued to laugh.

CHAPTER 23

BOOM BOOM...BOOM

The night before Dan was to return to work, Fionna was feeding Halia her bottle and chatting with Malani on the phone while Dan gave Aida her bath and helped her rub kukui oil all over her skin. Her eczema had come back in full force with the cold weather, and she was miserable.

Fionna had fixed her an oatmeal bath with lots of Tutu's oils. Dan had read to her while she soaked for the prescribed time and tried not to scratch.

Dan and Fionna were consumed with guilt over forgetting to put her kukui and coconut oil on her after her baths each night. Exhaustion had set in when Halia had begun crying endlessly unless she was being held upright and casted.

They'd tried everything, but she only calmed under either Dan or Fionna's soothing casts. Fionna kept insisting that Halia was in pain. A trip to the pediatric medio had revealed an ear infection, which had been promptly healed. Dan determined that the only way they were ever going to have any energy was if one of them took all of the night feedings so the other could sleep a full eight hours, and that had helped. They'd taken turns and were almost functional again.

Fionna was set to begin learning to teach pole and strip exercising on Tuesday. She was telling Malani all about it on the phone.

Thanksgiving was Thursday, and to Dan's delight, Kara and Zach were hosting this year instead of his parents. That meant the food would be edible, since Fionna and Kara were doing the cooking.

The Stylers were going to Monterrey to visit Gretta's mother. Fionna's step-grandmother was not doing well, and Mr. Styler had pulled Dan to the side the night before when they'd come to play with the girls for a little while and explained that he didn't believe that Gretta's mother would make it much longer.

Aida looked and felt much better after her bath and after Dan covered her in Tutu's oils.

He tucked her in as Fionna changed Halia's diaper and put her in her swaddle wrap.

They met in the hallway, and Dan laced his fingers in his wife's and guided her back to the couch.

"Both of the girls are in bed," she stated almost in disbelief. "I'm not sure what to do with myself. I talked to Nana after Malani, and she sounds so much better. She was talking and laughing. Daddy and Mama got there a few hours ago, and Mama said that she thinks they're going to move Nana back up here with them. She's so much better when Mama's there."

"That's great, baby." Dan was thrilled. He hoped Fionna's father's assessment had been incorrect. Having her grandmother close by would delight his wife.

"They're bringing her back next Friday."

If she was well enough to travel, Dan assumed she really was much better. "I can't wait to meet her in person."

"I know. I just want her to meet Aida and to hold Halia and see what a great daddy they have."

Dan kissed her cheek, and a thought began rapidly taking shape in his mind. With a cocky grin, he brushed more kisses on her neck. He felt her jaw move into her beautiful smile.

He brushed another kiss along her ear. She shivered deliciously. "If I run to the bank and get a stack of fifties, do you think I could get a lap dance, Mrs. Vindico?" His voice turned low and raspy in his rabid desire.

"Maybe." Her eyes lit with excitement. "But you don't need the fifties. I'll take payment in sexual favors." Her hungry gaze dared him to make another demand.

Dan growled in her ear as her breath began to pant. He traced his fingers over the low-cut T-shirt she was wearing and held her eyes with his own.

"I want you to go upstairs for me, baby doll. Put on that see-through purple top and bottom thing that makes you look like a walking wet dream. The one that has the strings that I can pull and watch it all fall off you. Then I want you to come back down here and shake it for me. Show me all of those luscious moves. We'll see just how long I let you dance before I throw you on the couch and fuck you so hard you get wet when you think about it tomorrow."

"Oh god, yes." Fionna headed toward the stairs. "I don't care how tired we are. We're having more sex."

"Yes, ma'am, now go." Dan watched his wife's gorgeous body respond to his commands. Her rhythms swam with desire.

She headed up the stairs, and Dan lowered the lights in the living room. She wasn't treating the neighborhood to a dance. That was only for him, and he planned to thoroughly enjoy himself.

Fionna made her reappearance in the lingerie Dan had requested. A hungry growl exited his lungs as she shoved him back in a wingback chair near the window.

"You know the rule, Mr. Vindico," she sassed as he let his eyes trace slowly down her curves.

"I don't like rules," Dan informed her defiantly. Her entire body trembled in need, and though he was most definitely flirting, he also wasn't stretching the truth.

"No touching," she cooed as her tongue traced her top lip seductively.

"I'll touch whatever the hell I want, baby doll. You're mine." He beckoned her with his finger.

Fionna used her hand to turn on the speaker system in their living room that her phone was hooked into. A rather provocative song played, and Fionna lowered the volume to make certain they didn't awaken the girls.

"Come on, baby doll. Show me," Dan challenged.

Her eyes lit in delight as she strutted her way over to him. Her hips began to sway to the music as she allowed the rhythms of the song to work through her own. Dan's eyes goggled. He'd never seen anything hotter. Her hands slid seductively over her own breasts and waist, then she turned and shook her luscious ass for him, making him groan in need.

She spun and leaned down in front of him with her back arched, shaking her cleavage in his face.

"Mine," he demanded hotly as he jerked the long velvet ribbon tied between her breasts and watched them spill out of the top he'd asked her to wear. Fionna let the tiny top, that covered nothing at all, slide from her shoulders. She spun and flung it in Dan's face.

"Now shake them for me." He tossed the top away. A moan she couldn't seem to stifle spilled from her lips. It drove him wild as she dragged her breasts over the slight stubble of his chin. His eyes rolled back in his head as he caught her scent. He longed to jerk the tie side panties from her and bury himself inside her.

But she backed away, shimmying her tits in his face. Dan gave her looks that said he wasn't going to last much longer. He was about to stake his claim. She jerked his T-shirt over his head and ran her hands down his chest. Then she spun. She threw a come get me look over her right shoulder. She held his gaze with her own as she untied the panties herself then backed up to Dan before releasing the velvet ties altogether.

She sank down and began grinding her body around his throbbing erection demanding her attention. Unable to wait, Dan edged his jeans down enough to get the job done. He traced his fingers from her mound to her backside, listening to her moans become desperate. Her breaths were short, and her head was thrown back in wild abandon. She continued to sway her hips over him. Every time their skin touched, Dan felt the spark of electricity course through him.

He wrapped his hands around her waist.

"I need to be inside you, honey. I hope you're ready," he growled. Making certain he wasn't going to hurt her, he quickly spun two fingers in her opening. She was ready. Dan's heart pounded as the liquid sex dripped around his fingers.

"You're so hungry for me, baby doll." His voice was low and thrumming. "I'm gonna fill you full. You're already dripping for me. I'm about to pound that sweet pussy. It's been too damn long."

"Oh god, yes," Fionna gasped as she swung her long chestnut hair back and slapped Dan across the face with it. It drove him wild. He smacked her ass as she shook it for him once more.

Dan wrapped his hands around her waist.

"Mine." He jerked her over him as he thrust up inside her.

"Yes!" she moaned as she began riding him.

"Faster, baby, be a bad girl for me," Dan demanded, slapping her ass again.

Wanton abandon lit in her eyes. "Harder," she ordered, and Dan nearly lost it all.

"Do you need to be punished, baby doll? Have you been a bad girl? Do you need to count them for me? Need to be reminded who owns this pussy?" He lifted his body up off the chair and slammed hard and fast into hers.

"Yes." Relief perforated her gasp.

"Count," he demanded. He watched her ass jiggle as he spanked her again.

She barely got out the word, "One," before an explosive boom thundered through the house. Electricity crackled in the air. Fionna screamed and halted her grinding. The entire street went pitch black and deathly quiet.

The Vindicos' house lit. All of the casted electrical wiring that Dan and his father had installed in his home began working. He'd installed it years before when he was certain Wretchkinsides would eventually find his home, and Dan wanted every advantage. He'd never pulled the casts from the wires because he wanted his family to always be safe.

Dan's brain rejected the images he was seeing. The majority of their neighbors were standing near their yard staring in shock. Their lighted windows drew everyone's gaze to Fionna riding in Dan's lap. Her back had been arched deeply, and her head turned back begging him for more. Dan grabbed a nearby quilt and threw it around her as she cringed in horror.

Halia began screaming as Dan tried to determine what had happened.

"Go get the baby." He jerked his jeans back up. All thoughts of lap dances and carnal pleasures were gone. He helped Fionna stand and prayed their neighbors weren't still watching her stumble and wince as she took a step. She wrapped the quilt around her.

"Daddy!" Aida wailed as she ran from her room.

Dan lifted her up and guided her head into his neck to try and let Fionna get to their bedroom to redress without Aida noticing that she was completely naked.

He sprinted to the nursery and patted Halia until Fionna whisked in wearing sweat pants and nothing else. She lifted Halia into her arms and soothed her.

"What happened? It went boom, and my windows shook, and Sophie was scared," Aida explained.

"Let Daddy go find out." He had to know what had happened even if it meant facing the Leslies and Fred Scheckles after the show they'd just seen. "Just stay in here, baby." He tried to save Fionna further embarrassment. "I'm going to pull the lights. No one else has power, and we need to look like we don't either." He drew the electricity from the casted emergency lights into his hand.

Hot tears steeped in shame worked from Fionna's eyes, effectively breaking Dan's heart.

Drawing a deep breath and whispering that he was so sorry, he kissed her forehead and led her into their bedroom. She crawled into the bed with Halia to hide from the world. He laid Aida beside her baby sister. All three of his girls formed a tight ball of protection as they clung to their mother. Fionna's soothing Receiver's cast formed around them.

"I'll be right back. Just stay right there," Dan soothed.

CHAPTER 24
DUELING CHRISTMAS DEGREES

Incensed fury lit through Dan as he stomped out of his house to view Fred Scheckles giving him a stupidly lascivious grin. He was holding two large three-pronged electrical cords.

"What the hell happened?" Dan demanded. Chris Leslie offered him a consoling slap on the back.

"Is Fionna okay?" he whispered.

"No."

Chris grimaced, probably from Dan's fury.

"You. Talk!" Dan demanded of Fred Scheckles. His wife and his baby girls were huddled in bed together all crying, albeit for different reasons, on top of what had just been interrupted, and it had Dan reeling in drowning frustration and unmitigated fury.

Matthew and Hannah Leslie had been outside with their father and were staring at Dan. Their expressions held concerned confusion, and Dan wanted to melt into his own driveway.

"Can I get you a cigarette there, neighbor?" Fred laughed hysterically at his own joke.

Dan's fist flew back. Chris attempted to grasp his arm, but his hands didn't make it around Dan's biceps. "Okay, obviously I can't stop you from hitting him, but let's find out what he did before you make him unable to speak."

"Not that anyone who just saw what he interrupted would blame you." A man Dan recognized as living a few doors down cringed. Dan rolled his eyes, clenched his jaw, and watched his neighbors all take several steps back.

Carrie rushed out their front door carrying Annabelle on one shoulder. Parker, the Leslies' five-year-old son, was on her other side with his chin trembling. He reached for his father.

"What happened? It's his fault, isn't it?" Carrie tried to bounce Annabelle and hand Parker to Chris all in the same motion. She turned to Dan. "Is Fionna okay?" His scowl seemed to be all the answer she needed.

"I'm not exactly sure," Fred stammered. "I was certain I wired it up right."

"Wired what?" Dan bore down on Fred once again.

"The Christmas lights, of course." Fred gestured back to his home. Dan let his eyes move from Fred to his home.

A woman dressed in a snap front robe with her hair in curlers and wearing fluffy house slippers was standing in the doorway bellowing, "Freddy, you forgot to leave a space again." Her body was obscured by a dozen light strings that Fred had wrapped around their home. Every available space was covered in colored Christmas lights along with the exits from their home. At least a dozen massive, inflatable Christmas decorations lay lifeless in the yard. Fred Scheckles had effectively trapped his family in his own home with Christmas lights. Had Dan been able to reason through his incensed anger, he would have laughed.

"So, you blew all the breakers in your house, moron? Why the hell is all of our power out?" Dan seethed.

"You probably don't know this, but I have an electrical engineering degree from SDEEMU, Go Emus," he chanted suddenly. Dan squeezed his eyes closed and added to his own fantasies of choking the life out of Fred Scheckles. "That's South Dakota Electrical and Engineering Management University, for those that might not know. We ranked 146th in small colleges in the Upper Midwest," Fred stated proudly.

Chris Leslie shook his head in abject disbelief as he rubbed his face with the hand not holding Parker.

The man who'd offered Dan understanding for wanting to pound his fist into Fred's face headed to the large transformer box situated near the street in the Leslies' front yard. "Are you freaking kidding me?" he gasped. "You cut the lock on a transformer box? Are you insane? That's against the law. Look at this. He overrode the junction box on his house and tried to tap the feed in here. He blew the whole transformer. This will take the power company days to fix."

"Now, do you have an electrical engineering degree there, Mr. Langer?" Fred scoffed.

Langer's eyes narrowed. "Yes, I do have an electrical engineering degree. I also have a masters in industrial and systems engineering from Virginia Tech…Go Hokies," he spat in enraged indignation.

"Oh," was Fred's ingenious response.

Suddenly police cars and emergency trucks from Potomac Electric Power flew onto the street.

Two police officers headed into the Vindicos' yard to the gathered crowd of neighbors. One recognized Dan. The other didn't.

"Sir, it's twenty degrees out here. Do you frequently walk around without a shirt on?"

The other officer shook his head violently and whispered, "Shut up, man. That's Dan Vindico. He used to be Chief of Elite Iodex," in the accuser's ear loud enough for Dan to hear.

"Oh, I'm sorry, Chief Vindico. I'm new to the force," the officer corrected. "Do you know what happened?"

Dan held out his hands to Fred. "He happened."

Garrett's squad car joined the others. He slammed the door and stomped toward Dan. "I just saw your address flash across my screen. What the hell happened?"

Suddenly, Aida rushed from the house in her fuzzy pink footy pajamas.

"Daddy, Mommy is still crying and so is baby Halia," she fussed in alarm. Dan let his eyes close in abject defeat as he lifted Aida up into his arms.

"You idiot. She just had a baby." Carrie Leslie dove toward Fred.

"She knows she's going to have to leave. They can't have a newborn there with no heat." Carrie's hand flew out toward the Vindicos' house as fury lit her eyes. "Just look what you've done."

"Sir, this is a disaster." One of the linemen from Potomac Power sauntered up to Garrett and the other officers. "He's blown the transformer. It's completely fried. It's going to take us days to fix this. I have to get in parts, and we're running on skeleton crews this week because of Thanksgiving. You're talking busted pipes from no heat, and no electricity on this entire street for days."

Visibly drawing on every last ounce of courage available to her, Fionna walked out of the house holding a screaming Halia. She'd pulled on one of Dan's Iodex sweatshirts.

"I can't calm her down. I'm too…" Fionna tried to explain that she was too upset to calm Halia while she refused to meet anyone's eyes. Dan handed Aida to Garrett and took Halia. He calmed her quickly.

He let his soothing cast work his way through the blankets Fionna had wrapped her in. Then he laid Halia up on his shoulder and pulled Fionna into his chest to let her hide in him.

"It's all right," Carrie soothed. "It's perfectly normal to be emotional right after having a baby." She had absolutely no idea why Fionna was so mortified. "Especially when your across the street neighbor is an imbecile," she screeched at Fred. Chris tried to wave her off.

Fred looked astonished that everyone was angry. "Don't you have any Christmas spirit? And why did Dan's house light up all of a sudden?"

"Generator, right, Dan?" Garrett stepped in.

Dan nodded. "It lights for a few minutes if the power goes out, but it's out of gas," Dan lied.

"Sir, we're going to be taking you in," one of the officers informed Fred.

"No, wait, he's the head of the CIA, and he said I could," Fred began babbling and pointing at Dan. "I have a degree," was the last thing Fred Scheckles uttered as he was shoved in a squad car.

Garrett knew there was more to it than what he was understanding. Fionna wouldn't be sobbing over a power outage.

He raised his eyebrows to Dan in question.

Dan shook his head. "Later," he mouthed.

"Fionna, I'm so sorry." Carrie was still overwrought. "Is there anyone you could go stay with?"

Garrett and Dan shared a knowing glance. Dan and Fionna were more than capable of running their home with the energy from their bodies, but it was against Realm law to flaunt one's abilities to the Non-Gifted or make them wonder about the Gifted Realm.

"I'd let you crash, but I have a one-bedroom apartment. I'll give you and Fi my bed, but I don't know where you'd put the girls," Garrett lamented. His shield was actively soothing Aida. She was snuggling into his embrace and dotting kisses on his cheek and neck.

"Why don't you go back in and start packing," Dan soothed Fionna. "I'll figure out where we're going to stay." Getting her out of their neighbors' sight seemed the best choice.

Fionna took Halia and returned inside.

"Mommy needs me to help her," Aida explained to Garrett.

"Okay, baby girl." Garrett set her down and watched her race after Fionna. "What the hell happened?" He spoke through his teeth as he edged Dan away from all of his neighbors.

"Our neighbors just got one hell of a show in our living room when the street went dark and my casted lines lit up."

Garrett tried very hard not to double over laughing. "You know Fi may never leave your bedroom again, right?"

"If you had any idea what they just saw, you'd know that she may have us moving to Kauai tonight."

"Where are you going to stay?" Garrett glanced around at Dan's neighbors. They were all studying him closely.

"No one has the room except my parents. Her dad and Gretta are out of town, and their guest bedrooms either have one twin-sized bed or are crammed full of bakery supplies. I cannot fucking believe this."

"All right, deep breath," Garrett ordered. "If you calm down, she will too. Take her to your parents' house. Tuck her up in your old bed and keep her casted until she stops freaking." He laid out the perfect formula to help Fionna begin to recover.

Dan squeezed his eyes shut. The last woman who had been in his bed in his parents' home was Amelia. *That was a lifetime ago, Vindico, get it together. She needs you,* he commanded himself. Giving Garrett a nod, Dan drew a deep breath.

Langer stepped toward Dan and Garrett. "I don't think we've officially met. I'm Seth Langer," he introduced.

"Dan Vindico." Dan offered Seth his hand but withdrew the offer as Seth cringed.

"Maybe another time," Seth hesitated.

Dan nodded his understanding as Garrett cracked up.

A man from Potomac interrupted, "I suggest you all find yourselves somewhere else to stay if you can. We'll get it taken care of as soon as we're able. Let your faucets drip while you're away. You can file suit with the man the police took in for the damages and hotel bills if you want, but there's no guarantee you'll get it back, so don't stay above your means thinking he'll end up paying for it."

"Why don't I help you pack?" Garrett shoved Dan toward his home.

CHAPTER 25
MI-6, MOTHERS, AND MEMORIES

Two and a half hours later, Dan guided his family into his parents' home. He still couldn't fathom how his life had turned so bad so quickly. Tears continued to leak from Fionna's eyes. Dan tried to reassure her unsuccessfully.

"We are moving tomorrow," Fionna decreed in the car on the way over. As reasoning with her seemed impossible, Dan had just gone along with it.

This had come after Betty Scheckles had climbed her way through the mass of tangled Christmas lights and worked her way to the Vindicos' home. She'd pled with Dan to get Fred out of jail. According to her, Freddie had informed their family that Dan was a British spy who had perfected the American accent. She'd asked that he contact MI-6 and get the king to release her husband.

Governor Vindico helped Dan unload the vast number of suitcases, bags, cradles, seats, diapers, formula boxes, and toys his girls would need over the next few days. "Please tell me Fionna isn't crying because she has to stay here." He sounded devastated.

"Oh no, that's not it. We really appreciate you and Mom putting us up," Dan assured his father.

"Mrs. Vindico, would it be all right if I made a cup of tea?" Fionna was begging Dan's mother when Dan and the governor made their way back inside the house weighted down with luggage and baby equipment.

"Of course," Mrs. Vindico agreed though it appeared she was very curious as well to know why Fionna could barely manage to quell her tears.

"Long night, Mom," Dan assured her as he let his parents tend to the girls for a moment, and he followed Fionna into the kitchen.

"Baby, I am so sorry," he vowed for what seemed like the hundredth time. Nodding, Fionna finally fell into his arms and let him shield her from the world.

"It's not your fault." She seemed to regain a little bit of her composure.

While keeping her pressed to his chest, Dan reached in the cabinet beside the refrigerator and extracted a mug. He leaned to the sink, filled the mug, then heated the water with his hand. He stepped back to the box Fionna had packed of things from their kitchen. She clung to him as he made each step. They both chuckled. Dan dipped the Nanea tea bag from the box of Tutu's teas into the mug and kissed the top of her head.

"And then a boom went really loud and then my windows went like this," Aida was regaling her grandparents with her eventful night. "And then Halia screamed really loud and then I said Daddy," Aida called making Dan's parents chuckle.

"I'm sorry I freaked out, and I know you don't want to spend the night here," Fionna whispered.

Dan kept his arm around her. "It's certainly not your fault either, and I want to stay wherever my girls are." The truthfulness of his statement brought him solace.

"Aida needs to go to sleep. She has to go to school in the morning." Fionna headed into the living room. "All right, baby girl, it's time for bed." She smiled at Mrs. Vindico who was feeding Halia a bottle.

"Do I get to stay in Aunt Kara's room with the Barbies?" Aida quizzed.

"Uh," Governor Vindico glanced nervously at Dan. He seemed to have discerned that Dan might not want to sleep in his old bedroom. "Sure, if it's okay with Mommy and Daddy."

"Yes, I'll need her to stay in Kara's room since I moved my new exercise bike into Meredith's room, and Lindley hasn't moved her things out yet," Mrs. Vindico decreed. "I put clean sheets on your and Kara's beds when you phoned, Daniel."

Fionna laced her hand through Dan's. "Thank you," she offered politely. "We can just put the bassinet in Dan's room with us."

"If you'd like, you could put the cradle in Lindley's room. Then she'd just be through the bathroom from you and Dan," the governor pointed out. "If you'd sleep better without her in there with you."

Not certain he wanted his little girl anywhere near Lindley's room, Dan considered. Shaking himself from his disorienting reverie, he lifted Aida into his arms.

"We'll have to leave a little earlier for school tomorrow, so you need to go to sleep," Dan instructed.

Aida blew the Vindicos kisses and leaned to kiss Fionna's cheek.

"I love you, Mommy." She wrapped her arms around Fionna as Dan held her lower half in his arms.

"I love you too, sweetheart. Go on to sleep. Maybe we can play with Aunt Kara's Barbies tomorrow," she guided. Aida nodded her understanding that she was not to play with the old toys in Kara's closet before bed.

After tucking Aida in, Dan returned to the living room in time to hear, "Now, I read an article in *Women of the Realm* that said that babies who aren't breastfed have more ear infections," ring scoldingly from his mother.

Dan marched to Fionna's side. "I think I need to put all of my girls to bed. Now." He scowled at his mother. "Why don't you get Halia, and I'll carry the bassinet up?"

"Do you need all of these bags upstairs, Fionna?" the governor asked.

Fionna blushed. "Yes, sir. I'm sorry. Babies require a lot of stuff, and I'm high maintenance too, I guess."

Chuckling, the governor shook his head. "I raised three daughters. I'm well aware of everything you all require." He winked at her and hoisted the many bags Fionna had thrown their belongings in into his capable arms. "Dan, you can just ride into

Venton with me, and I'll take you back by your house tomorrow afternoon to get your car."

Dan convulsed slightly. Staying in his parents' home, eating their food, sleeping in his old bed, and being taken to school by his father threatened to make him ill. He started a mental list of different ways he could drive Fred Scheckles to distraction as he stomped up the stairs.

Mrs. Vindico had done an excellent job of getting Halia to sleep, and Fionna laid her gently in her bassinet set up in Lindley's old room.

"Can we get you anything else before we head to bed?" Governor Vindico asked.

"No, but thanks again for all of this," Dan offered. "I'll chill cast Halia's bottles for the night, so we'll have them in here when she wakes up. I'll try to get her quickly, so she doesn't wake you and Mom."

"We're thrilled you're here. We'll be fine. We could even get up with her if you and Fionna would like to sleep for longer than a few hours at a time."

As intriguing as that sounded, Dan doubted Fionna would allow his parents to be inconvenienced.

"Maybe tomorrow night. Fi's a little harried," Dan tried to explain.

"Just let us know."

Dan forced himself into his old bedroom by sheer strength of will. He tried to remove the memories from his mind altogether.

Fionna was running a brush through her long hair. "Are you sure this is okay?" She sounded concerned.

"Wherever you are," Dan reminded her. "Are you okay with this?" He gestured to his old bed and wondered if Fionna might not want to sleep somewhere that Dan had used more times than he could count for the purposes of making love to a woman who was not her.

"It's a little odd." She wrinkled her nose. She moved to Dan, pushed her hands under his shirt, then let her soothing rhythms flood through his back. "She's a part of you though. I love you, so I love her."

Dan wrapped his arms around his wife, holding on to the only thing that really mattered. His past was gone. His present was in his arms, and he wasn't letting her go. "Aside from everything else, I'm not certain how we're supposed to fit in a double bed." It felt better to be discussing the oddities of the situation instead of pretending they didn't exist. He'd put on approximately seventy-five pounds of pure muscle since the last time he'd slept in that bed thirteen years before.

Fionna giggled. The sound soothed Dan's soul. She'd been so distraught. He was thrilled she seemed to be regaining a little of her equilibrium.

"It's okay. I'll just sleep on top of you," she teased hesitantly. She seemed to want to know if it was really going to be all right, if Dan was going to really leave the past where it belonged and be with her. If he really could let everything else rest in peace.

Giving a lusty growl in her ear that delighted his wife and had her rhythms lilting in happiness, Dan seated himself on the bed and pulled her into his lap.

CHAPTER 26

TENDER CONFESSIONS

She wiggled her backside for him as he rubbed it. "Dan Vindico's teenage bed." She laughed again. "Are there *Playboys* with Pamela Anderson or Kara Monaco or the *One Tree Hill* girls under your mattress with sticky stuff on them?"

Dan laughed and nodded. "Could very well be," he admitted sheepishly. "But if you're looking for Pamela, I'd check the bathroom cabinet."

Fionna laughed heartily.

"I love you," he vowed suddenly. He was simply unable not to tell her.

"I love you too." She stared up at him like he was the answer to every question she'd ever asked. He still couldn't fathom how she could possibly love him like that. "Do you think your mom will get mad if she catches us making out in your room?"

He winked at her. "Why don't I leave a bite on your neck, and we'll see if she hyperventilates in her morning coffee."

Fionna cracked up. He cradled her close, certain he could never love anything more.

"I don't know about you, but I'd say this has been one hell of an evening. Why don't you go do all of the stuff you do in the bathroom every night that I can't figure out, and then I'll try to wedge myself in around you in the bed."

He needed to hold her. He desperately needed to replace the memories. He wanted solace from the world, and he longed to cast his shield around her because she needed that.

Dan followed her into the bathroom.

"I didn't know you found my bathroom time confusing."

He squeezed her backside as she walked ahead of him. She shook it for him. She was definitely making a comeback.

"Guys shave and brush our teeth. That's about it. I don't know how you keep up with the order of everything you do in here every night. I can only assume, based on the ingredients in all of your products, that you're making some kind of fruit salad."

Keeping her laughing was the only way he was going to survive the week. "Natural products are best for your skin. You should know that from Tutu. If I don't do all of this, I become very unattractive. Trust me."

Dan shook his head. "I don't think so. You are beautiful inside and out, and you always will be."

He felt her energy spin in elation as she leaned up on her tiptoes and kissed his jawline. With a delighted smirk, she pulled open one of the bathroom drawers. She poked her lip out in a pout. "Aww, no Pamela."

Unable to recall a time in his entire life that he'd enjoyed being at his parents' home, Dan laughed. Needing to join his past and his future, he decided to really let her in. She was his. She'd given him everything. She'd made him the man he was. She'd saved him from himself and from the demons he carried that tried desperately to bring about his demise on a daily basis.

"Do you have some deep desire to see some Playmates, sweetheart?"

Her eyes lit as her mouth formed a naughty grin. "Yes!"

Dan shook his head and popped open the cabinet at her legs. She stepped back and placed her hand over her mouth as she watched him. "Oh my gosh. I'm so oddly excited."

He crouched down and leaned deep into the cabinet. "She may

have found them and thrown them away," he warned her, still reveling in her delighted giggles. "Nope." He laughed as his hand grasped the rolled-up magazines, all well over a decade old, that he'd shoved behind the water supply lines and the sink basin.

He extracted several *Sports Illustrated Swimsuit Issues*. Elle Macpherson and Beyoncé were showing off their curves on the covers. Under those were three copies of *Motorcycle Babes* and then a *Playboy* staring Sara Jean Underwood as the centerfold.

Fionna shook her head. She was still giggling hysterically. "Your mom never knew they were in there?"

With his face glowing a deep crimson, Dan hemmed, "I'd go with knew, but vastly preferred to remain in deep denial. Hang on, there's more." Dan cringed as he suddenly remembered. He used the end of his toothbrush, just like he did as a teenager, and edged a magazine out from behind the medicine cabinet that hung over the toilet.

"Oh my gosh," Fionna gasped as Dan handed her a copy of the Arlington Angels expanded program from the mid 2000s. The women were posed throughout the program all wearing the customary Angels short shorts and positioned to look very sweet but all well aware of their sex appeal.

"This is so fun." Fionna was nearly jumping up and down in the bathroom as Dan laughed at her outright.

She grabbed a screw-top jar of the moisturizer her grandmother made and took Dan's hand. She led him to the bed, still carrying the magazines. "You're sure you're okay?"

"I'm fine, baby doll. You can feel that," he reminded her as he joined her on the bed.

"You feel nervous."

"Okay, but I'm still fine."

"Can I ask you stuff and if you don't want to think about it or talk about it, just say no? You can ask me stuff too. I'll tell you whatever you don't already know, which I think is most of it."

"I guess."

"First kiss?" She studied him. He knew she was reading through his emotions, but the question didn't bother him.

"Age or location?" Dan found it odd that he didn't mind the recollections as long as they were with her.

"Both."

"Twelve and her swimming pool." He gestured his head toward the Richmonds' home. "How about you, Mrs. Vindico?"

"Thirteen and at the Kokee Museum on a field trip," she supplied.

Dan wondered if there was some reason she'd left out a rather pertinent piece of information. "With?"

Fionna glowed pink and squeezed her eyes shut.

"Not Kai."

"Are you kidding me? He's been drooling over Malani since his family moved from Oahu when we were all ten."

"Okay, who then?" Dan didn't really care about when Kai and Malani had fallen head over heels for each other.

"Uh, well," Fionna hemmed.

"Fi, come on."

She wrinkled her adorable nose as, "Josh Riker," fell from her lips and she cringed.

"Please tell me you're joking." Dan shook his head at her. "My deputy is the guy who first kissed you?" Realization lit in his rhythms. "That's why he shoved penis-head into the lockers." Dan now had all the pieces of the puzzle. Fionna covered her mouth and tried to quiet her abashed laughter. "You might've mentioned that before I called and thanked the guy for stepping in for me so I could move you back to the island."

"I know, but then you might not have called, and I really thought you should." She sounded like she'd just committed a heinous crime.

"I still would have called. I just wouldn't have been as nice." Dan grabbed her backside and scooted her closer to him.

"Okay, second base." Fionna seemed genuinely interested in hearing about Dan's sexual development.

"I don't know. Fourteen, maybe, and believe me, I was an asshole who just kept trying to go farther and farther," he explained with a regret-filled sigh.

"And who got to play with these first?" Dan slid his hands over her breasts and watched another crimson flush creep from her neck to her cheeks.

"That would have been Will Haydenshire," she confessed with a slight shudder.

"Same day as third base?"

"Yeah, after my mom died, I withdrew. It sort of stunted my sexual development, I think. I rebelled, but not in that way at first. Maybe that part was good. I don't know. It messed me up pretty badly," she admitted. "I went from no experience to…way too much too quick."

Dan felt the customary fissure in his chest whenever he thought of his baby reaching the brink of irrecoverable depression in early adolescence.

"I'm sorry," he soothed.

She began flipping through the old Angels program. "She wasn't nice," Fionna pointed to an Angels enforcer who Dan had no knowledge even existed. "She quit after my first season, but at my tryouts, she was very not nice."

"From you, I'm going to take it that very not nice means she was a real bitch," Dan translated for her.

She laughed and gave him a sheepish nod. "Okay, first blow job?"

Drawing a deep breath, he shook his head as he tried to recall. "I honestly don't know. It wasn't with Amelia, and you know everything after that was a blur until I met you."

"Really?" Fionna seemed shocked.

"She wasn't into that."

Fionna immediately sensed there was something Dan wasn't telling her. She studied him for a long moment. "You know,"—she closed the program and set it aside as she took Dan's hands in her own and drew from him—"I've never said this out loud, but after Mama died, I was so lost and so scared. You already know I refused to even leave Tutu's. I wouldn't do anything," she confessed as tears welled in her eyes. Dan wiped them away with his thumbs and tucked a few loose strands of hair behind her ears.

"I know, baby."

"Then Daddy decided we were moving." She let the anger she'd felt as a teenager finally work its way through her soul and out of her mouth so that it could be healed. "He took me away from everything I knew and loved. He took me from Malani and Tutu and Papa and the farm. I'd never even been to the mainland. He never understood," she managed in a choked whisper. "He didn't believe Tutu, and he didn't believe that I can't really survive without Kauai. Gretta saved my life by sending me back every summer. And now you're saving me by moving me back home. I think that's why I rebelled against Daddy so badly as a teenager. I only made life worse for myself, but that's why I did it. But then I realized that if I'd never left Kauai, if I'd never moved to DC, I would never have become an Angel, and so much more importantly, I never would have met you. Even with every horrible thing I lived through, I swear I'd do it all again to get what I have now."

She fell onto Dan's shoulder and let him hold her and stand between her and the corrosive world if only for a moment.

"Fi, can I tell you something?" Dan begged her. The need for her to know everything in that moment was so strong he was unable to shut it away. He hadn't even acknowledged this truth until recently.

She lifted her head. "Of course."

He shook his head and waged war against his own tears. "This is the worst part of the whole fucking thing." Raw emotion gripped his throat and squeezed the air from his lungs.

"It's okay. Whatever it is." Fionna let her eyes close. Her cast flowed through him, and he could breathe.

"It's not okay," he argued. "It will never be okay, but I don't think we ever would have actually gotten married. I don't even know how much longer we would have been together. We fought all the time.

"I kept going to Paris and Moscow because I didn't want to be at home, and I couldn't tell her that. I loved her so much, but it wasn't enough. There were a lot of nights I ended up at Will's because I walked out and slammed the door in her face," the harrowed confession poured like acid from his tongue. "She'd moved back home twice. If I'd just ended it when I wanted to, she'd still be alive. Her parents would have their daughter, and she'd have found some guy who could have made her happy. It just wasn't me."

"I'm so sorry." Fionna shook her head in disbelief. "I never knew that. Whenever I saw you with her, you felt happy. I could feel how much you loved her."

"When did you...?" Dan was shocked that Fionna had seen him with Amelia.

"You usually brought her to the formals at the academy, and I was usually there." She shrugged. She'd noticed him, but it had never gone the other way. Additional guilt and regret added to its loading burden.

Dan lifted her chin. "Thank you for loving me and for letting me tell you this. I never told anyone, not Fitz, not Dad, not Will, not Garrett, not anyone. I refused to even accept the truth until just a few months ago. We were great until we graduated and moved in together. We were too young, and I was a pompous prick. She knew but wouldn't call me on it. I wouldn't have listened if she tried."

Fionna shook her head. "It's okay. You were really young, and as horrible as it was and it is, we can't change it. You did every single thing you could to try to fix it, and it just can't be fixed."

"We had another fight that night before I left. Not one of our huge ones. I didn't storm out or anything. But the whole time I was at work, in the back of my mind, I was trying to figure out how to tell her we needed a little time apart. That I was going to move out and that we needed to sell the house," he convulsed as another round of tears overtook him. "I called her because I was a fucking coward and wanted to do it over the phone. She didn't answer. That's when I knew something was wrong. I rushed home...and she was gone." He shook his head, still unable to believe how everything had fallen apart so quickly.

Drawing a deep steadying breath, he squeezed Fionna's hands until she was staring up into his eyes and seeing into the depths of his soul. "It didn't matter how much I loved her. It didn't seem to matter how much she loved me. We couldn't make it work and then..." his voice shattered as he tried to share the moment that cemented them together for eternity. "Then I walked out of Anglington's with you, and..."—he shook his head—"I knew why it never would've worked." The tears he'd been fighting became his victor. "She wasn't you." When he finally managed to use his voice again, Dan kissed her cheek and tasted her salty tears. "I'm not sure how we got there from my first blow job."

A broken smile spread across Fionna's face. "You never know where porn and putting on a show for your neighbors might lead you."

"I never thought I'd say this, but I do now have a deep appreciation for my mother's obsession with window coverings." Air filled his lungs. The weight he'd carried on his shoulders and in the permanent scars of his heart began to lighten their load in the light of her love and of his terror-ridden confession.

"We should put those big white shutter things in the new house."

"Especially if Josh Riker is going to be coming by our house frequently." He wiped away the last of her tears.

"Thank you for loving me, and for moving me back home, and for understanding how badly I need to be there," spilled from her lips as she lost all sense of teasing banter.

"Thank you for you and for my girls and for making my life worth living." His words seemed to heal and bind her. He guided her face upwards with his index finger and devoured her mouth. They stayed lip-locked for several long minutes until she pulled away panting for breath.

"I love you so much," she whispered.

"I'll never deserve that," Dan vowed.

CHAPTER 27
DIMENSIONS

She shook her head and crawled in his lap. "Look, I can fit in my ball again."

"Right where you belong." Dan cradled her to him curled tightly in her cocoon.

Her eyes fell on one of the *Motorcycle Babe* magazines.

"I seriously considered having mine surgically enhanced." She pointed to the cover girl splayed across a Honda Fireblade showing off her overtly fake assets.

"Why?"

She tucked her head under Dan's chin. "I guess I thought mine weren't big enough. Chloe got hers done. I thought that's what I should do too."

"Fi." Dan leaned back to study her. "Your chest is gorgeous. Why would you mess with perfection?"

"When you've been objectified your entire career, it's easy to begin to think that your worth is entirely dependent on your looks. I haven't always had a great self-image. I still don't."

"That's why you're so worried about your weight." He felt stupid for never realizing that.

She nodded against him. Instead of telling her again how stunningly beautiful she was, he asked, "Is there anything I can do or say to you that would make you believe how amazing you are? Inside and out? Anything at all?"

"You are doing something. I know I don't always believe you when you tell me, but when you tell me that I'm beautiful and how much I mean to you, it does wonders. And you're taking me back to my island. You're taking me back to the people who know me as me, not Fionna Styler, the famous Arlington Angel. I let myself become that identity because I'd lost my own until you found me again. I'm still struggling.

"To the American Realm, I'm a two-dimensional image posed in a program." She gestured to the old Angels program on the bed. "I'm always supposed to look and act a certain way. I didn't understand that I could be me when the cameras weren't there, so I tried to always act and look a certain way. I tried to do what I thought would make everyone else happy because I can feel when they're happy, and I hoped their happiness would make me less miserable. I lost myself completely. It's part of being so far away from my island for so long, maybe. I never felt like I belonged here, and it was a lonely place to be for a long time before I met you and took you home that night. But now, I know that you're where I belong no matter where you might be."

The horrors of the past could never be explained or reconciled, but they were in the past, and each and every event was woven together into a future. Dan's future was curled up in her ball in his arms, and that was all he would ever need.

He gathered the magazines into a pile and tossed them in the trash can near his old desk. "I'm sorry," he whispered. "I'm sorry that I didn't understand what you've been going through and that I was a part of the machine that turned you into a two-dimensional persona. I'm sorry for every woman I objectified before you. I was an idiot."

She shook her head. "You did exactly what our world teaches everyone to do. All that matters is the image. You have no idea how happy I am that I'm not challenging anymore. I didn't even know how damaging it was until I quit."

"I'm still sorry. I want to make it right. I want you to understand how much you mean to me, how brilliant you are, how amazing you are. Mostly, I want you to understand that you give away a part of yourself every single time you put someone else's happiness over your own."

"I know."

"Good."

"Other than Garrett, you're the only person who has never asked me to do that for them. You're the only person in my whole life who didn't come to me with a list of expectations for how I should make them feel. Thank you for loving Maylea and not just Fionna Styler."

"I love every version of you, past, present, and future, and I always will."

"Dan?" whispered from her.

"What, baby?" He wondered what had her nervous suddenly.

"Would it be okay if we went to bed but didn't sleep?" The plea was full of desperation and longing.

"That sounds perfect." His pulse began to hammer and longing took hold. The need to join his past and his future in the present began to swirl in his shield as he laid her beside him and pulled the light from the lamp. He needed her to feel how astounding she was.

"I need you," poured from her lips without pretense. Dan slid his hands down her waist and lifted the shirt she was wearing from her.

"I want to feel you in my arms. I want to be with you." The need was so great his entire body ached with hunger. She was everything he would ever need. She filled the hollow emptiness and brought life's blood to his veins. She filled his heart and his soul. He pulled off his own shirt and jeans before sliding the sweatpants down her legs. A moan echoed from his lungs. She was exquisite, and there was no longer anything blocking him from all of her.

"I'm going to touch you, sweetheart," he guided her. The desperation to permeate her perfection welled inside of him. He crawled over her and gazed deeply into her eyes. Her body trembled beneath his.

Her rhythms revealed her fear. He knew she was scared of the past and of their gut-wrenching confessions and scared of the unknown the future kept hidden away. She was frightened that somehow, someday she might no longer be enough for him. Dan was determined to quiet every fear in her heart, to assure her mind and her body and her soul that he was hers forever.

His shield bled from his pores, encapsulating her in his protective love and adoration. She began to drink it in, inhaling his overwhelming love and commitment in the very air she breathed. She reveled in his weight pressed against her.

He traced her tenderly with his fingertips. There was no need to rush this. She was his, and this time in this place, was about making love with his wife without the show and without the customary lust. There was certainly a time and place for that, but it wasn't here in the bed that had raised him with the woman who had saved him. Not this time.

He slipped two fingers inside of her slowly and listened to her gasp from his tender care as he began to seek her release. She needed him to make it all go away, to make their past fade away in light of their present and their future.

"My god, you are so damn beautiful," he vowed in a reverent groan as he swirled his tongue around her nipple and then drowned it in his mouth. She panted for breath.

Her body shuddered from the sensation of them together. He pushed harder, touching her in places made only for him, bringing relief to the needs coursing through her veins and filling her energy. The liquid form of her began its slow drip down his fingers, and a shuddering growl Dan was certain his parents probably heard thundered from his chest.

"You are so fucking perfect." He caught her right breast in his mouth, pulling and licking, sucking the energy from the storehouse, letting it fill him and bind him back together. She made him whole.

Her skin was satin under his pliant touches as their bodies began to meld in the heat of their all-encompassing love.

"I want to taste you, baby. You're the sweetest thing I'll ever have in my mouth."

"Yes," she gasped. Dan worked his mouth down her body. He sucked her inner thighs, drinking in the Receiver's cast pulsing from her skin. Unable to wait, he licked up her slit. The liquid heaven of her energy poured into his mouth.

Fionna's back arched. She clung to his shoulders as he drank. She seemed terrified he might move away from her, but he had no intention of doing anything that removed her flesh from his.

The only thing coming next was that he was going to make their bodies one. He was going to penetrate her and fill her with all of him. Fill the empty spaces with his love as she healed his wounds and completed him. She released with a harsh gasp. Her body broke free and the nectar of her coursed around his tongue. He longed to drown himself in it.

Suddenly, her own cast joined with his rhythms. Her soothing energy, able to restore any pain and bind any wound, able to soothe the inconsolable, surrounded them, pulsing as one with his shield. It was unlike anything Dan had ever experienced in all the times he'd been with her. Their combined rhythms were in every gasped breath.

Dan moved up her body and cradled the back of her neck in his hand.

"Look at me, Maylea," he whispered. Her timid brown eyes stared into his. "Spread your legs for me, sweetheart. I need you. I need to be inside of you." Her thighs separated as he covered her in all of him, protecting her from the intruding world, from prying eyes, from everything that had no place anywhere near his baby.

She would be vulnerable only to him. He caught her hands and pinned them over her head as he kept his eyes locked on hers.

"Are you ready for me, baby doll?" He kept her body intertwined in his own. "I need you so damn bad," he confessed as he rocked his body, rubbing his cock against her.

"Please, please, I need to be yours."

With that, he stared into her starving eyes. "I know what you need. I'm gonna make it better." He dropped low and made his claim, piercing the very heart of her, rocking her body with his own as he filled her. "You feel so fucking good," he gasped in her ear.

As many times as he'd penetrated her before, he would never be able to fathom how their bodies formed together so perfectly. "It's incredible." He pushed farther, claiming every inch of her all for himself.

She trembled as she wrapped him up tightly in her. Dan felt his past slip away like sands through his open hands—every terror-filled night, every endless day, all of the pain and anger and wrath, it washed from his soul as he fell heavy into her open arms.

Thrusting and driving her, Dan felt her swell. She encased him in her perfection and love.

"That's it, baby. That's it," he guided her. "You're all mine. That's my good girl. I've got you. Let it come for me."

Her breath washed from her. She flushed as her body began begging his for continued relief. With a sudden gasp, she writhed. Her orgasm drove his and they came together, unable to feel where he stopped and where she began as their energy rolled together in perfect accord.

Refusing to withdraw, Dan crushed her against him. He kept her tucked in the safety of his arms and the protection of his shield. "I need more, baby doll. Can you take me again?"

"Oh god, yes," she gasped and clenched around his strain again as his secondary bands rushed blood back to his groin.

"I love you so much," he vowed, staring down into her eyes as he took her again. He rode the waves of his Maylea with unrelenting force. "All mine," he spoke the words she longed to hear, and her energy flooded around him.

She tensed her pelvic muscles, pulling him deeper still, milking him, and he shook from the sensation. "My good girl takes me twice and begs for my cum, don't you, baby?"

"Please," she groaned. "I need it." Her head shook back and forth on his old pillow. Her orgasm tore through her, and she gasped out his name in ecstasy as he filled her full the second time.

After several long minutes, he eased himself beside her on the bed and pulled her to him. They lay in peaceful serenity before she begrudgingly slid away.

"Don't," he begged in a choked plea. "Sleep naked with me. I miss that so much. I want to feel you on my skin while we sleep. I'll get the baby. Just for tonight, please," he continued to beg, unable to stop himself.

Fionna grinned and curled back beside him as he laid the sheets and blankets over her and tucked her safely on his chest.

"I love this too," she whispered. Her index finger traced slowly over his chest. The sensation was heavenly. "I feel so safe in your arms. You would never let anything hurt me."

"Never, Maylea," he assured her. Her energy rolled in placid contentment. She could feel his love and his tempting shelter. She was flooded full of his dual releases.

"When we move, will you only call me that?"

"I'll only call you that now if you want." He hoped she wasn't upset that he didn't use her nickname more often.

"No, I like it when you call me Fi, especially in front of neighbors and stuff." She shuddered slightly. "But I am Maylea, you know, and you're the only person in my entire life who knows the real me and loves each and every part of me." She tucked herself tighter into his embrace.

"I do, so fucking much." Dan was overcome with the knowledge and the love he felt from his Maylea.

CHAPTER 28

TIME'S PAST

They awoke at two, and Fionna sprang from the bed. "Halia! Why didn't she wake up?" she panicked.

Dan raced after her through the bathroom. She flung open the door to Lindley's room and bound to the bassinet. Their little coconut was waving her arms up and down. She seemed fascinated with the fact that her entire little body moved when she brought them up and down. She was cooing happily, wide awake but not crying.

Fionna clutched her chest and gasped for breath.

"What do we do? She isn't crying." Dan lifted his precious little girl into his arms.

"She's hungry, but she got distracted with her arms." Fionna giggled as she took Halia from Dan.

He grabbed one of the chill-casted bottles he'd arranged on the dresser and heated it.

They returned to Dan's bed, and Fionna cradled Halia in her arms, giving her the bottle. Halia sighed in contentment as she snuggled into Fionna's breast. Dan leaned and kissed Fionna's cheek and then Halia's. Fionna turned her adoring gaze on Dan as Halia reached for his hand. He placed his index finger in her tiny fist as she continued to suckle the bottle.

The next morning, Dan returned to his bed carrying Halia once again. He'd changed her diaper after Fionna had given her another bottle at five. She was babbling and didn't seem to want to sleep anymore.

Dan wanted desperately to carve out just a little time with his family before he had to go back to work. Aida knocked on the door, and Fionna let her in as well.

They all piled in Dan's adolescent bed. Positioning himself in the middle of all of his girls, Dan cradled Halia in his lap as Fionna and Aida laid on either side of his broad chest.

All too soon it was time to get ready to go. Fionna placed Halia in her portable swing and began making breakfast. Dan helped Aida get dressed and then took a shower.

He entered the kitchen in time to hear his mother rebuke his wife. "Arthur likes oatmeal for breakfast. I read in *Women of the Realm* that men in their fifties should eat oatmeal. It's better for his colon health than bacon and eggs."

The governor was shaking his head. "Fionna has gone to a lot of trouble, and it looks delicious. I'll have oatmeal tomorrow." His mouth appeared to be watering as Fionna fixed Dan a plate of fried eggs, bacon, toast, and a fruit salad that had come from their home.

"Thanks, baby." Dan kissed her cheek. "Fi's an outstanding cook, Mom. Sit down and eat," he commanded. He narrowed his eyes to let his parents know that if his mother kept up her reprimands, he'd have something to say about it. He was almost certain he knew why his mother's energy bands were so visibly irritated. She'd heard Dan and Fionna the evening before and wasn't pleased with their nighttime activities.

"I was just trying to help out," Fionna stammered. Dan poured her another cup of coffee, adding cream and honey just how she liked it.

As he tasted his own mug, he knew Fionna had fixed the coffee as well. Mrs. Vindico's coffee generally resembled tar and could be used for the purposes of paving roads. Dan grew up eating his mother's oatmeal. It held very little taste, due to her inability to use a salt shaker, and was the consistency of mortar. He chuckled at his father inhaling the bacon and eggs.

"I'm going to take Aida to school, and I'll ask them to send her on the bus that comes here this afternoon," Fionna explained.

"I'll be more than happy to watch little Halia for you. Since you've chosen not to nurse, I suppose you're able to leave her whenever you want." Mrs. Vindico was not letting Fionna's decision not to nurse go.

Fionna rolled her eyes but made certain that only Dan saw. He winked at her and squeezed her leg under the table.

"I was thinking I might go to the academy for a couple of hours to help Dan out. Would you mind watching her around lunch time? I'll just take her with me when we drop off Aida. I'd like to spend some time with both of them."

"That's fine. I'll go ahead and get ready. I remember when I was nursing Daniel he'd hardly let me shower before he wanted to eat again."

Dan promptly choked on the piece of bacon in his mouth as his body convulsed in a spasm of revolt.

Fionna covered her mouth to try and trap away her laughter as she handed Dan a glass of water. "Yeah, I know. He's like that sometimes." She barely managed the teasing quip before she began giggling.

The governor promptly cracked up. His laughter echoed around the kitchen. Certain that he was glowing crimson, Dan shook his head at his wife in mock indignation. Mrs. Vindico completely ignored all of this.

After helping Fionna load Halia's car seat in the Mercedes and kissing all of his girls goodbye, Dan begrudgingly climbed in his father's Land Rover. The remembrances were almost more than he could bear. Keeping the thought that Fionna was coming for lunch planted in his mind, Dan sighed as his father backed out of the driveway.

"It's been a long time since I drove you to school," his father commented with a chuckle.

"We'll be out of your hair soon, I hope."

"You're not in our hair. You're our son," his father sounded offended. Not having a response to that, Dan nodded but didn't speak. "Did you and Fionna sleep all right?"

"Yeah, Halia actually slept several hours straight which was nice."

His father kept glancing at Dan.

"What?" Dan finally demanded.

"Nothing." The governor shrugged. "I was just thinking that it sounded like you had a nice evening."

"She's my wife, Dad. I think I'll keep our night between the two of us."

"I certainly don't want to hear about it. I'm just surprised you're in such a bad mood."

"I'm not looking forward to going back to work," Dan admitted.

"I'm sorry you hate Venton so much. I'd hoped you'd get to a place where you enjoyed it, but it just doesn't seem to be you."

"I'm having lunch with Governor Haydenshire tomorrow," Dan broached. "I'd really like you to come along."

Deep disappointment etched his father's face. "Sure."

"What happened with Wilshire's separation trial?" Dan remembered that he'd filed for separation from Ellen.

"Stephen granted it. He ordered them counseling and gave her three-quarters of his paychecks. He left the retirement accounts for future deciding," Governor Vindico explained. "Oh, and Friday,"—the governor shook his head—"you won't believe this when I tell you. Terry Bryant applied for one of the open Duco mentors' positions, and he went as far as to petition Stephen for the job."

"What?" Dan gasped in disbelief.

"I told you." His father chuckled wryly. "He's coming in for an interview today."

"That's insane. Why the hell would he want to work with his ex?"

"I'm interested in hearing his reasoning today, but we've had three Duco mentors quit in the last month. I can't figure that out either."

They pulled onto campus, and Dan made a hasty exit from his father's car. To his shock, Will Haydenshire was sauntering over to him, laughing.

"Did you get put on restriction and your car taken away?" he teased as they shook hands.

The governor chuckled as he offered Will his hand. "He did have two girls in his room last night."

"Yeah, well, Danny seems to have a thing for little Hawaiian hotties." Will slapped Dan on the back.

"Hey, that's my little coconut you're referring to."

"Please tell me you do not call Fionna your little coconut."

"No." Dan smirked. "I call her my Hawaiian hottie among other things."

"Thank you for doing this." The governor rolled his eyes at the banter.

Will scoffed. "We're glad to help, and I get to hang out at Venton with Dan. I never thought that'd happen again."

"What are you doing up here?" Dan asked.

"I had Warren send over his best team. I'm having the school audited. The accountants are on mandatory leave. The Senate team is going over every penny until we figure out what the hell happened up here, and I wanted Will to run the show," the governor explained as they all headed into the admin building. "I'm tired of looking at those books. I want to know why Wilshire was putting so much money into the academy, and the books aren't telling me."

Will Haydenshire was an outstanding accountant. Despite all of the antics they'd pulled in school, when he'd been hired on at the Senate Bank, he'd climbed the ranks quickly and now worked directly under Buffett, the bank president.

"Hey, Lily Ana took her first steps last night," Will announced. He seemed uncomfortable with the governor's praise. He pulled out his cell and showed Dan and Governor Vindico the quick video of Lily Ana taking three steps unassisted right into her daddy's arms.

Dan laughed as she applauded her own efforts after Will scooped her up.

"She looks just like you." Governor Vindico grinned.

Will beamed. "She's got her mama's spunk, so I'm worried."

Dan's cell phone rang, and he answered Fionna's call. "Hey, baby," he soothed. Fionna began ranting before Dan made it through his greeting.

Dan listened to Fionna's outrage on how she'd been informed by the school board representative that Aida could not change buses and that a request to have her moved would require a bill with the Vindicos' new address on it.

When Fionna explained that they were only visiting Dan's parents for a few days, Ms. McBeechum had delighted in informing her that a request to switch Aida to a new bus would take two weeks to process.

"So then, Halia starts screaming while I'm arguing with that horrible woman about whether or not they'll allow me to have my own daughter in the car pickup line instead of driving back to our house so I can meet her bus to just drive her back to your parents' house where the bus picks up and drops off every morning," she shrieked.

"I'm sorry." Dan shook his head in disbelief.

CHAPTER 29
WILL

A few hours later, Dan fell back into his office and tossed his class notes on his desk. Sullivan had done a decent job of preparing the kids for their exams, but they had a lot of catching up to do.

A knock on his office door had Dan's smile returning. He swung it open, but his face fell as soon as Fionna stomped inside.

Will followed her in. "Let's go sit at our old table." He didn't seem to have noticed Fionna's irritation.

"Sure, just let me figure out what's wrong with my Hawaiian hottie." Dan winked at her.

A half grin formed on Fionna's face. "No, come on. I want to be in there when the students come in. I'll tell you while we eat."

"Hey, Fionna, how are you?" Will chanted.

"Hey, Will." Fionna giggled. "I'm good. I'm just irritated with my daughter's school and my mother-in-law."

"Oh, this should be good." Will offered Fionna his arm.

"I don't think so, Haydenshire. You keep your hands to yourself." Dan grabbed Fionna's hand and guided her to the cafeteria.

"He will never let that go, will he?" Will grimaced.

Fionna shook her head. "Dan has this kind of really overprotective thing going on."

Will feigned shock. "An overprotective Shield. How odd."

They seated themselves at the table where Will, Dan, Wes, Garrett, Levi, Mason Tucker, and Quentin Davenport ate lunch every single day of their school careers.

"What did my mother do?" Dan took in the cafeteria lunch before him. He'd carried Fionna's tray for her though neither of them were terribly excited about eating the Venton Academy spaghetti and stale garlic toast.

"Well," Fionna huffed as Dan and Will leaned in. "She found that stuff you threw out last night."

"Dammit, I meant to put that out in the dumpster this morning."

Will's brow furrowed as he spun spaghetti on his fork without much enthusiasm.

"Porn from my teenage years that I located in my bathroom last night to appease my wife's curiosity," Dan explained.

Will laughed as he nodded his understanding. "Last summer,"—he began shaking his head—"Lo calls me up, and he's like yeah, so Rainer and I are gonna finish the old guesthouse and move in out there. Can you come over and help us clean it out tomorrow? And I'm like sure, I'll be there." Will rolled his eyes. "So, I have to drive over to the guesthouse super early and crawl through three decades of dust before we ever made an appearance at Mom and Dad's to dump the vast collection of magazines we all hid out there." Dan was already nodding as he recalled their magazine stash for camping trips. "Brooke was laughing at me so hard she was crying." Will shook his head, clearly disappointed in their teenage fascination.

Fionna rolled her eyes at both of them. "Anyway, I get back to your parents' house and get Halia calmed down. I lay her down for a nap and go to take a shower, and when I get out, there are like ten books stacked on your bed. They're all from the eighties about building a strong marriage and ways to work with a medio to have your milk ducts work again even if your milk is dried up because you made a mistake by deciding not to nurse. One of the books is actually called, *Ways to Say No and Strengthen Your Marriage.* It's about abstaining for three months and bonding by talking instead. You're supposed to use the attached workbook which she also had in the pile."

"Until this moment, I've always been against book burning," Dan sighed.

"You sure as hell won't find any books like that at the farm. Mom and Dad can't abstain for three days." Will laughed at his own allowance.

Fionna continued to fume, "What's wrong with talking *and* having sex? I like having sex."

Will doubled over as several students that had taken seats nearby overheard Fionna's announcement. "Oh my God, please tell me she's coming to eat with you all week."

Fionna blushed violently. Dan was certain that she was the cutest thing he'd ever laid eyes on.

"Everyone gets out at one Wednesday, right?" she quizzed.

"Yeah, I only have to teach my morning classes and then we're out until next Monday," Dan reassured her. "Are you working out tomorrow with Kara or do you want to come back up here?" Dan wasn't certain that Fionna would want Will to know about her class, so he tried to be discreet.

"I'm trying to figure out how to get out of your parents' house without telling your mom where I'm going."

Suddenly, her brow furrowed as a small group of students passed directly in front of them. She closed her eyes discreetly in concentration. With a sigh, she shook her head.

"What?" Dan asked.

"She's nervous, and he's really horny. He's pressuring her," Fionna whispered as Dan and Will watched the boy in question edge everyone away from the girl and try to single her out.

Will sighed. "I coulda told you that, and I'm not a Receiver."

Dan shook his head. "He's one of mine. I'll talk to him after lunch."

"Any ideas?" Fionna quizzed Dan, taking him back to his question about her dance class the next day.

"Would you rather her keep our little coconut or do you want to take her with you?"

"I'd kind of rather your mom keep her. I'm still a little afraid of that nursery. It looked really nice, but she's so tiny and..." Fionna trailed off, unable to describe her desperation to protect their baby girl. Dan kissed her cheek.

"Where do you work out?" Will asked.

"Catalyst," Fionna informed him with a sweet smile. "It's actually a pole dancing strip workout. I'm really enjoying it."

Will gave Dan a goading smirk. "You married well, my friend." He lifted his Dr Pepper in a toast to Dan.

Dan accepted the toast. "Yes, I did."

"Actually, Brooke would be all over that. She's been wanting to join that gym but didn't know what to do with Lily Ana. Do you think she could go along tomorrow? If you're leaving Halia there, I'm sure Lily Ana would be fine."

Fionna's excitement was evident to everyone at the table. "That would be so much fun! Tell Brooke to come. She'd love it!"

"I'm trying to envision this conversation." Dan laughed. "Hey, honey, I ran into Fionna today, and she's taking pole dancing classes, so I signed you up."

"Hey, you're not the only one who married well, Danny Boy. My baby likes to shake those hips, and she's all about keeping our marriage strong."

"No way," Fionna gasped. Will and Dan both stopped laughing and followed the path of her eyes. "Is that?"

Dan nodded. "He applied to take one of the Duco mentor positions. He even petitioned your dad for the job." He gestured to Will as Terry Bryant approached with Governor Vindico.

"Why in God's name would you want to be up here every day with the woman who's been cheating on you for years with the chancellor?" Will spat.

"We're about to find out."

Dan's father gestured to their table. Everyone turned to smile at the approaching governor politely.

"Terry, this is my son and daughter-in-law, Dan and Fionna, and a good friend of theirs, Will Haydenshire. He's running the audit for me."

"Nice to meet you all," Terry offered as he shook Will and Dan's hands. He took Fionna's extended hand politely, and Dan watched his

212

wife offer the smile she reserved for people she wanted to remove herself from.

Dan was seated right beside her. His release was still inside of her, and part of her energy was still on his body and in his soul. He felt her internal shield set. Fionna jerked her hand from Terry's.

Dan's jaw clenched, and he leveled a cold glare at Terry Bryant. Will, who'd been one of Dan's closest friends since early childhood, picked up on Dan's disdain. He furrowed his brow but then in an almost automatic response turned to block Fionna from view.

"Terry's interested in picking up the three open Duco classes. We have assistants teaching them now," the governor explained. "Will was head of Duco Order when he was here. He's a Vice President at the Senate bank now," Governor Vindico added proudly.

"Oh yeah, I know. I watched you all grow up in the press. I'm sure your dad's pleased with your position so young," Terry offered.

An air of injustice rang in Terry's tone. Will's strength of his Predilection and even stronger work ethic would never have been viewed as the reason he'd been named one of the Senate Bank vice presidents at barely thirty years of age and several months before his father had been named Crown Governor. People vastly preferred the story that his father had arranged Will's promotion. Fionna scowled at Terry.

Will offered a polite chuckle and seemed to decide to let people think whatever they wanted.

"Katherine mentioned you'd just been off for paternity leave. Congratulations." Terry seemed to have realized his mistake and turned his polite endeavors on Dan and Fionna.

"Thank you." Dan kept his arm around Fionna.

"We were just heading to the mathematics building and decided to cut through here. The weather's brutal," the governor commented as conversation seemed hard to come by.

"Good luck with your interview." Will offered the signature Haydenshire smirk.

Dan noted the play. You may not want to give me any credit for my accomplishments, but I'm a Vice President of the Senate Bank and you're on a job interview, now aren't you?

With a nod, Terry Bryant followed Governor Vindico out the exit doors on the opposite side of the dining hall.

"Prick," Will sneered.

"He's gross and mean," Fionna vowed.

"No doubt," Will agreed. "Why on earth would he want to work here other than to be a complete douchebag to his wife? I know she cheated or whatever, but my God, be a man, don't plaster it all over Facebook and then show up here looking for sympathy and revenge. Take responsibility for your part, dig through the shit, and either fix it or move on."

Dan was struck by Will's wisdom. He'd grown up. They all had. And he had a great deal to offer the world. He'd been raised by Stephen and Lillian Haydenshire after all. His parents' wisdom and common sense had certainly been passed on.

"What do you mean his part?" Fionna quizzed.

Will shrugged as he visibly forced himself to consume the spaghetti on his tray.

"Something drove her to that, don't you think? Maybe I'm an idiot or whatever, but it seems to me if your spouse thinks you're the shit and you're taking care of them—making them feel loved and supported, being there for them, and making sure they know that they're valued—they wouldn't go looking for any part of that from somewhere else. It just can't be as complicated as everyone wants to make it."

"I think you're right." Fionna laced her hand through Dan's. "We were able to pick out what Wilshire did that got her going from those emails," she whispered. "I was so horrified by what she did to him and their kids I didn't really consider what drove her to that. And you were so mad at Wilshire, even when you told me how long it had been since he and Ellen had been together. It was still wrong, but he was in a bad place. But Terry is really an awful person. It rolls off him in waves." She tucked closer to Dan. Whatever she'd felt from Terry Bryant, it had her wanting inside of his shield. Dan kissed the side of her face and wrapped his arm tightly around her. "Your dad shouldn't hire him. Will's right. He's only here to get back at her."

"I'll tell him, sweetheart, but the order's hurting. Three Duco mentors abruptly quit. We've got seniors being taught by assistants. They're going to struggle to get jobs unless we get them a mentor."

Suddenly, Fionna's eyes goggled, and she spun in her seat.

"What?" Dan forgot about Terry Bryant in light of whatever Fionna had just felt.

"Who are they?" She gestured her head to three girls who'd just walked quickly behind her. They were talking rather aggressively.

"I'm not sure. Glance around the room. Study other people. Then tell me what you felt," he guided her in a low intonation. With a slight nod, Fionna followed Dan's instructions while Dan intentionally began a conversation with Will.

Will played along and never gave Fionna a second glance.

The governor reappeared. "Stephen just called. We thought the lawsuit between The Neutrons and Lee Winder was going to be settled out, but it appears they're going to trial. It's set for three. Do you mind working a little late then I'll come back and pick you up?"

"It's okay. I'll go get Halia and then pick up Aida and then we'll come get you."

"I can take you home," Will came to everyone's rescue. "You just need to go by your place and get your car, right?"

As Dan did not want Fionna trying to drive back and forth so many times in one day while trying to juggle Aida and Halia, who would need to be fed somewhere in all of that traveling, Dan nodded. "Are you sure you don't mind? I usually head out around 3:30."

"Nah," Will scoffed. "I can cut out early. I miss my girls too, and we'll be up here for the next few weeks. The books were much worse than I imagined. It's no big thing."

"I appreciate it."

"Thank you, William. I'm sure if you'd like to come over for dinner this evening, Marion would love to see Brooke and the baby," the governor extended the polite invitation.

Dan tried not to chuckle as Will cringed. No one who grew up eating Lillian Haydenshire's cooking could manage to choke down Marion Vindico's. Dan was still in awe of the fact that his father ate it on a daily basis and thought it was delicious.

"No sir, but thank you. We can't tonight. Brooke had her *Moqueca* going when I got up this morning. I've been looking forward to it all day."

Dan was fairly certain he wasn't lying. He seemed genuinely thrilled.

Governor Vindico chuckled. "You know, when you and Dan were about seventeen and your dad and I got called up here because you two decided to cast all of the mentors' cars and relocate them to different parking lots around the school,"—he reminded them as Fionna laughed at them outright—"your dad said it was going to take quite a woman to tame you, but he had faith she'd come along. Seems like Brooke was up to the task."

Will grinned. "I'll tell her you think so."

"I've got to get this interview over with and get to the Senate. I wish I could just bring myself to fire Wilshire and hire someone new. But if I terminate him, he loses his retirement. I can't make myself do that to Ellen. I keep trying to talk him into resigning, but my God, he's as stubborn as an old mule," the governor huffed. "Me trying to be a governor and the chancellor is running me ragged. " He waved his goodbye, and Dan and Will immediately turned back to Fionna.

"What did you feel?" Dan asked.

"They're high," Fionna whispered.

"Are you serious?" Will gasped.

Fionna gave a morose nod. Dan was certain just a few of the news stories of things Gifted teenagers had done while using were reeling through her mind. Last year, he'd worked a case where a seventeen-year-old had done meth and then summoned off an electrical line. It had killed him instantly.

"Only Dad can call for a test, and only urine tests are allowable— not hair samples. They did a urine analysis a few weeks ago. They think they're safe. I'll see if he can do another one." Dan pulled his cell phone from his pocket, but Will shook his head.

"The accounts are frozen. We're trying to get the audit done before payday, but the paychecks are the only allowable withdrawals for a while. Venton can't afford another test, and even if they could, the money can't be accessed to pay for it," Will lamented. He turned to Fionna. "What does someone being high feel like to a Receiver?"

"It makes their rhythms tense oddly, and their emotional strands split." She glanced back at the girls who were still laughing. "That's why people use, I think. To stop feeling what they've been feeling and to feel something they can't access without the drugs."

"Why isn't she enough?" Will gestured to Fionna. "We all watched her challenge for years. We know how powerful she is."

Dan returned his cell to his pocket. "You know the way the courts are set up. Receivers can give testimony, but as soon as the Dinkerton Report came out that proved Receivers' own emotions can affect their reads, the defense lawyers roll that study out and everything they've said gets thrown out the window by the Senteon."

"I'm sorry. That's the only thing I'm picking up on," Fionna sighed. "I'll walk around some and see what else I can feel."

"You have nothing to apologize for. I appreciate you helping me, and even if we can't catch them using, now I know people that might be very interested in having the tests covered up."

"I'll come back up here Wednesday," she offered. "Can I please bring Halia with me? I'll be with you the whole time."

Dan shook his head. He hated telling her no, but suddenly, he didn't have to.

She shuddered and chill bumps charged down her arms. She clung to Dan.

Dan and Will turned to find Clarence Pendergrath staring her down. He rolled his eyes derisively as he flung a lunch tray down on a table nearby.

"Wow," Fionna managed. "He really hates you."

As much as Dan didn't want her to have to feel that rolling off Pendergrath's son, she understood why the girls couldn't come back to Venton, and why no matter what happened, he couldn't work there much longer.

"Maybe Kara could watch Halia for a little while Wednesday," she corrected.

"He blames me for his old man's death and for everything that's happened to him. I can't give him access to you or the girls. I know I'm ridiculously overprotective, but this time I don't think I'm overreacting."

CHAPTER 30

AND BROOKE

Dan walked Fionna back to the car while trying to shield her from the freezing November winds.

"Can't say I'll miss this," she admitted. Fionna wasn't built for Virginia winters. She was his own personal sunshine with the breath of the palm trees coursing through her veins and the warmth of ethereal light spilling from her skin. He wanted to take her home. He wanted his girls away from the harsh, chilling world and in the safety of serenity of their family farm where they could grow and explore without worry or fear that around any corner could be awaiting revenge.

Dan spent all two hours of his lab class reviewing maneuvers they would have to perform on the final examination. When class was over, he pulled Jeff aside and walked with him down the corridor.

"Do you know her name?" He gestured to one of the girls Fionna had outed at lunch.

"Yes sir, that's Libby Ellington. Her mom's the Senteon representative from Maryland."

"Great," Dan sighed. He received another sneering scowl from Clarence Pendergrath just before Clarence spun and positioned himself in front of Libby, halting her progress down the hallway. She giggled flirtatiously and then stumbled into the wall, serving to make her laugh harder. Clarence caught and steadied her. "Even better," Dan spat.

"She's probably only after him because it would infuriate her mom, don't you think? I mean, his dad was an international criminal."

Dan gave a begrudged nod. "You're going to make one hell of a detective."

A few minutes later, he fell into Will's Volvo, thankful to be going to acquire his Ferrari.

"Bad day, honey?" Will mocked.

Dan laughed. "Yeah, are you gonna take care of that for me or would you like to take me to my wife?"

"I'll let Fi take care of that, but why don't you bring the girls over tomorrow night? I haven't actually seen the little coconut, and Brooke's missing Aida."

"Are you sure? Should you talk to Brooke first?"

Will shook his head at him. "As if I didn't already ask her, which is why I'm now extending the invite."

"I'll ask Fi. It sounds good though. Thank you."

Brooke was from Rio and spoke Portuguese. She and Aida adored one another and whenever they were together spoke to one another in their native language, which delighted both of them. Dan and Fionna were both trying to learn Portuguese, but neither had gotten as far as they'd like. They certainly weren't fluent yet.

Brooke had come to Venton her senior year as an exchange student from Brazil. Her parents had divorced, and Brooke was constantly put in the middle. She'd decided to take herself out of the situation altogether and applied for the Venton exchange program.

Brooke Bethancourt had stepped onto campus the first day of Dan and Will's senior year, and Will Haydenshire had been sold hook, line, and sinker. Always a player up until that moment, he gave it all up for her. Dan chuckled as he recalled Will volunteering to show Brooke around Venton on her first day and then taking her over to the farm for dinner that night.

"What?" Will asked.

"I was just thinking about you telling Brooke you'd been assigned by the academy to be her student guide and that you'd take her around campus and around town for the first few weeks since she was new to the school." Dan shook his head as Will cracked up.

"To this day, that remains one of the most brilliant damn things I've ever come up with."

Dan had to agree it was certainly original. "Is Brooke going to go back to McCarron anytime?" Brooke had been a kindergarten teacher right up until the moment she'd gone into labor with Lily Ana.

"I hope not." Will rolled his eyes. "If she wants to work, I'm all for it, but I hope she doesn't go back to McCarron."

"Why?"

"You have no idea what kind of shit the school board heaps on the teachers there. You've got people on the board who have never taught and then they make all of the guidelines for the people actually in the classrooms. I can't stand to watch her come home in tears every day again.

"She was so worried about her kids, but she couldn't really teach them because it's all about standardized test scores and the school board trying to keep the kids from learning anything uncomfortable. She'd get yelled at by the board for not following the guidelines, only the guidelines weren't teaching the kids anything. I finally went up there and said my piece when some bigot got in Brooke's face and informed her that there was a reason she'd been given all of the ESL kids. When Brooke tried to explain to her that she didn't mind having the kids that hadn't learned English as their primary language, but that she didn't speak Spanish and most of the kids did, the woman informed her that everyone who wasn't really an American, and came from *lesser nations*," Will snarled, "could speak Spanish and that Portuguese was Spanish so Brooke needed to figure it out."

"Are you kidding me?" Dan gasped.

"No, and I was not kind, believe me. I had Garrett wait on me outside in case they called the police. I was just gonna have him come in and get me."

"McBeechum," Dan guessed.

"Yeah." Will sounded surprised.

"We've had a few run-ins with her as well."

"I shouted until the principal made the bitch apologize to my wife, and then I sat Brooke down and begged her to quit. Not to sound like an absolute asshole, but I make really good money. I didn't want to come off like a prick, but it made me sick to watch her go on like she was. But she wanted to stay for the kids until Lily Ana was born," he sighed. "She was the best damn kindergarten teacher they had, and they're driving all of the good ones away with their insane regulations and constant testing."

They talked all the way to Dan and Fionna's neighborhood.

"Thanks for the ride," Dan said as Will pulled into the driveway.

"No problem. Hey, which one is the nut job?" Will gave him a smirk Dan recognized only too well.

"That'd be them." He pointed to the Scheckleses' home directly across the street from Dan and Fionna.

"You know, we could have a little fun for old times' sake." Will waggled his eyebrows.

"I might take you up on that." Dan tried not to think of how satisfying it would be to drive Fred Scheckles to distraction. "Hey, you never told me, did Brooke let you walk the dock that night you took her to the farm for dinner?"

Will laughed and shook his head. "Are you kidding me? Brooke made me work for every inch I gained. Why do you think I married her? I took her out on the dock, used all my best moves. Hell, I even talked about the moon or some shit, and then I kissed her and reached my hand up my shirt. She slapped it away so fast my head spun. Then she told me off in Portuguese, wagged that finger in my face with her hand on her hip, and I was sold," Will recalled with a wistful look in his eye.

Dan laughed. "I'll see you tomorrow."

"Yeah, go on to Mama and Daddy Vindico's. Don't abandon your wife and kids."

"I was trying to figure out a way to drive by Vindico Manor and have Fi throw the girls in and jump in while I peel away."

CHAPTER 31

FAMILIAL COLLISIONS

Dan unlocked the door to his parents' home not certain how to feel. His girls were there, and he wanted to see each of them and hold them all in his arms, but his mother was there as well. With a sigh, he flung open the door and stepped inside.

His screaming daughter's pitiful wails pierced the air. Her entire precious face was red and contorted in fury. Fionna was walking her in the living room trying to soothe her. Aida had her hands over her ears, and Mrs. Vindico was shouting at Fionna that the baby was crying because Fionna wouldn't nurse her.

Dan raced to Fionna and pulled Halia from her arms. She quieted, tucked into Dan's broad chest, and began sucking her fingers as she grasped Dan's tie in her tiny fist.

"I told you she was crying because she missed Dan," Fionna fumed to his mother. "She's never been away from you for that long. She was worried you weren't coming back."

Dan kissed Halia's sweet head. "I thought she didn't have object permanence down yet."

"Clearly she does," Fionna sighed. "Maybe she's advanced or maybe it's that you're her father, not an object."

"Daddy's right here, baby." He tucked Halia tighter in his arms. "I'll always come back," he continued to reassure his infant daughter. He had no idea if she understood anything he was saying, but she calmed as he spoke. He sank down on the sofa and pulled Aida against him as well. She gave him a delighted grin as she laid her head against his chest as well.

"I told you, Halia, Daddy will come back after work and that's after I come back from school," Aida explained with a hint of exasperation as she patted Halia's diaper.

"How long has she been crying?" Horrifying guilt took up residence in Dan's gut.

"A while. She's not sure where she is, and she couldn't understand where you were," Fionna explained.

"Well, my children never cried like that." Mrs. Vindico marched into the kitchen to burn dinner.

Rolling his eyes, Dan drew a deep breath as Fionna rubbed her temples. Dan noted several copies of *Women of the Realm* in their customary location on the coffee table. They were all folded back to specific articles. The one on top was what caught his eye.

"Aida," Fionna eased. "If you want to go play with Aunt Kara's Barbies some more before dinner, you can."

"Okay." Aida leapt off the couch. "Mommy played Barbies with me the whole time Halia took her nap, and Grandma found me some robot things that were yours, but Mommy and I can't work them."

Dan's brow furrowed. "Bring me one."

She returned a moment later carrying a basket of Transformers.

"Awesome," he gasped. Fionna laughed.

He transformed one for Aida while he keep Halia cradled on his shoulder. Aida wasn't very impressed with the car that turned into a robot and went back to Kara's room to play Barbies.

"Maybe we'll have a little boy next, and he'll play Transformers with you," Fionna offered.

"Nah, I like being surrounded by my girls even if you can't work Bumblebee."

Fionna leaned back to make certain Mrs. Vindico was in the kitchen. She was talking on the phone with someone from her bridge club by the sounds of it, so Fionna lifted the stack of *Women of the Realm* magazines and placed them in her lap.

Fionna's jaw tensed. "Apparently, your mother overheard…"

"You mean eavesdropped," Dan corrected.

"Okay," Fionna agreed with an eye roll. "She heard me on the phone with Candace when she called to confirm my appointment for next week." She squeezed her eyes shut and wrinkled her nose.

Dan thought she was rather cute when she was embarrassed. Candace was Fionna's esthetician, and in Dan's opinion, she did excellent work. But he could only imagine his mother's horror over finding out that Fionna got a Brazilian wax every few weeks.

"After Halia woke up from her nap, I brought her down here to give her a bottle and spend a little time with her since I'd played with Aida most of the afternoon. I sat down on the couch, and these were lying beside me."

Holding up the first issue, Dan shook his head and tried not to laugh since Fionna was clearly upset. The title of the article was, "Are Wax Salons Safe."

He took the magazine, that in Dan's opinion had never printed anything even remotely factual, and began reading. He continued to chuckle. According to the article, that gave no real points of reference or had any actual examples to support their claims, when women went in to have their "unmentionables" waxed, cameras could be hidden in the rooms. It also alleged that wax studios might not be clean and could cause infection.

"Unmentionables? They make it sound like you're having your lingerie waxed." Dan flipped the tabloid closed and glanced over the cover.

"This also says you can cleanse your liver and lose forty pounds in thirty days by drinking grape juice," he pointed out. "Oh, and that you can raise your child's IQ twenty-nine points by feeding them the hamburger macaroni casserole on page 127." Dan shuddered as he held up the photograph of the casserole that contained a layer of browned hamburger meat between two gelatinous layers of macaroni and cheese.

"Don't laugh. That's what we're having for dinner," Fionna informed him. Dan scowled in horror. "She's worried about Aida's IQ," she fueled the fury burning in Dan's gut. "I tried to get her to let me cook, but she wouldn't." She shook her head in defeat. "Then there was this one,"—she handed Dan the next article—"which led me to believe your mother might've been snooping in your bathroom after I left this afternoon."

Closing his eyes in abject defeat, Dan drew a deep breath. "I'm sorry, baby. She's impossible." He was certain she was correct. His mother would have gone through her things if given the opportunity. The article pertained to the shaving cream Fionna preferred that was currently in the shower.

The Angels often hosted different in-home party companies that would come to the arena during the ladies' lunch break and host a show. The team often ordered items being sold and split the party prizes amongst them.

The parties that pertained to relationship enhancements were their favorites, and many, many years before, Fionna had purchased shaving cream from one of these companies. She'd fallen in love with it and continued to order it.

The shaving cream and after lotion made her legs so soft Dan was certain the product was somehow actually infusing her legs with silk. He often placed the order for her if he noticed she was running low. The smell drove him wild, and her legs wrapped around his body, soft and smooth, made him ache. But the label had a fairly racy picture and elaborated on the fact that the shaving cream could be used on more intimate areas as well.

The Red Alert story for the month of August in *Women of the Realm* was alerting women to the fact that shaving creams sold by Romance Me were knocking more solid, upstanding companies that had been producing shaving cream for decades out of the market.

It alleged that the women of the American Realm were over-sexed and trying too hard to please their partners by making their legs soft. It insisted that they should return to other products even if they didn't work as well because the companies had better moral fiber.

"Who writes this shit?" Dan rolled his eyes. Performing the same move, Dan flipped the magazine closed to take in the cover. He laughed out loud as he read that you could lose twenty pounds in a week by eating pizza, and in the ultimate of ironies, there was an article that was dedicated to ways to make your skin softer and less dry in the winter.

"Wait, it gets better," Fionna informed him with a fitful huff. Dan shuddered as he awaited the next article.

She handed Dan the next magazine folded back to an article on whether or not couples in the American Realm were having too much sex. It went as far as to list other things that could be done before going to sleep at night like reading, watching TV, working crosswords, knitting, or planning out the next day in a day planner.

Fury began to course through him as he read that apparently men who had sex more than once a month were less attentive, more likely to watch porn, and less likely to go out to sporting events and therefore not leaving their wives in peace on the weekends in hopes that if they stay home they might be granted sexual favors.

Fionna pointed to a small box on the floor beside Halia's diaper bag. "Your mom put that together for us."

Inside the box were crossword puzzles, a few *Reader's Digest* condensed books that had belonged to Dan's grandparents, several curtain catalogs, and a large clothing store catalog that sold all of Mrs. Vindico's favorite brand of clothing.

Dan's mother thought Fionna dressed too provocatively and didn't care for the fact that when Fionna was on the farm or alone with Dan or with the girls, she was often topless. There was also a new roll of yarn and two knitting needles.

With a dramatic eye roll, Dan flipped to the front of the magazine to read the list of cover stories that included placing raw potato slices on your neck to remove a double chin and the directions for creating something called a bean cornucopia for a five-minute delicious dinner.

He stood and marched to the large brick fireplace in the living room while keeping Halia cradled to him tenderly. "Mom, the baby's cold. I'm turning on the fire," he called. His mother waved him off as she was still on the phone and didn't want to be interrupted.

Fionna doubled over laughing as Dan lit the logs with his hand and then promptly tossed the magazine in as kindling.

"That's her favorite magazine," Fionna managed to scold through her laughter.

Dan reseated himself beside his wife. "What's next?" he huffed.

"I saved the best for last. Are you ready for this?"

"Let me have it, baby."

"Okay, when you read this and figure out where this came from, please remember not to start shouting because our little coconut is on your shoulder, and she's had a really rough day."

"Got it, coconut, shoulder, give me the article."

"It's just marked there." Fionna showed him the dog-eared page. Taking a moment to study the cover first this time, he saw that apparently the magazine had hosted a reader poll and come up with the best frozen casseroles and gave the prescription for losing five pounds in one day by eating grapefruit and then how to lose an additional nineteen in one week. Ways to organize your kitchen cupboards were on prominent display along with a section on interpreting daydreams, but then Dan's eyes goggled as he saw the small tagline at the bottom of the magazine cover.

"She better not have," he spat.

"Coconut," Fionna reminded as Dan laid the magazine on his knee and flipped to the article in question.

Frenzied rage spilled through Dan as he forced himself to read the headline.

"Woman to sue sex toy company for medical compensation." The article went on to inform the readers that just as *Women of the Realm* had been preaching for years, sex toys like vibrators were only for promiscuous, unchaste women and that they had no place in the home of any upstanding citizen of the American Realm.

Their proof came in the form of a woman who was called out for not having a subscription to the *Women of the Realm*, and who'd been hospitalized after using a vibrator with her husband that ended in her receiving an electrical shock. Her husband apparently decided to up the charge on the device and over-torqued the vibrator, resulting in a slight electrical burn.

Having no need to read the article about a couple who needed to revisit an introductory electrical energies class, Dan tossed the magazine aside. His eyes were blazing in fury.

"She went through your bag." He tried and failed to modulate his voice as to not awaken Halia.

"I assume," Fionna admitted. "I didn't pick up on her feeling any deceit or anything though." She was clearly trying to give Dan's mother the benefit of the doubt.

"But you packed one. There is one in your bag." Dan tried not to sound like he was interrogating his wife.

"I definitely did not pack one, but there is one in my bag. I have lots of them, and it was probably in there from when I was traveling all the time with the Angels. I didn't mean to bring one." Her face colored rapidly.

"Even if you had intentionally packed one, there's nothing wrong with that. She had absolutely no right to go through your things, and the reason you didn't feel any deceit or remorse from her is because she doesn't feel any. She thinks she has every right to go through your bags."

"I talked to Carrie when I picked up Aida from the bus stop. She was getting their kids. They've decided to go ahead and leave for Vermont to visit her parents. Staying in a hotel room with five kids is more than she can handle, but she said that the Potomac Power guy told Chris that the transformer wouldn't be finished until Friday. We have to stay here all week, so just please don't freak," she begged. "I can't handle all of the confrontation right now. I'm exhausted, and Halia is scared."

"She had no right to do that, and she sure as hell has no right to make her passive-aggressive comments about the things you packed or about our relationship." He held up the magazine for a split second before he tossed that issue in the fire as well.

"I know, but I should've gone through the bag before I started adding stuff to it." Shame was evident in her rhythms which only furthered Dan's infuriation.

"No," he vowed adamantly. He lifted her chin gently with his hand. "You have nothing to be ashamed of, and there is nothing wrong with a woman who is comfortable in her own sexuality or with a couple who prioritizes their physical relationship."

Fionna nodded, but her playful banter had been replaced with harrowing embarrassment as she began to really consider what Dan's mother had done to her.

The governor arrived home just then. Mrs. Vindico waved to him with a kind smile though she continued to talk on the phone.

He moved to the liquor cabinet in the dining room and fixed a whiskey sour before returning to the living room to greet Dan and Fionna.

"Bad day?" Dan gestured to the drink as Fionna handed him a bottle for Halia. She was beginning to grunt but was still clinging forcefully to Dan's tie. He reclined her in his arms and gave her the bottle before she began her customary wail.

"Just exhausted. I can't wait until Wednesday. I can definitely use a little vacation." He took a long sip of the drink he'd prepared.

"Not to add to your burdens..." Dan began. Fionna adamantly shook her head.

"What?" his father sighed.

"Would you like to speak to Marion about her going through Fionna's bags or should I?" He ignored Fionna's objections.

"Your mother wouldn't do that." The governor gave Dan a dramatic eye roll.

"Okay, then I will."

A moment later, Mrs. Vindico whisked into the living room. "Hi dear, how was your day?" She began straightening pillows in the already pristine living room.

"Long." The governor pulled her in and kissed her cheek as she moved about the room.

"I found a recipe for a new hamburger macaroni casserole that's supposed to be excellent for the little ones, so that's what I fixed for dinner. You'll like it too though. You'll probably feel better after dinner."

Dan highly doubted that after he'd seen the photographic evidence of what they were about to be served.

"Sounds good, sweetheart. I think I'm going to eat and then head on to bed. I'm bushed," he whined.

"Well, that's what comes of a man your age working two extremely important jobs. You're going to have to find someone else to take over Venton."

"That's easier said than done." The governor made no effort to hide his irritation.

"Mother," Dan demanded, and Fionna cringed in horror.

"What?" was his mother's terse reply.

"Did you go into our room and go through either mine or Fionna's bags today?"

"Of course not," Mrs. Vindico scoffed.

"Right, right. Let me guess. Fionna's bag was on the bed or the desk or somewhere and you just happened to notice that it fell over so you cleaned it up for her."

"Yes, as a matter of fact, I did notice that one of your bags was knocked over when I went in to make your bed and to place a few books I thought you might enjoy reading in there. I'm sorry. I was not aware that going into a room of my own home to tidy up was a crime."

"Stay out of our stuff, Mother. That's an invasion of privacy. We are adults, and we do not need you commenting on the way we run our lives," Dan growled.

"I do not feel that the activities that you participated in my home last night were respectful or appropriate," his mother spouted. Fionna turned the shade of the deep antique pink couch they were currently seated on.

"We are married, Mother. My God, what else do you want?" Dan's shouting startled Halia. Her little body flinched, but then she went back to suckling her bottle a moment later.

"Must you two do this tonight? I've had a long day. Marion, stay out of their stuff, and Daniel, you two keep it down," the governor bellowed. "Can we have dinner?"

"Certainly." Mrs. Vindico craned her neck to place her nose in the air and marched back into the kitchen.

CHAPTER 32

STEP BALL CHANGE KETCHUP

A few minutes later, everyone was seated at the table with Halia still in Dan's arms, since she'd protested being put in her bouncy seat. Mrs. Vindico presented the odd concoction of unseasoned hamburger meat spread between two solid gelatinous pieces of burnt macaroni noodles covered in cheese that had solidified into a substance suitable for sculpture carving.

Aida looked horrified as Mrs. Vindico cut a large hunk of the horrible casserole-like item and hoisted it onto her plate. Dan put his arm around her and discreetly informed her that he would make her a peanut butter and jelly sandwich as soon as dinner was over.

"Thank you," she whispered as she continued to stare at her plate in confusion.

In an effort to try and calm the situation, Fionna used her fork to cut a hunk of the horrible hamburger cheese concoction on her plate and forced a bite.

"Fi, baby, you don't have to…" Dan started but halted as his wife shot him infuriated glares.

Dan watched her chew and then swallow down the casserole with copious amounts of water like she was forcing down some kind of medication. "Brooke and Will would like us to bring the girls over for dinner tomorrow night." Her eyes lit in relief. "They haven't seen

Halia yet, and Brooke misses Aida." Dan winked at Aida who was giving Fionna hopeful gazes.

"That would be fun." Fionna nodded. "Brooke texted me about class tomorrow. She wanted to know if I'd like to go to lunch with her afterwards, but I told her I needed to get back here and spend some time with Halia before we pick up Aida. But if we go over for dinner, that's even better. Is that okay with you, Mrs. Vindico?"

"I'm sorry, dear. I wasn't paying attention, something about Will and Brooke," she seemed to recall. Dan rolled his eyes and made certain his parents saw his disdain.

"Aida, would you like some ketchup? You need to eat. It won't help your IQ just sitting on your plate. Your daddy used to cover almost every dinner in ketchup when he was your age. Do you remember that, Arthur?" Mrs. Vindico chuckled.

Governor Vindico nodded as he wiped his mouth. "I considered buying stock in Heinz for a while," he teased.

"Mommy makes yummy ketchup," Aida offered. She didn't seem to know the correct response and was worried she was going to offend someone.

"Do you make your own ketchup?" The governor sounded genuinely interested as he helped himself to seconds of the hamburger casserole.

"Oh, uh, yes sir." Fionna stared at him in stunned disbelief.

"Marion, I think that oven is running too hot again. I'll cast it this weekend. This cheese is a little overdone," he lamented but continued to eat.

"I know you're exhausted, Arthur, but I phoned Kara today and told her that we're just having Thanksgiving here since Dan and Fionna are already here. Obviously, we'll need the oven working."

"But I'm still making the turkey and dressing, right," Fionna pled.

"Yes, she is." Dan dared anyone to object.

"I certainly won't argue. Just don't get your feelings hurt if it doesn't come out quite right. It took me a few tries to get the turkey just perfect. It's not an easy dish to prepare," Mrs. Vindico warned as she rode her martyrdom until it gave up the will to live.

"Oh, I won't," Fionna assured her.

"More than a few tries," Dan huffed under his breath. Fionna bit her lips together to keep from laughing.

Mrs. Vindico turned to Fionna. "Kara told me you two have been taking a dance class."

Fionna's eyes goggled momentarily, but she cleared her throat and nodded. "Yes, ma'am. It's great exercise."

"Kara took ballet and tap when she was a toddler, but I never knew she'd want to take it as an adult."

Dan bit back laughter.

"Hopefully she won't wet her pants at this recital." The governor made everyone laugh.

"I think we're going to take Will and Brooke up on their invitation to dinner tomorrow night," Dan brought the conversation back.

"That will be good. We're hosting bridge here tomorrow evening."

"Marion, I've been telling you for weeks how exhausted I am. I don't want to host the bridge club," Governor Vindico whined.

"I'm sorry, Arthur, but I've already agreed. I'll just pick up a few of those hors d'oeuvre trays from the supermarket," she explained as if that would lessen the load of holding down two full-time jobs for Dan's father.

"Fine, but not too late, please."

"If you wouldn't mind watching Halia for me while I go to my class and my instructional session, I'd be happy to fix you some food for your meeting," Fionna offered sweetly. "I could go by Daddy's and get you some of his finger sandwich trays."

Dan grimaced. He didn't want his wife catering his mother's bridge club, especially after his mother's gross invasion of Fionna's privacy.

"That would be nice, I suppose. I'd be more than happy to keep Halia. We had a lovely little discussion while you went to have lunch with Dan."

Dan assumed his infant daughter with no real ability to debate and disagree would be viewed as the perfect conversationalist for his mother.

"What did you say you'd be doing after the class?" Governor Vindico asked as he continued devouring the casserole. Dan wondered momentarily if the governor's taste buds had just up and died during the early years of their marriage.

"Oh, uh, I'm going to be learning to teach the class occasionally. I start training tomorrow."

"Did you dance when you were younger?" Mrs. Vindico asked.

"Yes, ma'am. I practiced hula from the time I could walk until I started challenging at the academy."

"I wonder why they didn't want Kara to learn to teach. She started taking tap at Miss Elaine's when she was three and kept with it until just after kindergarten."

Dan allowed himself a moment of spite to envision his mother's reaction to learning that Kara was teaching people to pole dance and strip.

"I think it's great you and Kara are doing that." Governor Vindico nodded. "Seems like fun."

"Yes, sir, it is fun," Fionna agreed with a mischievous smirk.

CHAPTER 33

PEANUT BUTTER AND JELLY BLESSINGS

Later that evening, Dan lay on his childhood bed with Halia fast asleep on his chest. He was grading an exam review sheet that Sullivan had assigned.

"She really missed you today." Fionna grinned as she emerged from the bathroom having taken a long shower and washed her hair.

Dan brushed a tender kiss on the top of his little coconut's fuzzy brown hair. She looked like a tiny pink ball all curled up on Dan's chest in one of her fuzzy pink sleepers.

"I missed her too. I missed all of you." He was shocked by how long the hours felt when he was away from his girls.

Halia had clung to Dan. She'd cried whenever he handed her off to anyone. He'd given her the last two bottles and given her a bath in the kitchen sink before she'd fallen asleep on top of him.

"Is it hard to have three girls who adore you and always want to be curled up on your chest?" Fionna teased him as she climbed into bed beside him and Halia.

"No." Dan steadied Halia with his hand while he leaned to kiss her mama. "It's pretty much my definition of heaven."

Fionna's cell phone rang, and she scrambled from the bed to answer it before it awoke the baby.

"Hey, Em, are you back?" Fionna quizzed. She'd been eager to hear about the Angels' trip to the orphanage in Brazil. Dan and Fionna had packed numerous boxes of toys and books for the Angels to take with them.

This had all been photographed for their work with the Auxiliary International Adoptions program but neither Dan nor Fionna were after praise. The kids needed toys and books and blankets, all of which Dan and Fionna were only too happy to provide. Rainer and Emily, along with Governor and Mrs. Haydenshire, had joined in and made a large cash donation to the cause.

"Oh, you got back at five. I wonder what you've been doing for the last four hours," Fionna chanted before she began giggling. Dan shook his head. He was sure it had taken Rainer Lawson approximately two and a half seconds to have Emily stripped and in bed after the Angels' jet landed.

"No, we didn't tell her. I was worried with her getting used to having Halia," Fionna explained what Dan assumed was a question about whether or not they'd told Aida about the Angels' return trip to the orphanage.

Fionna gasped, and her hand flew to her mouth suddenly. Dan set down the paper he was grading.

"Oh my gosh. Thank you!" Tears began pouring from her eyes.

Not certain what to do, Dan sat up. He kept Halia on his chest as he tried to determine what had made Fionna cry.

"No, no, I want her to have it now. I'll think of something. Hey, do you think Will would care if you and Garrett came over there and ate with all of us tomorrow night?" Emily's response had her nodding and smiling through her tears.

"Thank you! You are the best! I'm gonna go tell Dan," she announced. "Love you too."

"What was that all about?" Dan quizzed.

Fionna shook her head, and then covered her face with both of her hands and began to sob.

"Baby, what happened?" Dan gently laid Halia down on the bed and embraced his wife instead.

"I just can't believe this," she gushed as she tried to quell her own tears.

"Please tell me what happened," Dan begged.

Fionna drew a deep, steadying breath. "When Aida was at the orphanage, there was this little bunny stuffed animal that she always slept with. She wasn't allowed to bring it with her when Rainer flew her up here for the wedding because you aren't allowed to take toys from the orphanage. After we adopted her, I planned on seeing if I could find her one that was similar here, but she never mentioned it and she seemed so happy with Sophie.

"But since we sent all of those stuffed animals and toys, the nuns sent Aida back a few things that she loved from her time there. So they cleaned up her little bunny and they sent that back with Garrett along with *The Paperbag Princess* in Portuguese and a few other things they found in the little shack house where her family lived. They released Aida's file to Garrett so he has that as well, and there are photographs of her family that they must've found in the house."

"Wow," Dan choked.

"I know." Fionna began sobbing again as Dan held her closely. He wanted desperately to wake Aida up and drive her over to Garrett's to get her things. He wanted her to have them right then. He didn't want to wait until the next evening. She'd had so much taken away from her. Dan couldn't bear the thought of her being without anything at all. He loved her too much to allow her to suffer ever again.

"Let's just go get them," he urged.

She beamed at him through her cascading tears. "Emily has the box, but Garrett is the one who got it all for us. He should be there to see her open it. He loves her so much."

As it was Garrett who had managed to get his baby girl what would certainly become some of her most treasured possessions, Dan certainly wouldn't deny him.

"God, I just want to take you all home. I want her back in her room with her stuff. I want her to crawl into bed with us in the mornings and for there to actually be room for all of us. She's been without all her life, and she loves our house and your cooking and her fairy princess bed. That's where she needs to be, and I hate leaving all of you every day. I miss out on so much," he lamented. "And God only knows what my mother will pull next."

Fionna chuckled as she shook her head. "I know this is a lot with a newborn and Thanksgiving and everything going on at McCarron that Aida doesn't understand. She knows she's falling behind."

"Wait, what's going on at McCarron?" This was the first he'd heard of Aida falling behind.

"We talked about it while we were playing this afternoon. Her class is having a Thanksgiving feast Wednesday afternoon. Most of the kids in her class have heard the story for years, so when she asked Ms. Powell to explain it, everyone laughed, so she wouldn't ask anything else," Fionna lamented and Dan's heart fissured. "I'm going to go to the bookstore on the way to class tomorrow and buy her a few books about it, and I promised her that I would be there for her feast."

"I'm coming too," Dan vowed.

"It starts at noon. You'll be at work," Fionna reminded him gently.

"No, I will be at our baby girl's school for her Thanksgiving feast," Dan corrected. "I'll let my class out at eleven. I drive a Ferrari, and every freaking traffic officer in the commonwealth owes me a favor. I will be there in time to eat with her."

"I think they're singing some Thanksgiving songs as well."

"Then I'm not missing that."

"Best dad ever."

"I'm gonna go put our little coconut in her crib then I'm gonna put their mama to bed with me," Dan soothed.

He carried Halia across the bathroom and laid her in her bassinet. He kissed her cheek and then covered her and heat casted the cradle before returning to Fionna.

Sliding into bed, he smiled as Fionna curled up on his chest.

"Do you think your mom knows we snuck the girls back down and had a peanut butter and jelly party?" She giggled.

"The picture of Aida devouring her sandwich with jelly all over her cheeks would make anything my mother had to say worth it."

"I love you," Fionna vowed suddenly.

"I love you too, baby."

"Thank you," she whispered.

"For what?"

"For you, and for our life, and for my girls, for everything because

I've never been happier, and I don't care what you say—I know it wasn't me. It was all you, and I could never thank you enough for all you've given me." Tears worked from her eyes down Dan's bare chest.

"Fi, baby, I still don't think you have any idea what my life was like before you."

"I know, but we've been given so much, and I'm just so thankful to be here in your arms and to be the mother of your little girls. I feel so blessed," she confessed in a choked whisper.

"We are," Dan agreed. "We really are."

CHAPTER 34
HONEST OPINION

Jogging into the Admin building the next morning, Dan glanced at his watch. He'd started his morning off sweet talking his wife into taking a shower with him, which she'd agreed to after a good bit of coercion.

Dan wouldn't have been so relentless except that he could tell she wanted a little time alone together but was terrified of what Dan's mother would have to say if she found out. Then he wanted to give Halia her bottle and spend a little time with her. He was trying to ward off another bout of crying that afternoon, then he drove Aida to school wanting to spend time with her as well.

They'd discussed Thanksgiving, and she'd been delighted that both of her parents would be there to see her sing the next afternoon.

But all of this had resulted in him missing a faculty meeting and being a half hour late to work. As he was currently living with the chancellor, that was going to be hard to get out of.

"Dude, it's awesome," he heard Chance vow to both Jeff and Ben who were laughing at him outright.

"That is probably the stupidest thing I've ever seen," Ben corrected him.

"Nah, man, you don't get it. Jeff, you and Becca should totally go get one. It, like, cements you."

"My marriage certificate and my ring along with our child cement me and Becca, and you and Arial have only been dating six months," Jeff razzed still shaking his head. Dan was pleased Jeff appeared to be in such a good mood but wondered what they were discussing.

"Hey, hey, Mentor Vindico," Chance called, "you want to see my new tat?"

Dan raised his eyebrows as he unlocked his office door. "Sure." He couldn't have cared less, but he probably should've so he lied.

Ben Cobson asked, "You and your wife have matching tats, don't you, Mentor Vindico?"

Dan's brow furrowed as he tried to decide whether he was going to answer that question. Curiosity won out, and he nodded.

"Yeah, two of them match, why?" Dan quizzed.

Jeff laughed. "Okay, but their tattoos look cool and also mean something to them, which is why you should get them in the first place. That really is dumb. I'm sorry."

Arial located Chance just then and rushed toward them.

"Wanna see them together," she gushed excitedly.

Ben and Jeff visibly fought their laughter and managed a nod. Dan watched as Chance extended his inner forearm to reveal a black line tattoo in the shape of two bumps. As Arial lifted her forearm to meet Chance's, he understood. The bottom of the heart shape was on her arm.

He ran his hand over his mouth in effort not to guffaw.

"Okay, I gotta go to class," Arial chanted as she kissed Chance's jaw and then raced down the corridor. With that, Ben and Jeff lost it. They doubled over laughing.

"You look like you have boobs tattooed on your arm, and hers looks like some kind of weird angle that points to her stomach when her arms are down," Ben sneered.

"Dude, you just don't understand love at all." Chance headed down the corridor after Arial.

As soon as he was out of earshot, laughter erupted from Dan.

"Please tell me they were drunk." Ben and Jeff both shook their heads.

"Nope, completely sober. He's just a dumbass," Jeff explained.

"Wow."

"Hey, Mentor Vindico, does anyone know what all of your tats mean or are they all some big secret?" Ben quizzed as they followed Dan toward their first period class.

"You're a moron too if you think he's telling you about them," Jeff commented.

Dan had taken his shirt off the afternoon before in their intense lab class where they were doing several combat maneuvers that would be on their finals. He'd noticed several of his students admiring his ink though no one had asked about his numerous tattoos.

"My wife knows what they all mean, and I think we'll just leave that with her."

"Told ya," Jeff quipped.

"I had to try."

After his History of Defense class, Dan raced to the Ferrari, eager to meet Governor Haydenshire for lunch. Truthfully, he wasn't certain if his father was at Venton or at the Senate, but they were all due at Frye's in a half hour. Dan summoned and made the Ferrari fly as he moved onto the interstate.

He slid into the customary booth in the back of Frye's a half hour later. His smile from putting the Ferrari through its paces was still firmly in place.

The Crown Governor fell into the seat across from him just a moment later. "I started to drag an Auxiliary mediator up here with me, since I have a feeling I'm about to be negotiating your move with your father," Governor Haydenshire said wryly. Dan hesitated to admit that the Crown Governor was at least partially correct.

Dan quickly pulled his cell phone from his pocket. "Hey, have you seen any new pictures of Halia? She really is adorable."

"Uh-huh, I had a feeling." Governor Haydenshire rolled his eyes. "Of course I did have a pretty big clue when I received the packet of documents from Victoria Kalakona's office this morning."

Dan grimaced. "I was hoping to have lunch with you before those got to your office." Suddenly, a waiter appeared carrying the Crown

Governor's sweet tea with lemon. He took Dan's drink order and disappeared quickly.

Victoria Kalakona was the Senteon Representative from Hawaii, so she was the one that had to sign the contracts for Dan to become the sheriff of Kauai.

"Am I to assume that Daniel Vindico has asked me to lunch to inquire of my humble opinion about the documentation I received this morning and about him moving his wife and beautiful daughters almost five thousand miles away?"

"If that's not asking too much."

The governor gave him a broad grin. "I'm honored," he vowed. "Now, would you like my honest opinion or would you like to wait on your father, so that I have to toe the party line, so to speak?"

"No." Dan shook his head. He glanced toward the parking lot, making certain his father's Land Rover wasn't pulling in. "Please, I want your honest opinion. I know he doesn't want us to move, so please." Dan gestured for Governor Haydenshire to go on.

"Truthfully, I don't want you to move either, but I assume you won't be selling your shares of the Angels, so I'm hoping you'll have the family back a few times a year anyway."

"Yes, sir, that was my plan. Fi's parents are here as well, and we'll certainly miss everyone. But, I really, really hate teaching, and my girls need to be on Kauai. I have to take care of them. I know that if Mrs. Haydenshire needed anything at all that you'd even give up the Crown Governorship for her."

"In a heartbeat." He paused and seemed to will Dan into filling the silence.

"When you fired me…" he began.

"As I recall, you resigned," the governor corrected.

"Fine," Dan sighed. "When I resigned, you said 'anywhere but law enforcement, it isn't good for you,'" he choked out the memory. "I just wondered if maybe you'd changed your mind." He wondered if maybe Governor Haydenshire had noticed how hard he'd tried to become a better version of himself.

"I'm stunned," Governor Haydenshire admitted. Dan's brow knitted. "I'm stunned that you care, honestly, and I mean that with all of the respect I have for you which is a tremendous amount." The governor shook his head. "It's been a hell of a year, I suppose."

A year. Dan's breath caught. Praying that Halia would just give him a little time, Dan had some shopping to do before he left for his parents' home to pick up his girls after work.

"Yes, sir. It has." The realization of all that had happened to him since Thanksgiving the year before settled firmly in his mind.

"I gather that Mrs. Vindico would like to return to her homeland, and if math serves me, I believe your youngest daughter just might be carrying the Hawaiian energy rhythm strains as well."

"Yes, sir." Dan grinned as he briefly recalled Halia's conception on their wedding night.

The governor drew a long sip of his tea. "I wondered what had you jumping at the chance to teach at Venton. That never seemed to me to be something you might find fulfilling, but then I realized,"— Governor Haydenshire studied Dan—"you took the job for the summers. You'd taken the job for Fionna. That won't ever work, son, not that it wasn't an admirable thing to do. But if you're working for the off hours, your profession will never fulfill you because you're constantly fighting against it for more of those hours that you're without it. It's a balance just like anything else, but you asked me if my opinion had changed.

"I think I would have to say that my original opinion was incorrect," he allowed. "I don't think I was giving your beautiful bride all of the credit she deserved, and I know I wasn't giving you even half of what I should. I was concerned. You'd walked through hell a dozen times. You'd lost a child in the process and damn near lost your queen of hearts. I think I was feebly trying to keep you all safe so that you could heal."

Dan nodded his understanding and his appreciation.

"There's some quote that Regis used to throw at us all the time about what you do in your spare time being what you should do for a living." Governor Haydenshire chuckled as he recalled the former Crown Governor's words. "I suppose there's some truth in that, but it seems to me that you cherish every single second you can squeeze in with Fionna and your girls, and the few times I've either seen you at

Venton or after you've left work, you look like you've been sentenced there as some sort of punishment. So, if you want to go back into law enforcement in a much smaller capacity, I understand, and if that's what Fionna wants then I certainly won't stand in your way. But I will also not be offering you another job in the National Iodex office. I do actually agree that you need a change of scenery, but if you quote that to your father, I will adamantly deny it.

"I'd also like to point out that in your spare time, you've taken up several detective jobs assigned from your father and myself and recruited yourself a small task force by means of my son and Jeff Strenton," he pointed out though he didn't seem upset by that in any way. "So maybe, if it's in you then it's in you, and you should stop trying to swim upstream and just work on maintaining your strokes. Don't let it drown you again, and I think you'll be fine.

"Here comes your old man now, actually." Governor Haydenshire gestured toward the parking lot. "I'll help you do this, but think about what I said. Make certain that wherever this life takes you location-wise or career-wise that you aren't working solely for your vacation days and that you're with your girls as much as you can be. They are very obviously your center," he reminded Dan just before turning to smile at Governor Vindico as he slid out of his jacket and fell into the booth beside Dan.

The waiter returned with Governor Vindico's customary water with lemon and asked the men if they were ready to order. After placing orders without having to look at the menus, conversation resumed.

"I'm sorry I'm late. I decided I might give Dean another chance to resign before the holidays, but I didn't get very far." Governor Vindico shook his head. "Of course, my son was late to work this morning because he spent a half hour coercing my sweet daughter-in-law into showering with him, so maybe tardiness runs in the family," he harassed.

Governor Haydenshire laughed and shook his head at Dan. "I can't say I haven't done the same with my wife," he admitted, making everyone laugh.

"Trust me, I had a lot more fun in the shower than I would've had at that faculty meeting."

"What are you going to do about Terry Bryant, Arthur?" Governor Haydenshire quizzed as their food was delivered. Governor Vindico rolled his eyes.

"Bryant and his wife are quite a pair. He's petitioned the school governors, and I received an email this morning from Governor Sherman that they want him hired and to start right after Christmas break. They not only know of the desperation for another mentor in Duco Order but feel that it might show the students the importance of marriage and working together, even though neither of those are the reasons that Terry Bryant wants to work at Venton."

"You can override their decision, Dad," Dan reminded him.

"Yes, I can, but having the power and using it are two entirely different decisions. Sometimes listening to your subordinates and withholding your own power can speak a great deal louder than exerting your own will over those whom you rule."

"Hear, hear." Governor Haydenshire raised his tea in a mock toast before he drew a long sip.

"All right, well, I imagine I'm about to be told that you *are* moving my granddaughters to the other side of the world, and Stephen is going to tell me that you're being a good husband and the man that I raised you to be and that you'll be back several times a year. So, are you quitting or are you going to finish out your contract?" Governor Vindico demanded.

"You know your general disdain for bullshit, Daniel? You got that from your old man." Governor Haydenshire smirked.

Dan decided to shoot straight with his father. That's certainly what he would want if the tables were turned. "I'm staying until I figure out what the hell is going on at Venton. I won't have all of this falling in your lap, and there is still a tremendous amount of planning before we can actually move. As far as I'm concerned, I'll be finishing out my contract, but I have accepted the position of Sheriff for Kauai Iodex, and I'm due to report in June."

"Fine," Governor Vindico sighed. "Here's what I've decided." He turned to Dan with challenge in his eyes. "If you and Fionna are moving to Kauai, then your mother and I are purchasing a vacation home out there. I want to spend time with you, son. I miss you. I want to see your girls grow up. I plan to serve another few years as a governor, and then I'm going to retire. Your mother and I would like to travel, and we'll be spending a few months each year out in Hawaii with your family." He dared Dan to object.

Although he was shocked, Dan let the information settle on him slowly. "If that's what you want, it's fine with Fionna and me, but you don't have to purchase a home. There are several guest cottages on the farm that you would be welcome to use whenever you visit," Dan reminded his father of Tutu's open invitation to his family. "You'll get to do a lot more traveling if you don't try to purchase anything in Kauai. That'll set you back more than you'd think. I hate to see you retire early though."

He could tell his father had been prepared for battle and was shocked by Dan's acceptance and his invitation.

"If this year has taught me anything, it's that I haven't been doing the best job I could as governor."

Governor Haydenshire and Dan both set to disagree, but he waved them off. "Do you think if we're out there for weeks at a time that you and your mother could find some way to get along?"

Dan ground his teeth. "She went through Fionna's bags, found some rather personal items, then decided to mark pages in a tabloid magazine which she presented to my wife while she was giving our baby her bottle. If there was a passive-aggressive kingdom, she would be their incredibly intrusive queen."

Governor Haydenshire choked on his Philly Chicken sandwich as he tried not to laugh. He swallowed copious amounts of tea in effort to clear his throat.

"You have to give your mom a little latitude," Governor Vindico insisted. "She doesn't see you as an adult. She's trying to look after you and Fionna as well. Sometimes she gets a little overzealous, but she does mean well."

Dan shook his head. "Guess what? We are full-fledged adults with children of our own, which by the way, she was so hell-bent on me settling down and having kids, she does realize that in order to have her grandchildren we have to have sex."

With a slight grimace, Governor Vindico ate a few bites of his baked potato before he replied, "She does understand that, Daniel. She just doesn't like that fact thrown in her face."

"Fine," Dan huffed. "Tell her to stay out of my wife's things."

"Honestly, this is going better than I'd envisioned." Governor Haydenshire reminded them that he was still sitting there.

"Are you bringing the girls to the Venton Christmas Party?" Governor Vindico asked.

"No," Dan lamented. "And no offense to either of you, but yet another reason I will no longer be working at Venton would be the fact that my baby girls will never be within arm's reach of Pendergrath's son. If you think I'm overreacting, talk to my wife about what she picked up off him when she was up there yesterday."

"I'm sorry about what Fionna felt. I have high hopes for Clarence. He needs some better influences, and he certainly needs an education. I feel like if given better opportunities he could turn his life around," Governor Haydenshire apologized. "But we do have to give him time to mourn his father. He's lived a lot to only be eighteen. That takes its toll."

"I think we'll just agree to disagree on him turning his life around."

Dan knew that Governor Haydenshire had made some kind of deal with Pendergrath to keep Logan from losing his badge for killing Alexi Pravus in cold blood. Not that Dan had any issue with Logan's actions, and he had no right to complain about Governor Haydenshire saving him as he'd also saved Dan from punishment for killing Wretchkinsides with black energy. But Dan suspected that Clarence's appointment to the academy had fallen under the prison deal the governor and Pendergrath had hatched out before his trial.

He glanced at his watch under the table and wondered how long he could shop before Fionna would either become suspicious or his mother would drive her insane, and he would need to go home and referee.

Governor Vindico was still fuming over Dan's final decision about moving and the fact that he'd already accepted a job, so he began to pout in the booth beside Dan.

"Have you found out anything else about Venton?" Governor

Haydenshire broached. He seemed to understand that they weren't going to get very far with Governor Vindico.

Dan went over the things Fionna had picked up on the day before and why another drug test couldn't be run until the audit was over. He explained about Sullivan's additional test. "I'm swimming in evidence, but I have no idea who is involved. I'm sorry, sir."

"Once the foundation cracks," Governor Haydenshire sighed. Governor Vindico nodded his begrudged agreement. "It's certainly not your fault, Daniel. I know you'll get Venton sorted out. I just hate that this is drawing so much attention." He discreetly slid his eyes to Governor Vindico. Dan nodded. "But, on to brighter horizons. What has to be done to get you and your girls moved to Kauai so you can get a fresh start?"

Dan appreciated his optimism and knew that he was trying to get Dan's own father to realize that perhaps Dan's future wasn't in DC, maybe it was on a small island in the middle of the Pacific.

"We could sell or we could rent out the house here," Dan began. "I thought about talking to Patrick."

Governor Haydenshire thanked the waiter for refilling his tea with a kind smile. "It's a great house. It would be an excellent rental property. Great school district. That would provide you a steady income, and you know Patrick would keep it up." He was never afraid to vouch for his children, especially when he knew they were worth their salt.

"We plan to sell both cars and start shipping stuff over there after we finish the new house. Fionna's grandfather just doubled his farm size so there are a few places we could build. The blessing on the new land was several weeks ago, but Fi would like to be at the blessing for the foundation of our new home, and of course there will be another when we move in." As he discussed these things with relative calm, he wondered what his father was hearing.

Things that Dan accepted readily that Fionna and her family had introduced him to, the spirituality of the lands that had seeped into Dan's soul as he worked the farm all summer. The faith of Fionna's grandparents despite the losses they'd survived. The faith of his wife that never faltered. It had changed Dan thoroughly though he often wondered if his parents would ever really see him as anything more than a pompous teenager with a smart mouth and a great disdain for his family.

"We have to get the plans drawn up and sent over. Fionna's grandfather will work the crews. They're building at a drastically reduced price since we don't have to purchase the land and everyone on the island loves Papa and Tutu," he elaborated. Governor Haydenshire smiled at Dan's declaration. "Aida will go to the same elementary school Fionna attended, and she already has friends there." Dan hoped to remove the deep scowl that had formed on his father's face.

"And you'll have help with the little one?" Governor Haydenshire asked.

Dan nodded. "Fionna's grandparents are still going strong. They kept up with Aida all summer, and Fi's best friend and her husband live just a quarter mile down the road on a smaller farm. Fi and I are their daughter's godparents."

"We will miss you, but if Lillian and I can do anything to help, don't hesitate to call."

If I leave now, I could go to several of her favorite stores before I need to head home, Dan strategized.

"I hate to cut out early, and thank you both for everything, but Fi asked me to pick something up for her while I'm in town. If it's okay, I might run."

"That's fine. Enjoy your afternoon. I think your dad and I need to discuss Venton and a few other things," Governor Haydenshire agreed.

Dan offered him an appreciative smile. He knew the Crown Governor was going to try to soften the blow of Dan and Fionna moving away and probably try to guide Dan's father into making a few swift decisions regarding the academy.

Throwing down enough money to cover his lunch, Dan shook the Crown Governor's hand and then slapped his father on the back. "I know you're upset, but I have to do right by my wife and kids. That's what you taught me. We'll see you when we get back from Will and Brooke's tonight."

CHAPTER 35

PURITANICAL PINEAPPLE

Thanksgiving had been early in the month the year before, and it was late this year which meant that in two days' time, it was the anniversary of the beginning of him and Fionna. His wife was a powerful Receiver who would most certainly remember the date and hold it in high esteem. Dan needed to go all out. His mind reeled backwards as he drove toward the shopping district of Pentagon City.

The dimly lit bar, the way his pulse had hammered when he'd watched Fionna Styler sashay in on Garrett Haydenshire's arm. Dan had wanted to unzip that leather miniskirt from the moment his eyes had wandered from her beautiful eyes to her luscious pout then across her cleavage.

With a chuckle, Dan realized that she'd amped them up quite a bit with a push-up bra in order to catch his attention, but when his eyes landed on her luscious ass caught up in a tight leather skirt, he'd been done for, no turning back.

Letting that night play back through his mind, Dan's mouth still watered and his heart still raced whenever he thought about his beautiful Maylea. He knew that the likelihood of his baby ever even being able to zip up that tight black skirt again after giving birth to his little girl was slim, but he didn't need leather skirts and push-up bras. He didn't need her to look the way she did in Angels programs. He'd never wanted the 2-D version. He needed her just the way she was. He needed Maylea. She was more beautiful now than she was on the night that he'd followed her home and she'd taken him to bed and brought him back to life and out of the tombs he'd existed in for years.

Deciding to go ahead and alert Fionna to the fact that he would be a little late, Dan phoned her from the car. "Hey, baby doll, how was your class?"

She giggled. "It was really fun and then I went by Daddy's and got your mom's sandwich trays. Then Halia and I decided to take a little nap together," she explained.

"Good girl," Dan urged. She gave him a quick moan as he indulged just one of her sweetest kinks.

"It *was* good. We were getting in some good snuggles, and we slept for about a half hour before your mom decided to dust your room," she managed before she began laughing in disbelief.

"While you were asleep?" Dan gasped.

"Yep." Fionna continued to laugh, but Dan was furious. "But now Halia and I are making some mango salsa for your mom's party and then we're going to get her bottle and then I thought I'd make some of my curried grilled pineapple rings. But your mom is looking up an article where she thought she might have read that pineapple was an aphrodisiac and therefore we would not be able to serve that at bridge club." Fionna made it through her plans before she began giggling again. As much as Dan adored hearing his wife's laughter, he was infuriated with his mother.

"I was going to say that I needed an hour or two in town to pick up a few things, but clearly I need to come home."

Fionna's laughter halted. "No, we're fine, but what are you picking up?" She sounded excited. As much as she might deny it and as much as she did love to give to other people, Fionna Vindico loved receiving gifts as much as Dan loved spoiling her.

"Christmas is coming up." Dan dodged the question rather well he thought.

"It's not even Thanksgiving yet." She knew him too well.

"Maylea," Dan scolded.

"Oh my gosh, your mom's going to the couch," she whispered. "Her face is all red. I think she just read what pineapple actually does in the sex department."

Dan cracked up. "You might want to get her a paper bag."

"If she doesn't throw out all of this pineapple, then I'm either going to grill it or just eat it all and then give you a treat." She sounded like she was in the mood for a little mischief. Dan gave her a shuddering growl.

"You're always a treat, baby doll. Sweetest thing I've ever drank," he assured her in a low hungry intonation. It occurred to him that the more puritanical his mother became, the wilder and more rebellious his wife got. Maybe the week at his parents' wasn't all for naught.

"Stop it, or I'm gonna have to go play with that item I packed that she's all appalled over."

"I'm coming home." His entire body seized from the image of his wife lying in his adolescent bed, splayed out with a vibrator in hand. His breath came in rapid pants like he'd just run miles as he let the fantasy play out in his mind.

"Stop it. I'm going to finish these appetizers and then get ready for Will and Brooke's tonight. Then when we get back here, I'll let you play, but you go shop."

"You're sure you don't mind?"

"I'm fine. Halia and I are talking."

"Don't tell her what pineapple does, please," Dan teased just to hear her laugh again.

"We were discussing our new house," Fionna whispered into the phone, clearly not wanting Dan's mother to overhear their conversation.

Extracting himself from the car, Dan chuckled. "And what does our little coconut think should be in our new house?"

"A big kitchen, and lots of porches, a playroom for her and her big sister, oh and a master suite with lots of different places for her parents to play too."

Dan grinned as he entered Guinevere's Lingerie and Erotic Gifts. "Tell her all of that is already taken care of and that Daddy loves her and will be home quick."

"Love you," Fionna called.

"Love you too, baby." Dan ended the call.

CHAPTER 36
WITCH'S BREW

"May I help you find something, sir?" a woman several years older than Dan, with her slightly greying hair pulled up in a sophisticated twist, approached before he was two feet in the store.

"You probably know my wife. I'm here for our anniversary or one of them at least. I was hoping to find several things she might like," Dan explained. Fionna loved lingerie, and on the few occasions Dan had purchased some for her, she'd been elated.

As it was their anniversary, so to speak, he felt less guilty about the fact that it was just as much a gift for him as it was for her, though he intended to pick up a few things just for her as well.

"Yes sir, what's your wife's name?"

"Fionna Vindico."

"Ah, yes. She's a doll. You're a lucky man. She seems to have just as much charm and wit as she has beauty," the woman gushed.

"I am extremely lucky."

"I seem to recall Fionna being in a week or so ago. We usually keep a card on things our customers have their eye on. I'm Contessa. I'd be happy to help you."

"Thanks. That would be great." He understood why Guinevere's was one of Fionna's favorite stores. It was classy and sophisticated. It seemed to celebrate femininity and cater to the art of making love rather than hiding the store in a shady neighborhood playing to the crude side of just having sex. It reminded Dan of lingerie shops in Paris that Fionna adored.

Contessa was flipping through an elaborate cherrywood file card box while Dan glanced around the store. His eye landed on several silk handcuffs, some adorned with wispy fuzz and others just plain silk tie-ups. Chuckling, Dan was impressed at the relative ease with which the store seemed to accept the many sides of carnal pleasures.

Still studying his surroundings and trying to locate something perfect for his wife, Dan's eyes landed on a few female shoppers.

There was another man working with a different saleswoman. It sounded like he was trying to push his wife or girlfriend into being a little wilder. His solution seemed to be racy lingerie. *Might want to talk to the woman in your bed and not a salesclerk, man,* Dan thought with a slight eye roll.

"Here we are," Contessa brought Dan's attention back to the large marble counter fitted with antique cash registers.

"She has several cards actually," Contessa stated with a smile as Dan laughed.

"That's my baby."

Contessa checked the cards and then showed Dan the things Fionna had admired when she'd been in the store recently. "She's looked at this several times." Contessa lifted a black, see-through, baby doll gown that would show off Fionna's backside to perfection. The back was nothing more than a set of six crisscrossing silk strings. Contessa flipped the hanger to show off the front of the gown which had gathered straps just above the breast cups. Dan's mouth went dry as he took in the cutouts that would reveal Fionna's nipples.

"Uh, yeah." Dan nodded. "Let's start with that."

"Would you also like the matching panties? They have an open panel," she effectively sealed the deal.

"Absolutely," Dan agreed as she chuckled. "But listen, Fionna just made me a daddy again. I need this to be the size she is now. I do not want her dissolving in tears because it doesn't fit." He shuddered as he considered how that might play out.

Contessa nodded. "She's been in since your daughter was born, and we remeasured her. This is her size."

"She's lost a few more pounds in the last few weeks."

"The good thing about this is that it isn't tight, and she should be able to wear this size for a while."

A relieved sigh exited Dan's lungs as Contessa handed the nightie to a young clerk to be wrapped.

"Anything else, Mr. Vindico?"

"Was there anything else she mentioned she liked?"

Contessa consulted the cards again with a nod. "There were a few sets she admired. She likes the apron there on the mannequin." Dan's lungs seemed to shrink. He was unable to draw a full breath as he fought to keep his trousers from straining as he envisioned Fionna servicing him in a tiny black see-through apron with white edgings.

"I cannot buy that for her," he choked. If she wanted to purchase that to surprise him, then he would try not to drool all over her when she made her appearance, but that wasn't one he would purchase for her.

Contessa moved on. "If the apron isn't exactly what you had in mind, I'm certain you know that she's a fan of most of the garter stocking sets. Your wife has a lovely sense of style. She enjoys all the feminine details."

Before Dan could agree, he heard an audible, derisive huff. Spinning around, he glared at none other than Mentor Katherine Bryant. "Do you have something to say about my wife?"

Contessa's eyes flashed in concern.

"Of course not, *Mentor* Vindico. I'm not looking to get myself fired. I was just shocked you scoffed at the apron there. That seems right up your alley."

Dan's blood boiled as he narrowed his eyes in hate-fueled spite. Forcing himself to draw a deep breath, he locked his jaw to consider his words. "I have no idea why you seem to despise me so much, Mentor Bryant. You don't know me, and you sure as hell don't know my wife. I had nothing to do with your affair, and on that note, would you be in here purchasing something for the chancellor now that he's legally separated, or are you trying to slither back into your husband's bed now that Wilshire's freed up? Does that make him less appealing?" Dan spat viciously. "I'm here shopping for my wife. I didn't ask for your opinion or for you to even make your presence known, so just stay away from me and away from my girls—all of them."

He turned his back on Katherine's infuriated scowl. "I'm sorry, ma'am. What else was Fionna interested in?"

"Uh," Contessa stammered before regaining her composure. "This way." She directed him toward the back of the store. "She's looked at these massage candles several times." She pointed to a line of seductively scented candles that once heated could be poured out and used for a heated massage. Thinking that sounded like something they would both enjoy, Dan sampled the scents. He picked out two he thought Fionna would like and that he would love smelling on her and had those added to the nightie.

"Perhaps one of our boudoir sprays. Does Mrs. Vindico wear perfume?" Contessa gestured to a display of linen and perfume sprays.

"She has a favorite, and I don't think she'd be interested in any others." He wondered momentarily what Katherine Bryant would make of that as she was still stalking around shopping for revenge.

"She loved this boudoir set. One of our staff noted that she's tried it on three times." Contessa held up a delicate aqua lace camisole top with spaghetti string straps. It was paired with matching lace and ruffle hipster panties. There were diminutive bows between the cleavage portion that gathered under the breast line and on the sides of the panties. It would ruffle around Fionna's waist and had a scalloped hemline around the panties that obscured everything for Dan's eyes only. It was sweet and deliciously innocent, and she would look phenomenal in it. Wondering why she hadn't purchased it, Dan lifted the hanger from Contessa's hands to study the set and the price tag. It wasn't even expensive. Dan's brow furrowed.

"She's tried it on three times but didn't buy it?"

"It clings in the middle there with the delicate lace patterning. She made a comment about her weight the last time she was in and tried it on. I only remember because I was so shocked that she would worry about her weight. I guess we all have our hang-ups though. I tried to tell her she looked stunning in it, but she chose something a little looser."

Dan's heart sank. "Are you absolutely certain that I can get this in the size she is right this moment?"

"Yes, sir, that's the one she tried on. It might even be a little loose now if she's dieting."

"I'll take it," Dan leapt. "And I like that." He pointed to a long silk negligee. The top was a delicate creamy lace. Dan envisioned Fionna in the gown with her nipples pulsating under the lace and the rest of her covered in deep coral. *Just until I get it off her.*

"That's lovely. We didn't have it when Fionna was in last, but I think it suits her. She'd like that you picked something on your own."

Another audible scoff came from Mentor Bryant's direction, but she was talking on her phone. Suddenly, Dan's secondary Predilect flooded warning alerts through his body. It forced his shield back. The sensation was always so odd. Dan's heart thundered out its disapproval. He gripped the counter to steady himself as he adjusted to the switch.

She's waiting for something, Dan realized. His mind raced. His eyes closed and he let his Visium Predilection consume him. *She's furious and out for revenge.* His shield fought the only conclusion that he could access.

"I'll have everything wrapped for you in just a moment," Contessa assured him. Dan's body spasmed in horror as he began to consider what Katherine Bryant might be up to. Contessa lifted a gown from the rack and headed back to the cash registers.

Letting several rather explicit curse words hiss from his mouth, Dan grabbed his cell phone as it buzzed in his pocket.

"Hey, baby." He moved as far away from Mentor Bryant as he could without exiting the store.

"What's wrong?" Fionna demanded. She always knew.

"I need you to come into town as fast as you possibly can. See if my mom will watch Halia or bring her with you. I need you to meet me at Guinevere's right now."

"What?!" Fionna gasped. "I'm on my way but why?"

"I'll text you why," he whispered furtively. "Just please hurry for me."

"Mrs. Vindico, I need to run a quick errand. Would you mind watching Halia for a moment? I'll be right back. She'll still be sleeping I'm certain," Fionna pled with Dan's mother.

She began her diatribe on the fact that Fionna was leaving Halia once again.

"Okay, thank you," Fionna cut her off. "I'll be back in just a little while." Dan heard her car door open. "I'm on my way."

Dan's parents' home was in one of the nicest subdivisions near Pentagon City. It wouldn't take her long to arrive. Dan sent over the text and prayed that she wouldn't try to read it while she drove. Then he waited.

"Was there anything else you'd like today, Mr. Vindico?" Contessa asked. Dan tried to see out the large storefront windows, but they were covered by expensive brocade fabrics in order to conceal the delicate nature of the store's stock.

"No, ma'am. Thank you so much for your help. If you'd just get those wrapped up for me quickly." Dan pulled his wallet from his back pocket and handed Contessa one of his credit cards.

"Certainly, sir. Fionna's going to love them." She hurried the woman gift wrapping Dan's purchases.

He let his eyes slide discreetly to Katherine Bryant. She was still on her cell phone. His entire body flooded with revulsion. He called her several less than savory names under his breath as he began pacing and praying that Fionna would make it in before Bryant finished concocting her witch's brew.

CHAPTER 37
SURPRISE

The door flew open, and Fionna raced inside. Fury lit through her features and flooded her energy. Dan pulled her to him and hugged her tightly.

"They're pulling up now," she whispered into Dan's chest. It was too late.

"I figured."

Shock lit Contessa's eyes as she returned to Dan to give him the bags and his credit card, but white-hot fury exploded from Mentor Bryant as she watched her carefully orchestrated plan begin to crumble.

Contessa smiled. "Well, Fionna dear, how are you? It's good you didn't come rushing in a moment or two before."

"He's so sweet. He doesn't have to get me anything. He spoils me rotten," Fionna gushed rather loudly.

"It seems you two have a match made in heaven."

"We definitely do." Fionna turned her enraged wrath on Katherine Bryant who was edging closer.

There were a few other places Dan had wanted to peruse before he went home, but they would have to wait.

"I'm going to take you to my car. I'll bring you back up here to get yours in an hour or so. We'll get Meredith to pick up Aida at the bus stop," Dan strategized.

Fionna swallowed down her anger and her fear. She trembled slightly as she began to consider what was set to be in the Gifted papers the next day had Dan not realized what was going on. She put distance between herself and Bryant. Dan knew it was an effort to push back the emotions rolling off Katherine.

Dan took both of the large shopping bags from Contessa and turned them outward to make certain the Guinevere's signature corset logo was on full display. He wrapped his arm over Fionna's shoulder and flung open the door. Fionna leaned up and kissed his jawline as cameras began clicking.

They halted almost as soon as they'd begun. Dan forced himself to walk slowly and gaze at his wife as if he'd never noticed the press vans circling their prey. He opened the passenger side door for her and made a show of helping her in before he climbed in the driver's seat and sped away.

"I cannot believe that…ugh," Fionna growled in abject fury, but she was still unable to call Katherine Bryant a bitch. "That was an all-time low."

"Remember a few days ago when you asked me if I wanted to buy my way out of my contract and move early?" Dan spat.

Fionna nodded.

"Well, I do. Let me figure out what the hell is going on at Venton, and then we're moving. I'm not dealing with the likes of her and her moronic husband any longer."

"She was delighted. I could feel it when I walked in. She was actually willing to sell herself out yet again just to make it look like you two had something going on. She's miserable and mean."

"This is what I kept telling everyone about Wretchkinsides," Dan finally let the fury flow from his lips. "People with nothing left to lose are the most dangerous. I swear I'm not trying to scare you, but what we just did isn't going to stop her. Something is going to come out of all of this. I just don't know what."

Dan and Fionna rushed inside the house. Fionna lifted Halia from her bassinet though she'd just begun her customary grunting. After

Dan asked his sister to pick up Aida from the bus stop and promised that they would pick her up from Tim and Meredith's, he began trying to console his wife.

She clung to Halia while giving her a bottle. Dan could tell she was fighting the harrowing fear and anger that coursed through her body. Wrapping his arm around her, he forced his shield out over her and their tiny daughter.

Halia pulled away from the bottle to try to grasp at the fierce green energy surrounding her. She cooed her delight.

"Only you, baby. You know that," he reassured. "Don't let her do this to you. No one else. Not ever. This,"—he rubbed Fionna's back with one hand and Halia's head with the other—"this is all I will ever want or ever need."

"I know," she choked back tears as she gazed down at their child. It appeared Halia was, at that moment, something Fionna considered to be her strongest tie to Dan. It crushed him that her faith had been shaken. It made him violently ill when he began to consider what would have come of Katherine Bryant timing it perfectly so that she made it appear that she and Dan left a lingerie shop together.

"Fi, come on, I went in there for you," Dan reminded her.

"I know," she whispered, but Dan was only serving to make her feel more guilt. "I just can't stand her, and I can't stand that you work with someone like that. Her husband is no better. I hate that everyone always wants to take pieces of us away. They want to own a story that has nothing to do with reality, and they don't care what it does to me or to you or to anyone. I want to go home." She gave in to the tears that had been looming on the horizon since the evening before when she'd realized Dan's mother had gone through her things.

Holding her and whispering how much he loved her, Dan knew that the house ten miles from his parents' was not where she wanted to go. Her roots were much farther away, deep in the lush volcanic soil and the rhythmic salty waters of the island of Kauai.

Dropping his cast, Dan left her for a split second before returning back to the sofa with his laptop.

"Let's get this done. I want to go home too."

He opened the five house plans that they'd been working from and the document containing his notes on all of them.

"Let's pick the one we're going to start with and then we can modify it. I'll send them to Papa tonight, and tell him to let me know what we need to do next and when we need to be there for the foundation blessing."

Fionna lifted Halia to her shoulder and began patting her back. Deep relief flooded through her energy. She was going home. She was taking their girls home, and Dan wanted to go just as much as she did.

"Okay." She drew a deep breath. "I don't like how closed off the kitchen is in that one, but I did like that your office would be off the kitchen and living room and that the porch is accessible off both of the girls' bedrooms," she pointed out. "But we weren't sure about the girls' rooms being on the other end of the house from ours."

He switched to the next set of plans.

"I love that French door entryway, but I'm not crazy about that kitchen either."

"I would like a separate entry and exit into my office. I plan on running Kauai Iodex from our home quite a bit, but I don't want my officers disturbing you and the girls."

He opened the next tab.

"I love all of those porches. That's my second favorite one," Fionna confirmed.

"I think having a lanai between our actual home and my office might be perfect, but why don't you just tell me your favorite and we'll use it."

"This one." She pointed to the screen. "The kitchen is perfect."

It was a rather large ranch style that would fit in well on the farm.

"I don't think we'll need a fireplace on the back lanai," Fionna giggled.

"Papa thought you would like that. He's afraid you're going to miss Virginia winters." Dan chuckled over the fact that Fionna's grandfather loved spoiling her almost as much as Dan did.

"I don't deserve either of you." Fionna seemed to regain her equilibrium.

"I heartily disagree, and I'm certain he would as well."

"I do really like the idea of a playroom being right outside the girls' rooms." Fionna pointed to the screen as Halia located her own fingers and began soothing herself to sleep with her other little hand on Fionna's breast.

"I like to sleep holding on to those as well," Dan teased. "We can add porches here and here." He returned to the plans on the screen. "And expand the kitchen width and length. So, is this the one?"

A broad grin lit Fionna's beautiful face as she nodded.

"I love those closets," Fionna squealed.

Dan grinned. Off the large master bathroom was a closet that was big enough to be a room unto itself. It held its own built-in bench seat, and Dan planned on adding shelving for her expansive shoe collection and a small rack for his own clothing. The huge closet also connected to the laundry porch which Dan thought was ingenious. He liked the plan as well even if it might be more room than they would ever need.

"Your girls won't be born on the island, Daniel." Tutu's cryptic prediction played through his mind once, and he amended his original thought on the size of the home they were going to build. If Fionna was going to give him more than one son, the entire farm might not be big enough. He was shocked at how the thought of expanding their family again excited him.

"And it has a three-car garage." Fionna brought Dan back to present. "So, there's room for my stud's Agusta motorcycle that he looks so freaking hot driving." Dan shook his head at her.

Keeping Halia balanced on her shoulder, Fionna snuggled into Dan's embrace.

"I'm sorry your surprise was ruined, and I'm sorry I freaked out. I just…can't imagine what the papers would've said tomorrow."

"Me too," Dan sighed. "But hopefully you'll like what I bought."

"I love that you went there for me, that you think of things like that. I really am the luckiest girl in the world. I think that's why it freaked me out so much. I can't imagine my life without you," she confessed in a harrowed whisper.

"You will never be without me, so please try to stop worrying."

CHAPTER 38

MEMORIES

After exchanging their cars and picking Aida up from Meredith's, Dan drove his family over to Will and Brooke's. He and Fionna had decided to lay aside the vengeance being thrown their way in light of getting to be with Aida while Garrett and Emily presented her their gifts.

Dan carried Halia bundled in her warmest blankets on his shoulder while Fionna grabbed the diaper bag and they moved quickly to the front porch.

Garrett answered the door and they bustled inside.

Aida hugged Garrett and then rushed into the kitchen and was greeted excitedly by Brooke in Portuguese. Lily Ana rushed to her uncle Garrett in a crawl. Then she stood and tried to walk to him, but she fell back and landed on her diaper, still not having walking perfected just yet. Garrett chuckled and picked her up before she cried. She snuggled into her uncle's chest with a great deal of exuberance.

"Hey, come on in." Will grinned. "Beer," he offered Dan. Nodding, Dan accepted as Halia began raring her head back to see everyone in the room.

"She's so beautiful," Brooke gushed as she and Fionna hugged.

"Thank you." Fionna beamed over the assessment.

"Do you want a beer, Fionna?" Will offered.

"Just a Dr Pepper, thank you." Fionna grinned as Will handed her the drink and lifted Aida up onto the countertop so she could watch Brooke baste the large platter of Brazilian ribs. Fionna had been studying Brazilian cooking since the summer before. She wanted to teach Aida to cook meals from her homeland, but she was struggling with some of the techniques.

"I've been working on the *refogado*," she explained to Brooke.

Brooke nodded. "Everything delicious starts there." She smiled at Dan. "We had so much fun this morning. I can't tell you how excited I am to go next week. You should see her shake it, Daniel. She's part Brazilian. I told her this."

Everyone laughed as Dan nodded.

"I've seen it. Trust me, she's hypnotizing." Dan waggled his eyebrows as Fionna blushed.

"Da-yee," Lily Ana demanded of her father. He reached and extracted her from Garrett's arms. She pointed to Halia on Dan's shoulder.

"Bay-yee," she announced.

"Do you want to see the baby?" Will asked. Lily Ana opened and closed her hand repeatedly as she reached for Halia. "You have to be sweet to Halia." Will carried her closer to see.

Everyone watched Lily Ana lean forward and pat Halia's back gently.

"Hi, bay-ee," she gushed in an exuberant whisper.

"Aww," Fionna and Brooke both swooned.

Halia stretched and yawned in her father's arms as she turned her head to locate Lily Ana.

A moment later, she was working herself into frustrated grunts. It was several minutes past time for her next bottle. Fionna extracted one from the diaper bag and began heating it in her hands.

As Halia began to cry in earnest, Lily Ana's face fell.

"No, bay-ee!" she ordered, complete with shaking her little finger at Halia.

"Baby Halia is hungry," Will explained.

"No!" Lily Ana continued to demand.

"She says this all the time. No, no, no. Everything is no." Brooke shook her head at her daughter.

Rainer and Emily knocked on the door, and Brooke welcomed them in. Emily hugged her brothers and sister-in-law then she and Fionna embraced for several long minutes.

"Yeah, we're gonna be visiting Hawaii a lot, I think." Rainer gestured to his wife and Fionna as he accepted a beer from Will. Dan laughed his agreement that Fionna and Emily would need to see one another on a regular basis.

Emily had placed a wrapped box on the counter just before she and Fionna began hugging and jumping around Brooke's kitchen. Aida greeted Emily with equal exuberance, making everyone chuckle.

"Can I hold her?" Emily gestured to Halia who was rapidly consuming her bottle in Dan's arms.

"Sure." Fionna grinned. Dan handed Halia and her bottle to Emily. After feeding her and burping her, Emily gave Rainer the look that said *we could have one too if you wanted. Please, please, please.*

"Em," Rainer sighed. "Remember you love challenging for the Angels, and only being twenty-one, and liking to sleep."

"Yes, but she's so adorable."

Everyone inhaled Brooke's delectable dinner of Brazilian ribs and Feijão Tropeiro, an outstanding dish made of Brazilian beans, sausage, and collard greens.

"This is delicious, but I know Dan's disappointed we're not playing bridge with his parents' bridge club tonight," Fionna teased.

"This tastes like I ate it before," Aida announced.

"Maybe you ate it when you lived in Brazil, sweetheart," Fionna explained.

Aida nodded. She appeared to try very hard to access a memory she couldn't quite manage.

After consuming the delicious meal, everyone settled into the living room.

Fionna nodded to Emily. Dan handed Halia off to Garrett as he and Fionna sat beside Aida on the couch.

"Hey Aida, did you know that Garrett and I were in Brazil for a couple of weeks?" Emily eased.

"Why?" Aida's brow furrowed.

"Well," Emily's voice softened, "we went back to work at the orphanage where Fionna and I met you last year."

Aida crawled in Dan's lap and clung to him.

"Mommy," she corrected Fionna's name. Dan's heart fissured as he cradled her to him.

"Yes, Mommy," Emily assured her. "I'm sorry."

"I don't want to go back there," Aida choked.

"No, baby, you're not," Dan assured her as everyone joined in.

"Aida Mae, you're staying with your mommy and daddy forever, baby girl." Garrett rushed to her.

"And you?" she begged.

Garrett met Dan's eyes. "Of course," he promised.

"You're never going back there, ever. I promise," Fionna vowed.

Emily wiped away tears of her own as she, Rainer, Will, and Brooke vowed their reassurances as well.

"You are staying with your mommy and your daddy forever, but everyone at the orphanage wanted to send you a present, so Garrett and I brought it back for you," Emily rushed her explanation.

"You're not allowed to bring things from the orphanage," she stated the firm rule.

"Your mommy and daddy and all of us packed up a bunch of toys and books and blankets and things for the children that still live in the orphanage, and they had a few things that they wanted to send back to say thank you."

"You did?" Aida asked Dan. She sounded a little hurt.

"We did, baby. We knew they needed new toys and books, and Mommy and I wanted to thank them for taking care of you before we got you."

Aida's grin soothed his soul as she threw her arms around his neck.

"May I see my present, please?" she asked Emily.

Emily handed her the small, wrapped box.

"It's not even my birthday or Christmas yet."

"I was thinking maybe it should be big sister day," Fionna announced. Aida bit her lip as she nodded.

"Open it, baby girl," Garrett encouraged, still knelt down beside Aida with Halia on his shoulder.

Aida pulled the paper away from the unassuming cardboard box. Everyone braced as she lifted the sides open.

"Davi!" she squealed. She lifted the small stuffed animal bunny from the top of the package and hugged him tightly to her chest. "I missed him so much." Tears of joy fell from her eyes, and everyone in the room blinked back their own. "Can I keep him here with me?"

"Davi is going to stay here with you forever," Fionna vowed. "He can sleep with you in your fairy princess bed just like Sophie."

"Thank you!" Aida kept Davi tucked to her chest and gave Garrett a one-armed hug.

"Look, there's more," Emily directed her.

Aida kept tight hold of Davi. She lifted out three slightly damaged photographs with her brow knitted deeply. The edges were singed.

"That's Mamãe and Pai." She gently touched the photograph of her parents. They were much older than Dan and Fionna but were hugging each other and smiling. Happiness exuded from their faces, and a boulder of emotion clogged Dan's throat as he stared down at Aida's biological father and saw the eyes of his precious little girl.

"I forgot to remember," Aida confessed as her chin began to tremble. Fionna lost it, and Dan shook his head, unable to hold back his emotion any longer as he turned Aida to hold her.

She wiggled back down and looked at the next photograph.

"These are my big brothers," she explained. Aida's siblings were much older than she was. She must've been a surprise many years later.

"Do you remember their names?" he asked her.

"Carlos," she pointed to the eldest Santos child. He appeared to be fifteen or sixteen when the photo was taken. "And Miguel," she moved down the line. "And Daniel," she pointed to the youngest son. "That's like your name." Aida turned to Dan who nodded.

All of the children were in tattered clothing, and the photo was taken in front of what appeared to be a two- or three-room shack that had been Aida's home until she was four and moved to the orphanage.

"That's me." She flipped to the last photo, a picture of her father holding a toddler Aida up on his shoulders. She appeared to be around three at the time of the photo.

"We can put those in a very special place in your room so you can see them every day," Fionna promised her.

"Thank you. I want to look at them every day so I don't forget to remember again," Aida pled.

"There's one more thing," Emily urged as Rainer handed her a tissue to dry her tears.

Aida hesitantly handed Fionna the photographs of her family.

"I'll keep them safe. I promise."

Aida turned back to the box and then her mouth fell open as she lifted the well-worn copy of *The Paperbag Princess* in Portuguese from the box.

"I get to keep this?"

"Your daddy ordered ten copies all in Portuguese to send to the orphanage so you could have this one," Garrett complimented Dan's actions though it was by no means necessary.

"Thank you!" Aida slowly turned the pages.

"Would you like me to read it to you, my sweet Aida?" Brooke offered.

"Yes, please."

Dan didn't want to let her go. He wanted to hold her safely in his arms. He wanted to set his shield over her and promise her that he would never let anything bad happen to her ever again. He didn't want her to slide from his lap with her bunny and her book and cuddle in beside Brooke. But he said nothing as he watched Brooke begin the story in their beautiful native language.

"Thank you," Aida whispered as she gave Brooke a hug after the story was over. *"Você é bem-vinda minha querida, Aida,"* Brooke soothed as she kissed Aida's cheek.

Aida beamed but then rushed back to Dan and Fionna.

"This is my mommy and my daddy, Davi," she introduced them to the rabbit. "And you can come live at our house too."

"And you can see Aida's room and sleep in her fairy princess bed and meet Sophie, her very special baby doll," Fionna supplied.

"I think Davi missed me too," she whispered to Dan.

"I know he did, baby." Dan lifted his sweet girl back up into his lap and felt everything in his world settle into perfect accord as she tucked her bunny under her arm and then hid her face in Dan's neck.

Aida spun in Dan's lap after several long minutes of hiding in her daddy's arms.

"Davi needs to meet Halia," she announced.

She paced quickly to Emily who was giving Halia her next bottle.

"This is my very, very favorite bunny, Halia, and I will let you play with him if you promise to be very, very careful."

"Why don't you and I go out after your feast tomorrow, and we'll find Halia her very own bunny. That way you'll both have one," Fionna offered. "You don't have to share yours with Halia. It's okay to have things that we keep safe and don't share."

Dan heard the wisdom and the underlying plea in his wife's words. She also had every right to keep things that she didn't want to share safe and away from prying eyes and curious hands. She had a right to have things that were never meant for their neighbors or his mother or the entire American Realm to be privy to. He made a vow to himself to be a better Shield of the things she kept closest to her heart.

Aida nodded. "That's a good idea."

"Are you having a feast tomorrow, Aida Mae?" Garrett quizzed.

"Yes, we're singing three songs about Thanksgiving and then the bigger kids put on a play in front of where we stand for singing."

Garrett chuckled and scrubbed her head.

"Mommy went to the bookstore and bought me books that Daddy is going to read to me in bed tonight so I understand about Thanksgiving even though I would rather him read me my other *Paperbag Princess* book because when he reads it to me I feel the sunshine in my tummy, and I haven't felt it there much since our house got broken and we had to go stay with Grandpa and Grandma."

"Your house will be fixed in just a few more days, sweetheart. I promise," Garrett pledged. He turned to Dan and Fionna. "Hey, if it's too much over there, you know Mom and Dad would love to have you out on the farm."

"I should have thought of that sooner." Will shook his head. "I'm sorry."

"No, that would hurt Dan's parents' feelings," Fionna assured them.

Drawing a regret-filled breath, Dan nodded his begrudged agreement.

"Hey, then why don't you all come over for football Friday?" Will offered.

"Yeah, that'd be great," Rainer leapt on the bandwagon.

"What's football Friday?" Fionna sounded intrigued.

Emily grinned. "Mom will be cooking for the next two days straight, and we always go serve Thanksgiving dinner at the shelter, but on Friday, Dad won't let Mom in the kitchen. He pretty much waits on her hand and foot, and he makes us pancakes for breakfast then all of the Haydenshire boys, and anyone else they can drum up, play football all morning and then watch football games all afternoon. We eat Mom's Thanksgiving leftovers for lunch, and then Dad orders like thirty pizzas for dinner. It's fun. We just hang out. We'd love for you to come," Emily was on the verge of begging.

"I haven't been in years," Dan added. "But I'd love to. I think by Friday we're going to need a long break from Marion and Arthur."

"Can I bring anything?" Fionna asked.

"Just the baby girls and maybe a few toys for Aida unless she wants to play football." Will chuckled.

"Can Davi come?" Aida whispered.

"Of course," Emily assured her. "You can introduce him to Abigail if you want to, but I have a question for you."

"Okay." Aida looked eager.

"Would it be alright if Rainer and I came to see you sing at school tomorrow?"

Aida was visibly delighted as she turned to Fionna.

"Am I allowed for Emily and Rainer to come see me sing tomorrow?"

"Sure, sweet girl," Fionna vowed.

"Can I come too?" Garrett asked. Aida leapt from Dan's lap and into Garrett's. "Yes!" She threw her arms around his neck. Garrett's eyes closed as he cradled her in his arms. Dan grinned as he understood that Garrett didn't need permission to come.

CHAPTER 39

A HELL OF A YEAR

A little while later, Dan loaded Halia and her car seat into the Mercedes. He helped Aida up into her pink flower seat and buckled her in as well.

"See you tomorrow." Dan offered Will his hand.

"Nah, man, did you forget? The Senate's closed tomorrow. It's just Venton that's open."

"I never took the day off." Dan had always looked forward to the day before Thanksgiving because he could work in the quiet and then sleep in his office and work most of Thanksgiving day before making his begrudged appearance at his parents' house for Marion Vindico's mockery of the Thanksgiving meal.

"Yeah." Will seemed to remember that as well. "Been a hell of a year."

Dan was still stunned at how one woman, one fate-filled night, one bullet, one trip to Kauai with his angelic bride, and two beautiful little girls could have made his life everything he'd ever wanted. And that it had all somehow taken place in one year's time.

He lifted Fionna's hand to his lips. "I love you so much."

"I love you too, Daddy," Aida assured him from her seat where she was hugging Davi tightly.

"I love all of my girls," Dan vowed as Fionna beamed.

Driving slowly, Dan longed to take his family home. He wanted to tuck Aida and Davi up in her fairy princess bed and read her to sleep. He wanted to lay Halia in her nursery after feeding her and rocking her to sleep, and then he wanted to cradle his beautiful bride in their bed where they all felt safe and secure and at peace. He needed to prove to her that he would be a better Shield than he'd proven to be in the last week. Bitter regret ate at him.

"Football Friday sounds fun," Fionna said. "I'm excited about spending the day with Emily and Mrs. Haydenshire. I wanted to ask her all about our new house and things that would be good for little ones."

"I'm more excited about that than Thanksgiving too," Dan assured her.

Fionna offered him a sorrowful gaze as she drew a deep steadying breath. The drive was over much too quickly. Dan led his family into the house. He carried Aida. She was yawning and rubbing Davi's ears between her fingers. Fionna lifted Halia out of her car seat and cradled her tenderly in her arms as they moved through the cold night air.

"Here they are," Governor Vindico announced as they entered.

Dan's heart sank as he saw who was awaiting them in his parents' formal living room. Amelia's parents, the Richmonds, were smiling up at him kindly.

"We didn't mean to interrupt bridge," Dan offered but his voice held no tone. He kept Aida tucked up in his arms.

"No, no, we just overstayed our welcome hoping to see your little ones," Mrs. Richmond explained. Dan would never understand how Amelia's parents could ever be kind to him when it was entirely his fault that their daughter had suffered the way she had.

"Grandpa, look!" Aida held out Davi. "Garrett brought him back for me from where I used to live," she explained before she remembered to smile at the Richmonds. "Hi," she offered politely as she shrunk into Dan.

"Hi there, sweetheart." Gerald Richmond offered her his kind smile.

"That bunny looks like you must love him very much." Faith grinned as well.

"Yes, ma'am. I slept with him every single night at the orphanage because he made me feel so much better when I missed my mamãe and pai and I wanted to bring him when I came here, but you aren't allowed to bring toys from the orphanage and I decided that I wanted to see Emily and Mommy more and Sister Mary Francis said Davi would be there when I got back, but I didn't have to go back cause Mommy and Daddy adopted me and I wanted to ask for Davi but they gave me so many things I didn't think I should," she explained without so much as a breath. "But now I get to have Mommy and Daddy and baby Halia and Davi, and Garrett is coming to my singing tomorrow."

Faith Richmond clutched her chest. "Dan, she's just adorable."

"Thank you," he choked.

Governor Vindico beamed at Aida. "What are you in tomorrow, sweetheart?"

"My Thanksgiving feast, and I'm singing three songs with my class," Aida explained.

"Well, Grandma and I will be there as well," he assured her.

"Oh, wow," Aida gasped. "Thank you!"

Fionna revealed Halia who was sleeping sweetly wrapped up in her mother's arms. Faith wanted to hold her, Dan realized, and he selfishly prayed that Fionna wouldn't offer. His body didn't seem to know how to respond to such a thing. The cataclysmic collision of his two worlds. He didn't know how to exist in both.

Fionna immediately picked up on his panic and kept Halia tucked in her arms.

"It was so nice to see you both again," she assured the Richmonds. "But we should get the little ones to bed."

"Of course. It sounds like Aida has a big day tomorrow," Faith agreed with a hint of disappointment in her tone.

A moment later, the Richmonds made their exit and journeyed back to the house next door.

Dan tucked Aida in Kara's old bed and read several books on Thanksgiving to her. He listened to her questions and answered them the best he could. But very soon, she was sound asleep, clinging to

Davi and her blanket. Dan kissed her cheek and sealed heat in the fibers of her bedding before tiptoeing out of her room.

CHAPTER 40

VENGEANCE WROUGHT

At eleven thirty the next day, Dan delighted his class by wishing them a Happy Thanksgiving and dismissing them early. He raced to his car and flew to McCarron. He joined Fionna, Emily, Rainer, Garrett, his parents, Governor and Mrs. Haydenshire, Governor and Mrs. Willow, Wes, and Lauren in a long line of seats.

He tucked Fionna under his arm as the lights in the cafeteria lowered and the kindergarten students were revealed behind the thirty-year-old brown felt curtains to sing "Gobble, Gobble Goes the Turkey."

Aida's class along with the other second grade classes appeared after the first graders made their exit, and one little boy in an exuberant dance step fell off the stage and had to be consoled by his parents.

Dan, Rainer, and Garrett all wolf whistled when Aida's class began to sing.

Aida giggled and waved as she heard her admirers. Dan blew her a kiss which she returned to swoons from the audience. Mrs. McBeechum, however, was not impressed with the sheer number of admirers that Aida had and scowled Dan's direction for most of the play.

Fionna handed Halia off to her grandfather to be given her bottle so that she and Dan could eat Mrs. Powell's Thanksgiving feast with Aida.

"Oh, Mr. Vindico." Haley's mother rushed toward Dan. "I just wanted to thank you again. Marc's just got his final exams left and then he's been hired on at the precinct all thanks to you."

"Congratulations." Fionna wrapped Haley's mother up in an exuberant embrace. "I'm so glad to hear that."

"That's great," Dan agreed, offering her a kind smile.

"I don't know what we would've done without you."

"I didn't do much."

"I'm going to be a big sister too," Haley informed Aida. Haley's mother chuckled and nodded. Dan and Fionna offered their congratulations.

"I can teach you how. You mostly have to pat them and tell them not to cry and then when they cry anyway you have to know how to put your hands over your ears tight like this." Aida demonstrated.

Fionna and Aida headed off in the Ferrari to try and find a bunny for Halia while Dan took Halia back to his parents' home in the Mercedes. Fionna had been busy preparing for the next day's meal right up until the moment she had to leave for the school. Mrs. Vindico was furious over the mess in the kitchen.

"Mom, I'll clean it up. She's trying to cook Thanksgiving for everyone and be the phenomenal mother and woman that she is. I'm sure she planned on cleaning it up when she's finished." Dan settled Halia in her swing and then began cleaning his mother's kitchen. He worked quickly and then gave Halia a bottle just a little early in hopes that she would sleep while Dan took her to finish his anniversary shopping for Fionna.

"We'd be happy to watch her, son." Governor Vindico sounded offended that Dan was taking Halia along.

"I know, but I want to spend a little time with her." His tone left no room for argument.

"No, now, Arthur, let Dan take her. I need your help. I've got to get a few dishes made for tomorrow as I don't have a great deal of faith that anything she's making will be edible."

"Fi is an outstanding cook. She's cooked the full Thanksgiving meal many times before. It will be delicious. You've been doing it for years. Why don't you just take the year off?" Dan hoped his mother would take the bait.

"We'll see," Mrs. Vindico sighed as she began pulling out mixing bowls, measuring cups, and prepared boxed mixes for macaroni and cheese and mashed potatoes. Dan shuddered as he made certain Halia was bundled up in her hat and blankets and then headed to the car.

He went by the jewelry store and waited as they attached the birthstone charm he needed. Then he arrived home just a few minutes after Fionna and Aida.

"Halia, look!" Aida was ecstatic as she laid a similarly sized and shaped bunny as Davi in Halia's car seat on top of her leg. Dan and Fionna beamed over her exuberance.

Governor Vindico entered the room. "Dan." He sounded devastated. Dan raised his eyebrows to his father, but his face fell as he took in the governor's deeply troubled scowl. "Could you come up here for a moment please, son?"

"Sure." Dan left Fionna with the girls and followed his father back to his office.

"What's wrong?"

"I just had a chance to look at the papers, but you need to see this." He spun a copy of *The Realm Times* for Dan to see.

His eyes goggled as he took in a large photo of him and Fionna exiting Guinevere's the day before. That wasn't the worst part by a long shot. The paper stated that a source close to the Vindicos, who happened to be with them in the store, gave a full interview on the things they'd purchased.

"I knew she was going to do something." Dan read that according to the source, the Vindicos had purchased numerous items used in light forms of S&M including tie-ups, handcuffs, whips, and paddles. She'd also informed the papers that Dan seemed rather abusive and demanded that Fionna purchase outfits that he liked including a racy apron to do his bidding.

Dan tossed the paper back on his father's desk. "You know none of that is true. Katherine Bryant was in the store when I went in to buy some lingerie for Fionna. Nothing more. Our anniversary is tomorrow—dating, not marriage obviously."

"Whatever you bought is between you and Fionna, but I would like to know how you want to handle this. I'm certain most of your students have now seen it."

"Fionna's going to come unglued." Dan rubbed his temples. His blood began to boil. "I don't understand how I became such a shitty Shield in the last year. I can't seem to keep her safe anymore. It's driving me insane."

"You're an outstanding Shield, Daniel. There's just too many people that are rabid for information on the two of you. I'm sorry for the part I play in that."

"It's not your fault." Dan told the entire story from running into Mentor Bryant in the store and then figuring out what her first plan had been and how he'd thwarted it. He left out the details as to what he had purchased but explained everything else.

"A Mrs. Contessa DeRyan stated that it was store policy never to share customers' purchases, but did add that Mentor Dan Vindico was very loving and attentive to his wife and did nothing to give her the impression he was ever anything but a consummate and adoring husband." The governor read from an excerpt under the fold that most people would never see. "What do you want to do?"

Possibilities formed rapidly in Dan's mind. They could sue Katherine Bryant for invasion of privacy or libel although that would mean that they would have to prove that what she said was libelous. The lawsuit would probably shut her up for a while, but lawsuits were also an outstanding way to lose a great deal of money.

He could have Jack Stariff send her a cease and desist which seemed like an excellent first step. If she didn't keep her mouth shut, then he and Fionna would pursue legal action. Dan doubted that she planned on making more engagements with the press, however. This was a crime of opportunity, one that would probably never happen again. But a letter from the top lawyer in the American Realm would show that he meant business, and the action would most likely make it to the papers. Fionna's horrified embarrassment over the entire thing infuriated Dan more than anything else.

"I'm calling Jack. I'll have him send a cease and desist to Mentor Bryant," he strategized. "And, you know, two can play at this game. If she wants to embarrass my wife then I can fix it so every single student at Venton Academy knows what she did and what lengths she'll go to when she's gotten her feelings hurt." Dan narrowed his eyes in indignation.

"Be careful," the governor warned. "I believe you have a saying that goes something like, if you lie with dogs, you're likely to get eaten alive. If you're willing to listen to your old man for once, I'd suggest that you file a formal complaint with the school governing board. You might kill two birds with one stone. That may force them to reconsider Terry Bryant as a viable candidate for mentor," Governor Vindico suggested. "You could present your receipt to the board proving your purchases if you and Fionna would be comfortable with that. It would prove that her claims on what was purchased were false which would discredit everything else she said as well."

Dan felt violently ill. How could he have landed his wife in a situation where they were having to share yet another part of their intimacy. He shuddered slightly as he recalled the fact that half of their neighbors had already seen them in the act.

"Why don't you wait to tell Fionna? Give her a little reprieve. It looks like she'll be cooking the rest of the afternoon, and tomorrow is Thanksgiving. I doubt they'll run another article saying the same thing tomorrow so..." The governor's strategy drowned out in his own considerations.

"No." Dan shook his head. "You don't keep things from Receivers, especially one you're married to and intimate with. If she felt me keeping something from her, which she certainly would, that would only make all of this a million times worse."

The governor nodded his acceptance of what Dan was saying.

"I'm sorry I keep asking this, but would you mind watching the girls for a couple of hours," Dan asked.

"We don't mind watching the girls ever. We're their grandparents. We want to be a part of their lives. Go figure out how you want to handle this and tell Fionna how sorry I am. Stephen and I never realized that the Bryants would blame you for what happened to their marriage."

Dan's cell phone rang in his pocket.

"Are you okay?" Garrett asked. He'd obviously seen the papers.

"Not really."

"Figured that. How's Fi taking it?"

"She doesn't know yet."

"Who the hell is the source close to the Vindicos?"

"Katherine Bryant was in the store when I went in yesterday. I didn't see her until it was too late."

"Do you want me to come over? We could take her out to eat or something. She's going to freak."

"No, thanks though. I just need to get her away from everyone for a little while. I need to be a better fucking Shield."

"Dan, come on. You're the only fucking Shield strong enough to protect her powers."

"I've been doing a piss-poor job of that lately."

"You're outnumbered and without a badge. I get the feeling that the Venton disaster is bigger than anyone knows. If I can help, let me know. No one that's ever met you thinks you're abusive, and that's what's going to bother her most. Give Rainer a call. If anyone has experience with this kind of shit, it's him." Garrett reminded Dan that Rainer and Emily's honeymoon had been plastered in every Gifted newspaper, magazine, and blog all over the Realm.

"That's a good idea." He would take all of the advice he could get.

"Tell Fi I love her, and if you decide to enact some kind of revenge, call me," Garrett vowed his allegiance.

"If this had been her husband, I'd beat the shit out of him. I'm not sure what to do with her."

Garrett laughed. "You beating the shit out of someone might not make you appear non-abusive." An audible huff was Dan's only response. "Call Rainer and then take Fi out somewhere. Try to stay away from the cameras. I'll talk to Dad," Garrett instructed.

"Thanks."

Ignoring his father's quizzical gaze, Dan touched Rainer's name on his phone.

"Hey, man, I'm sorry," was Rainer's greeting.

"I was hoping you might have some idea on how I could fix this." It was distinctly odd to be asking advice from Rainer, not that he didn't respect Rainer immensely, but it was a role reversal to say the least.

"I've definitely been there. Emily cried for about seven hours straight and then off and on for most of the day. You were there. You saw her," he reminded Dan.

"Yeah, I remember. How'd you get her to stop?" Dan asked the question he really wanted an answer to.

"I was so pissed at everyone and at myself. The whole thing made me sick. I didn't feel like I deserved to be her Shield, but she's a Receiver, just like Fi. She's going to draw her reaction from you. Whatever emotion you're feeling, that's what she's going to reflect. When I eased up on myself, she got better. Then there was the whole putting it all back together deal, trying to resurrect what we both felt people had torn apart. I'm sure you'll know how to do that. You know her better than anybody."

"Yeah, I hope." He didn't like the feeling of his confidence draining in light of someone attacking his marriage.

"Is there anywhere you could go talk? Some place she feels safe and that means something to you two."

Dan let their past whirl through his mind. It wasn't the first time he'd lamented the fact that he and Fionna had started as a one-night stand, and when they'd promptly realized that they were meant to be, Dan hadn't been able to take her out anywhere as he was constantly afraid that if Wretchkinsides found out about Fionna, he would hunt her down and kill her as well.

A thought occurred to Dan, but it didn't seem enough to heal the damage that had been inflicted.

"I'll think of something," he replied.

"Good luck, and tell her Emily definitely understands. If you want to come over here, you're welcome," he offered.

"I think she's going to want to hide away for a while."

"We did a good bit of that. I'm pretty sure the Uber Eats guy and the pizza dude were the only people who knew where we were for a solid week." Rainer chuckled. "Cold pizza and kung pao chicken are an interesting breakfast combo," he added hoping to cheer Dan up. He chuckled though he didn't feel much like laughing.

"You know she's already picked up on something, but she's afraid to interrupt." Dan was certain that Rainer, more than anyone else, knew what being married to a powerful Receiver was like.

"I'm sure. Let me know if we can do anything."

"Thanks. We'll see you Friday."

"What are you going to do?" Governor Vindico asked as soon as Dan stowed the phone back in his pocket.

"I'm going to take care of my wife and of my marriage, and I have learned a few things over the last year so I'm going to prove that to her. I'm going to talk with her and listen to her and let her decide how she wants to handle this."

"Let me know what you decide. Bryant can be brought in for reprimand Monday morning if you alert the academy governing board by Friday."

"Let me talk to Fi."

CHAPTER 41
FAMOUS

When they arrived in the kitchen, Aida was helping Fionna make pumpkin pies, but Fionna was distracted. Worry shadowed her features.

"Hey, baby, will you go out with me for just a little while?"

"Just one sec." Fionna wiped her hands on her apron and pulled two skillets of cornbread from the oven cooked to a perfect golden brown.

Halia was asleep in her swing, and Aida knew something was wrong as well.

"I want to go too," she whispered. Dan kissed her cheek.

"We'll be back in just a little while."

Governor Vindico came to Dan's rescue. "You come play checkers with Grandpa, Aida."

"Where's Mom?" Dan asked.

"She's...lying down." The governor bristled. Clearly, Mrs. Vindico had already seen the article and was in her room freaking out over what the Realm might think of either Dan being an abusive husband or that he and Fionna were much kinkier than they actually were.

Fionna whipped off her apron. "I just fed Halia, so she'll probably sleep in there for a couple of hours." She gestured to the swing.

"We'll be fine, sweetheart," the governor reassured her.

"I'll finish the dressing when we get home and then maybe Dan can help me get the turkey out of the brine and then help me finish up."

"Of course." Dan nodded. "I'll stay up all night with you if you need me to. Let's just go though, okay?" His urgency frightened her. She already knew something was wrong, and his desperation to fix it spiked panic into her rhythms.

Dan revved the engine on the Ferrari. The raw power coursed through his veins and soothed a little of his fury and spite.

"What happened? What did your dad tell you? Tell me," Fionna demanded.

"I'll tell you. I promise, but not in the car," he soothed. "Do you want go home for a little while? I'll get takeout from Cheng's."

"*Can* we go home?"

Dan saw the desperation in her eyes. She'd wanted to go home from the moment they'd arrived at his parents', and he wanted to hold her and cradle her. He longed to stand between her and the world while he explained what had happened.

"I'll make sure no one knows we're there," Dan assured her as he picked up speed and phoned in their usual order from Cheng's. He rushed in the restaurant and returned with their dinner. *If I didn't have to break her heart by telling her what that bitch did, this would be a really nice way to spend the evening.*

He searched for anyone lurking around as he drove down their street. The weather had cleared up, and all of the rain and humidity had the temperature much warmer than the typical Virginia November, but no one was outside playing or enjoying the afternoon. The street appeared deserted just as Dan had been hoping.

He summoned and raised the garage door. Sliding the Ferrari into place, he lowered it back. No one needed to know where they were. He wanted to hide her away, let her cry and fume and scream, if she wanted, and he would never allow anyone to see her like that. Just like when she was under him, vulnerable and exposed. He would be her Shield even if he'd done a terrible job of that the past week. He would keep her safe. He would make this right.

She drew a deep, restorative breath, and the beginnings of a smile formed on her beautiful lips as they stepped inside. He set the food on the kitchen counter and lit the fireplace. He heat casted several of Fionna's favorite quilts while she ran upstairs to put on sweats.

After lighting several of the candles in the living room that she loved, Dan followed her upstairs to their bedroom. He changed into sweatpants and an Angels T-shirt then guided her back down the steps. He'd heat casted the pipes and most of the house before they'd left so it wasn't freezing, but the fire was soothing.

He decided not to chance lighting any of the lamps. He didn't want to alert anyone to the fact that there was anyone in the house or make anyone question how they had electricity when no one else did.

Fionna grabbed forks from the kitchen while Dan unpacked the food and chill casted two of the Dr Peppers from the non-functioning refrigerator. "Before you tell me what happened, can I have like two minutes to be here and not have to feel anyone's emotions but yours?"

"Of course." Dan set a shield cast on the doors. No one was going to intrude. He'd take nothing for granted. He would prove to her that he would be better. They settled on the couch and began eating. She visibly reveled in being in her space.

"Okay, now, what happened?" she asked begrudgingly several minutes later.

"Katherine Bryant struck, and I am so sorry. We'll handle this however you want, okay?"

Fionna sat down her box of shrimp chow mein. Dan reached in his laptop bag that he'd shoved the paper in before they'd left his parents', unfolded it, and handed it to Fionna. He braced, not certain what might be coming.

Her eyes goggled as she vibrated in her fury. "Is this some kind of joke? Who would believe this?" she demanded. "Why would she do this? It's completely untrue. Why does she hate us so much? It isn't our fault she had an affair," she continued to shout. Suddenly, her fury erupted into tears. Dan pulled her to him, holding her tightly to his chest.

But a few minutes later, she shocked him. "You know what? No." She shook her head and wiped away her tears. "I refuse. I won't do this."

"You won't do what, baby?"

"I will not shed anymore tears over that woman. This is insane." She flung the paper off the couch. "If I want you to tie me up, then that's okay. If I don't want that, that is also okay, but it is no one else's business what we do or what we buy. I am so sick of being on the front page because people want to make up lies about us, because they think they have a right to know things about us." Her jaw clenched, and she narrowed her eyes. "But I will not have anyone saying that you are abusive. That isn't fair to all of the women in the world who do have abusive spouses. It's just like you said—she has nothing left to lose, so now she's going to make our lives miserable because she's jealous. How do we make her stop?"

That wasn't at all what Dan had been expecting. He'd braced for tears and fury not logic and control. "You're so fucking amazing," he vowed.

"I am not amazing. I am furious."

"You're handling it better than I did."

Fionna shook her head. "She's so hurt and broken that she's bleeding all over everyone else. I almost feel sorry for her, but I will not have anyone saying that you're abusive. Can't we sue the paper or something?"

"We can if you want, but libel cases take a while to get through the courts. The papers fight to keep it from coming to trial endlessly because the longer they drag it out and talk about it, the more money they make. I'd like to be living in Kauai before it would ever come to trial. Do you want to bring all of this with us?"

"No, but I also don't want anyone knowing anything about any part of our intimate lives. That's for us. I'm so tired of people thinking they have a right to know whatever they want to know about us. Why won't everyone just leave us alone?"

Regret stabbed through Dan. "I've been the governor's son for most of my life. You were one of the most famous Arlington Angels ever to challenge. I've tried so hard to carve out a life for us away from the cameras, but somehow, we keep getting thrust back in front of them. I don't know how to stop it. I can't even keep my mother from going through your stuff. I'm so fucking sorry."

"I don't think we can stop it. I really want to hate Mentor Bryant, and I've never hated anyone," Fionna fumed. "But I do hate this town, and I want to go home."

"I'm trying to get you there as fast as I can." No one would blame her for seeing the dramatic difference in the harsh intrusions that DC brought them constantly compared to the idyllic peace and privacy they had on the farm. "If you want me to quit now and we move into one of the guesthouses, I will, but there will be problems there as well. We'll still be the governor's son and the famous Arlington Angel."

"I know, and those are important aspects of our lives. I don't want to erase them. I just wish those titles didn't make people believe that they have a right to our private lives."

"Then why don't we talk about how we want to handle this?"

"I want to strangle her, and I am very anti-violence." With a stubborn huff, Fionna retrieved her food and then wiggled closer to Dan. He seated her between his outstretched legs and swathed them in the quilts in the serenity of their home. "What can we do?"

"We can take the high road and pretend it didn't bother us or that we didn't even see it. We could not give her the attention she's wanting, or I can call Jack Stariff right now and have a particularly nasty cease and desist letter sent to her. You know, something like, if you don't stop wrongfully attacking my clients, the Vindicos, they will sue you, seek fines and imprisonment on the grounds of libel, sue for invasion of privacy, have your car impounded on a daily basis, and send their newborn daughter's full diaper disposal bags to your office at Venton Academy, etc. etc."

Fionna's giggle soothed his soul, but she was still devastated. She was trying to be brave and quell her anger. Her fear and embarrassment had Dan longing to do anything to make this better.

"I can file a formal personal complaint with the Venton governors. She would be brought up for reprimand, but if I do that, I will probably have to provide the receipt of what I purchased to prove that she lied, since there was a picture of us leaving the store."

"Dan," Fionna choked, and he stopped talking abruptly. "Why did you go in there? Did you really remember tomorrow?"

"Did you think I'd forgotten? Last year, you changed my whole world all for the better. You saved my life. I would never forget that date, but it did sneak up on me with everything we've had going on. I wanted to spoil you a little. I wanted to go out and get a few things I hoped you'd love and that we could share together, because as long as you know how much I love you, I really don't give a damn what the Realm thinks."

Fionna tucked her head under Dan's chin.

"I love you too much to let people think you're abusive. That was awful." This time the tears became her victor. Wrapping her up in his protective embrace, he didn't need to eat. He just needed her to be all right.

"Okay." He rocked her softly as his shield surrounded them. "We can try talking to her in front of witnesses. I can see how far we get, or we can take this to the school governors. It was a spiteful, bitchy thing to do, and calling me abusive is libel, plain and simple."

"But if you file a formal complaint, we have to tell them what you bought me?"

"It's the easiest way to discredit everything she said. It's the paper trail."

"I don't want anyone else to know that. That's for me and you and no one else, just like you said. I'm so tired of people taking pieces of us away."

"I know, but only the school governors would see the receipt, and it would prove beyond a shadow of a doubt that she was lying, at least about what she said we purchased, which would cast doubt on everything she said and did. On the other hand..." Dan hesitated. "I can't promise you that calling her hand on it will make her stop. We may only be feeding the fury and the jealousy she has.

"If I've learned anything, it's that the right thing or the most logical thing may not always be the best thing. Vengeance is a dangerous game, trust me. I played it for a decade. So, I want to sit here and hold you and talk about this until we really know where we're heading from here. I don't want to do anything else that might hurt you or get you thrown in the middle of all of the animosity that seems to come with every freaking job I take."

"Do you think this could affect your new job?"

It touched the deepest wells of Dan's weary heart that she wanted him to have the job he so desperately wanted, and she was afraid something might stop him from achieving their plans.

"I don't think so, sweetheart. It's pretty rare that news from DC makes it to Lihue, but that would be another reason to fight this and clear my name."

Dan let his mind work in reverse. He went over everything Rainer and Emily had done to fight the gross injustice against them. Rainer was never working for monetary gain or to own an island. He'd worked to show the world that he wouldn't allow them to rob Emily of her privacy and of the things shared between them. He couldn't take away what everyone had seen photographic evidence of, but he made a statement to the world that he wouldn't allow his marriage or his wife to be ridiculed and mocked or taken advantage of. "I think we should call Jack."

Fionna looked relieved that he didn't want to take the high road any more than she did. He pulled his phone from his pocket. Jack answered on the second ring. Dan casted his cell phone so that Fionna could hear the entire conversation.

"I was hoping either you or your lovely wife would be calling me, although I'd love to hear from you even when we're not about to go to war."

Dan wondered if he should have called Jack more often since he'd left the Senate. He and Dan had certainly worked together quite a bit as he was the top Senate prosecuting attorney.

"You've got both of us, and I'm sorry I haven't called."

Jack chuckled. "Never apologize. I taught you better than that."

"I went into the store to purchase lingerie for my wife. I never dreamed it would lead to so much trouble."

"No good deed goes unpunished," Jack chided. "Now are we fighting the whole yarn or just the part about your being abusive?"

Dan raised his eyebrows to Fionna. "I don't want to make people think that if they're into that, that we think it's bad, but that isn't what he bought." Fionna sounded somewhat confused. "I want people to just let us live our lives. I want to stop being so interesting to everyone that when they don't get a story, they make one up."

"That's a steep order, Fionna. I'm sorry to say, but it's the truth."

Dan stepped in. "At the very least, I want Katherine Bryant to stay the hell out of my business and away from my girls. She was in the store when I went in, and she took the opportunity to become the source close to the Vindicos. She blames me for outing her and for getting Wilshire ousted. Is there any way we can accomplish those things?"

"Blaming you is vastly more appealing than looking in the mirror, I'd say. I can get a cease and desist out and have Portwood draw up a restraining order tonight if you want. That would keep her away from Fionna and your daughters, but if Fi or the girls are up at Venton, that could get tricky." Jack began listing out their options. "The cease and desist will enumerate your plans to proceed with a lawsuit if she decides she'd like to become a source close to the Vindicos again."

"Dad wants me to file a formal complaint with the Venton governors. He's trying to keep her husband from gaining employment there, but that may only piss them off more," Dan lamented. "But there is another possible complication."

"What's that?"

"I was hoping not to spread this around just yet, but I was offered a position to become the Sheriff of Kauai Iodex. I'm to report in June. We're building on Fi's family farm there, but I really don't want to go into that job with suspicion that I'm some kind of abusive douche that should really just be beaten with the rock any guy that would hit his wife lives under."

"Anyone who's ever met you or been in the same room with you and Fionna knows that you're not a rock-dwelling douchebag, but let's go ahead and see if we can't clear your name. File the complaint and request the reprimand. I'll represent you. If the two of us can't scare her enough to get her to lay off, then this isn't going to end well for her."

"Okay, and go ahead with the cease and desist and the restraining order. Fionna doesn't need to be up at Venton anytime soon, not if it leads to this kind of crap."

"You got it. I'll get it over there tonight. She can chew on that along with her turkey and a healthy side of bitter regret tomorrow," Jack sighed.

Truthfully, Dan thought that was a little low, but he didn't comment. There was a reason Jack Stariff was a cutthroat lawyer. One didn't earn the title by being nice.

"Fionna, I'm sorry for all of this, sweetheart. We'll get it taken care of. You just take care of you and those beautiful girls," Jack soothed kindly.

"Thanks, Jack." Fionna did sound more confident. She seemed to revel in the fact that people who knew Dan knew he was not abusive and were more than willing to help them.

"Stephen mentioned that your family was going to the farm for football Friday. I'll be stopping by. I make an appearance every year for Lillian's pecan pie and that whiskey cream sauce she makes. We can go over the formal complaint Friday if that works for you."

"That's perfect, and you can see my girls." Dan remembered that Jack had never seen Halia.

"If they're half as sweet as their mama, you're going to be beating boys back with a bat, Daniel, so watch out."

"Don't I know it."

Fionna blushed but seemed very pleased with the assessment.

"Hey, congrats on your new position. I never really saw you as much of a mentor, truthfully."

"I wish somebody had told me."

"We had to let you figure that out on your own. I usually golf for a couple of weeks each spring at the Prince Club in Waikiki. I did some work for Arnold decades ago. We still keep in touch, so if I catch a commuter, I'd love to see you when I'm on the islands," Jack urged hopefully.

"That'd be great," Dan assured him. "Just let us know when you're flying in." He was genuinely thrilled that people that meant a great deal to him seemed more than willing to visit his family in Hawaii.

"I'll see you Friday. Kiss all your girls for me."

"Will do. Thanks, Jack."

CHAPTER 42

RESTORATION

Dan tossed his cell onto the couch and wrapped his arms around his wife. He gently kissed her cheek. "That was from Jack," he informed her. "And this is from me." Dan guided her face tenderly to his own and brushed his lips across hers. He felt the customary spark, his life's pulse, there in the delicate kiss.

"I want more from you," she whispered, and with a reverent groan Dan leaned and devoured her mouth.

They broke apart after several long moments both panting for breath, and Dan debated. He longed to strip her down and lay her out on the couch, cover her with the warmed blankets and then with him, and wrap her up in the heat they created together. But he doubted she felt like being exposed even to him at that point.

"Hey, baby doll," he whispered as she wound her body around his and tucked her face in his neck. She wanted to hide away just as Dan had suspected.

"How about we go for a ride just the two of us? Get away from all of this for a little while."

He saw the intrigue spark the wildfire in her eyes. His heart thundered in his chest.

"Where are we going?"

"Nowhere, everywhere. I just want to be all alone with you for a little while. No one knowing where we are," he explained his plan for the next hour or so.

"I still have to cook everything."

"I'll help you do anything you want when we get back. Just come with me for a little while, please."

Her sweet smile had him reeling as she nodded.

"Go put some jeans on for me, baby," Dan instructed. He swatted her backside as she headed toward the stairs.

"I just told Jack we weren't into that," she teased and then giggled at her own joke.

"Yeah, well, Jack and an entire Gifted army couldn't get me to keep my hands off your sexy ass."

They changed into jeans, and Dan wrapped his riding jacket around Fionna. It was rather large on her. She wrinkled her nose and moved to the closet after handing the jacket back to Dan. She emerged with a leather jacket Dan had never seen her in before. It was a smooth white leather with a slight fur collar. It clung at the waist, and she couldn't quite zip it up over her cleavage. Dan gave a shuddering growl. She looked phenomenal.

"Why haven't I seen this before?"

She grinned. "I used to wear it all the time. I kind of forgot I had it and then I was full of Halia so I couldn't wear it." She pointed out that for most of their relationship she'd been pregnant.

"You look so damn sexy. I hope you don't mind me pulling off on a trail somewhere and taking a little break from the drive."

Dan shrugged into his riding jacket and led her to the garage. Praying no one was around, he summoned the door open and handed her the helmet he'd bought for her.

"It's been a long time."

Dan nodded as he threw his leg over the bike. "Hold on tight, baby doll."

"When we move back to Kauai, will you take me out on it in, like, some cutoffs and a bikini top?" she teased him.

Dan revved the motor and made her laugh. "No," he called over the metallic thrum. She laughed as he backed the motorcycle out of the garage and closed the door quickly. He let the image of her on the Agusta in a string bikini and cutoff shorts with her arms wrapped around his chest play out in his mind as he let the vibrations of the bike surge through his soul. He'd never let her ride that way. That was too dangerous, but it made for a hell of a fantasy.

A moment later, they were flying. Her body pressed to his back. Her hands circled tight around his chest as he took her away from all of the stress and turmoil.

It *had* been a long time. Dan picked up speed on a deserted road. Fionna had ridden with him a handful of times before she'd gotten pregnant. They'd agreed that she was not to ride on the Agusta while carrying their child, so it had set idle in their garage for long periods of time.

A half hour later, Dan pulled into Great Falls Park. He slowed as he took the winding lanes through the park. The ground was covered with wet leaves, and the park was empty in the late fall. He felt Fionna squeeze her arms around him tighter. Smiling against his helmet, Dan picked up pace until he located a hideaway tucked in an outcropping of trees inaccessible by car.

Shutting the Agusta down, Dan slid from the seat in a rather smooth glide and then turned and re-straddled. This time he faced his wife who was pulling off her helmet. Dan hung the helmets on his handlebars and gazed at Fionna.

"I've never parked on a motorcycle." Timid hunger burned in her eyes. She was wary. The world had taken away so many pieces of her, of them, and her soul was wounded. Dan wouldn't and couldn't allow that.

"It's way better than in a car," he informed her.

"Why is that?"

"I already have your legs spread, baby doll." Dan gave her a cocky grin as he leaned and caught the back of her neck with one hand and angled her head in for a kiss. He lowered the zipper on her jacket with the other. A moment later, he was cupping her breasts with his right hand, plying them gently with his fingers. A furtive, rapacious moan spilled from her mouth into his, and Dan pulled her closer.

"What if someone sees us?" choked from her.

"No one knows where we are. I promise I will never let anyone else make you feel like you're on display. I swear to you. I'll do better."

Dan worked his lips to her ear and brushed her hair behind her back.

"I want you to grab me, baby," he commanded.

"Oh, yes," Fionna gasped as she ran her palm over his strain then spun her index finger lower, teasing his sack. A thundering groan echoed from him as she continued to grope. "No one else will ever know, baby doll," he vowed. "No one will ever know how hard I get for you, how bad I ache, and how you're the only thing that makes it better. You're the only cure. Only I and only you will ever know," he growled in her ear as she began to writhe on the bike.

"No one knows how you drip for me," he continued his reassurances. She shuddered against him, gasping for breath that seemed to elude her. Their passion, their love, the nuances of them together belonged to no one else no matter how intrusive the world might be, and he would prove that to her. He jerked the zipper of her jacket farther down.

"No one will ever know what we have. How you tremble and swell when I pound into you and how damn good that feels. Those sweet sounds you make for me when I bring you," he vowed in reverence. "How tight you are. How bad I crave you. No matter how much this world wants to take from us, they'll never know."

A quaking, convulsive groan poured from her lungs as she lowered the zipper on his jeans and sought his strain.

"That's it, baby doll. Grab me. Feel me throb for you," he commanded. "All for you, all for that sweet wet hole that belongs to me," he continued his needy promises. "And for that hungry mouth. My god, when you suck me it's like heaven and hell all tied up in your perfection. It feels so fucking good, but it makes me so damn greedy for your tight little pussy I lose all restraint.

"No one will ever know the things I know. You're so fucking sexy. You drive me wild. Nobody knows what a good girl you'll be for me. Nobody knows where I mark you, sweetheart. No one knows how hard I claim you, and no one ever will."

"I need you," she finally pled in desperation, and Dan knew he was getting through.

"What do you need, baby doll?" He jerked her into him with force. Sucking her neck, he left a faint hickey. "You want me to take it away. Want me to fill you full and make it feel better?"

"Yes, now, I want you. I just don't want to think anymore. Just take me," she begged in heated need.

"Not here, baby doll." Dan hoped he wasn't being mean. "I'm going to take you back home, then you're gonna ride me. Then we'll go back to all of the other bullshit going on."

"Now," she ordered.

"Yes, ma'am." Dan quickly reversed his seating, zipped his zipper, and kicked the Agusta to life.

Staying on the straightaways this time, Dan summoned and casted the bike so they were home in under ten minutes.

It seemed unlikely that the lights would suddenly come on in the house again, but he wasn't taking any chances anymore. He led her to their bedroom. She shimmied out of her jeans and the G-string underneath.

Dan lifted her to their bed and pulled off the jacket and shirt she was wearing. He jerked her bra away from her and gazed at her, naked and luscious, dripping wet, and fevered hot for him.

"So damn gorgeous," he growled as he stripped as well. "I can't decide if I want to eat you out or fuck you hard, baby doll."

She writhed and whimpered.

"Both." He jerked her legs apart and pulled her ass to the edge of the mattress, as he fell to his knees.

"Yes," she groaned in quaking, all-encompassing desire.

"No one will ever see this," he vowed in awe as he stared at the pulsing pink perfection of her. He spun his tongue just inside her lips, lapping it around the entrance to what Dan was certain was heaven. "My good girl likes this, and only I know that." Dan traced the tip of his tongue in tiny circles around her clit, and she went wild. He moaned against her, lapping at it and then leaning and sucking her fervently. She came undone as she let him take everything else away. No one had any idea where they were or what they were doing.

"I'm not finished, baby. I'm still hungry," he demanded as her body bucked and rolled under his greedy touch. "All mine," he commanded as he tugged her right lip tenderly with his teeth and her energy tensed on the verge of climax again. He released her lip and moved to the tender spot between it and her leg. "And my baby loves this," he growled. "So fucking sexy when you wear my mark." He sucked her hard and left his brand of ownership.

She came undone again, and her energy filled his mouth.

Dan fell to the bed beside her.

"Mount me," he ordered, unable to wait any longer. She climbed over him, straddling herself over his straining need.

Dan wrapped his hands around her waist and bucked upwards as he pulled her over his strain.

He growled in fiery passion as her body consumed his.

"Ride me, baby doll. Hard like my good girl," he ordered, and she began grinding her body against his rhythmically.

Dan's eyes rolled back in his head from the exquisite feeling. He held her body to his strain, forcing himself in deep, and she released again. It had been too long, and she'd burdened enough stress lately. She'd needed release for some time it seemed, and he planned on taking excellent care of her.

"Such a good girl. They just keep coming, don't they, baby doll. You want some more. I've got all you need." She threw her body back. She was flushed and glistening from the effort of her ride.

"Now, I'm gonna take care of you." He grasped her waist and flipped her underneath him. He kept himself buried deep inside of her perfection. "Just lie there and take it like my good girl." He spread her legs wide with his hands and pounded into her.

"Oh, god, yes." Her wild moans nearly drove him over as he watched her hair splay across the sheets and her head jerk back and forth from the heavenly sensations he brought her.

"I'm gonna," she gasped.

"I know, sweetheart. I feel it. Let it build for me," he assured her as he closed his eyes and willed his body not to give it up yet. She was astounding. Her body's responses to him were all consuming, and he longed to fill her full of his energy, full of his release.

Her back arched. Her energy peaked, and her temperature shot upward. "Sweet little pussy milking my cock. I'm gonna fill you full."

With one final ragged plunge, Dan exploded inside of her, thankful that his release had pushed her over.

He collapsed on their bed beside her. He was struck for a moment as the erotic haze cleared from his mind by how much he missed being in their bed naked with her.

Dan pulled her to his chest and cradled her in the serenity of their bed in their home where they so desperately wanted to be.

"So, there was some shit going on, but I can't seem to remember what," Dan teased and reveled in her giggle.

"We're gonna fight this and make her say she was lying, right?" Fionna demanded.

"We'll try, but like I said, all that matters to me is that you know and our girls know how much I love you." Their erotic energy spiraled and dissipated around them.

After a few bliss-filled minutes, Fionna sighed. "We should probably go get our little girls."

"I've got my girl right here, and our little ones will be just fine for a few more minutes." Dan was certain the girls were being well taken care of. He may not get along with his mother, but she was an excellent caretaker as was his father.

"I still can't believe someone would be so spiteful and vindictive," she lamented. Dan hated that she was still so worried after everything they'd shared.

"We're going to take care of this." Dan wanted to get her mind off Katherine Bryant. She had no place in their bed in their sanctuary. The thought made Dan feel vile.

"I'm all right until somebody attacks you, and then I kind of want to be mean," Fionna admitted.

Dan kissed the top of her head. "I appreciate that, but I feel like I'm the one that's let you down over and over again this week." He watched the sparkle in her eyes dance from being in his arms. Her cheeks glowed pink, and her beautiful curves were swollen and swathed loosely in the sheets and around his body.

"I love you, and I'm the luckiest guy in the Realm. I don't think I'll ever be able to show you what you mean to me."

"You show me in a thousand little ways every single day." She lost all sense of teasing. "When you hold me either because something upset me or frightened me, or just because you want to be near me, when you get up at night with Halia and try to keep her quiet so I can sleep, when you read Aida a story, when you bring me my coffee in bed so I can be lazy, or just lie in bed with me so we can just be together, and you're moving our whole family five thousand miles away so I can be home. You show me constantly."

"Good. I want to show you constantly."

Fionna brushed a sweet kiss on his cheek before settling back onto his chest. "When do I get to see this lingerie that's caused such an uproar?"

Dan sighed over the entire debacle. He eased his hands up and down her back. "Tomorrow."

"I got you something, but it's just kind of little," Fionna admitted sheepishly as she wrinkled her nose.

"You gave me you and then on top of that hunk of perfection you gave me two beautiful daughters, and there is nothing else I'll ever need."

"We better go see our beautiful daughters," she insisted.

Begrudgingly, Dan handed his wife her clothes. He took a long moment to gaze at her naked, sitting in the bed with her cheeks flushed and her lips still swollen from his hungry kisses.

"What?" An abashed grin formed on her face.

"You're beautiful. You take my breath away."

"Stop. You're gonna make me cry."

Garrett Haydenshire

Garrett grimaced when his phone rang in his pocket. He was sure it was Fionna, and it killed him that he didn't have a good way to fix this insanity for her.

As he stared at the screen, concern replaced his disappointment. It was Connor. His little brother only called when something serious was on his mind.

"Hey, is everything all right?" Garrett asked.

"Uh…yeah…I think so."

"Doesn't sound like you're too sure of that. What's going on?"

"I…uh…I was thinking…maybe…that I might…uh…bring someone for Thanksgiving dinner tomorrow night. And also maybe to the food bank with us, but probably not," he rushed out the last few words like ripping off a bandage.

Garrett considered his response carefully. "If I ask you something about whoever you're bringing, will you tell me the truth?"

"I guess so."

"Is this someone you've convinced yourself *we'll* like, or is this someone you actually like?"

The silence took on its own pulse, but Garrett refused to speak. Connor needed time to work through this, and Garrett would be there every step of the way.

"Someone I like," Conner finally admitted in a hard choke. "His name is Reid."

Relief washed through Garrett's shield. "Good. I can't wait to meet him."

"Yeah, about that. I was kind of wondering if maybe you'd like to meet him tonight, just you know, maybe like break him into the family a little at a time or something."

"Have you introduced him to anyone else already?"

"No."

Garrett was supremely touched. He grinned and checked his watch. "I'd love to. Are you thinking my apartment, Lesco's, or something a little farther away from our familial entourage?"

"Farther away."

"Got it. How about 2Fifty in Riverdale Park?"

A relieved breath left Connor's lungs. "Yeah, that's a good idea. Maybe Levi could come too. You know two of all of us before *all* the all of us. Levi will be cool."

"Everyone is going to be cool. I promise. I'll call Levi and we'll meet you there. An hour good?"

"Yeah. And Garrett…"

Garrett waited. He knew what was coming.

"Thanks."

"You're my little brother. All I want is for you to be happy." He hoped that Connor would grasp that no one in their family was going to be thrown by this. The Realm might be another matter entirely though, and Garrett knew that was where the apprehension was really coming from. That's why he wasn't sure he wanted Reid to come to the food bank. The press always made a show.

"We'll see you there," he assured Connor. He ended that call and touched Levi's name on his contact list.

"What?" Levi half-snarled.

"Damn. What is wrong with you?"

"Nothing."

"You remember that I'm a detective, right? What's wrong?"

An exhausted and audible breath left Levi's lungs. "Uh…found out a few weeks ago that Sarah was cheating on me." Devastation shattered the words. "Apparently the press just found out as well."

Garrett's eyes closed in defeat. "I'm sorry, man. Anything I can do to help? Want me to fix it so her and whoever her boy toy is they get a parking ticket every single time they open their car door?"

Levi forced a chuckle. "No, but thanks for offering." He paused for a beat. "Can I ask you something?"

"When have you ever not been able to ask me something?"

"I think I might've met someone…else. I mean…someone who isn't Sarah. I mean I definitely met someone who isn't Sarah. She's…"

"Not Sarah," Garrett offered since he seemed stuck in his explanation.

"Yeah." Relief flooded through the single word, and Garrett understood more. He'd long suspected that Levi was with Sarah because he thought she was the kind of woman he *should* be with, not one he actually liked. "She's better. Way, way better. But…uh…she's Non-Gifted. Her name is Olivia."

Garrett nodded. "Have you told her about us?"

"Kind of."

"Kind of?"

"I'm sort of doing it slowly. Letting her ask questions. Stuff like that."

"All right, would you and Olivia like to come meet me and Connor at 2Fifty. He's got someone he wants me and you to meet before he introduces him to the family tomorrow."

"Him? Did you say him?" Levi sounded as ecstatic as Garrett felt.

"His name is Reid."

"I'll be there, but I'm not quite ready to drag Olivia into the drama that comes with being the Crown's kids just yet. Plus, I want this to be about Connor and Reid. Like I said, the press just broke the Sarah story. I don't want them showing up and making this any harder on Connor. I'll sneak out without them seeing me. It's not about me. This is huge. What time?"

"I'm heading out now."

"I'll be there." He chuckled. "I'm so fucking proud of him."

"You and me both, bro. But listen to me, I still want to hear more about Olivia. Whenever you *are* ready to introduce her to the Crown's kids, I'll be there."

"I might bring invite her to dinner tomorrow. I'm a little worried that Abby will try to push energy onto her though."

Garrett chuckled. "I'll try to delicately explain what she's doing, or we can just let Emily hold her. She's her favorite anyway."

CHAPTER 43

THE RECEIVER AND THE ENFORCER

~DAN VINDICO~

They slid into Dan's parents' home and overheard an argument.

"Good grief, Marion." The governor stomped toward the living room. He halted abruptly as he almost walked into Dan. "You're back," he announced. "I just put Aida to bed. She fell asleep while I read to her, and Halia's in her bassinet. Your mother fed and bathed her."

"Thank you." Fionna forced a slight smile. Her energy was fraught with terror over the emotions spinning in the house from the fight. Dan doubted very seriously that Aida was asleep unless the fight had begun once she was completely out.

"Is everything all right?" Dan laced Fionna's fingers in his own, letting her draw from him. Her rhythms continued to tense.

"What did you two decide to do about the article?" was the governor's response.

"I'm going to file a formal complaint, and I want a disciplinary trial which is only going to piss her off more," Dan sighed. "We talked to Jack. He's sending a cease and desist and having Landon draw up a restraining order."

"That's good." The governor's mood seemed to improve. "I hope the Venton board will see what kind of a rat's nest they'd be getting into if they hire Terry Bryant. They're both insane. I swear."

"Jack's going to represent us in the hearing, so I'll need to let him know the time." Dan studied his father, searching for clues as to what they were arguing about.

"I plan to set it during your off period on Monday morning." Dan nodded, but his eyes shifted to his mother. She was stomping toward them. He recognized the obstinate defiance in her rhythms. He edged in front of Fionna. His shield pulsed in warning.

"Dan, Fionna, I would like to have a discussion with you in here." She stabbed her fingers toward the living room.

Dan rolled his eyes. He'd been lectured in the living room of his parents' home for most of his life. He wasn't able to recall being on the receiving end of one of his mother's tyrannical lectures that hadn't ended in a screaming match and then with him bolting and slamming the door behind him.

"I'd tread carefully if I were you," he threatened both of his parents. He would leave. He would not allow his mother to attack Fionna. He would jerk his girls up out of bed and have them on Haydenshire Farm in a heartbeat. His father seemed aware of this fact. His mother didn't appear to have even heard him.

"Dan." Fionna shook her head, and she willed calm through his hand. This would certainly be interesting. His mother was a rather strong Vis Virres Predilect, but she'd never gone up against the strongest Receiver of their time. Fionna didn't argue. She remained dignified and calm. Her strength was in her resolve and in her grace and dignity.

She would allow Mrs. Vindico to spew her insanities out like an overgrown child and then she would come in and make her points calmly and rationally. You didn't have to agree with her, but you did have to listen. Dan would make certain she was heard. The fire and the water could both be all-consuming, and together they were impenetrable.

"When your son announces that they're having Thanksgiving at Stephen and Lillian's, don't come to me." The governor fell into his chair and crossed his arms.

"Fionna, dear," Mrs. Vindico sneered, and Dan narrowed his eyes. "I'm really not certain how you were raised. I understand that you did not grow up here and perhaps things weren't done properly in Hawaii." Fury flooded through Dan as his eyes flashed, but Fionna grasped his bicep and shook her head.

Dan's entire body vibrated in fierce wrath as he leveled a hate-filled glare at his mother. "I'm telling you, Mom," he warned.

"Let her finish," Fionna soothed.

"I did try to let you know that perhaps your and Daniel's excessively physical relationship was inappropriate, and I believe we saw today that I was absolutely correct," she drawled out what Dan was certain she considered a bitter triumph. "Daniel, stores like that should not even exist, and I simply cannot believe that you not only visited one but made numerous purchases judging by the size and number of bags you were carrying when you allowed yourself to be photographed exiting that kind of place." She shuddered. Dan's mouth fell open, but he was speechless for the first time in his life.

"There will always be temptations, but we do not need to give in to the temptations. There is simply no sensical reason to spend money on things like nightwear or other kinds of inappropriate things…and things like that." She stumbled over her words, apparently unable to discuss sex toys. "I did try to be more discreet by showing you articles about the kinds of things you're using and the appointments for treatments you are receiving and how dangerous they can be. Some of the things in Dan's shower are not only inappropriate, they're immoral."

The governor grimaced. He shook his head and rubbed his temples.

"Feeling and looking sensual seems to be very important to you, and I don't think that's appropriate for a married woman. Dan is your husband, and you are his wife, not his plaything. Even your underwear are lascivious in nature." She convulsed slightly. Fionna bit her lips together trying not to laugh, but Dan wanted to strangle his mother. "If I may be perfectly honest," she began again.

"When have you ever not?" Dan snarled.

"You show entirely too much skin in your low-cut tops and short skirts. Even when you were pregnant, you wore tight clothing and bikinis of all things."

"Are you finished, Mother?"

"No," Mrs. Vindico defied.

"Your father felt I should inform you of my decision first, so I am going to recommend you to an Auxiliary counselor. I feel that your marriage is unhealthy and too physical." She concluded her abject martyrdom.

Dan's eyes goggled in stunned disbelief. "Are you fucking kidding me?" he erupted.

His entire body shook in savage rage as he rose off the sofa.

"Fi, go get our stuff together and wake the girls up. We're leaving right after I tell my mother exactly where she can go when we leave."

"Maybe," Fionna stated calmly. "But there are a few things I'd like to say first."

"Fine, but let me say this. If you go to the Auxiliary department, who by the way we work for—work that makes a difference all over the world. They don't really seem to give a damn how much sex we have because you see, *Marion*," he sneered his mother's name. "Children without homes and without food… Those are things that matter. Problems that we can help solve. What my wife wears or whether or not you have an issue with our relationship is all trivial fucking nonsense that you need to get the hell over. But if you go ahead with this insanity, you won't be seeing me or my girls anymore. I'll call up Iodex in Lihue and tell them I'll be reporting in before Christmas, and you will not be welcome on the farm. Ever."

"Fionna, sweetheart, what did you want to say?" the governor soothed. Giving him a kind smile, Fionna turned her gaze on Dan's mother.

She drew a deep, steadying breath. "First of all, Mrs. Vindico, I do hate that you have concerns about me and the way that I choose to do things. But I listened to you, and now you are going to give me the same courtesy.

"Please understand that I don't like sharing these things with you. It's an invasion of my privacy and of Dan's privacy, but you already invaded that when you decided to go through my bags and Dan's shower," she reminded his mother softly. "Sometimes, when we take it upon ourselves to bulldoze our way into other people's lives, we find out things we would rather have not known. I think that's what you're experiencing now.

"But since you did go through our personal things, I think we should discuss them. I know this will be difficult for you to believe, but I am probably more upset that Katherine Bryant decided to take out her jealousy and vengeance over her own missteps on Dan than you are. But, like I said, when we bulldoze our way in or heap our troubles on others, we end up with an even bigger mess to try and clean up."

Dan bit his lips together in awe of how his wife had just drawn a parallel between the chancellor's mistress and his mother. Mrs. Vindico was being taught a lesson without her being consciously aware of it.

"But I am not upset that Dan went into Guinevere's to purchase things for me. He does that because he loves me and because I love lingerie." Her cheeks colored slightly but she pressed on. "I disagree with your statement that I shouldn't purchase things like that. He's my husband, and I want there to be more to sex than the act itself. That is our choice, and quite frankly, you don't get to have a say in it. I intend to always make our physical relationship a priority. You don't have to agree with me, but I love your son more than life itself. It's an important part of our marriage.

"I wish everyone could have it as a strong part of their marriage despite what *Women of the Realm* might say," she shot but didn't wait for rebuttal. "We didn't want to share any part of our relationship with you or with anyone else. We certainly did not want the press or the Realm to intrude. But just like the reporters, you went through our lives, involved yourself in things that should only be between Dan and me, and now you presented your opposition to things that were none of your business, but you don't want to hear our side or even our explanation even though you've forced this conversation.

"You want us to fit into a mold you've decided we should fit in, and that will never work. But I will share this with you. Dan loves me and has ultimately taught me to love myself. The person I really am." She laced her fingers back through Dan's and gazed up at him with a smile. Somehow, she was always able to see him beneath the burning fire and the volatile fury.

"And he taught me that there's nothing wrong with owning my femininity and being proud of it. He appreciates the distinctly feminine things that I love to do. He doesn't try to change me. He embraces and even enjoys the things that make me, *me*," she vowed. "I'm not ashamed of who I am. I'm not ashamed of my body even if I occasionally wish I looked a little different. But he's the one who taught me not to be ashamed, to be proud of who I am, and that I don't have to become whoever the Realm wants me to be.

"I'm not ashamed that I share a strong, intimate, physical relationship with my husband because I think that's extremely important. We do have a very healthy marriage, Mrs. Vindico, no matter how you want to see it. And I want you to know this as well—I am very hurt that you would even consider seeking counseling on our behalf simply because we don't do the things you want us to do. But if you do go on with trying to force us to look, or do, or be what you want instead of who we are, it isn't going to work.

"Please consider all of the ramifications of your actions before you act, because I have lived my entire life being told that I should fit into molds that were never made for me, being forced to look and act a certain way. I won't do it anymore. I spent most of my adulthood having people want to take me apart piece by piece and then only use the ones they approve of to build me back the way they think I should be. I will not be broken into pieces ever again. Dan loves every piece of me. I love every piece of me, and it has taken me a long, long time to do that. But I have a great deal of experience fighting against the people who want to set up rules for me that only serve themselves. It won't end well for you. You do not get to pull us apart and put us back together into a two-dimensional version that you think is acceptable to the Realm."

The governor stared his wife down and gestured to Fionna. "Keep listening, Marion. Really hear what she is saying to you."

Fionna smiled at the governor. "If you haven't heard anything else I've said, please remember that because Aida is adopted, if you go to the Auxiliary department for whatever reason involving Dan and me, that it could complicate our adoption and it will most certainly complicate our relationship with you. I don't want that, but he's a Shield. I would never ask him to not protect us because that's who he is. And just like he loves every piece of me, I love every piece of him, even the darkest places that he wishes weren't a part of him. If Dan decides that we are safer not being around you, then I will support his decision. Sometimes we want to judge a flower by a picture in a magazine"—she gestured to the stack of *Women of the Realm* magazines on the coffee table—"instead of for the beauty that it holds all unto itself. A wildflower can be just as beautiful as a rose even if it is an entirely different flower," she concluded.

"And that is what Maylea actually means to me anyway," Dan vowed. Nodding and smiling, Fionna went on.

"If Dan wants us to leave, then we're going to leave. I'm his wife, and I support his decisions because I respect him and I love him and because he respects and loves me and always, always looks out for me and my best interests. To me, those might be things that you could be thankful for in your son's relationship with his spouse instead of tearing apart the things that don't involve you and that you have no say in."

Dan squeezed Fionna's hand as he turned his glare back on his mother. "I told you on Kauai that we weren't going to be one way when we think the press is watching and one way when it's just us. We're just going to be ourselves, and you don't have to like it, but you do have to keep your mouth shut," Dan commanded. "There is nothing in the world wrong with me buying my wife lingerie. What was wrong was that someone tried to butt into our lives and use the press to their advantage. Garrett told Rainer after the insanity with his honeymoon that just because something shouldn't be photographed doesn't mean that it shouldn't happen, and I'd say that applies rather well here. Now, do you have anything else to say before I pack my family up and leave?"

"Please, don't leave," Governor Vindico pled. He looked like he was being rent in two.

"I will not have my life picked apart and my wife reprimanded. Certainly not by my own mother, and I haven't heard an apology."

"All right, fine. I certainly don't want anything to jeopardize our little Aida, so I will not say anything to the Auxiliary department, but we waited too long to have Lindley helped, and I do think your relationship is too sexually charged. I'm sorry, but that's how I feel," Mrs. Vindico pouted.

"You're not sorry at all, Mother. You're angry that she dismantled your argument piece by piece."

"Your father is a Realm Governor, and you, apparently, have just become the sheriff of an entire island. You do need to think about your reputation. Your father has certainly never purchased me lingerie. What would people say?" she shrieked in horror.

"I don't give a damn what people say. People will believe what they want to believe, so after the papers today, people will either think oh, I guess the Vindicos were shopping at Guinevere's, or they will say he's abusive and kinky, but I couldn't care less." Dan kept his tone just under shouting.

"People who know me and people who worked for me or will work for me will see who I am or already know that I love Fionna more than life itself and would never hurt her or demand anything from her at all. Don't you see, Mom? I didn't do anything wrong. There is nothing wrong with having an intimate relationship with your spouse, but people are going to talk no matter what you do, so why not live your life and let them talk?"

"Fine, it's not as if I've ever changed your mind anyway, but I disagree with your reasoning. I still feel that your relationship relies too much on the physical side. That will change over the years. What will happen then?" Mrs. Vindico challenged. Dan's brow knitted. He was impressed that his mother, in all of her convoluted ways, was actually trying to strengthen his and Fionna's relationship.

"There is a lot more to us than sex. We said it was important, not the only thing. And I'm certain that our relationship will change and grow with us. It already has as we've married and had children. I don't think anyone who's spent any time on our farm with Tutu and Papa would ever be able to argue that desire goes away as you age. So, just like they have, we both intend to keep it a vital part of our lives, but if for some unfathomable reason our entire physical relationship went away tomorrow, I would still be completely and wholeheartedly devoted to her and only her. Please stop worrying, and like Fi just said, be thankful for who she is and the way we are and the marriage we have and the good that we can do for each other and for the entire Realm."

Never liking to admit she might've been wrong, Mrs. Vindico crossed her arms and formed her face into a pout. "I do think perhaps a policy of 'if you don't want others to see it, then don't do it' is best. I believe you've seen this now."

"I don't mind people seeing me buy lingerie for my wife, and we have a right to our privacy. We don't need you trying to tell us what to do, or how to dress, or which shaving creams to buy, or how and when to have sex. So, how about if other people don't want to see it, then stop nosing into things that are between me and my wife and no one else?"

Governor Vindico shot his wife a look that said he'd tried to stop her, but she wouldn't listen.

"And you don't feel that you flaunt that aspect of your relationship even a little?" Mrs. Vindico challenged.

"Maybe." Dan shrugged. "If we do something in front of you that makes you uncomfortable in your home then please respectfully and quietly ask us to stop. Other than that, mind your own damn business."

"Fine." Mrs. Vindico marched toward Fionna. Dan's eyes narrowed. His shield tensed and sizzled in fury.

"Marion." The governor's eyes goggled. His rhythms tensed toward panic. "Whatever you're about to do, don't do it."

But she refused to listen. She jerked the collar of Fionna's sweater outward and studied her neck. She found what she was after.

"This is not the first of these that I've seen. That is entirely more information than I need," she vaulted angrily.

Fionna's hand covered the slight purple marking on her neck. Her face glowed crimson, and fury surged through Dan. He jerked Fionna's shirt out of his mother's grasp.

"Once again, you're sticking your nose places it doesn't belong. You couldn't see that. You took a guess. Now keep your hands off my wife," he roared.

"When she parades around here in nothing more than your T-shirts I didn't have to look hard to see them on her legs, Daniel," Mrs. Vindico shouted.

"I did nothing of the sort!" Fionna was in her face. "You saw my legs when I was in the bed with Halia and you came in to dust. I can feel you lying every single time you do it," she reminded Dan's mother. "And you will not stand there telling bald-faced lies about me. Do you understand what I'm saying to you? I'll take my girls and leave, and I'll make sure you never see them again."

Dan had assumed as much. Fionna might fix breakfast at home in nothing but one of Dan's shirts and a skimpy pair of panties, but she hadn't left Dan's room without being fully covered at his parents' home.

Fionna turned to Dan to explain. Fury rolled in her rhythms. "I wore one of your shirts to nap in."

"You don't have to justify wearing anything at all," Dan growled.

She shook her head. "I am once again having to share things that I shouldn't have to share. Quite frankly, I resent that, Mrs. Vindico. I wore his shirt because I like to wear them, but Halia was missing him again." Fionna turned back to Dan before continuing. "I thought smelling your cologne might help her. I was trying to soothe her until you came home so she wouldn't cry like that again because I know how guilty that makes you feel. She's felt so confused since you went back to work, and we came here. You make her feel safe. I lay on your bed and kept her on my chest, but with her on me and her blanket and the bedding on me, I got warm, so I kicked off the covers. I didn't think anyone would come in," she stammered in frustration.

"Marion, you went in Dan's room while she was sleeping?" The governor gasped.

"I didn't know she was asleep. I knocked several times, but when no one answered, I got concerned. The point is that they shouldn't have been there in the first place, and she certainly had no business being in our son's bed with so little on."

"She is my wife!" Dan thundered.

"He wasn't even here!" Governor Vindico panicked as it became more and more clear that Dan and Fionna and the girls were leaving.

"I should have expected that you would take their side as well. Whatever Daniel wants," Mrs. Vindico drawled spitefully.

"No, not whatever Daniel wants," the governor joined Dan's acrimony. "Dan didn't do anything wrong and neither did Fionna. They are adults with children of their own. This is not like when he was seventeen. She's his wife, and she may be more comfortable with things than you are, but they're right. It isn't any of our business."

The juxtaposition seemed to genuinely confuse Dan's mother.

"I would never have lain in a bed in your parents' home without being properly covered."

"Mrs. Vindico, that's the entire point of all of this," Fionna commanded everyone's attention. "Dan and I are not you. It doesn't mean one of us is right and the other is wrong. We're just different, and I am perfectly happy to try and be respectful of our differences, but I expect the same respect from you."

"And I do not think that is asking too much," Governor Vindico commanded.

"Fine, but I do not feel that your and Dan having intimate relations in my home is respectful of me any more than I feel that you sleeping in his bed with little to nothing on is respectful."

"This is insane," Dan barked. "We are leaving." He began shoving burp cloths and blankets into Halia's diaper bag.

"I do not want you to leave, Daniel. Your wife just said that she wanted to show me respect, so I thought you should know what I expect."

Dan laughed in her face derisively. "I'm sorry, Mom, but your rules are just a little more than I'm willing to follow. That should sound familiar. You are, after all, the reason I was so hell-bent on moving out of here at barely twenty years old and pressuring Amelia into moving in with me."

"Oh, so that's all my fault as well?"

"That's what I just said."

"Dan." Fionna sent her soothing cast through his forearm as she caught him in her grasp.

"So, you two will just never get along, is that it?" the governor implored. "You can't even make it through one week being in the house a few hours a day without you purposefully being intrusive, Marion, and you doing things just to spite your mother, Daniel?

"I've had enough. Marion, they are married. There is nothing wrong with them doing whatever they want to do in Dan's bedroom. I certainly haven't noticed anything at all, so I assume that what you saw, you saw at a time that you should not have been near her. And, Daniel, you aren't always easy to live with either, son. You came into this world looking for a fight.

"Before Fionna, it was Amelia constantly, before her it was special ops training, before that it was the car, or being at the Haydenshires, or the phone. My word, son, we gave you your first ten speed bike when you were eight. Your mother told you not to go past the end of the street. You went around the entire golf course, all eighteen holes, three times. All I'm asking is for you to either find a little common ground and stick to that or try, for my sake and the sake of our family, to be polite and respectful of each other's beliefs and of their privacy, Marion. You don't have to agree with each other. You just have to keep your mouths shut."

With that, Aida appeared carrying Davi and her blanket. Her chin was trembling, and tears pricked her beautiful brown eyes.

"Mommy feels sad and like when your face feels hot," she explained in a pained whisper as Dan lifted her up into his arms. Fionna moved to them. Her cheeks were, in fact, fevered from her embarrassment.

"Do you ever think, Mother? Do you ever stop and think about how you make other people feel when you butt into their lives and then try to enforce your beliefs on them?" Dan menaced.

"Mommy is the best person in the whole world, I think," Aida tried to explain to her grandmother. "Because she came to where I used to live and took care of me and taught me how to not feel so sad. And then I came to live here, and she makes the sunshine in my tummy and in Daddy's tummy and Halia's. And she makes Papa smile big like this." Aida forced a broad grin.

"And she makes Tutu laugh and Aunt Malani feels so happy when Mommy is there. And Garrett feels not so sad when he's with Mommy. And she takes care of everyone, and she doesn't get mad and yell if you do something wrong or on accident. And she plays with me and when I don't feel good she holds me and reads to me and then I feel better. And she makes 'Aida cookies' and has tea with me and she makes Daddy so happy too. He feels happy all the time if Mommy is there, but if she isn't there sometimes he feels sad and afraid. But I make him happy too. I can feel it." She sounded very pleased that she soothed her father's soul.

"You make me so happy, baby." Dan held her tightly in the safety of his powerful embrace.

"I don't want you to fight," Aida choked.

Suddenly, a tiny, frightened wail made its way down the stairs.

"I'll get her." Fionna rushed up the stairs.

"Go with Mommy. Tell her I'll be up there in just a second," Dan guided Aida.

"I'll help with Halia. She feels scared." Dan set Aida on her feet and watched her race after her mother.

"There are things that matter, Mom, and there are things that don't," Dan vowed in a choked whisper.

"I do understand that she is a wonderful woman and that she makes you happy," Mrs. Vindico decreed. "But I do not understand the way that you two choose to conduct your life. Just like I told you in Kauai, I don't understand it, and I do not agree with it. I cannot fathom how you just don't care what other people think about you and our family."

"I'm not asking you to understand it. I'm asking you to stop making judgement calls on my wife and on our life. Because when it comes right down to it, you have no say. She is everything to me. She is my other half. I cannot fathom life without her, and I am happier than I have ever been. Why can't you just be happy for me?"

"I am your mother, and whether you want to admit it or not, your flagrant disregard for the fact that there are people out there determined to embarrass you and our family is causing problems."

"I am taking care of the problems and of the people out to do whatever to my family, but I will not change because you or anyone else thinks I should. So, maybe Dad's right—we should just drop it and agree to disagree."

"I don't know why I talk. You never listen."

"The feeling is definitely mutual."

"I'm going to bed, Arthur," Mrs. Vindico informed haughtily.

"Are you staying here?" the governor sighed.

"Whatever Fi wants is what I'll do, and that will always be the way it works."

CHAPTER 44

ELUSIVE PERFECTION

Taking the stairs two at a time, Dan entered his childhood bedroom to find his wife cuddling his girls in the bed. Halia was giving her sweet rhythmic suckles on a bottle, and Aida was playing with Fionna's hair.

They turned to gaze at him as he entered.

"Hey." He joined them on the bed.

"Are you okay?" Fionna handed Halia over to him. She pulled away from the bottle, and to Dan's delight, gave him an attempt at a milky, drooly smile.

"I am now," he vowed as he offered Halia the rest of her bottle which she latched on to instantly.

"Are we staying here, or do I need to pack?"

"Whatever you want," Dan assured her.

"All right," she whispered. "Baby girl, I think Davi is sleepy, and I know Sophie is wondering where you are. We need to put you back to bed because tomorrow when we wake up, Mommy is going to cook, and you and Daddy and Halia can watch a parade."

"I don't know what that is," Aida confessed.

"It's a lot of fun. There will be big floats of characters that you like and singers and dancers, and you can see it on the television tomorrow. And you get to wear your pretty jumper."

"The one that makes me and Halia match."

Fionna had ordered Aida and Halia matching outfits for Thanksgiving. Dan wasn't certain who was more excited about them, Aida or Fionna.

"Do you promise not to fight anymore?" Aida turned her pleading eyes on Dan.

"I promise, baby. Mommy and I are going to put you to bed, and then put Halia back to bed, and then I'm going to help Mommy cook all of the food for tomorrow."

"Let's talk about your mom." Fionna patted the bed beside her when Dan returned from laying Aida down.

"Do we have to?"

She chuckled. "We do because the tension you two exist in is exhausting both me and your dad."

"I'm sorry."

"I know. But listen to me, your mother has spent her entire life searching for a rule book, when life doesn't give us that."

Dan considered her words. "That's why she quotes *Women of the Realm* like the Bible."

Fionna nodded. "And the sad part is that people who are so desperate for rules, either for themselves or for others, are people who have felt shame and they're terrified to feel it again. Someone somewhere in her life made her feel that she was only worthy of love if she was perfect. She's so afraid of feeling that way again she'll do anything to avoid it, even making up ridiculous rules and trying to make people in her proximity follow them."

"Her Predilect is a huge part of that though," Dan pointed out.

"True. She wants both people and food to do what she wants them to do *when* she wants them to do it, and neither work that way. Patience is definitely not her virtue. But this whole thing in the paper is her worst nightmare. She lives and breathes by what other people think about her. It's really very sad. She's lost herself in nothing but her perception of other people's opinions. I don't think she has any idea who she is anymore. Instead of the world doing it for her, she turned herself into a 2-D image, and now she doesn't know how to deal with all of us who are real. Being real comes with regret, and shame, and anger, confusion...and lust." She grinned. "She doesn't want to experience any of those things."

"Because they make her feel like she's not in control."

"It would be very much like trying to make a Shield watch someone he loves be hurt."

A little while later, he wrapped his arms around Fionna's waist as she stood at his mother's kitchen counter crumbling cornbread with her hands.

"I love you," he whispered in her ear. Her energy spun around him in contentment.

"I love you too, and I can't lift the turkey out of the brine," she confessed. Chuckling, Dan headed out into his parents' garage and brought in the huge pot Fionna had used to brine the turkey in all day.

They worked late into the night, talking and laughing quietly as they went. Fionna spun and fed Dan a bite of the caramel cream cheese frosting she'd been stirring with a large wooden spoon.

"Yum." Dan lapped it up. It was outstanding. Then with a naughty glint in her eye and a delicious grin, she stuck her finger in the bowl and then dragged it just over her exposed cleavage.

"Even better." Dan pulled her close and bathed her chest with his tongue making her giggle flirtatiously.

Eventually the icing made it onto the pumpkin cake. The turkey went into the hot oven for an hour and was then turned down to cook all night.

"I'll just come baste it whenever Halia wants her bottles," Fionna decided. "And I'll make the pear tart tomorrow."

"You've cooked enough for an army, baby doll. Come to bed with me. You're going to be exhausted tomorrow."

"I just want it to be perfect. It's Aida and Halia's first Thanksgiving, and I want your mom to like it. This just feels really important." She tried to explain what she was feeling, but Dan already knew.

"Because it's our first Thanksgiving as a family, and it's been quite a year." Dan let her thoughts and feelings take wing on his tongue.

"Yeah," she confessed, suddenly overwhelmed with emotion. Dan wrapped his arms around her to try to pull the overwhelm into his shield.

"I love that you want our girls to have the perfect Thanksgiving and that you want our family to have traditions. But sweetheart, we could be at home without electricity eating cold pizza on the couch, and it would be perfect to me because you're there and my baby girls are there." Dan willed her to recognize the power of their all-encompassing love.

"I know." She laid her head on his shoulder and let him tuck her away from the world for a moment.

"Let's go to bed. I want to hold you, and tomorrow, we'll have our first Thanksgiving as a family, the first of many."

"It was my mom's favorite holiday," finally poured from her lips in a harrowed confession.

Dan nodded his understanding as he let his shield encapsulate her.

"I don't know how I ever survived without that," she admitted as she reveled in his energy surrounding her completely. "It's amazing."

"You know," he whispered as he kissed her head, "you're the only other person I've ever wrapped up in here with me." This seemed to surprise her momentarily. "You and the girls."

"Then we're the luckiest girls in the whole world."

He grinned at that. "Come to bed. I'll keep you in it all night if you want." He was perfectly willing to stay up all night and guard her heart and her body if that's what she needed.

CHAPTER 45

GIFTS

Fionna crawled back in the bed just after five. Dan yawned as he pulled her back onto his bare chest.

"Coconut or turkey?"

She kissed his cheek. "Both." She nuzzled her head on Dan's chest, making him smile.

He yawned again and let his hands work down her curves. He stopped at a few of his favorite locations. "This is the first time I have ever woken up in this bed and thought something smelled delicious."

Fionna laughed, but something else was on her mind. She traced timid patterns down Dan's chest with her index finger.

"So," she began. Dan recognized her flirtatious sass, and the customary smile formed on his face. "On this day one year ago right now, you were what?"

"Probably out running." Dan's brow furrowed. "But after that, I was probably still pouting about being on mandatory leave and getting ready to go watch the Angels challenge, which by the way, you were the only Angel I watched that whole day."

Her energy spun in elation as she waggled her eyebrows.

"And you, Mrs. Vindico?" he quizzed.

"At five in the morning before we had our little coconut, I was most definitely sleeping. But I got up, and made coffee, and planned out my strategy of how to get you to come home with me." She hid her face in his chest after her admittance.

Dan chuckled and kissed the top of her head. "And what was this strategy?"

"I was worried because I'd gotten waxed like a week or so before, so nothing would really have come out. I remember thinking that. Then I got ready for the challenge, which we lost," she sighed. "Then I talked Garrett into coming over and helping me get ready for the after party. That included a trip to Guinevere's."

"You took Garrett Haydenshire to Guinevere's to get lingerie for me?"

"Yep."

"And what did he tell you to get?"

"He told me things you might like."

"I'm going to need an example." Dan tried not to enjoy how cute she was when she was embarrassed.

"I don't know," she lied.

"Come on, I made a fool of myself begging you to take me back to your place and then begging you to come with me to Sydney. Tell me what Haydenshire told you." He tickled her ribs making her wiggle and shriek.

"Your mother is up, Sheriff Vindico. She informed me she was certain Ryan would like her pumpkin pie more than mine, so she was making him one special." Her tone was a mix of irritation and hurt.

"I'm sorry, sweetheart." Dan shook his head. Fionna had fixed two of her outstanding Hawaiian pumpkin pies the night before.

"It's fine." Fionna tucked closer to Dan in the bed.

"No, it's not fine, but I still want to know what Garrett told you."

"We had a long debate because I wanted to wear that low-cut, creamy silk blouse which meant that I needed a skin-colored bra. But Garrett said you liked black lace and that you were an ass man. So, I needed a skin-colored push-up bra and a black lace G-string. I thought I should wear a matching set, but he said you wouldn't care."

"Right on all counts, although I am concerned that Haydenshire knew all of that about me."

"He stayed with me all afternoon and told me all about you. He's the greatest guy best friend ever, ever!" Fionna vowed adamantly. "He was really worried about me."

"Because of me?" Dan was stunned. Garrett Haydenshire knew him better than just about anyone. Surely, he didn't think Dan would have done something awful.

"Not like that," Fionna assured him. "You were in a really bad place. I was in a really bad place. I think he was worried if we didn't fall in love, we were only going to get worse. And he was afraid if you pushed me away, I would get even more depressed."

"As soon as I saw you, I wanted to be near you. My shield wanted to protect you. I'd ignored wanting you for months, but my shield knew you had all of my missing pieces."

"And we put each other back together." Fionna squeezed him with everything she had.

"So, fast forwarding a year, would my beautiful bride like her anniversary gifts now or would the queen like to sleep a little more before the princesses rouse?"

"What are the possibilities that the queen and the king could have coffee in here alone together and then open their gifts?"

"I live to serve her majesty." Dan slid from the bed. He kissed her cheek as he made his way downstairs to fix coffee.

"Morning." He dumped out the coffee already in the maker that his mother had fixed. It had an odd aroma and was beginning to separate.

He grimaced as he watched his mother, dressed in her heavy, velour, pea green, zip-front robe circa 1988, dump canned pumpkin into a bowl of rice cereal and chocolate chips and then begin mashing it together.

"Daniel, I just made that coffee," was her irksome greeting.

"Uh-huh," Dan agreed with the statement as he began making drinkable coffee.

Casting the maker, Dan had a pot of coffee that smelled delicious as he poured two large mugs and added honey and half and half.

"There is dried milk and powdered creamer in the cupboard. I don't know why Fionna insisted on picking that up at the store." Mrs. Vindico gestured to the cream as Dan poured it.

"Because Fionna knows that this is how we like our coffee in the morning. Why does it matter what she got at the store? Why do you care?"

"You should drink what we have. It's impolite, and where are you going?" Mrs. Vindico demanded.

"I am going to have coffee with my wife in my bed before our children get up and before my wife starts cooking again."

"Your father will be down soon. You and Fionna should have coffee with us. You're being rather rude, don't you think?"

"No," Dan quipped. "I want to have coffee with her. We'll be down in a little while." With that, Dan headed up the stairs, listening to his mother's customary huffs of offense.

When he returned to his room, he found his beautiful bride sitting on his bed holding a box and looking excited.

"Coffee for my queen." Dan handed her one of the mugs. She giggled as she drew a long sip of her favorite beverage.

"Uh, was your mom having a mixing bowl of rice cereal for breakfast or was she putting that in the pie?" she quizzed as Dan settled on the bed beside her after gathering the boxes from Guinevere's and a long, black, velvet box from a jewelry store downtown.

With a slight shudder, Dan assumed Fionna must've seen his mother pouring out the cereal when she'd been downstairs basting the turkey.

"Mom's pumpkin pie, which I'm sure you'll be shocked to learn came from a recipe in *Women of the Realm*, consists of a store-bought pie crust, a large can of mashed pumpkin, like a hundred and fourteen packets of Sweet'N Low, a bag of chocolate chips, and rice cereal, mashed together and baked to a blackened crisp," Dan informed her as she tried not to gag.

"Why Sweet'N Low if you're putting chocolate chips in?"

"Ah, see, there you go with logic and reason again, baby doll. That won't work here." Dan kissed her cheek as she continued to laugh. "Open your gifts, Mrs. Vindico."

"I am really curious." She pulled one of the boxes from Guinevere's into her lap. Fionna swooned as she lifted the long coral negligee from the box.

"Oh my gosh. This is beautiful." She caressed the delicate lace bodice.

"I can't wait to see you in it," Dan agreed.

"Thank you." She shoved the box aside and threw her arms around him. A moment later, she was on her knees, and his face was buried in her cleavage.

Dan began licking what she'd forced on him. Giggling, she backed away.

"Bring those back." Dan grasped her waist and dragged her back toward him.

"You have a gift as well."

"I like this gift," he informed her as he lifted her shirt and returned to his task. Laughing hysterically, she wiggled herself free.

"Would you behave?"

"I can't think of a reason why I would."

"Because if you don't, then you will only be allowed to eat me for Thanksgiving."

Dan gave her a lusty growl. "That's just rewarding bad behavior, sweetheart."

She opened the aqua boudoir set next. She lifted it out of the box and stared at it lovingly.

"I'm too big to wear this." She shook her head. "No. I'm not saying that anymore. It's too small for me," she restated. "I'm trying so hard to accept myself where I am."

"Try it on."

"Now?"

"Please. I know you're going to be stunning in it."

Fionna hoisted Dan's T-shirt and her Angels sweatpants off, and after Dan took a moment to explore the fact that she'd worn nothing underneath, he urged her to try on the lingerie.

She tugged the top on and shimmied the panties up. Dan moved from the bed to stand beside her. Grasping her shoulders, he spun her until she was facing his dresser mirror.

"You are so beautiful," he vowed as he lifted her chin gently and forced her to look in the mirror. "You're just absolutely stunning."

"Thank you for always making me feel beautiful," she choked as she spun into his chest. He wrapped his arms around her. His breath was coming in rapid pants as he gazed at her only slightly obscured in the delicate lace.

"I love it," she finally admitted.

"I'm glad because I really want to peel it all off you very slowly. You look virgin sweet, baby doll. I want to open you up all for me."

Her eyes began their begging storm as her breath came faster. "I want to go home," she finally pled.

"Tomorrow night, and when we get there, I want you to put this back on and we'll see how long I make it before I rip it off you," he dared.

She shivered deliciously, and Dan had to remind himself that both of his parents were awake and very nearby.

"Open yours," she urged softly.

"Only if you leave that on."

"Okay, fine." She seated herself back on Dan's bed and handed the wrapped box to him as he joined her.

"I feel bad. You got me such nice things, and this didn't really even cost me anything," she fussed.

Dan shook his head. "You gave me you, remember." He popped the tape on the end of the box and eased the paper off. He could feel the nervous energy rolling off her in waves. Furrowing his brow to study her, he pulled the top off the box.

"Careful," she panicked suddenly. Dan eased the box onto the mattress and then pulled the tissue paper back.

"Is this...?" His heart pounded. He swallowed down raw emotion as he lifted the black leather tri-fold badge case from the box. There was a pistol case in there as well.

"It's your Iodex Sheriff's badge. I sent Josh your picture from your Elite badge, and he sent me the rest. A year ago, I wasn't really ready to be an officer's wife. Your job terrified me. But you've really changed, and I know how much you miss it. I think this is what you were put here to do in some capacity. Still can't shake the feeling that there's more to this than we're thinking, but this time, I wanted to give you all of this from me because I love you so much. I'm so proud to be your wife. The fact that you want to go back to my island and keep everyone I love safe means the world to me.

"I'll always worry about you, but I'm ready now. Because it's who you are, and I just couldn't ever love anything more." The vow fell from her lips without pretense or force. It flowed from her heart.

Dan opened his new badge and ID complete with the Kauaian Iodex seal and sheriff marked on the badge. The box also contained a brand new standard issue Glock, several navy blue Iodex T-shirts with the seal on the pocket, and another copy of Dan's sheriff's badge to be worn around his neck.

"God, baby, thank you! This means the world to me, not only because of what it is, but because you gave it to me," he vowed adamantly. "You're just amazing."

"You just better be careful and not ever, ever get hurt," she ordered.

"Hey, if you tell me not to go, I'm not going." He wanted her to know that he remembered the deal they'd struck.

"Okay," she allowed somewhat hesitantly.

"I really want to put one of those shirts on," he confessed.

"You wear one of your new shirts with your boxers there, and I'll wear this nightie and then we'll see what your mom says." She giggled.

"Sounds like a plan to me. The girls in their little turkey dresses and us in this." He gestured to her in the delicate sweet albeit see-through lingerie.

Unable to help himself, Dan lifted the gun from the box. He made certain it was empty before he began examining it.

"It's never been shot?" he quizzed.

She shook her head. "Nope, it's a virgin. You get to pop its cherry," she sassed.

Dan moaned, cracking her up all over again.

Forcing himself to return it to the box, Dan handed Fionna another of the boxes from Guinevere's.

"I want you to wear this tomorrow night too," he informed her wryly.

She tore the paper away and opened the box. "I've been wanting to try these," she exclaimed as she opened the candles.

Laughing, she held up the one that Dan was fairly certain she would love.

"Naked Hawaiian Princess, how appropriate."

"Sounded right up my alley." Dan waggled his eyebrows. "I will say though that since we started calling Halia our little coconut, I can't buy you sexy stuff that's coconut-scented," he explained as he recalled one of the other available scents for massage candles. Fionna laughed as she nodded her understanding.

After she opened the black nighty complete with a crotchless thong and nipple holes which seemed to thrill her, Dan stopped her progress before she opened the last gift.

"Hang on." He moved from the room and carried a very sleepy little Halia back into the room with him. She looked confused momentarily as she settled back on Dan's chest to resume her slumber.

"She helped me pick it out so I thought she should be in here," he explained.

"I think you're just a really good daddy, and you know she's been missing you since you went back to work and you wanted to hold her and keep her with you today," Fionna informed him. Dan nodded his allowance of that.

"Can't keep much from a Receiver, I guess." He kissed Halia's sweet head and reclined back so she could sleep in her customary ball on his chest.

With that, Fionna rubbed her index finger along the velvet box.

"I really hope this is what I think it is because I freaked out yesterday when I couldn't find it."

He grimaced. "I was hoping you wouldn't look for it."

She popped open the box to reveal the diamond and pearl tennis bracelet Dan had given her for her last birthday. It had Aida and Dan's birthstone pendants hanging from it, and it was Fionna's favorite. Dan had taken it back to the jeweler and had Halia's citrine stone added to it as well.

"It's beautiful." Tears welled in her eyes. The stone he'd chosen was a deep cognac color and hung perfectly beside the tanzanite and Dan's lighter citrine stone. "Thank you." She caressed the stone and then leaned over Halia to give Dan a sweet intimate kiss. "And I think it matches my new lingerie perfectly."

"You should wear that today along with this." He tugged on the tiny lace shorts she was still wearing.

CHAPTER 46

FEATHERS

After offering to help numerous times and being told to watch the parade with the girls, Dan settled on the couch with Halia on his shoulder and Aida's head in his lap as she watched the Macy's Thanksgiving Day Parade.

Fionna pulled the huge platter of cornbread dressing from the oven, and Dan inhaled deeply. He was shocked how peaceful he felt in his parents' home. He couldn't recall another time he'd felt that.

"Okay, let's go put on your jumpers," Fionna called as she moved into the living room.

Aida crawled out of Dan's lap, and he stood to carry Halia upstairs as well.

The girls in matching gingham jumpers with their names sewn into the fabric and matching bow headbands even brought a smile to Mrs. Vindico's permanent scowl.

She'd become more and more irritated with each and every dish that Fionna set on the table. When the governor offered Dan the carving knife with a great deal of pride after declaring that since his wife had prepared the main course that year that he should do the carving, she'd left the kitchen with a fitful huff.

Aida and Olivia raced upstairs to play Barbies in Kara's old room while the final preparations were made. Dan handed Halia off to

Meredith momentarily, but her face contorted in a horrified sob, and Meredith handed her back.

"She is such a Daddy's girl," Fionna soothed as she gazed at Dan as he cradled Halia once again. She'd stop crying instantly, which delighted her father, but he hated that Meredith was disappointed.

Dan fed Halia a bottle. She fell asleep while she ate, and he tucked her in the bassinet then moved to the dining room to join his family.

Noting that neither he nor Fionna had a drink, he stood and moved to the adjoining kitchen. "What do you want to drink, my sweet Maylea?" He dropped ice cubes in a glass. His eyes goggled as he realized what he'd said. He offered Fionna an apologetic gaze as everyone but his parents and Aida stared at him in confusion.

Fionna shook her head slightly though her cheeks flushed.

"I thought you only went by your little nickname on Kauai," Mrs. Vindico smarted.

"No. Dan calls me that a lot," Fionna choked out, and guilt took up residence in his gut.

"I like for Daddy to call Mommy Maylea," Aida commented. "It's her name, and it makes her feel happy," she explained.

Kara and Meredith seemed to understand that Fionna didn't want to discuss her nickname. Tim and Zach didn't seem to care. They were much more interested in heaping food on their plates, but Lindley leapt as soon as she sensed Fionna's discomfort.

"What, you have like a Hawaiian name or something, or is that your safe word?" she sneered.

"I'm so sorry." Dan set his and Fionna's drinks at their places and seated himself beside his wife. He wrapped his arm over her shoulders, trying to give her a place to hide.

"It's just a nickname," Fionna scoffed, trying to pretend that it was no big deal in an effort to get Lindley to drop it. It certainly wasn't just a nickname. It was who she was, and it had been given her by her mother. It was a sweet sentiment meant for only her and Dan, when they were off the island anyway. Dan glared at Lindley, daring her to continue her biting remarks.

Ryan was chuckling over Lindley's comment.

"This turkey looks so juicy, Fionna. I can't wait to try it," Governor Vindico tried to change the subject.

"Thank you. The brine is really the key," Fionna explained.

"I really think it can only count as a pet name if that's what he calls you when he creams your face or jizzes in your juice," Lindley chanted.

"Lindley," Governor Vindico roared as Ryan doubled over laughing. He shook his head at her.

"Shut the fuck up, Lindley," Dan demanded through his clenched teeth, making certain Olivia and Aida didn't hear him.

"Suck it, Maylea," Lindley came right back. Fionna shuddered slightly. Her energy drowned with embarrassment and disappointment. Regret surged through Dan.

"Dammit, Lindley," he shouted.

"Lind, come on baby, she's not laughing, okay," Ryan soothed as he gestured to Fionna. "Let it go. Don't get Dan all pissed off, okay."

"Let's just eat," Kara commanded as the dishes began being passed around the table.

"The soup's really good, Care Bear," Zach vowed.

Dan kept his left hand laced through Fionna's as he whispered his continual apologies.

"It's fine. I mean, they'll all visit us on Kauai at some point," Fionna pointed out in a forced whisper. "This *is* really good, Kara," Fionna agreed more audibly as she gestured to the potato and leek soup Kara had prepared.

As Dan consumed his third helping of turkey and dressing, Fionna was beaming from the praise she'd received over her cooking. Mrs. Vindico and Lindley were the only people at the table not gushing about her food.

"Daniel, would you care to inform your sisters about your upcoming move?" Mrs. Vindico challenged.

Cocking his jaw to the side and taking in Fionna's sympathetic gaze, Dan finished the last few bites on his plate and then tossed down his napkin.

"Fine." He drew a sip of his water. "I've accepted the sheriff's position for Iodex in Kauai, so Fi and I and the girls are moving this summer."

"Fi, no," Kara pled.

"I'm sorry. I was going to tell you later. I didn't think we were going to discuss it over Thanksgiving," she stated rather pointedly.

"I don't want you to move away." Olivia's lip turned in a pout, and she grasped Aida's arm.

"I know. I'll miss you too, but you can come to our farm, and I'll show you all of the fun things to do," Aida tried to soothe her cousin.

"Perhaps this wasn't the best time," Dan challenged his mother.

"It's still a ways off." Governor Vindico glanced around the table. "Kara." His eyes landed on her. "You look like you've lost some weight, sweetheart. Fionna was telling your mother and me all about the dance class you're taking." Kara's eyes goggled in momentary confusion. Fionna shook her head slightly.

"Oh, uh, yeah, it's really fun and a great workout." Kara regained her composure. With a slight giggle, she drew another sip of her water. "You should see Fionna. She's amazing." Blood pooled in Fionna's cheeks though she seemed to enjoy the inside joke.

"What? Are you two in some kind of loose hole tap class or something?" Lindley spat in a vicious tone. Fionna's eyes goggled as did Dan's and the governor's.

"Lindley, your nieces and nephew are at the table with us in case you failed to notice that. Now, could you please shut it unless you have something positive to add to the conversation," the governor commanded. Ryan laced his fingers through Lindley's and calmed her.

"I'm positive I'm tighter than they are," Lindley hissed under her breath. Ryan kissed her cheek and whispered something in her ear that had her beaming.

Still fumbling for conversation, Governor Vindico smiled. "Well, Marion, I think we have quite a bit to be thankful for this year, don't you? Two of our kids got married this year. We got three new grandbabies." He winked at Aida.

"Mrs. Powell gave us each a big feather that we cut out of construction paper and we wrote on it what we're thankful for," Aida leapt into the conversation. "Then we put them on a big turkey on the bulletin board."

Kara beamed at her. "What were you thankful for this year?"

"I'm thankful that I have a mommy and a daddy and they love me so much, and I love them so much. And I have a baby sister and a house and blankets at night if I'm cold, and a fairy princess bed, and stories to read, and Sophie, and Davi my bunny, and lots of clothes that don't pinch and lots of shoes that don't hurt my feet. And Mommy makes yummy food and my tummy never hurts at night anymore 'cause I get to eat until it's all filled up and then Daddy makes the sunshine in it. And I have Garrett and he's right here with me instead of only being able to come sometimes. Mrs. Powell let me have three feathers because I had so much to be thankful for," she gasped. "On one of my feathers I wrote all of you."

"Oh." Kara clutched her chest.

"We're so thankful that you are in our family now too, sweetheart," Governor Vindico assured her.

"Yes, dear, we are so thankful, but please put your napkin in your lap," Mrs. Vindico corrected.

"Yes, ma'am. I'm sorry I forgot." Aida quickly placed her napkin on her little legs. Dan rolled his eyes as Fionna chuckled under her breath.

As dessert was being served, Halia began her customary grunts of hunger. Mrs. Vindico set her very odd-looking pumpkin pie concoction in the center of the table and retrieved a server. Rolling his eyes, Dan set Fionna's pumpkin cake with the cream cheese caramel frosting along with her Hawaiian pumpkin pies and Meredith's pecan pies on the sideboard.

"Thanks, Dan." Meredith grinned at him.

"I'm going to get my little coconut." He halted Fionna as she was making her way to the stairs. "I got her. You eat," he soothed. With a smile, Fionna returned to the table.

Fury lit through Dan when he returned to the table carrying Halia to discover that everyone had been served Mrs. Vindico's pie while the rest of the desserts sat idle on the sideboard.

Shaking his head, Dan handed Halia to Fionna, prepared her

bottle, then proceeded to cut a slice of the cake for himself, Aida, and Fionna.

"Oh," Zach leapt. He held his plate for Dan to add cake to his as well.

"This is really delicious, Marion. You should try it," Governor Vindico gushed as he inhaled a piece of the cake he'd gotten Dan to cut. "I'm sure Fionna would share the recipe."

"Of course." Fionna smiled. "It's Daddy's actually, but it's one of Dan's favorites," she added. Mrs. Vindico scowled as everyone inhaled dessert.

~

After the dishes were done, Dan fell onto the sofa lamenting how much he'd eaten. Fionna handed him his cell phone that had been lying on one of the bookshelves in his parents' living room. He read the text from Chris Leslie and smiled.

> Just talked to a guy from Potomac. Power should be back on at eight tomorrow night.

Fionna was beaming, and Dan thought she might actually jump up and down. Chuckling, he pulled her down beside him and tucked her into his chest.

"That is far and away the best Thanksgiving meal I've ever eaten, and I will now have to spend the entire next week at the Venton gym."

"Thank you, but I'm not certain that's really saying all that much." She wrinkled her nose and blushed as she tried to joke but immediately felt guilty for making fun of his mother's cooking. Dan laughed more over how adorable his wife was than what she'd said.

Fionna fixed Aida and Dan turkey sandwiches around eight before she tucked Aida into bed and joined Dan in his room as they packed their things to return home the next evening.

CHAPTER 47
HAYDENSHIRE THANKSGIVING

~EMILY HAYDENSHIRE~

Emily sat wrapped in a quilt up in the barn loft freezing. She pulled the quilt tighter around her and pressed heat out through her pores. Then she heat casted the additional quilt she'd brought out with her as well.

She didn't want Conner to be cold. She knew he wanted to talk to her alone. She knew he would know right where to find her. She even knew what he was likely to ask. She was a Receiver after all. She'd wait patiently until she turned blue to give Connor time to work up the courage. She'd been waiting to have this conversation with him ever since he'd ended things with Katie a year before.

Guilt plummeted through her rhythms. She hated that she'd ever introduced them. She should have focused on Connor more. She should've known. But he hadn't figured it out himself. There was nothing to feel but his confusion.

She saw his shadow cross the moonlight path just outside the barn, and she smiled.

"Hey, Em?" he called as he moved from the moonlight into the darkened barn.

"I'm up here. I brought you a quilt and some hot chocolate."

The ladder gave its customary creaks as he climbed up and joined her. "You didn't have to do all of that."

"I wanted to." Emily pressed more heat out from her energy bands and unwound the quilt from her shoulders. She wrapped Connor in it before she grabbed the still-folded one that wasn't quite as warm. Then she handed him a warmed mug of their mom's hot chocolate.

He smiled at her. "Kinda reminds me when you used to make me and Logan play tea party with you."

She chuckled. "Thanks for putting up with me."

"I guess you were worth it."

"That one time I mixed Tang in with some of Mom's tea it was pretty good," she remined him.

He laughed. "Yeah, but there were a few times you tried to get us to drink lake water."

Emily cringed and decided to change the subject to what she knew Connor really wanted to talk about. It definitely wasn't lake-water tea. "We all really like Reid," she assured him. "He's great."

Connor managed a nod as he drew a long slip of the hot chocolate and swallowed it down. "Yeah, he is great."

"How long have you been seeing him?"

"Uh…I guess almost a year now."

Tears welled in her eyes but she blinked them away. They took up residence in the tight knot of regret in her throat instead. "Did I…do something or maybe say something that made you think that you couldn't tell us? Did any of us do something like that? If we did, we're all so sorry."

He shook his head. "No. I just don't really want the press to find out. They're gonna be brutal. I don't want Dad to have to go through it anymore than I want Reid to. I just wish I could live my life."

She squeezed his arm. "I've definitely been there, but they aren't going to scare him away. I promise."

Connor's deep brown eyes, a perfect match of all of her brothers, lifted to hers. "Why?" he whispered.

Emily's brow furrowed for a moment. She closed her eyes and tried to get a deeper read on Connor's frantic emotions. "Are you asking me why they won't scare him away?"

He managed another nod as he dropped her gaze, and realization shimmered in her rhythms.

"Because he loves you."

Relief flooded through Connor. "Are you sure?"

"There is no emotion stronger than love. I felt it instantly as soon as he got here. I felt it from both of you."

Connor cocked his jaw to the side. His eyes closed. "Can I ask you something about that?"

"You can ask me anything about anything."

"When uh…when you feel that he loves me…or…you know, you feel that I love him, does it feel different than…the way Will feels about Brooke or Rainer feels about you?"

The tremble of her shoulders betrayed the tears she could no longer hold back. "No," she vowed. "God, no. Not at all. I swear. It feels and looks and everything is the very same. The bands of love are identical. It doesn't matter who they're coming from or who they're going to." She threw her arms around his shoulders. "Please believe me. Please don't worry about that. You are exactly the way you're meant to be."

He embraced her like clinging to her might be the very thing that saved him. She squeezed her eyes shut and held him tighter. She'd never let him go. "You love Reid exactly the way that Dad loves Mom, and Will loves Brooke, and Patrick loves Lucy, and Logan loves Adeline, and Rainer loves me. It's no different."

After a few minutes, he eased his grip. She refused to be the one to break the hug so she waited until he dropped his arms.

"Can I ask you something else?" he managed.

"Anything, remember?"

"What did Dad feel when Reid walked in?"

"Relief."

Connor's brow furrowed. "Relief?"

"Yeah. Pure relief flooded through all of his emotional bands and everyone else's too."

"You're sure?"

"Never been more certain. We're all so relieved that you felt like you could tell us. That you were going to give us a chance to show you how much we love you and how much we love Reid because you love him."

"Thanks, Em."

She grinned. "Anytime."

"This conversation might even make up for the times you tried to make me drink lake-water tea."

Emily shook her head. "I doubt that, so if you want to keep talking about all of this, I still owe you big time."

CHAPTER 48
TRADITIONS
~DAN VINDICO~

The next morning, Dan had all of his girls up early, promising that Governor Haydenshire's pancakes were worth it.

Fionna beamed as Dan pulled through a Starbucks drive-thru and handed her a large breakfast blend with extra cream and honey.

When they arrived on Haydenshire Farm, Dan cradled Halia in his arms as Aida knocked on the kitchen door.

"Well hey, baby girl," Governor Haydenshire greeted Aida as she rushed to Garrett.

"Did you wear that just to irk your mom?" Garrett lifted Aida high in the air as he gestured his head to Dan's Kauaian Iodex T-shirt.

"You know it," Dan allowed. Governor Haydenshire shook his head as he chuckled. He was flipping pancakes on three griddles lined up on the massive island that ran the length of the Haydenshires' kitchen.

"Let me see her." Mrs. Haydenshire headed to Dan. He lowered Halia from his shoulder and cradled her in the crook of his arm as she slept soundly.

"She's beautiful," Mrs. Haydenshire swooned.

"Just like her mama." Dan grinned as everyone chuckled and Fionna blushed.

"Ni-on-na," Keaton shrieked as he raced into the kitchen wearing navy blue footy pajamas.

"Hey there." Fionna lifted Keaton up into her arms as Dan shook his head slightly.

"All right, there's Rainer and Emily." Governor Haydenshire gestured his head out the front windows to the approaching Hummer. "Let's eat up and get playing. I've been looking forward to this for months. No work. Just my kids." The governor slapped Dan on the back. He added him in with all of his others, just as he always had. "And this year you're here, so I will not be receiving phone calls from Moscow," he chastised.

Dan knew he deserved the reprimand he'd received the Thanksgiving before when he'd cussed out the Russian board of governors, assaulted numerous Iodex officers, and fled the country.

Fionna beamed and kissed Dan's cheek.

"Totally worth it, I think," she whispered.

"Definitely," Dan agreed. If he hadn't gotten suspended for two weeks and ordered to not only attend the Summation challenge, but also the after party, he never would have fallen for Fionna.

Rainer and Emily fell into the kitchen both laughing. Emily's cheeks were glowing pink, and she was gazing at Rainer like he was simply too good to be true.

Governor and Mrs. Haydenshire shared a knowing glance as Rainer planted a kiss on the top of Emily's head.

"Jeff and Becca are on their way," Emily announced as her father handed her the second plate of pancakes, bacon, and eggs. Mrs. Haydenshire had been given the first.

"Oh good. I was hoping they'd come." Mrs. Haydenshire seemed thrilled with the added guests.

Soon, everyone was seated or standing in the Haydenshires' kitchen, devouring the delicious breakfast. Dan noticed a guy who was hanging out beside Connor. He smiled and offered his hand. "I'm Dan Vindico. This is my wife, Fionna, and our daughters Aida and Halia."

Connor grinned. "This is my boyfriend, Reid."

Fionna beamed. "It's so nice to meet you!"

Dan nodded and smiled. He wondered how long they'd been a couple. Garrett hadn't said anything about Connor finally coming out.

"We're all so glad you're here, Reid," Governor Haydenshire vowed. "Do you prefer defense or offense?"

Reid chuckled. "I'm good most anywhere, sir. Thanks for having me."

Mrs. Haydenshire nodded. "You are welcome on Haydenshire Farm any time you'd like to be here."

The family all echoed the sentiment.

Jeff knocked on the door and then led Becca inside, accepting the warm greetings they received.

"Thank you." Becca beamed as the governor handed her a plate as well.

"How are you feeling, sweetheart?" Mrs. Haydenshire gazed at Becca's slightly swollen midsection.

"A little better. I haven't been back to the hospital at least." She gestured to Adeline who nodded her agreement as she chewed her food.

"I pretty much go to school, take my three classes, and then go home and rest until Jeff gets home from work. I'm kind of bored out of my mind."

"I keep telling her that she's working way harder than I am," Jeff said as he rubbed his hand over her bump.

"Smart man." The governor nodded.

"Hear, hear," Dan agreed.

"Oh Dad, Portwood said he and Julie might drop by for a little while," Logan seemed to remember suddenly.

"The more the merrier as long as Landon can throw a pass."

Dan noticed Jeff's grimace.

Logan shook his head. "He's crazy about you. If it weren't for Julie, he would marry you, I swear. You've solved cold cases we've had open for years. Stop freaking about the hacker dude."

"Seriously, we stand in awe of your mighty powers." Rainer made everyone laugh.

"Thanks." Jeff blushed violently. "But this guy is driving me nuts. He's amazing, but if he just keeps people from hacking, then we can't arrest them. I have no idea who or where he is. He could be in the freaking South Pole for all I know."

Dan kissed all of his girls before he went out to the Haydenshires' back field to join the dividing teams.

Fionna, Emily, and Adeline sauntered out after a couple of hours. They brought water bottles that they chilled and handed out.

"So, can we play?" Emily teased her brothers.

"No," Will and Patrick declared simultaneously.

"That's very sexist," Emily informed them, but Dan knew she didn't really want to play.

"No, it's self-preservation." Garrett quickly downed a bottle of water. "If we let you play and I tackle Fionna, Dan beats the shit out of me. Then Adeline has to heal me all up, and that's a game delay. Not to mention the real reason which is the fact that you suck *so* bad." Everyone laughed at Rainer's trying very hard not to.

Dan shook his head. "Nobody tackles my baby, except for me." He winked at Fionna. "Where are our babies by the way, Mrs. Vindico?"

"Halia is lying on a blanket with Abigail. I've decided it's her first play date," Fionna announced. "And Aida Mae is showing her doll catalog to Brooke and Becca."

"I do not suck at football," Emily smarted.

"Em, go away. Rainer can tackle you later," Connor sneered.

"You can play if you want, baby." Rainer pulled Emily under his arm. Her face scowled as he backed away.

"Never mind. You stink." She pretended to gag.

The girls returned back into the house and a second game began. But a half hour into the game, just as Dan had thrown Will to the ground and forced the ball from his hands, Fionna returned.

Dan leapt up hearing his little girl's tiny wails.

"Sorry. She's a little confused again and…shh, shh, Halia, it's okay. Daddy's right here," Fionna broke off midsentence trying to soothe Halia.

"Baby, I'm filthy." Dan didn't know what to do. He was covered in dirt and sweat. Halia's head turned instantly toward Dan's voice.

"She's scared, and she wants you." Fionna's voice edged on desperation.

"Just don't tuck her and run, Daniel," Governor Haydenshire teased as everyone joined Dan on the sidelines to drink more water.

"I think if you leave the game to attend to your baby, the previous fumble doesn't count." Levi was irked that Will had turned the ball over.

"Actually, I think that rain means the game's over," Logan lamented as the first drops of a rain shower began pelting the shirtless men. Dan did in fact tuck Halia into his chest and run her back into the house.

CHAPTER 49

TATTLE-TELLING

The band of starving, sweaty men raced into the kitchen to devour Mrs. Haydenshire's Thanksgiving leftovers.

"Daniel, go shower, son. Representative Kalakona is coming over for pizza in a little while. She wants to talk with you and Fionna," Governor Haydenshire announced as Dan kissed Mrs. Haydenshire's cheek as she handed him a huge slice of her phenomenal pecan pie drizzled with whiskey cream sauce.

"Clearly, I need that recipe as well." Fionna giggled.

"What does she want to talk about?" Dan shoveled pie into his mouth.

"It's pretty much whiskey and heavy cream with a little maple syrup mixed in until it tastes good," Mrs. Haydenshire explained.

"She's hoping to get to know your family, I expect, and I think she has an offer she's hoping you'll take," Governor Haydenshire explained.

"Your boss is coming over," Fionna panicked as she finally listened to the governor instead of Mrs. Haydenshire. "I look terrible."

"You always look beautiful," Dan immediately argued.

"Sweetheart, Victoria knows we're just hanging out today, and I'm going to sit in my chair and talk to all of my girls in these sweats, while Stephen serves pizza to the Hawaiian Representative to the Senteon," Mrs. Haydenshire soothed. "And I am not going to care at all. Join me."

"Wait, wait, wait. Dan's new boss is coming over." Garrett smirked.

"Garrett," the governor warned.

"Oh, come on, I feel certain William and I could come up with some stories to regale Representative Kalakona with." Garrett threw his arm around Will's shoulders as everyone laughed.

Dan shuddered slightly as he considered the stories that could be told.

Aida rushed to him in the kitchen. "Did you win football?" she asked. Dan shot Will a goading grin.

"We were just having fun," he teased.

"Careful, or I'll take Garrett up on his offer of recalling your adolescence for your new boss," Will harassed.

Aida's tiny, adorable nose wrinkled.

"You smell…not like you normally do," she explained.

"Okay, okay, I'm going to shower." Dan shoved one more bite in his mouth and raced up the Haydenshires' stairs.

Dan felt sixteen again as he stepped out of the shower attached to Will and Garrett's childhood bedroom. He laughed out loud as he discovered that not only had someone stolen the towel he'd laid out, but they'd taken all of the towels from the closet in the bathroom and had removed his clean clothes from the counter.

"Fi!" He leaned his head out of the bedroom door, keeping his body hidden behind it. Raucous laughter echoed up the stairs.

"Garrett, what did you do?" he heard Fionna scold.

She raced up the stairs and began giggling hysterically as Dan stepped back, letting her in the room.

"This is my favorite thing for you to wear," she teased.

"Could I get a towel, please? I'm freezing."

Fionna rushed from the room and returned with a towel he assumed she'd located in one of the hall bathrooms.

She heated it for Dan and then shot him hungry looks as he ran it over his body. Moving to him, she traced her fingers up his shaft and then looped them over his head.

Dan growled heatedly.

"I was going to say I need my clothes, but if you're offering I'll do without." He grabbed her hand and wrapped it fully around his strain.

A growl spilled from deep within Dan's chest as he willed her to keep her hand wrapped tightly around him. He tried desperately to remember where they were and that there was a house full of people one floor below them, two of which were their daughters.

Fionna leaned and he was done for. All thoughts of who else was there made a rapid departure from his mind. His head fell back as her tongue flicked over his shaft.

She gave a whispered moan as need leaked from his head into her mouth. She lapped it up.

"You like that, don't you, baby doll? I'm gonna fill you full of it."

"Fionna Styler Vindico, I swear if you are doing what I think you're doing on my bed, I will send Aida in there right now," Garrett threatened.

With a spiteful smirk, Fionna moved to the closed door. "Now, which one was Garrett's bed?" she chanted.

"Fionna," Garrett spat.

"Then where are his clothes?"

"Garrett Alexander Haydenshire, for heaven's sake, son, you are thirty-one years old. Give the man his clothes," Dan heard Mrs. Haydenshire command from the bottom of the stairs.

Dan wrapped the towel back around his waist as he heard the lock pop. Garrett waltzed through the open door.

With an eye roll, he stomped to the old desk in the room and opened the bottom drawer. He tossed Dan's jeans and polo to him.

"You weren't supposed to come up and make him not want to get dressed. He was supposed to have to come out buck-ass bare and beg for his clothes," Garrett huffed.

"Will you never grow up?" She shook her head. "Only I get to enjoy the gorgeous sight of my hunky husband all sexy and naked," she chanted as Garrett pretended to gag. Dan fought the blood pooling in his cheeks as he dressed quickly. "Also, don't mess with us, Haydenshire. I'll tell your mom on you."

CHAPTER 50
PELE'S TEARS

A few minutes later, Dan and Fionna reappeared downstairs to be greeted by Jack Stariff, who was devouring a piece of Mrs. Haydenshire's pie. Fionna was beaming and holding Dan's hand. He guided her into his lap on the large sectional sofa that took up most of the Haydenshires' living room.

"My God, he just looks abusive, doesn't he?" Jack joked derisively.

"Not certain I would joke about something like that, Jack," the governor scolded. "But I agree the claim is preposterous."

"Ms. Bryant did receive the cease and desist and the restraining order. I did, however, fix it so that your beautiful bride will be able to attend the disciplinary meeting Monday morning."

Fionna nodded but her brow furrowed.

"I'll keep her," Emily leapt.

"Okay, problem solved." Fionna shrugged.

"Maybe," Jack lamented. "Bryant is *extremely* unhappy."

"Well, you know, when you're the one who created the shit storm, most of the time you're the one who drowns in it," Garrett spat.

"I add all of those adorable little phrases to his baby book." Mrs. Haydenshire shook her head at Garrett as everyone laughed.

"She's furious with you and your father. I'm not supposed to know this, but a friend of a friend let it slip that she and the chancellor have had more than a few clandestine meetings in the past couple of months, prompting his filing for separation, I expect. It seems that's the one relationship in her life that she works on. Her kids are apparently still furious with her," Jack lamented.

The governor shook his head and wrapped his arm over Mrs. Haydenshire. He scooted her closer as she smiled at him.

"Of course, your father won't be able to govern the disciplinary hearing. Obviously, Stephen, I didn't think we should ask you to step in at the academy," Jack said. Governor Haydenshire nodded his agreement. "I'll have to see who might be willing to oversee the academy governors with the meeting, but what I need to know from you two is, what are your goals for this hearing?"

Dan hemmed as Brooke handed Halia to him. She'd begun fussing again, and Brooke had given her a bottle while Dan and Fionna talked with Jack.

Fionna explained, "I want her to tell everyone that she's a liar and that Dan has never and would never be abusive. I want her to confess that she was planning on leaving the store with Dan, and that's why she'd called the press because she was going to make it look like they had something going on."

Dan chuckled as he kissed her cheek. Jack was trying very hard not to laugh at her outright as was the Crown Governor.

"Even I'm not that good." Jack winked at her.

"How about we want her to stay away from us, and we want her out of our affairs. A public apology would be great, but I doubt we'll be getting that, although having her make an admission of guilt to the school governors would be good. It might make them realize the kind of vindictive behavior she's capable of." Dan tried to lower his wife's expectations just a little.

"Remember that I have no real evidence that says she's the one that phoned the press. Now, I am working on that, and I do have a description from the manager of her, and obviously you had words with her," he pointed out. "Did you have that receipt, Daniel?"

"I'll just keep it with me until Monday morning when I hand it off to whomever is running the disciplinary meeting if it's all the same."

"Sure, that's fine," Jack assured him. "I understand."

"We all do, Dan." Governor Haydenshire offered Fionna a kind smile. "The fact that you're having to present it at all is insane."

"Yes, it is, and I keep telling all of you you've just tapped the well of what Katherine Bryant is capable of. She feels unloved and trapped in her marriage. She is also jealous. She feels very wrongly judged and, most importantly, deeply embarrassed. A woman with those kinds of emotions is capable of most anything," Mrs. Haydenshire explained in her calm, soothing thrum, though deep concern etched her eyes.

"She's not the only one who feels trapped, sweetheart," the governor soothed. "Arthur feels like he needs more evidence to fire Dean because if he's fired he loses his retirement which affects Ellen. Donating money to the school is not a fireable offense. The school governors are eager to cast Venton back in a more positive light, and they feel that hiring Terry Bryant might make people believe that they're helping the Bryants rebuild their marriage, even though that doesn't appear to be the case. I would love nothing more than to decree that neither Katherine nor Terry may be employed by the Realm, but that affects their children," Governor Haydenshire laid out all of the problems surrounding one man's indiscretions. "People want to chuck rocks in the pond and pretend the ripples won't reach the shoreline."

After going over the things he planned to say and present at the disciplinary hearing Monday morning, Jack thanked the Haydenshires and then left. Dan watched football most of the afternoon alongside everyone else.

"You sure you're up for your defense exam next week?" Dan asked Jeff. He was still impressed with how well he'd handled his early exams thus far.

"I hope," Jeff admitted. "I have both of your defense first semester exams left, and then I hope to take most of my second semester exams in January, and then I have to take my exit exam, and I'll be done," he announced with a great deal of exuberance.

"The exit exam is super easy," Logan chimed in. "Every answer is pretty much Crown Governor Lawson was the shit and then here's all the ways we were assholes that screwed up the Non-Gifted Realm over the years."

Rainer nodded. "I do remember thinking it was pointless. If I don't know what my dad did, then failing the exit exam is the least of my problems."

Everyone laughed as they recalled their own exams from Venton.

Lily Ana was sound asleep on Will's chest in one of the recliners. Governor Haydenshire had Abigail in a similar position seated nearby.

Aida was playing with the twins, and Halia was sleeping in her portable swing. Fionna curled up on the couch cuddling into Dan's chest, making his whole day.

"So, when you built this house you already knew you wanted to have several more children?" Fionna continued her conversation with Mrs. Haydenshire.

"Well," Mrs. Haydenshire hemmed as the governor chuckled. "I was pregnant with Levi when we moved in, and I'd miscarried between Garrett and Levi so I was on my fourth pregnancy. I didn't really seem to have any trouble conceiving." She made everyone chuckle.

"I did try to make it as easy as possible on you, sweetheart," the governor harassed his wife, cracking everyone up.

"Your service was most appreciated," she teased as the laughter turned to groans from her adult children.

As two pizza delivery guys brought thirty pizzas to the farmhouse, Representative Kalakona made her appearance.

Laying it on just a little thick in Dan's opinion, she brought leis for Dan, Fionna, and Aida. She presented gift baskets containing Kona coffee, mangos, Hawaiian chocolates, and macadamia nuts for the Haydenshires and the Vindicos.

Garrett chuckled as Fionna thanked Mrs. Kalakona. "She wants something big," he warned through his teeth. Dan nodded his agreement.

Mrs. Haydenshire smiled. "Victoria, you didn't need to bring us anything. Make yourself at home."

"I do know how cliched this basket is. Fionna, I phoned your grandparents to ask what we might get you, but they kept insisting that I didn't need to bring you anything. I did want to show you both how thrilled I am that you're coming back to my islands. I wanted to do something," Mrs. Kalakona insisted.

"This was kind of you," Fionna accepted graciously, but Dan caught something in her rhythms that had him concerned.

"You all take the kitchen table. We're going to eat in the living room, and Emily seems to have claimed Halia all for herself." Governor Haydenshire gestured to the kitchen table.

"Thank you, Crown Governor," Mrs. Kalakona assured as they sat down. "I also brought gifts for the girls."

"You didn't need to do that." Fionna was visibly uncomfortable with the level of persuasion being thrust upon her family. Her rhythms tensed in rapid pulses. Dan laced his fingers through hers, but even her immediate draw didn't soothe her.

"Of course I did. Like I said, I was thrilled when the Kauaian counsel told me Dan had accepted the sheriff's position. I grew up on the Big Island, and my husband's family has lived on our estate on Molokai for three generations. I can assure you, all of Hawaii eagerly awaits your family's return to our land."

"Mahalo," Fionna stammered uncomfortably. She was studying Victoria, reading the emotions of her energy. Something she was picking up on had her either confused or concerned. Dan couldn't figure a way to discreetly ask her what she was feeling though.

Aida seemed to sense Fionna's concern. She rushed into the kitchen.

"This must be your precious Aida." Mrs. Kalakona beamed as she leaned down to gaze at Aida. "I have you a present."

"Thank you very much, but you didn't have to bring me a present."

"These are just little tokens to say welcome to Hawaii." The representative handed Aida a small white box with an embossed pineapple on the lid. "I have one for your little sister as well."

"Halia can't say thank you yet, so I will say it for her," Aida pledged.

Nodding, Mrs. Kalakona shot Dan a look that said she too thought Aida was adorable.

Aida pulled the lid off the tiny box and smiled. "Look, Mommy, it's a bracelet," she gasped as Fionna knelt down to help her pull it from the box.

"It is and those look like peridots. They come from Hawaii," Fionna reminded her though Dan was fairly certain she knew that from living on Kauai over the summer.

"It kind of looks like yours." Aida turned to Mrs. Kalakona with a smile. "My mommy has a bracelet like this one only it has the *real* kind of green peridots that are very beautiful. These aren't the real kind, and Mommy's bracelet has diamonds in between them. My Papa gave it to her, because Mommy is his *pa'ipunahele*, and that means favorite love, and I'm Papa's favorite love too he says. And he told me that it came from a place I forgot to remember the name but I think it said tears," she trilled. Dan bit his lips together as Victoria Kalakona's face fell.

"Papkolea Beach," Fionna reminded her. "And the peridots are called Pele's tears. I think yours is beautiful just like mine." She fixed the elastic band with fake plastic perfectly round peridot lookalikes on Aida's wrist.

"Thank you." Aida smiled.

"You're welcome." Mrs. Kalakona sighed her defeat. She smiled at Dan and Fionna. "Shall we?" She gestured to the Haydenshires' kitchen table.

"Of course," Fionna agreed as the representative fixed herself a paper plate of pizza.

Dan fixed Aida two pieces of cheese pizza and settled her at the coffee table with Logan and Adeline. He returned to the kitchen table, wishing that he could settle Fionna in his lap and watch the recorded game from the day before that had just been turned on.

"Aida seems well versed in her Hawaiian language and history," Mrs. Kalakona complimented.

"Aida loves Kauai just like Fi and I." Dan wondered where this conversation was heading.

Kalakona shifted uncomfortably. "My husband told me that I needed to shoot straight with you. That you were no-nonsense. I guess he was right."

"Did you need help with something, Representative?" Fionna asked.

"I do," she allowed.

Dan decided to eat. He was starving and wanted to get this portion of his evening over with, so he could join his friends to watch the game. He felt rude being in someone else's home attending some kind of business meeting.

"I was hoping to come up with some way to make what I'm asking so appealing you wouldn't turn me down, but you seem just as tough as I've ever heard," she admitted.

Dan wiped his mouth. "I'm not certain what you heard, but I probably don't have an easygoing reputation if that's what you were hoping for."

"Easygoing is not what I'm looking for. I want someone who can get the job done," Mrs. Kalakona vowed. Wiping her hands on her napkin, she folded them on the placemat in front of her. "Dan, I would like to offer you a different job.

"I do understand that you want to be the Kauaian Iodex Sheriff, and I want that as well. I also understand that Fionna's ties to her family's land run very deep. They always have, and I expect that your children will develop those bonds to that land just as Fionna did and her mother, and her grandmother, and her great-grandmother. That's the kind of commitment to my people that I'm looking for. So, I am more than willing to allow you to run all of the Hawaiian State Iodex from Kauai if you'd be willing to accept that position." Dan's mouth fell open as she continued. "I'm also more than willing to match the combined salaries for both jobs. The job would also allow you Senate Jet privileges again."

"The Hawaiian Iodex has an entire complex in Honolulu," Dan stated the first thing that came to mind.

"Yes, and you would need to be there often, I'm sure, but we also have the greatest Gifted networks and computers at our disposal. I want your brains more than your brawn. I want to tighten our hold on crime. I intend to lower the entire state's crime rate statistics, and I know you're the man for the job. I also know that you want to be on the farm with your lovely wife and beautiful girls. I am willing to bring the Iodex departments from each island to train under you," she continued to bait.

Fionna stared up at Dan in disbelief.

"Thank you for the offer, Representative Kalakona, but I'll have to discuss this with Fionna and Aida." Shock continued to wash through him in waves. "You are aware of my past transgressions, correct?"

Victoria chuckled and nodded. "You would probably find me in the camp of vastly more disappointed with your show in Moscow last year than in the way you chose to handle Dominic Wretchkinsides, but if I may try to explain a little bit of why I'm so interested in your taking this position."

"Please," Dan agreed. He still couldn't access an emotion to associate with the offer. Excitement and hope bubbled in his gut along with apprehension and concern over what that might mean for Fionna and his girls. He desperately needed to know what Fionna was feeling from the representative, because whatever it was, it wasn't good.

"Despite being white, I consider myself Native Hawaiian." Dan noted Fionna's bristle, but he pretended to ignore it as Kalakona went on. "I was born there. My heart lives there on the islands. In everything I do in my career and personal life, I want to honor the traditions and beliefs of Hawaii. Crime takes away from my people and from the people who visit the lands in hopes of rejuvenation and relaxation. You and Fionna have formed your own ohana, but you have also joined Fionna's ohana. You spent the summer working the lands. You gave your baby a Hawaiian name. I know that Fionna has an inoa welo, but I also know that it must be very special to you. I've never thought that enough credence is given to the energy either taken or given when a name is spoken. Therefore, I will call you Fionna with hope that someday we will call each other by the names assigned us by those that know us best," she eased.

Fionna forced a smile, but her eyes were narrowed. "I appreciate that."

"I want someone that loves the land and culture as much as I do, that wants to preserve the people and their heritage. That can strike a balance between keeping our lands safe for the Hawaiian people and the tourists that we share our lands with."

"I'm honored that you think so highly of me, Representative. I think we just need a little time to discuss this and process everything."

"Please take your time and decide if this will work for you, but I know that Hawaii needs you, Dan, and perhaps we can balance everything so that Hawaii gives you life and you give her protection."

At that moment, Halia began sobbing, and Emily carried her into the kitchen.

"I'm sorry, Representative Kalakona. She wants Fionna," Emily apologized.

She handed Halia to Fionna and then made a quick exit.

"Oh, goodness." Fionna beamed as she cradled Halia closely. "You always want Daddy. I didn't think you ever wanted me."

Dan scoffed. "Of course she wants you. She just has you most of the time, and we don't have another Receiver that can tell you she wants you just yet."

Halia located her fingers and began sucking as she nestled into Fionna's chest.

"I spoke with your grandfather, and he mentioned that you're building a new hale. When are you breaking ground?"

"In a few weeks. We'd like to have the foundation blessing before Venton goes back for its second semester. Then Fionna's grandfather will be running the crews and we'll hopefully return for Spring Break to check up on everything. It's going to be a lot to manage with the girls and Aida's school, but we're eager to get home," Dan explained. His allowance that Kauai was home delighted both his wife and Representative Kalakona.

"It's seven thirty," Fionna reminded less than patiently as Dan and Will shouted at the television when Detroit missed a field goal. Kalakona had left not long after eating and told Dan to phone when he'd made his decision.

Dan took Fionna's hand and pulled her onto the couch beside him. He wrapped his arm around her. He felt selfish for trying to soothe her just long enough to see the last plays of the game.

She was onto him instantly of course. He chuckled as she rolled her eyes.

"Do you want to go, baby doll?" he offered. Fionna was just as desperate to get home as he was. They'd had a wonderful day at the Haydenshires', but Dan knew she was eager to discuss his job offer. He supposed he was as well, but shock was the only real emotion he could recognize when he thought about being the Commander of Hawaiian Iodex. It was more than he'd ever imagined after the circumstances of his resignation.

"How much longer does it last?" Fionna studied the television. Dan smirked then bit his lips together as Will, Logan, Levi, and Garrett laughed from making her comment dirty in their minds. Fionna rolled her eyes.

"Men are so much worse in groups," she huffed. Emily and Adeline nodded.

"Well," Garrett drawled. "There's three minutes left in the fourth, but the Cowboys have the ball on their own thirty. Their center just had a bad snap, and Detroit got called for encroachment so Dallas will probably gain five. It's twenty one even so could go into overtime."

"What did he just say to me?" Fionna demanded of Dan who cracked up.

"We can go, sweetheart." Dan helped her off the couch. They gathered the girls and their things and thanked the Haydenshires profusely for having them.

"If you want to bring over the house plans, Fionna, I'd be happy to look over them and we could talk about them," Mrs. Haydenshire assured Fionna as she hugged her goodbye.

"Thank you."

"Dan, if you need any help or advice, you know where I am." The governor pulled him in for a hug as well.

"I'll be calling, don't worry," Dan assured.

ABOUT THE AUTHOR

J.E. Neal (aka Jillian) vastly prefers coffee to tea, guac to salsa, the beach over anywhere else, and the world inside her head over the one outside her front door. She also loves not having to choose.

Driven by the question 'what if,' J.E. Neal's world began to manifest. What if there were people with powers the rest of us couldn't see? What if the energy of our world could be summoned and used at their will? Characters with these amazing abilities took shape in her mind. She created—and continues to create—an endless number of stories full of delicious escape from our reality where emotions are visible, desire is palpable, and danger is universal.

Learn more about J.E. Neal at JillianNeal.com

facebook.com/jilliannealauthor
twitter.com/JillianNeal_
instagram.com/jilliannealauthor

ALSO BY J.E. NEAL

TANGLE OF MAGIC

Tangle of Magic Boxed Set (Books 1-6)

Tangle of Lies (Book 1)

Tangle of Chaos (Book 2)

Tangle of Desires (Book 3)

Tangle of Fates (Book 4)

Tangle of Trust (Book 5)

Tangle of Ruin (Book 6)

ENERGY OF MAGIC

Shield and Shattered Cages (Book 1)

Shield and Faltered Steps (Book 2)

Shield and Splintered Oaths (Book 3)

Shield and Humbled Crown (Book 4)

Shield and Vile Serpents (Book 5)

Shield and Coveted Splendor (Book 6)

Shield and Guarded Shadow (Book 7)

Shield and Worthy Sinner (Book 8)

Shield and Sacrificial Heirs (Book 9)